TOMMY
the QUARTERBACK
a novel

DONALD GRECO

Jan-Carol
Publishing, Inc

"every story needs a book"

Tommy the Quarterback
Donald Greco
Published March 2025
Little Creek Books
Imprint of Jan-Carol Publishing, Inc.
All rights reserved
Copyright © 2025 Donald Greco
Front Cover Design: Tara Sizemore
Front Cover Photograph: © SeanPavonePhoto/Adobe Stock

ISBN: 978-1-962561-66-2
Library of Congress Control Number: 2025937975

You may contact the publisher:
Jan-Carol Publishing, Inc.
PO Box 701
Johnson City, TN 37605
publisher@jancarolpublishing.com
www.jancarolpublishing.com

To my sons Ben, Luke, and Nick,
who were lucky enough to call Angie "Mom."

Also by Donald Greco
Abramo's Gift
The Ghost Hawk

For Young Readers
What Ever Happened to the Smooth-Tongued Cats?

Part I

Neva

THIS CHRISTMAS WAS GOING to hurt more than others. Everything seemed to be falling apart around him. How could his life be such a mess? All the promise he had shown, all the dreams for his future, all the peace he sought, all the rewards he knew were waiting in his old age…and yet there was nothing there. Everyone he cared about was either sick, like Smokey, or burnt out like Med, or old like Lazarus, or lonely and hurt like Elly. And he was like all of them.

As he drove, he found himself instinctively drawn to the Silver Bridge. He parked his car in the small rear lot and entered through the back door. The lights were dim and the decor dark. Inside, he sat at a back table, one he usually sat at when a drink would feel its best. The woman who owned the bar came over to him smiling brightly. "Chief, you on duty?"

He shook his head. "Double bourbon and splash, Sherry," he said as he took off his coat. This wasn't one of those nights when he would talk much, so she nodded and turned away.

It was getting cold outside; maybe they'd have an ice storm later tonight. What was he going to do? Even if Carly didn't make a power play against him, what was his life going to be like when he finally quit? Jesus. It was like waiting around to die…The present was bad

1

enough, but the future was a dreary, empty prospect. And the past...
All it meant was that he was now lonely and guilty for having let Elly
grow up a stranger while he made a career, while he chased crooks that
no one ever cared were caught or punished. He had no wife, and there
hadn't been a woman in his life for so long...Hell, he wasn't any kind
of bargain, anyway. He was old and fat and alcoholic. Sherry brought
the bourbon, and he downed it easily. In a few minutes, he tipped his
glass toward her stealthily and she brought him another. This was going to be one of those nights, she knew. The chief wasn't feeling good,
and the booze was going to help him forget. "You better call Chief Malatesta, Charley," she said to her bartender. "Let him know he'll have
to send someone out after Tommy tonight."

"It's been a while since he's done this, huh?" said Charley.

"Yeah," she sighed, "...just every so often the past ten years."

"He ever makes any trouble?" said the bartender.

"Nah," she said. "When Gus owned this place, he'd take him home
by himself. Now, Bumpy Malatesta sends a cop out to get him...so no
one else'll see him."

About a half hour later, the back door opened and a familiar, formidable, stocky figure came through. He waved to Sherry, who with a
tilt of her head indicated that the chief was at his old table. The rain
was starting to freeze and so the bar was almost deserted. And Bumpy
was relieved.

He joined the chief at the table, throwing his blue officer's overcoat over one chair and sitting down hard in a chair opposite him.
"We have to stop meeting like this, Bump," the chief said wryly.

"Next time you want to party, why don't you invite me along, too?"
said Bumpy.

"So, what brings you to a place like this, Chief? You're supposed to be on duty, remember?"

"More important, what brings you here, Tommy?"

"I'm allowed. I'm not on duty."

"What's the trouble, *Paesan?*" Bumpy asked softly.

"I'm just smashed and can't remember how to get home, okay?" said Tommy, slurring his words slightly, but still seeming in control of himself.

"I mean the reason for this bender, Tom," Bumpy said seriously.

"No reason. I haven't seen Sherry for a while…"

Bumpy stared at him silently. This wasn't going to be easy. "Come on, Tommy; I'll drive you home."

"I'm not going home, Chief," said Tommy gruffly. "I'm staying right here with Sherry and having a few more drinks." Sherry looked over to them at the mention of her name. She also noticed that the chief's voice was getting louder. Tommy caught her eye. "Another one, Sherry."

"Tommy, for Christ's sake…" Bumpy pleaded.

"Have one on my tab, Bump."

"Make me a coffee when we get home. Come on, Tom." As he spoke, Bumpy touched his friend's arm slightly, urging him up. The chief roughly shrugged it away.

"Just let me be, Liborio! Don't you have anything better to do than escort drunks? Aren't there some crooks to catch?"

"Tommy, don't make this any harder…"

"Harder? Who the hell asked you, Chief? Jesus. What the hell's so hard for you? You got four great kids…Jesse's crazy about you. What do you know about hard? Why don't you just get the hell out of here and leave me alone." Tommy's voice was shrill, but it was plaintive rather than angry.

3

"God damn you, Tommy. You're coming out with me even if I have to strap you into that fucking chair with my own hands and drag you out...and you know I can do it. So, are we gonna go out to my car or not?"

Tommy sat back down. He had stood up to confront and tower over his tormentor. Bumpy sat down, too. "What's wrong, *Paesan?*" he said softly to his old friend. "You sick or something?"

Tommy was shaking his head as Bumpy talked. "Nah, Bump, I'm just old, you know? Just tired."

The black Cadillac stopped in the curb lane of the busy street, pausing for a moment to let some of the commotion pass by: cars, jaywalkers, a wayward cab. But in a moment, a burly man sprang from the front seat of the car and opened the opposite back door in an easy, practiced movement. The big man looked around, careful and watchful as good bodyguards should be. Out stepped a young, dark-haired man in a tailored blue suit, glistening black shoes, beige silk paisley tie, and pale white shirt. He had the practiced look of a busy man, looking hurried yet unhurried, determined but slightly bored. The younger man was in his early forties with dark, wavy hair, thinning slightly at the temples though not yet very noticeably, manicured nails, and the deliberate studied grace of someone born to command, someone with a destiny. With a quick sideways glance at the burly older man, who nodded imperceptibly in assent, the young man stepped up to the sidewalk and walked the few feet into the Youngstown police station.

Close watchers had seen the little ritual unfold time and again in Youngstown. A large car stops, a bruiser gets out first, surveys the scene, and nods an okay...all clear. This was the custom of the Mafia in every city. It was the custom of someone who had something to hide, who had something to fear. And the ritual had been affected now by others, the non-lethal rich who wanted to assume the air of power that subliminally proclaimed: Here was someone potent, who lived on the edge of violence. Fear and danger go before him.

Without stopping, he nodded to a sergeant who approached him smiling, with an extended hand. "Hi, Mayor, how's your dad?"

"Okay...better now," said the mayor-elect, unsmiling and still walking. At the far end, there was a long counter, the breadth of the room, cutting off all intruders who entered the lobby. Around the lobby were benches of polished granite, ancient and heavy things that seemed to anchor the room on all sides.

"Can I help you, sir?" said another sergeant as the mayor approached the counter. The mayor nodded to his bodyguard who answered for him.

"We're here to see the chief."

"Would you like me to ring up?"

"No!" said the bodyguard testily. "Buzz this open." He pointed to the tall gate doors with wrought iron reinforcements that were at the back end of the counter.

The sergeant pressed a button under the counter that caused a loud buzzing to emanate from the lock on the iron doors. The bodyguard pushed them open and stood aside as the mayor-elect walked through...up the elevator to the third floor, a quiet place, with none of the hectic movement of the first and second floors. These were the research and clerical offices of the force. And here was the chief's office.

The bodyguard knew where he was going, and the mayor-elect followed him with a bemused, preoccupied look. When they got to the office at the far end of the hallway, there were a pair of smoked-glass double doors set against the paneled wall. The bodyguard opened them and stepped aside as the mayor strode through. Then the bodyguard spoke to the secretary who was seated at a desk behind a railed partition that separated the waiting area from the office area. Inside there was another inner office, this time with a polished wooden door set into a door frame of rich dark wood. On it was a single brass plate, about the size of an eight-by-ten picture:

THOMAS P. MCCARRIE
CHIEF OF POLICE

"The mayor's here to see the chief," said the bodyguard with an air of newly minted command. The mayor looked a little uncomfortable, but nonetheless cool, as he watched and waited during the short exchange between the assistants. The secretary was a lovely, but not classically beautiful woman, of uncertain racial heritage. She had a wide, but non-Negroid nose, and a full mouth. She was taller than most Hispanic woman, possibly someone of mulatto heritage from the Caribbean. She was full-bodied, yet not fat, with a lush and understated sensuality... black hair and large black eyes, striking for a woman in her late forties. She had the fortunate skin tone that seemed to give her a permanent suntanned look... smooth, flawless, and golden brown. She spoke in a way that betrayed a slight accent. Maybe not an accent, but a Hispanic delivery of speech, restrained, even hesitant, and dignified.

"Was the chief expecting him?" she said quietly, seeming puzzled by the sudden appearance of the two men.

The mayor hesitated for a few seconds, then kept walking, the bodyguard surging ahead of his boss, trying to pull the door aside.

As the men strode past her, the secretary frantically tried to interpose herself at the door, but the bodyguard was through the door already.

Inside, the three of them confronted a man who had been standing, looking out the bay window behind his desk. The man had been gazing thoughtfully outside as he often did lately. He turned suddenly as the trio confronted him, bunched together at his office door. He glanced at his secretary, who returned a helpless, distraught look that told him that she was unable to stop the men from coming in.

"Thanks, Lucy," he said, nodding to her as she turned uneasily and left, closing the door behind her. "Mayor-elect," the chief said coldly.

"I've come for that talk I promised you," the younger man said, not even trying to be cordial.

"Have a seat," the chief said, gesturing to one of the two Queen Anne chairs in front of the fireplace on the far side of the room. The mayor walked over to a chair and sat down. His bodyguard stood behind him against the wall.

The chief looked at the two of them and smirked almost imperceptibly, yet enough to anger both men, as though they had not been let in on one of the chief's private jokes. "So, what's on your mind, Mayor?" the chief said almost flippantly. The bodyguard snorted, purposely loud enough for the chief to hear.

"Your resignations on my mind, Chief," said the mayor-elect, calmly, in an oft-practiced cooing tone. The younger man was working hard to restrain himself. He felt smug and potent...and yet this old man had gotten him almost out of control. All the good cards he had been dealt were not enough to soothe the rage and hatred he felt within him.

"Yeah," said the chief. "I'm almost sixty...so I figure a few more years..."

The mayor was losing his composure, almost on cue from another snort from his bodyguard. He was trembling as he spoke, "I want it this week...on my desk this week."

The chief ignored him and turned to the bodyguard. "Mickey? How thoughtless of me. I'll have Lucy bring you a cup of coffee...How about you, Mayor? A little Perrier?"

The mayor still seemed calm. "I mean it, Tommy. I want it before I take office." As he spoke, he turned to look at Mickey, daring him to accept the chief's feigned hospitality. "If you're smart, you go quietly and let me do what I was elected to do."

"But I'm not that smart, Carly. Hell, else I'd be mayor," said the chief mockingly.

"As mayor I can demand your resignation," said Carly.

"You can demand all you want, Boyo. Trouble is, I don't give a shit about your demands."

"You son-of-a-bitch," muttered Carly, flushed and trembling now. "I have to clean up the mess in this department, and I don't want some has-been wino like you around as chief."

"The only 'mess' in this department is gonna be after you put all your whores in good jobs...and all your dad's old numbers runners."

"I want that resignation this week, Tommy...or..."

Tommy chuckled. "Or what? Fire me? You don't have enough balls to fire me, kid. If you did, you might lose next time. And then you can't be congressman..." Tommy was counting on his fingers theatrically. "...or governor...or president. Hell, your old man would have wasted all that graft he laid on every crook and whore in the Valley. Who knows? You might even have to go to work for a living."

"Tommy, if you don't resign, I'll smear your name all over this valley...all over this state. You're nothing but a goddamned lush long past his prime – if you ever had one."

"Tommy the Quarterback," said the bodyguard, chuckling.

Tommy glared at the bodyguard for a second, then turned back to the mayor. "Look, Mayor, I'm busy. So, let's wrap this all up, okay? You want me to resign, and I want you to go fuck yourself. See? We just can't agree on things…"

The mayor stood up, glaring at his adversary, and advanced suddenly toward him as though to cause harm, and the bodyguard lunged after him. But Tommy stood his ground. "Carly," he growled softly, "even with this goon to help you, you can't be that stupid."

The mayor-elect swerved suddenly and headed for the door, opening it so that it slammed against the doorstop on the wall behind it, shaking the wall. Outside, he turned back to Tommy, who was still standing inside his office, and yelled back. "This week, you bastard! This week!"

Another door slammed, shaking the walls again, clattering the plaques and pictures against it. Carly and his bodyguard were gone. Lucy walked slowly back into Tommy's office, horrified as she had never been in her years as the chief's secretary. "Chief? Are you okay? Was that the new mayor?"

Tommy nodded and sat down in one of the fireside chairs. "He wants my resignation by week's end, kid."

She took a deep breath, more composed, standing directly in front of him. "Will you do it?" she asked hesitantly.

Tommy shook his head slowly, hardly moving it at all. "A couple years. That's all the sooner he's getting me out."

She nodded, straightening her dress, seeming to iron it with her hands against her outer thighs. "Would you like some coffee?"

"I'd like a bourbon and soda," he said wistfully. She stared back at him, saying nothing. "He said I was a wino, right?"

She smiled weakly. "I'll get some coffee," she said.

———◦•⬧•◦———

December rain made the chief morbid; but worse than that, to-night his nose would ache, and the pressure under his eyes, just about the time the rain came, would set his temples throbbing, and wind an invisible torture ring around his head. And knowing more pain would come tomorrow, made the pain he felt today all the worse.

Maybe I'll have a drink, he thought, as he headed for the oak library cabinet built into the entire west wall of his office. He opened the wainscoted doors outward; a nip from time to time, he thought. Hell, he was the chief. All those years, turning down drinks while on duty... Well, now he was the boss — at least for a while, and he didn't give a damn about the rules anymore.

He poured a finger of bourbon. and downed it quickly. It cleared his head a little, he told himself. But even if it didn't, he delighted in flouting the rules. And as though the effect of the bourbon were instant, he felt meaner and crankier, and in the mood for some mischief.

His secretary buzzed him on the intercom. "Yeah?" he answered.

"Chief Smolenski," she said.

A tall, slender man in his late fifties walked in unescorted. He was handsome and erect, neatly dressed in a dark blue uniform with epaulets and chevrons that signified deputy chief rank. He walked somewhat uneasily, but steadily. His hair was straight and white, and parted high on his head. He wore small, rimless glasses over a sallow face that had the sags and wrinkles that told of lost body fat. His hollow cheeks and wide prominent mouth might lead a close observer to surmise that the man had been sick. "How are you, Chief?" the man said.

"Fine, Smoke, how about you?" the chief answered, his tone questioning why his friend was there so early.

"Understand you met the new mayor," he said as he smiled wanly.

"Yeah, just what I needed to brighten up my day," Tommy sighed.

"He ask you to resign?"

Tommy looked at his old friend. "You could have bet your next month's pay on that."

"Don't even think it, Tom. It'll kill the department if he installs Laney in as chief. Christ, he'll be carrying bags in both hands."

"I'm not gonna do it, Larry…but he's gonna be trouble all the way. He's too dumb to know when not to fight."

"His old man must have greased people all the way to Columbus to get that kid in. And now he'll never know that his kid's still an arrogant jerk with no finesse. He'll never make the city work."

Tommy chuckled. "But, hell, he doesn't have to, Larry. You know that story: Keep telling everybody that it's working, and before they realize it isn't, Carly's running for governor."

Smokey sat down in one of the two dark leather easy chairs in front of the chief's desk. "Up so early, kid?" the chief said seriously as he walked around to the front of his desk and sat in the other brown chair, facing his colleague.

"Well," Smokey said uneasily, "we have something weird."

"Everything's weird, Boyo," the chief grumbled.

"We have to be careful with this one though, Tom." The chief nodded assent though still unsure of what his friend would tell him. "We caught two kids up at Spring Common with a quarter pound of cocaine in their car."

"I knew that," said Tommy. "Lucy had it on this morning's up sheet." The chief looked ruefully at his deputy, knowing he wouldn't like what Smokey still had to tell him.

"Did you get the names?" Smokey said. Tommy sighed, shaking his head. "A young kid and his girl," Smokey said softly. "...Bellino... Danny Bellino's kid."

"Oh, fuck!" the chief muttered.

The deputy grimaced. "Danny doesn't know. Hell, he's not even in town. I sent him out to Kansas City to that computer conference."

"How about his wife?"

"I'm gonna go see her. I just wanted you to know first."

Tommy walked toward the cabinet again. "Want a belt, Smoke?"

Smokey grimaced uneasily. "No, Tom, too early for me."

The chief poured another finger of whisky and drank it down silently, not looking at his deputy. "What the hell's their program? Running drugs, for Christ's sake?"

"I don't know, Tom. They didn't have a damned thing on them... no tools, no weapon, no money, no snorting stuff. I don't think it's theirs."

"Then whose is it?" Tommy said slowly, squinting his eyes as he talked.

"Tommy, they say they didn't do it, and I'll kiss your ass if they're a couple of runners."

"Where are they now?"

"Down in one of the old sweat rooms. We didn't put them in the cage... it would have embarrassed Danny." The deputy paused a few seconds. "There's something more, Tom."

"What?" Tommy sighed, turning back to Smokey.

"The president of Spring Common has called me twice already this morning. First time, he wanted them to get the chair. Second time, after he thought about it a little bit, he was worried about the 'adverse publicity.'"

Tommy snorted. "Hell, Lar, you've handled this kind of stuff before...just stall him till we get our act together."

"Yeah, Tom, I'll take care of it," Smokey said uneasily.

"How'd the president of Spring Common know when I didn't even know?"

"He said one of his campus security guys reported it."

Tommy was thoughtful for a few minutes. His hands rubbed the bridge of his nose, reddening further the visage that all his life seemed to show a constant flush. His glasses were hurting his ears again as if a headache wasn't bad enough.

"Danny's a good cop, Tom. You know much about him?"

"Not a lot. I know you like him. Both Bumpy and Pete told me he was a good man in Vice."

"He's honest and he's fair...and he keeps on learning."

"An honest Vice cop? I thought you and I were the only ones dumb enough for that."

"He's good enough to be sitting in your chair someday...if Carly Giustino doesn't do him in first."

"You're sure he's not one of Giustino's boys?"

"No way. And this thing could screw up his chances for captain next year. If I have anything to do with it, he's gonna get it."

———⦁⧁⦁———

On his way down the hall, the chief nodded to sergeants, secretaries, and patrolmen, and waved imperceptibly to captains and lieutenants. A young woman patrolman jumped up when she saw him. She smiled, opened the gate, and admitted him to the squad offices. He kept walking, following a corridor through the line of secretaries and stopped to talk to the day officer near the interrogation rooms. The officer escorted him down the green-painted corridor to the last room. The chief nodded to him as he unlocked the door and ushered Tommy in.

Inside were a young man, a boy almost, and a girl…obviously his girlfriend. Tommy surveyed the two of them; they were clean and attractive. The boy was sitting against a wall leaning backwards on a chair, and the girl, sitting near him, looking down at her hands folded in her lap. They looked like high school sophomores, Tommy thought.

The boy was angry and frustrated, and the girl frightened. "Who are you?" she asked. "What do you want from us now?"

The boy sneered. "This is Tommy the Quarterback, Neva," he said, looking defiantly at the chief.

Tommy walked toward the girl, but as he walked, in passing the boy, he kicked the chair out from under him, sending him sprawling to the floor. The boy was startled, and the girl screamed softly. The boy tried to pick himself up off the floor, doing a push-up to bring himself erect. Then, Tommy grabbed him by the scruff of the neck and hurled him toward the girl, forcing him to brace with his hands to keep from hitting the wall.

"Right. A smart ass," growled Tommy. "You call me 'Chief,' kid. This is my place and I'm the boss around here…Do you two know what you're in here for?"

"We didn't do anything," the boy said. "We never use dope, and we never saw that stuff before." Tommy turned toward the girl, but the boy was still talking. "You can't keep us in here," he continued. "You have to let us talk to a lawyer."

Tommy turned toward the boy again, eyeing him coldly. "A lawyer, huh?"

"It's part of your procedure. I know that," the boy said in calm defiance.

"Kid, maybe we ought to get something straight: Personally, I don't give a rat's ass if they throw you in the slammer till you're fifty." Tommy tried to calm himself, pausing for a few seconds. "But I know and respect your father. And he doesn't deserve a loud-mouthed son who can wreck his career just because the kid was too stupid to behave himself."

"But I told you we didn't do anything wrong!" shouted the boy, this time his voice cracking slightly, with the hint of tears in his eyes.

Tommy grabbed him suddenly by the front of his shirt near his neck, and roughly pulled the boy's face forward to look into Tommy's eyes. The boy was startled and frightened, and stared silently at Tommy. The girl let out a soft shriek and put her hand on Tommy's arm to restrain him. "Refresh my memory, kid. I could swear you're in here for possession of narcotics."

Tommy turned back to the girl. She was a lovely young thing; almost what Lucy would have looked like as a girl. Lighter maybe, but with the same beautiful dark eyes and black hair. "We didn't know about that stuff," she said softly, looking up at the chief's face. He could sense a gentleness there, a difference, like something in his memories of long ago, of a girl he had almost forgotten, and of a time when he had a chance for happiness with her, and chose someone else.

Tommy was calming down, soothed by the magical innocence of the girl. When he glanced at the boy, he could see a trickle of blood from one nostril where he must have struck him as he grabbed his collar. "Come sit down here," he said to the boy softly, gesturing to a seat near the girl.

When the boy sat down, he looked at Tommy and said, "You don't believe us, right?"

"I believe you," Tommy sighed. "But you have to understand something: You don't live in a vacuum. Your dad's in this world you live in...and your mom. And yours, too," he said, turning to the girl. "But so are a lot of people who don't give a damn about you, or whether you both go to jail. People out there who don't like me, or your dad, or anybody else who'll try to defend you. So, you have to let the right people help you...and if you've never told the truth before, you'd better start doing it now."

The boy softened, clasping the girl's hand as Tommy talked. "Does my dad know?" he said quietly.

"No, but he's gonna know damned soon," said the chief. The boy took a deep breath and looked at the girl. "What were you two doing out there at one in the morning?"

"He was working on a computer program," the girl answered. "We go there a lot on Friday nights because the system doesn't get as much demand on Fridays. I help him."

"The janitor lets us stay because he knows us, and we never cause trouble or leave a mess," the boy said.

"So, we went out to the car just like we always do," said the girl. "And by the time we got to Stadium Drive, the Spring Common police stopped us."

"And they found two bags of something...dope," said the boy.

"Was your car locked when you left it?"

"Yeah, I lock it out of habit. My dad always..." His voice trailed off as he spoke.

"Where was the dope?"

"In the car," the boy said with a quizzical look on his face.

"I mean where in the car?" Tommy said impatiently.

"Under the back seat," the boy answered. "I never took that seat out in my life."

"Was it easy to see?"

"No," said the girl. "There was a guard or something. It was under that... You had to take the back seat out anyways."

"You mean like a shroud over the fender under the seat?"

"Yeah," said the boy.

Tommy stared at the two of them for a moment. They looked so fresh, so young, so unlike the people they often got in that place: people wasted by years of running, cheating, drugs, guilt. No lines had been etched into their faces, no sags and weighted jowls, none of the intractable cares and worries of the world had faded their skin or stretched it over their faces taut and transparent.

"You swear to God you don't know anything about this?" Both shook their heads. "And you're not into dope... neither one of you... no brothers and sisters into crack?"

"There's just nobody," said the girl, looking at the boy who was shaking his head. "It's not us."

"Okay, you two just stay here for a while. I'll be back later."

"But what about my mom? My dad's out of town..." said the boy. "And her mom..."

"If you're telling me the truth, you'll see them soon," the chief said.

Outside, the chief walked hurriedly down the hallway to the desk of the day officer. "Where's Chief Malatesta?"

"He's in court, sir."

"How about Sergeant Williams?"

"He's down in his office."

Tommy walked down the long corridors he had traveled so many years. He knew every square inch of the building... every closet, every shelf, every sink, every light box. The thirty-three years he spent rising from rookie to chief had made the station as much his as a hive to a bee. He stopped at the smoked glass door. The sign on the door read: Sergeant Meadows J. Williams, Impounded Vehicle Office. Inside, Tommy confronted a young black secretary, sturdy, heavyset, but with a smile that seemed to come from nowhere to brighten a rather ordinary dark brown face. "Hi, Chief McCarrie," she said brightly.

"Hi, Lassie, is the boss in?" Tommy answered, nodding toward the door.

"Yes, sir, he sure is. Come on in," she said.

Tommy followed her a few steps as she opened the door admitting him to a cramped, messy office that had a large desk at one end, taking up almost the width of the rectangular room. Behind the desk was a tall, black man, about six-feet-five in height, with long slender arms and a gaunt physique that seemed to be that of an aging basketball player. His face was dominated by a thick moustache, more gray now than black. His small head was close-cropped, with hair seeming to gray only at the tips, as though covering his head with hoarfrost, all except at the ever-widening ring about the crown of his head which was bare and shiny. The man smiled at the chief, and stood upright quickly making a half-hearted attempt to come to attention until Tommy's hand shook an imperceptible rejection of that formality. "How are you, Chief?" said the man, towering over his visitor.

"Hi, Med. Long time no see," said the chief.

"Down here, anyway."

"This is a friendly visit, Meadows…just you and me."

Meadows nodded, knowing that there was surely an unstated reason why the chief of police would appear suddenly in the shabby old vehicle office. "Yeah, I hear you," said Meadows. "Something wrong, Chief?"

"Not with you, Boyo," said Tommy. "How're the knees?"

Meadows raised his eyebrows. "They want to do the other one now," he said. "I told them I got some time to go for my pension."

"You mean you're still worried about being put off the force?"

"It could happen, Tommy," said Meadows softly.

"Not while I'm chief," Tommy answered. But as he spoke, he could see the doubt and uncertainty in his friend's eyes. "I got a couple years almost, Med. I won't let anyone screw you on that."

Med nodded to himself, relieved to hear the chief promise what he always knew he would do. "The mayor doesn't have enough stick to get you out, huh?"

"Not quite...not for a while anyway."

"So, what's the Chief of Police doing down here in the motor room so early in the morning?"

"Danny Bellino's kid's in trouble, Med."

"I heard," sighed Med, still puzzled about Tommy's presence.

"Med, there's something screwy about the whole thing. That kid's no more guilty than you or me. Hell, he was studying at Spring Common with his girlfriend."

"But they caught him with quarter pound, Tommy."

"Yeah, I know," Tommy sighed.

"And you believe those kids, right?"

Tommy nodded. "I talked to them even. They didn't do it."

"That much dope is a hell of a problem, Tommy," said Med.

"Where's the car?"

"Across the street," said Med, expecting another question from Tommy.

"Do me a favor...Go over it...Strip the doors down...Check the windows. See if they used a slim-jim...What am I saying, huh? I'm telling you how to scope out a car..."

19

Med chuckled. "Long time, Tommy. You get a little busy sometimes."

"I have to know who planted that stuff in Danny's car, Med. You're the best one I can trust to find out."

"Give me a couple hours. I'll get right on it."

"This is between you and me, Meadows. Okay?" Med nodded. "I'll be up in my office," Tommy said.

Tommy waited in his office, tending to a few chores he had to do: a letter to the Command Officers Association, a note to the superintendent of the State Highway Patrol. *Things would change*, he thought. Soon, Carly's going to try to move Chris Laney up to deputy chief. Hell, he thinks he's running things now. And fewer things of consequence will cross his desk. He'd get ceremonial things, civic pride stuff. But he wouldn't be running the police anymore. Giustino would see to that. All he could do was be stubborn; if Carly wanted it, he would be against it. And he had to protect a few people…Smoky, Med Williams, Pete Mencken, Bumpy, Danny Bellino, all the guys who never screwed him, who fought the streets with him, all the guys who helped him be a good chief.

Lucy opened his door. "Chief? Are you okay? Do you have something you want me to do?"

"Nah, kid. I'm just waiting for some info. When Med Williams comes up show him right in."

She nodded as she turned toward the outer office. *God, she's beautiful*, Tommy thought as she walked away. *I wonder if she's still seeing that lawyer from the prosecutor's office. She's so efficient, so perfect. Hell, those guys ought to feel lucky just to touch her hand, let alone take her out.*

Tommy worked quietly, yet nervously, bothered by the time that was going so slowly. Just then, Lucy rang on the intercom. "Chief Smolenski," she said.

Larry Smolenski walked in hurriedly, confronting Tommy with a worried look. "What's happening, Tom?" he said.

"Did anyone give those kids some breakfast?"

"Yeah. They didn't want anything…just juice."

"I don't think they knew anything either, Smoke."

"So, what are we gonna do?"

"Med Williams is over checking out the car. If he finds any signs of entry it'd have to be a plant, right?"

"But if it was, then what?"

"If it was, those kids are going back home."

"Who knows about this, Tommy?"

"Bumpy, Med, Pete…all the gang. If no one else talks, then it's a secret, right?"

Just then, Lucy opened the door and Med Williams entered. "Chief," he said, nodding to Smokey.

"So?" said Tommy.

"Clear as day you could see scratches from a stick," said Med. "And something else…I found a hair in there…in the back seat where the crack was planted."

"What color hair?" asked Larry.

"It sure as hell wasn't from those kids…white…"

"Straight or kinky?" said Tommy with a smirk.

Med chuckled. "It wasn't mine, Tommy," he said.

All three men laughed softly and easily, old friends whose faith and integrity had been tested again and again over long years of friendship.

Suddenly, Tommy grew serious. "Med, get some people you can trust and have them dust that car top to bottom." Then, he turned to Smokey. "No paperwork on this one, okay?" Smokey nodded. Both men stared at the chief. "And I'm gonna take those kids home," he said.

Down at the garage, there were two cars parked in the chief's place: one, a black-and-white with the emblem and shield of the Youngstown Police emblazoned across the door…his show car, used on official meetings where dignitaries would attend. The other was a black Lincoln with a luxury interior and unpretentious outside. It was the plain car that was Tommy's personal car also, a perk of the job that no one begrudged him. The boy and the girl followed him through the cavernous garage to Tommy's black Lincoln. Tommy immediately went to the driver's side and opened all the locks with the turn of his key. Young Bellino stood aside to let the girl in. She hesitated for a moment, and Tommy said, "I won't bite you. Come on." With that the girl slid easily onto the front seat next to Tommy. Danny got in beside her and shut the door.

They drove in silence and bemused amazement for several minutes. Just then, Tommy stopped the car in front of a small restaurant known as much for its pastries as for its food. They looked at him warily. "I'm hungry," Tommy said as he got out of the car.

Inside, the restaurant was almost empty. Most of the early diners were on their way to work. As Tommy sat down, an old, small woman approached the table smiling. She nodded to Neva and Danny and spoke to Tommy. "Chief, it's nice to see you." She spoke in broken English laced with heavy Hungarian. She turned toward the young couple. "Are these your grandchildren, Chief?"

"No," said Tommy, "I'm just babysitting."

The woman twinkled. The girl smiled first and finally the boy smiled softly. "Let's get some breakfast. I want to talk to you…You know what I want, Mariska," he said.

Neva ordered a waffle and Danny ordered eggs and bacon. Tommy always ate a small omelet of eggs scrambled with paprika and onions.

"So, you two aren't a couple of crooks, huh?" he said, eyeing them both.

"I can't understand it," said Danny. "Why would anybody do that?"

"That's what I want to know... Do either of you have any enemies, bad enemies?"

"No," said the boy. "I don't think everybody likes me, but I don't know anyone who would do this."

"We aren't important. Why would anybody pick on us like that?" the girl said.

Tommy studied her throughout their talk. She wasn't well dressed, but she was neat. Her hair was not done to her best advantage. Yet she had large dark eyes and a wide mouth that made her smiles light up her face. *What some Hollywood makeup man could do with her*, he thought. She had something more than sheer beauty... a quiet reluctance; maybe it was humility. She had the look of someone poor who was struggling to overcome it. Although bound by the life she had, she was gifted enough and determined enough to be different. She would someday not be poor, and it would come of her own goodness, her gentility, her intelligence, and her honesty.

Danny was clean and healthy looking, easy middle class. He came from a good family who were comfortably well off- police lieutenant's comfort. At first, they would seem an unlikely couple. He was impeccable with white shoes and jeans; she looked like she was trying to be comfortable wearing someone else's clothes. And yet she was appealing. Slender and not too tall, she was the frail counterpart to the stocky Danny.

"You two been going together long?" Tommy asked.

23

They looked at each other. She smiled shyly, a lovely wide, glowing smile. Danny did, too, as though they shared a secret between them. "About a year," Danny said.

They were quiet for a few seconds. Tommy was wondering what they would do in the future, but Danny seemed to feel that he had to assert something. "We're going to get married when I graduate next year," he said, seeming to sense Tommy's wondering.

"How many in your family?" Tommy asked the girl.

"I'm the only one at home now. I have four older brothers and three sisters...all married except my brother in the Marines."

"And yours?" he said to Danny.

"A younger brother and a sister," he answered. "I'm the oldest."

"Do you go to school full time?" Tommy said to the boy.

"Yeah, and I work part time at the Kroger on Market Street."

"How about you?" Tommy said to the girl.

"I work full time. I'm a secretary at R. M. Murphy Construction. I take two courses at night every quarter. That's where I met Danny."

The old woman brought the rest of their breakfast. They exchanged a few more pleasant words, and then the woman left them again. As Tommy began to eat his omelet, the girl studied him. Finally, she said, smiling, "Why do they call you Tommy the Quarterback?"

Tommy looked at Danny who was smiling but slightly uncomfortable at the girl's insouciance. "Maybe I should have left you in jail," Tommy said to Neva, chuckling softly.

"We answered all your questions," said the girl, playfully.

"I was a quarterback at Ursuline when we beat Massilon one year... when no one ever thought we could. The whole team used to hang out together...we were mostly all good friends. We even went into the service together — about five of us. Anyway, one of the tackles who's now a deputy chief, Bumpy Malatesta, told the sergeant that I was a quarterback on our team. And the sergeant kept calling me 'Tommy the Quarterback'...and so did everyone else in our company. And some of the hometown boys took the name back to Youngstown — and it stuck — all through college, all through the police force. I've been waiting to get even with Bumpy ever since."

"He's under you at the police station?" the girl said, wondering why Bumpy had not been made to pay for his treachery.

"Yeah, but he's always been such a good friend — I was his best man — I can't bring myself to really get him good. I'll think of something before I die."

The girl nodded, seeming to take pleasure in the little story. She looked down at the breakfast that she had hardly touched. "You wouldn't treat us like this..." she said without looking up.

"I believe you," Tommy interrupted. "But you must know that some people like to have scapegoats." He turned to Danny, peering over his glasses. "And some wouldn't mind seeing the career of a promising young police lieutenant go down in flames just 'cause he's such a standup guy...and they're jealous."

The boy nodded remorsefully. "I would never do that to my dad," he said.

"And that's why you're having breakfast with me and not in jail talking to lawyers or police investigators," Tommy said.

After a few seconds in which each of them did some justice to their breakfasts, finally Neva looked up at Tommy, and without speaking, let him know that they were done.

Tommy had become enchanted with the girl. She reminded him of an Italian girl he once knew, someone he had been false to, someone whose goodness he had feared, someone whose freshness and honest love he had run away from. And Neva was the reincarnation of that girl he had long regretted losing…ingenuous, bright, and honest.

His life had never been the same, he thought, as the girl found him staring at her, curious about his thoughts. She could have been his granddaughter. She could have been Anita's parting gift to him. She could have been what saved him from his arid life…from marrying Janet, from all the pain he suffered, from all the lonely days.

Abruptly, Tommy stood up and walked over to the counter to pay the check. The boy and the girl waited for him by the door. The old woman thanked him for coming and reminded him not to stay away so long.

On the way, since Danny's house was closer, he dropped him off first. "You stay here," he said as he got out of the car, letting Danny kiss the girl goodbye and walk toward the house. Just like always, Tommy thought: Dagos always go in the side door.

Danny entered with a key into the brightly-lit house. The sky showed faint brightness in the early morning, but the windows showed lights that had been on all night. Danny's sister heard the door and entered the kitchen frantic to see who had entered. When she saw Danny, she turned and rushed out of the room. In a minute, she returned with her mother. For a second, she paused, looked at Danny with gaunt face and hollow eyes, and then looked at the chief. No one spoke for a few seconds. Her eyes glazed with tears as she looked back at her son, questioningly. "I'm okay, Mom," Danny said softly.

She looked at Tommy and he nodded. Then she hugged Danny to herself and cried softly and silently. His sister also cried a few steps from her mother and brother. In a few moments, she released her son and held him at arms-length before her. "What happened?" she asked, meaning the question more for Tommy than for her son.

"There was a problem with some drugs we found in your car, Mrs. Bellino," said Tommy.

"Oh...drugs?" she said, horrified, as she looked into her son's eyes before her.

"I didn't, Mom. It wasn't me."

Again, she looked at Tommy for reassurance. "He didn't do anything," he said. "But it does look like some kind of set-up."

"Has he been charged?" she said, fixing her gaze on Tommy.

"No charge. Have you talked to your husband lately?"

"About an hour ago. He's on his way home."

"Chief Smolenski talked to him also. When he comes home, tell him to get some rest...I mean that...and then come to see me tomorrow."

Tommy left them in a few minutes. Outside, the girl waited nervously in the car as he approached. "Is it okay?" she asked as Tommy got behind the wheel.

"Yeah," he said. Then, he started the car and backed out of the driveway. "You know I'm going to have to talk to you both again," he said.

"I know," said the girl. Then she was silent as Tommy drove. "Why did you believe us? Was it just because of Danny's father?"

"You know it wasn't just that," Tommy muttered.

"And we're not liars?" the girl said, softening her tone slightly as she spoke, seeming more personal and almost intimate. Tommy shook his head.

Her face brightened with a smile as they drove for several minutes without speaking. "Are you coming in to talk to my mother?" she said.

"Yes," said Tommy, not taking his eyes off the road.

Finally, she spoke again as the car neared her house. "You're a good man," she said. "Those stories they tell about you aren't true."

"Some are true," Tommy grumbled. "Even when you try to do good, some bad stuff slips in."

Neva smiled again, this time looking at Tommy, letting him see her face. "I'll make you coffee when we get home," she said.

The girl's mother was a slender woman with large dark eyes and thick black hair streaked with strands of gray. She had the same golden skin tone as Neva, but with thin lips and tired expression.

"It's okay, Mama," Neva said as her mother stared fearfully at her and looked skeptically at Tommy. Her daughter hugged her and stepped back to confront her. "Mama, this is the chief of police." Her mother gasped at the mention of the top policeman. But her daughter spoke playfully, with a slight smile playing across her lips as she spoke, "Tommy el Quarterback."

Her mother responded nervously to her daughter's mood. "Please sit," she said to Tommy.

Tommy grabbed a kitchen chair and pulled it away from the table to give him vantage of the two women who faced him. Suddenly the girl began to stir, preparing coffee. Neva's mother watched the girl's casual ease despite the presence of the chief of police in her kitchen. It was now daylight in the early morning.

"There was trouble, Mama," the girl said. "There were drugs in Danny's father's car. And we don't know anything about it."

The mother cast a sharp glance at the chief. "Do you believe this?" she asked.

"I believe your daughter," Tommy said. "Do you have any reason to believe that either your she or Danny were involved with drugs?" Neva looked sharply at Tommy, surprised at his question. The woman shook her head silently. "They didn't know it was in the car," said Tommy to assure her.

The girl sat next to him. Suddenly this man mattered to her. She hadn't had a father in so many years, so many dim recollections. This nice, tough man had been good to her, had believed her, and that was his greatest gift to her.

"We might have to go back to talk, Mama," said Neva.

"If they did nothing, why do you want to talk to them?" the mother said to Tommy.

"We have to see if they can remember anything, or tell us something that might help us find out who really did this. Those drugs were worth a lot of money."

The girl poured coffee for Tommy, and he nodded thanks and appreciation. "Why didn't you arrest them?" the woman said warily.

"I could have," Tommy said. "It would have been standard procedure. Do you think I should have arrested them?"

"Mama!" the girl chided.

"It was not because Danny's father was a policeman?"

"Yes, it was…and because I believed your daughter. Look…Danny Bellino's a fine young officer and a good man. And I don't want to see his career ruined because of this, understand?"

She nodded slightly, convinced that Tommy made sense. "So, it was more than the kids?"

"Mrs. Molinero, I told you I believe them," Tommy said.

Neva put her hand on her mother's forearm, and without a word calming her and reassuring her that Tommy was honest. She started talking to Tommy about his job, and as she did, her mother began to soften. The mother responded to Neva's instinctive, unguarded attraction to this older man.

The time passed easily, with Neva talking softly, sometimes teasing, sometimes taunting Tommy. Neva not only soothed her mother with her cheerful demeanor...but also Tommy. After a while, it was time to leave. The mother's tired, troubled eyes, the girl's relaxed and suddenly fatigued look, told him that. Tommy said goodbye and started back for the door that they had entered from the driveway. They knew they were not done with the police, but they knew also that there would be one man on their side that mattered.

Just before he left, he turned back to the girl, who had been following him. "You watch yourself," he said earnestly to her, "and make something out of that hot-headed boyfriend of yours."

She was smiling broadly before he spoke, but now she just looked at him with a slight smirk playing on her lips. "Tommy the Quarterback," she said softly. But before he could react, she hugged him and held him for several seconds. Tommy put one arm behind her shoulders and held her to him gently.

Suddenly this young woman with the strange, lovely face and slender body and thick black hair and luminous dark eyes had touched him, and found a way to instill some feeling into his tired life.

———•◦•——

Throughout the day, Tommy sat pensively in his office doing paperwork. Occasionally, Lucy would come in to him to ask questions and directions. He signed letters and read reports. He drafted a response to the FBI. He was sleepwalking he told himself. Med had come up with his report — no fingerprints in the car except those of the girl and the Bellino family. They did find a small piece — about a centimeter square — of latex, probably from a rubber glove.

Tommy sat thinking as he waited for Smokey to come to him for one of his daily reports. Who wears latex gloves but a pro? Who would plant something on Danny Bellino?

Lucy came back in. "Would you like some coffee, Chief?" she said.

"No, thanks, kid...Smokey isn't around, huh?"

"His secretary usually calls when he's coming up..."

As she spoke, Smokey opened the doors to the outer office. He walked more haltingly than he had early this morning, and looked drained and tired. Lucy closed the door behind her, leaving both men in Tommy's office. Tommy eyed his deputy chief uneasily. "How're you doing, kid?" he said as Smokey settled unsteadily into a chair.

"Okay, Tom," he said wearily, trying to hide his feelings as he always did.

"You have your chemo recently?" Tommy said, looking at the tired old friend who sat before him.

"You don't have to be on chemo to be tired, Tommy," Smokey answered with a slight edge in his voice, wishing to avoid the conversation.

"Yeah, I know, but I was just..." Tommy looked up at his deputy and was struck by the quiet dignity of the man. He was in pain and Tommy knew it. He knew all the body language of his old friend. He knew him as a rookie cop when Tommy was only a second-year foot patrolman. He knew it from all the danger they had been in, from all the moral support they had given each other. He knew him as a friend who was as decent and honest as any man he'd ever met.

"You want some time off, kid?" Tommy said quietly.

"No, I don't want any time off," said Smokey seeming to be jarred from some inner thoughts, answering in disappointment and hurt rather than in irritation.

"I didn't mean you aren't doing your job, Lar. I'm just asking if you want some time to rest at home."

Larry snorted. "Someday I'll have all the rest I need, Chief. No,

I'll be okay. I'm off the weekend; I'll rest up." He paused for a second, then looked directly at Tommy. "I had a treatment Monday."

Tommy took a deep breath. "Larry, I just want you to get through this okay. I need you, Boyo. You're the best damned cop this city's ever had."

"Thanks, Tommy. Yeah, a good spit and polish guy, but I've never been the investigator you are."

"I'm just more cynical, that's all. I've always looked up to you...and envied you."

"The carpet's getting a little damp, Chief," said Smokey, urging his boss to stop the accolades that made him so uneasy. And to stop reminding him of what he had to lose.

"I've seen Med. He told me they didn't find anything in the car. Just family prints...and a piece of latex, no doubt from a rubber glove," Tommy said.

"Bumpy said he thinks he has the guy who stabbed that high school kid on Wilson Avenue."

"Nice work, huh? Good old Bumpy," Tommy said.

<hr>

Later that night, Tommy was home reading, thinking about what Med Williams found...nothing. Nothing but the light hair and a spot of latex. And a lab analysis of the hair showed that the owner had taken cocaine. So, Danny's family had someone to fear. But to put a quarter pound in a car?

He'd have to ask Danny about his life: Who were his enemies? Who would plant so much coke just to wreck one cop's career? Or those two kids? Who would try to do them in? To the tune of so much cocaine? He shook his head. Too much to think about now. *I wonder how Elly's doing*, he thought. As he thought of her, he picked up the phone. He dialed and waited. He was always a little nervous about talking to her; they hadn't really been close as she grew up. But in later years, they discovered how much alike they were, and how much they needed each other in their own ways. Only lately, when both of them were lonely and vulnerable did they seem to find, in their misery, some time to talk heart to heart.

The phone rang and a voice answered. "Hi, Elly. It's your old man."

"Hi, Dad," she said, brightening.

"How are you doing, kid?" he said.

"Okay," she said unconvincingly. "Things are about the same here."

"And the kids?"

"Oh, they're fine…Carrie's taking ballet lessons and Mike's got a paper route; a small one, but it gives him some spending money."

There was a slight pause in their exchange, each knowing that there was something on the other's mind that was unsaid. "So, how's Tommy the Quarterback?" she finally said.

"The same, kid…mean as hell and cranky as ever. You know, I'm sorry I haven't gotten up to see you lately."

"I know you're busy, Dad. Just come when you can." Another pause, and this time Tommy was feeling all the things he wanted to say eluding him. Elly sounded tired.

"He was a damned fool to leave a girl like you, El," Tommy blurted out suddenly.

"Being a damned fool doesn't spoil your golf game, Dad…or make you any less of a ladies' man."

Tommy nodded silently. "Would you take him back?"

She shrugged to herself. "There are days when I think I would… even knowing all that he did. How about that for a dummy?"

"You that lonely, kid?" Tommy said.

"Kind of like my old man," she said, changing her somber tone slightly.

"I deal with it most of the time," he said. "But sometimes it gets me...like when I can't come over to see you and the kids at night."

"David got married, Daddy," she said, again in her hollow, somber tone.

Tommy didn't answer for a few seconds. "With that one he was carrying on with?"

"He says she makes him feel alive and creative. I guess he was feeling dead and stifled with me, huh?" she said, her voice cracking at the injustice of it all.

"If somebody had to tell him what he was giving up, it wasn't there in the first place, El," Tommy said. "And it wasn't any of your doing."

"I had to have done something," she said. "I wish I would have known if there was something I..." Her voice trailed off, and Tommy used the pause to change the subject to the kids again. They talked of Christmas and when Tommy could visit. After a while, they both knew that they had said all they could over the phone...until next time.

"Dad, please don't send any more money to the kids. You know I appreciate it, but it's more than they need. And I'm doing all right."

Tommy snorted. "Just trying to let them know I'm thinking of them, kid. I can't make the same mistake with them that I did with you. You're all I've got."

There were a few more seconds of silence before Elly suddenly said to Tommy as a goodbye, "I love you, Daddy."

"Thanks, kid, I love you too." Then he heard the dial tone. She wasn't all right. She was coping, straining under her loneliness...and she was hurt. And he knew it would never go away in Boston.

The next morning, Med Williams was waiting at his office when Tommy arrived at work. He was talking quietly to Lucy and drinking coffee. "Morning, Chief," he said, for both himself and Lucy. Tommy nodded and waved Med into his office. Lucy was already pouring his coffee.

"So, what's up, Meadows?" Tommy said, hanging his coat in a closet in the inner office.

"Not a damned thing, Tommy. That car was clean…a real pro job."

Tommy snorted. "Tell me something, Med. Why would somebody piss away almost a grand worth of coke like that? Only to nail a couple kids?"

Med snorted. "They had to be after Danny, right?"

"Unless they're completely screwed up…"

"You think Danny's wired?" Medford said somberly.

"No, but I don't like surprises either," Tommy muttered.

The chief and his sergeant talked for a few more minutes. Then, Med left, promising to keep Tommy posted on anything he heard.

At Christmastime, Carly Giustino held a press conference and gave two personal interviews on television, all of them oblique plaints against the police department. Tommy sulked in silence, still trying to temper his friends against the day he might have to give up his job.

Not so many bad things had happened in Youngstown recently — no bodies floating in the Mahoning, no drive-by shootings, no bombs going off. Larry Smolenski seemed to be getting worse. He was short-tempered but controlled. The department ran as it always did…efficiently. More computers were being brought in. Danny Bellino, over the shock of his son's arrest, began implementing the computerizing of almost every routine record-keeping task.

It was hard not to like Danny. He was the son everybody wanted: bright, friendly, straightforward, honest, and natural. And he worked hard. His family life had settled down, and his kids were back in school.

Occasionally, Tommy would recall the young girl. It had been so long since he had been enchanted by a woman…smiling, frowning, hurt, angry. It was as though she knew exactly what to say and how to say it. He thought of the wide mouth and the fine white teeth as she smiled. Hell, he had come to feel like a grandfather to the whole world: every woman younger, all sophisticated, all choosy and judgmental, all cold and calculating. But then he saw that warm, young girl whose unforced, gentle prodding began to take its toll upon his heart. Soon he remembered through a haze of cynicism how wonderfully charming women could be, how unique some were, how gentle, how captivating without effort. Soon he knew that he had not forgotten the pleasure of being in the company of a genuine and honest woman.

Med Williams began to stop by daily to talk…two old timers charging their batteries. It was going to be an easy year out, despite the machinations of Carly Giustino. It was obvious that Carly wanted him out, but that he didn't have the clout to fire him. So, he would try guerrilla warfare: thwart Tommy at every turn, elevate people who Tommy thought were incompetent or corrupt, and downgrade or ignore people who Tommy thought were honest and able. Carly's corruption would be slow and malignant, and long after Tommy was gone, Carly would have worked his will on the Youngstown police. He felt sorry for Danny and all the good cops he would leave behind, but he couldn't fix it all. There wasn't anything to do about the deliberate self-delusion of some people of Youngstown. How could they elect Carly? What makes good people close their eyes and hold their noses and rationalize their votes in favor of a weak, unprincipled mannequin who, without his father's ill-gotten wealth, would have been a hack lawyer doing divorces and DUIs for hoods and crack dealers?

Lucy came in with a tray of coffee. She didn't speak as she set the tray down on his desk. She seemed to make more trips in with coffee during these last few weeks. Tommy smirked, nodding his head slightly in agreement with himself. She was keeping him pumped with coffee and trying to make it tougher for him to crave the bourbon in the library cupboard.

Tommy had been staring out the window as she walked toward him. "What are you going to do, Luce?" he said, still not looking at her.

She stopped for a second, as if not understanding what he had said. But finally, she answered, "I'll find someplace...or maybe I'll retire if they make it too tough."

"But you don't want to retire, right?"

"I like my job," she answered quietly.

"They won't get rid of you; I'll see to that," said Tommy.

"As long as you stay, they won't," she said, looking directly at him.

"I'll find you something good before I'm gone," he said.

"Let's not talk about your being gone," she answered.

Later that morning, Larry Smolenski came upstairs to talk to the chief. He looked drawn and grave and sat down heavily in the chair in front of Tommy's desk.

"What's up, kid?" said Tommy.

"I have to go back into the hospital," Smokey answered.

Tommy was silent for a moment, staring at his friend, feeling helpless and at a loss for words. "Anything I can do, Larry?"

He was hesitant to respond. "Chief, I have some sick time and some vacation left. But I'm still a few months shy of thirty years on the force..."

"Jesus," muttered Tommy. "Lawrence, you mean to tell me you're worried about taking time off? You take all the time you need. Your checks will be delivered regular...by me...right to your goddamned house."

"But with sick time and..."

"I'll decide what you use. Far as I'm concerned, you're on special assignment for me."

"But Carly won't let you do it, Tom. You don't need that kind of aggravation from him."

"Smoke, far as I'm concerned, you don't have a damned thing to say about this. And Carly isn't gonna know the half of it. I'll snow that bastard so bad, he'll be on his ninth piece of coed ass before he even finds you've come back."

Smokey was quiet for a moment, staring at his boss. "I'm grateful, Tommy, but..."

"But nothing, kid. It's done."

Smokey nodded and left the room, flushed and relieved. Tommy sat in his chair staring at the papers on his desk. Suddenly, he was fearful. How could he ever go on without Smokey at his side? For thirty years, he saw him every day, was helped by him every day. And now the empty sensation of life without Smokey began to seize him. What would a morning seem like when he didn't get a visit from the top deputy chief? And never get one again?

The rest of the day, Tommy went about the routine jobs that confronted him. Once, Lucy came in to talk to him. "Chief Smolenski's sick again, isn't he?" she said.

Tommy nodded. "Yeah."

"Do you want me to get his mail again?"

"Yeah. Start tomorrow...and tell Chief Malatesta to come see me before he leaves today."

Later that afternoon the chief's office door suddenly opened and the familiar short, square man with huge arms and legs came into his office unannounced. "How are you, Tommy? Lucy said you wanted to see me?" He sat down in the chair near Tommy's desk.

"Smokey's sick again, Bump," Tommy said quietly.

Bumpy took a deep breath, looking out the north window in Tommy's office. "How bad?"

Tommy sighed. "He has to go in to the hospital for more treatment...something new."

"I've seen this before, Tommy. Often as not they don't ever come back out."

Tommy shrugged resignedly. "I need you up here, kid. You have to run things while Smokey's gone."

"Ahh, Tommy, I'm just getting that squad developed. If I let it go now, it'll be lost...How about Pete?"

"Pete's still coordinating that new narc group with the FBI. I can't shake him out...besides, I want you."

"Hell, Tommy, Smokey was the perfect guy for this. You know I get pissed off too easy..."

"I know you can do the job, Bump. And I sure as hell need someone I can trust. Carly'll want to slide Chris Laney in if you don't take it. *Capish?*"

"Shit," said Bumpy again, under his breath. "How long do I have?"

"Smokey's going in tomorrow. Maybe we can all meet and set up some agenda for you."

"You sure know how to fuck up a Christmas, Tommy."

———◆━◆◆◆━◆———

Tommy made it through the Christmas season. He bought gifts for Elly and her children, and for his cousin Ted, a priest at St. Martin's church in Warren, and for some old friends, hams for people he knew could use them, whiskey, grocery bags, and discrete handfuls of money for some people who it suited.

One gift was special, a pair of fur-lined, suede gloves for an old Black man who was the real, but not nominal, coach of the high school football team Tommy played on. He was gruff, patient, and never satisfied with anything but perpetual effort, constant striving for perfection. And Tommy was always a school boy to his coach whenever they visited together.

Tommy's tickets to Boston were already bought. Carly hadn't made any moves against him recently. *But now with the mantle of office upon him, he'll come at me,* Tommy mused. *Soon enough.*

His black Lincoln slowly came to a stop in front of an East Side house, once the neighborhood of many nations, but now the abode of Blacks, and some alien beings plying the drug trade among their own people. Some young men were standing in a group in front of the corner Straight-Eight Bar, about a hundred feet from the house. Curtains parted in other houses and Tommy sensed the eyes upon him. The men watched intently as the burly white man in a suit and black overcoat and black hat made his way across the street. Before crossing, Tommy had stood beside his car for a moment, looking up at the house, and up and down the street, not seeming to notice the young men, but noticing nonetheless. This man was someone official, they knew. Nothing but trouble could come to them by his acquaintance. But what would the police want here at Lazarus's house? And he couldn't be a doctor…and no minister would look with those policeman's eyes, back and forth and cautious, just as a cat would do before going out into someplace strange. Gradually, the men seemed to flatten themselves against the front of the bar, nervously eyeing Tommy in sideways glances. One man went inside the bar after a few seconds.

Tommy turned and walked through the chain-link gate that opened to about a fifteen-foot path and a set of stairs. On the porch, Tommy approached the front door of the house and knocked. An attractive Black woman came to the door and smiled when she saw Tommy. She quickly opened the door. "Hi, Ruby, how've you been?"

"Chief, nice to see you," she said, smiling broadly. "You're looking good, Tommy."

Tommy patted his stomach, showing how prosperous he was. "When you gonna franchise that place out, Ruby? It's a shame not to spread that good food all over the Valley."

Ruby beamed. "I got enough, Tommy. My kids don't want to do it, so one of these days…when I'm too old, I'll sell out…let somebody else do all that work."

Ruby was moving as she spoke, walking to an inner family room where an old Black man sat in a stuffed chair watching a college football game on television. "Daddy, Chief McCarrie's here to see you."

The old man snorted without looking up from the television screen. "He musta come this neighborhood to round some niggers into jail," he growled.

"Daddy, hush!" Ruby said, flustered by her father's outburst.

Tommy shook his head and winked at her. "If any niggers are going to jail, I'm gonna make sure one of them is a crabby old has-been football coach."

The old man scowled, then turned toward Tommy, with a quick glance at his distraught daughter. A smile played on his lips as he twinkled just a little. "He's mean as the day is long, Chief McCarrie. Ever since momma died, no one can deal with him."

"Laz, when are you gonna start behaving yourself?"

"Never, Tommy. It's a long struggle, but I'm gonna win." He glanced at his daughter, who was smiling now. "I raised all these kids, worked hard, and now they come 'round telling that I can't eat this, and I can't drink that, gotta walk more, gotta give up cigars. Bah!"

"Laz, it's time you gave up all that sinnin' you've been getting away with all your life," Tommy said.

Ruby snorted. "He keeps trying all the day, Tommy. World'll end when he stops sinning."

Laz chuckled. "I told you they ain't gonna win, Tommy. Now sit yourself down here," he said, pointing to the platform rocker opposite him. "Now tell me all about yourself, Chief of Police."

"Same old thing, Laz. Just biding my time till I'm sixty-two."

"You mean you're gonna skate till your sixty-two? Just like that?"

"I'm feeling pretty good…"

"That's not what I mean, damn you," Laz growled. His daughter had disappeared into another room and soon would be back with some of the pastries from her shop and some hot coffee. "I know the new mayor's got a big hard-on for you, kid."

"Does that surprise you, Laz? I put his old man in jail two times."

"You ain't gonna quit, are you, Tommy?"

"Nah, Coach, he's gonna have to fire me."

"You know he ain't got balls for that. So, what are you worried about?" Laz said knowingly, nodding his head in agreement before Tommy answered.

"He's trying to screw my friends and reward my enemies. I'm gonna take a lot of good people down with me...whether I go or stay."

"You ain't never been a quitter, Tommy. Remember that Campbell Memorial game? You won it in fourteen seconds?"

"Smokey won it. He's the one who caught the ball and ran forty yards...That was long ago, anyway, Laz," Tommy said wistfully.

"So, you ain't doing so well, then, kid?" Laz asked thoughtfully.

"Been better, Laz," Tommy said.

"Tommy, some things are always with you, things nobody can teach you...like staying until the job is done."

"I've pulled too many boners, Coach..."

"No one says you can't be dumb once in a while, kid. You just have to do it less than most."

"I'm tired, too, Laz. Maybe it's time for me to bail out."

"Bail out hell!" Lazarus growled. "Those sons-a-bitches can't wait till you're gone so they can fleece this valley and all them dumb sheep in it."

"But I don't have any leverage anymore. The only thing I got going is he's scared a little of firing me. He might not want a big battle right off the bat. But he's gonna move Chris Laney up...and nail Pete and Bumpy; you can count on it. And maybe Smokey, if he makes it."

"I heard about him down at the club this morning," Laz said.

Lazarus raised his chin and stretched his neck forward, a gesture he'd used all his life when he was thoughtful. Tommy watched him and recalled the sideline huddles of many a tight football game when Laz would rack his brain for just the right play...that always seemed to pay off. "I have to hang in there, too, Tommy. Sometimes I don't know why I do...with all this arthritis, all them hospitals, all the money it costs my kids. But here I am pissin' and scratchin'. Ain't that what we're all supposed to be doing? You and me?" Tommy nodded. "Cause life's too important to give it up, son. You're near twenty years younger than me. You can't start giving it up now."

"I suppose I'll hang in there a while longer," Tommy sighed. "Every time I see that bastard and his goons, I think of how these people in town are gonna get..."

"Fleeced," Laz interrupted.

"Fleeced," Tommy agreed.

"Besides, you have some good people you have to take care of, right?"

Tommy snorted. "You still have my office bugged, Coach?"

"Be fun if I did, kid. We just hear a hell of a lot down at the club. And I got some good spies watching over you. I know what you did for Med Williams."

"We winos have to stick together, Laz."

"You know I graduated high school with Meadows' father? You'd have liked him, Tommy. His son's just like him... quiet, sensible, honest, hard worker... only he likes the sauce just like his old man. Got killed in a car wreck when Med was just a kid in high school."

Ruby came back with coffee and sweet rolls. "If you behave yourself, Laz, Ruby'd have more time to make these wonderful things." Tommy held up a roll in front of him.

"She works too hard, Tommy. Then when she's tired, she comes after me," Laz grumbled.

"Somebody has to keep you in line," she said to her father.

Tommy reached into a bag and brought out a whiskey bottle and a gift for Laz and one for Ruby. "Aw, Tommy," Laz scolded, "I told you not to do this."

"No one twisted my arm, Coach. Besides, Ruby always gives me extra sweet rolls when I stop at her place."

They talked for a while longer, Tommy feeling warm and easy in the house of his old friend and mentor. Laz talked of all his kids and more of Ruby. Tommy remembered her as a little girl, beautiful and clean, one of the nice memories of his youth, when Laz would bring him home for supper to make sure he didn't lose more weight than he might. And now, through her marriage, her children, her widowhood, and through the years of caring for her father in his house, she still had that delightfully simple belief in God and goodness and hard work. She brought back not just memories, but feelings and hopes…a way of looking at the future and seeing light.

Later, after he had bidden Laz farewell, he stopped to talk to Ruby in the hallway. She always seemed like a little sister to him…one that he never had. "Well, we got one more year out of that old buzzard, huh, kid? Thanks to you."

"He's easy, Tommy. He likes to talk tough just to show you who's still the coach." She hesitated for a minute. "Only a few of you come to see him now, you know that? He thinks they've all forgotten him."

Tommy shrugged and shook his head. "He's one guy I can't ever forget, Ruby. Hell, we'd still be hustling pool and working in the mill without him…me, Bumpy, Pete, and Smokey."

"Is Smokey gonna make it, Tommy?"

Tommy shook his head. "I'm not sure, kid. It doesn't look too promising." He hugged her and kissed her on the forehead and headed out into the icy weather.

———

Lieutenant Daniel Bellino walked nervously down the long hall of the third floor of the police station. His face was drawn, and his eyes showed how tired and fearful he was. What would the chief tell him? Would this stop his career in its tracks?

As he neared the paneled wall where the chief's office was, his heart beat loudly in his chest. The smoked glass doors with Thomas P. McCarrie's name on them had never seemed so forbidding. It showed the authority of the community, the sanction of the populace, and it seemed to show them all arrayed against him.

These things didn't turn on fine points of law, of guilt or innocence; they turned on the perception that people had of your fitness. When you're a cop, if you even *seem* guilty, you're lost.

He opened the double doors and was met by the chief's beautiful, gold-skinned secretary. She admitted him into the chief's inner office, announcing his presence as she did with any caller who was there to see him.

Danny walked into the room and stood in front of the desk until Tommy motioned for him to settle into a leather armchair opposite the desk.

The chief was cordial, but not overly friendly. Most of what he knew of Danny was from others, people he trusted, to be sure, but not himself. This time he would try to find out what made this guy tick. If Danny was a smoother phony than Chris Laney, or if he was an honest cop who hadn't done anything wrong, then Tommy would know it. The instincts honed over thirty-three years of listening, would make a lie resonate in his psyche. And he would know then what he had to do.

Without almost any lead-in, Tommy asked Danny pointedly, "Do you know anything about that dope in your car?"

Danny took a deep breath, almost relieved to be able to say it first without interrogation or entrapment to squeeze the truth out of him. "No," he finally said, shaking his head.

Tommy stared into the younger man's eyes. "Would you know anybody who'd like to do you in?"

"I don't know, Chief. I guess there are some I've busted, but nobody stands out. Who would come out of the woodwork just to get a police lieutenant? Hell, we're a dime a dozen."

"How about Danny? He ever give you any trouble?"

"Not much...some teenage stuff...a speeding ticket...a fight after a football game. He's got a temper like my dad had...but he's not a bad kid at all, Chief."

"How about Neva?"

Danny was surprised that the chief knew the girl by her first name. "She's a girl Danny's lucky to have. I hope he marries her."

"So, you believe them when they say they don't know anything about the coke?"

"Yeah, I do," said Danny quietly. Then, as an afterthought, "But you believe them, too, right?" he said to Tommy.

"How do you and your wife get along?" Tommy said, ignoring Danny's question. He was being a professional investigator, and not allowing himself to be swayed by the natural charm of Danny.

The younger man seemed to squirm a little in his seat. "What makes you ask that?" he said, looking directly at Tommy.

The chief could feel the reaction as Danny answered. This was something in his life that marred the perfect appearance. He knew something about what Danny would tell him. "Just fishing, kid...routine investigation. So, what about it?"

Danny took a deep breath. "Yeah, a couple years ago. We just came unglued...six, eight months of arguing. Nothing vicious, just tiredness...irritability. We just couldn't talk without fighting."

Tommy could hear the strain in Danny's voice as he talked, could see the pain his question evoked in his young lieutenant's eyes. "How many years ago?" he said.

"Two almost…"

"You patch things up?"

"Yeah. We went to a counselor…and a priest."

"Did the kids see much of this?"

Danny raised his eyebrows and grimaced, an Italian gesture Tommy had seen on friends and foes alike all his life. "I'm sure they did… even though we tried to keep it to ourselves."

"How're you getting on now?"

"We're okay."

"Did you see anybody during this estrangement?" Danny seemed surprised at the question and looked questioningly at his boss. "Did you, Danny?"

"No," he said, looking away from Tommy.

"How about your wife?"

"Chief, what does this have to do with a bag of cocaine?" Danny said, now feeling angry as well as hurt. "My wife isn't into drugs."

Tommy really had two personae, one as the chief, Tommy the Quarterback, the gregarious public figure, the other was that of an experienced investigator — logical, intuitive, and alert. Few people who had known him as chief had ever seen him as an investigator…except the old gang. But seeing him would give clues as to how he became chief. It was a personality that always shadowed him and seldom came forth unless he was confronted by a mystery, not many of which had come his way in recent years. "Did she go out on you, Danny?"

Danny exhaled, seeming to have held his breath for several minutes. "Yeah, she did," he said, "…when we were separated."

"She had an affair with somebody?"

"No, Chief. She said she never slept with him...Jesus," Danny muttered under his breath as he felt the pain of the thought of his wife out with another man, much less having him touch her.

"It's pretty unusual in this day and age to keep company with a guy and not go to bed with him, Danny...Do you believe her?"

"With all my heart, Chief," he said, eyes glistening. "She told me he never touched her."

"She's very attractive as I recall," Tommy said, leading his subject to say more.

"Yeah," sighed Danny, showing annoyance at the comment.

"You have any reason to believe that she ever did this before?"

Danny shook his head. "I don't think she ever has, Chief. She's not the type...she found that out when she was with this other guy."

Tommy softened a little. "Do you know him?"

"No. He was in a class she was taking. He quotes poetry, likes wine...one of those guys who make a guy like me look like a clod."

"Those guys always look better through opera glasses, Danny," Tommy said. "...So, you're back together for good?"

"Yeah," Danny said softly.

Tommy eyed him for a few moments without speaking. Danny had taken out a handkerchief to wipe his eyes and blow his nose. *Even a life as perfect as this one, huh?* Tommy thought to himself. *This kid and his family look like a Currier and Ives painting. He was slender and nice looking, tall for an Italian, and intelligent. He was also genuine and decent. Why does evil intrude upon such a life?*

He had learned early in his career that appearances were never a window on reality. He'd seen vicious killers who looked like altar boys, maniacs who looked like Jaycee's men-of-the-year, and thieves and wife-beaters who looked like decathlon gold medal winners.

And now this nice young man with the picture-perfect family somehow has to deal with a bag of cocaine in his car and questions that evoke bitter memories of how he almost lost his wife. How strange that so many odd things intertwine and weave a life.

"Did you talk to your wife about the coke, Danny?"

"Yeah, Chief, she doesn't know anything about it," Danny answered tiredly.

Tommy stood up and went over to the bay window behind his desk and put one foot on the built-in bench in front of it. He watched the weather outside. Finally, he said, "I'll tell you what I think, Danny. There's a chance this thing is some kind of fluke...some screw-up with a drop- off at the college, or...it may be that someone has a hard-on for you, and they tried to do you in, or somebody wanted to do a job on Danny or Neva."

"You know, Chief, I talked to those kids for hours. They don't know anything about the drug trade. Neva's mother, my wife...nobody has a clue. I wish I could tell you something more; there just isn't anything."

Tommy turned back toward his lieutenant. "Tell you what: I'm gonna let this thing stay right where it is...in Limbo. If nothing more happens, we chalk it up as an educational experience and forget it." Then he looked directly at Danny, moving closer to him to make his point. "But if you haven't been straight with me, son, I'm going to find out...and then I'm gonna cut your balls off. *Capish?*"

Danny swallowed hard and nodded. "I swear to God, Chief..."

Tommy held up his hand to stop Danny from talking, moving it palm-front, sideways across the front of his body, as though giving an Indian sign for silence. Danny nodded again.

Tommy, by this time, was around the desk as Danny stood up. He reached for the younger man's hand and grasped it firmly. "I had to ask you those things, Dan. I know it was tough." Danny smiled weakly.

Larry Smolenski went into the hospital on Monday morning to begin cancer treatments again. Bumpy Malatesta became first deputy chief, much to his own chagrin. But he did his job with energy and care, and with the dedication that he expected from all those who worked for him.

All in all, the force ran smoothly. Tommy helped Bumpy by sharing some of the workload with him... especially the work that required reportage and phone calls. They both missed Smokey at the end of the day.

Tommy took his time getting ready to go home that night. Lucy had closed up the outer office as she usually did. He poured himself a drink from his cupboard. It was almost dark and it was barely five o'clock. The streets were busy and noisy in the rush hour, and the Youngstown winter weather was changing suddenly. Snow was beginning to fall, and that would make for the traffic division a nightmare on the beginning of the shift. Snow caused more horns to blare, more sirens to sound, and more rescue squads to course through the downtown streets.

Suddenly he heard the outer door open. *Bumpy*, he said to himself, not imagining anyone else who could come in. But soon his door opened, and Lucy peeked in, holding the door ajar slightly. "Chief? Is everything okay?" It was a form of address she had adopted over the last few years. It was more of a personal question, not used in workaday matters, but used, rather, when Tommy was found alone and brooding over troubles that she knew by instinct he was trying to drink away.

"Hi, Luce, what are you doing back...in this weather?"

She knew by his tone that he was drinking not to wash away any acute troubles, but rather the chronic problems of his life. "My car won't start, Chief. The auto club can't get to me for about two hours, so I decided I'd wait for them up here. I've got some work I can do."

"Where'd you call?" he asked.

"The Belmont Station," she said.

"I know that guy. I'll call him up to get him on it right away."

Tommy called and talked to the owner of the gas station. He had known the man many years, and had some work done on YPD cars there. Upon hearing Tommy's concern for Lucy Searles's convenience, the owner promised that as soon as one of his two trucks would return from the many calls they had been on, the truck would be out to start Lucy's car. "Maybe it'll be less than two hours now, Luce," Tommy said. She thanked him and turned away to hang up her coat. "Would a drink take the chill out a little?"

She stared at Tommy for a few long seconds. Then, she said, "I'll have some coffee."

"Do you really have a lot to do out there...that won't wait till to-morrow?"

She seemed puzzled, and he could tell from her expression that she didn't know what he was asking. "No," she said awkwardly, "I guess it can wait. It wasn't due tomorrow."

"Then bring your coffee back in, okay?" Tommy said, unsure of what she would say. She had worked for him for nine years, and in that time, he realized he knew very little about her. In the few seconds of hesitation born of the uncertainty of what he was asking, Lucy hadn't said a word. "This isn't a proposition, Luce," he said finally.

She huffed. "I didn't think it was, Chief." Tommy nodded and closed his eyes in assent. Silently she went into the outer office, and in a few moments returned, coffee in hand. Tommy had seated himself by the fireplace in one of the Queen Anne chairs that faced each other in front of the hearth. He had turned on the gas logs earlier in the afternoon and hadn't bothered to turn them off. One look outside and the glowing gas fire and artificial logs seemed just the thing to fight the gray sky, the snow, and the chill.

Tommy motioned toward the other chair, and she sat down, somewhat uneasily in the unaccustomed posture across from her boss. She was someone who never had trouble accommodating herself to a work life. In her youth she had known hard times, dinners of beans and bread, creditors haunting her mother, sickness tormenting her brothers and sisters. In her adulthood, she knew a weak, uncaring husband whose drinking and drugs had scourged their lives and made her child-bearing years ones of pain and fear for the future. Then, when Ed Searles died, Lucy had to raise two small children on a secretary's salary.

Only when she interviewed for the job with Tommy did she feel that life had given her a good turn. The chief, who had seen several women and one man during a long dreary afternoon, could hardly believe his eyes when Lucy was ushered into his office. Her quiet presence, her beauty, the combination of body and skin tone, hair and sensual features, were stunning enough. But when she began to speak, in measured, easy responses to his questions, when he heard her voice over the telephone and saw her handwriting, he knew she was the secretary for him.

Tommy had been smitten by her for many years, and had patiently endured the occasional chuckles and remarks from his poker buddies about her looks and inexplicable dedication to Tommy's welfare.

No one in their wildest dreams would accuse Tommy of doing what so many other bosses would do with so alluring a secretary. It wasn't in his makeup. Tommy was never a womanizer, nor an exploiter. He wasn't attractive to women, he felt. He was balding, and paunchy, and busy, and lonely. None of these things were fuel for a life of partying and easy love, or at least easy conquest.

He was endearing enough to be unsure of himself around her, to watch the language that she sometimes heard in his rage behind the big doors to his inner office, to inquire about her welfare and her family in gentle, yet sincere queries. He tried to be his best around her; he tried to be a gentleman.

They sat in silence for several minutes, both listening to the howl of the wind as it lashed grainy snow against the bay window of Tommy's office. In the distance, there were sirens going on and off. Beneath them, the squads of the night shift were going out on calls in hopes that before the next dawn, all streets would be clear of wrecks.

"Why did you stay out so late, Chief?" she said suddenly, as though she knew exactly what he would answer.

Tommy shrugged. "I just had a little work to do and was taking my good old time about it."

She smiled slightly. "You could have gone home. You know Chief Malatesta can handle all this."

"Yeah, I know," said Tommy uncomfortably, "but maybe…"

"But maybe they'll need your help?" She had become protective of his welfare over the years. Besides, it was easier to talk that way, maternally, than to talk as woman to man, after work in that quiet place.

"Did you call home? To let everybody know you were coming late?" Tommy finally asked.

"Yes," she said, "I left a message for Eddie. He has a lab tonight at the university."

"Yeah," Tommy said, "your daughter's not living there anymore, right?"

Lucy took a sip of coffee. Tommy had held the small, straight tumbler of whiskey all the time that Lucy was there. From time to time, he would sip at it. "You want me to drive you home, Luce? And then we can get your car tomorrow? Or maybe I can...."

"I'd like to know what's wrong with it, Chief...to see where I'll have to have it towed if it's bad off...But I can close the office if you want to go."

"I'm gonna hang around a little while longer," Tommy said. Again, they sat in awkward silence.

There were things he should have said before, that he never had time to say. But, as was his custom, he said them when they occurred to him, with only a little thought to whether the time was right. "Lucy, girl, you've been a good secretary all these years, and I want you to be well provided before I leave. So, if there's any civil-service job in the city you want to bid on, you go right ahead. I'm gonna wind things down over the next several months, and I can turn my work over to someone from the pool downstairs."

She smiled. "You wouldn't care if I left?"

"You know better than that, kid. I just don't..."

"What?"

"I just don't want to drag you down with me."

She huffed softly. "The only time I was ever up was with you, Chief."

"Look, you know the mayor's out to get me because I used to give his dad a hard time years ago. He wants me out. And if I go, you might go, too."

She was quiet for a few seconds. "Not might. When you go, I go."

He stared back at her. "Thanks, kid. I appreciate your loyalty, but it's gonna to hurt you in the long run."

"It wouldn't feel right to leave you now, Chief. Who will make your coffee?"

Tommy chuckled. "What *are* you going to do, Luce? You have to think it through. Just tell me what you want. I won't take it personal... you know that... and I'll help you any way I can."

Here it comes again, Tommy thought to himself as he glanced at her legs as she sat across from him. How long had he suppressed the fantasies about her body in his arms? He wouldn't even let himself think of them... the musk of her body, the scent of her as she was near him, the calm reassurance of her presence in the outer office every day, taking care of business, protecting his flanks, doing the mundane typing and bookkeeping tasks that had been thrust upon the chief. It was an act of duty not to let his imagination run away with him. "These have been good years," he said suddenly, after several seconds.

She arched her eyebrows, as if she didn't quite know the years he was referring to. Tommy caught her expression and hesitated for a second. "The years with you," he said. "You're the best secretary I've ever known."

"Why did you hire me?" she said, somehow mustering courage to ask what she never had before. It seemed strange sitting in this incongruous setting with her boss. She was uneasy in the relationship between them as people. He was always "The Chief," and she was always the devoted secretary. They had never even gone to lunch together, and now they were sitting after work, having coffee and just talking.

"I don't know," he said, looking away from her. "The way you looked, I guess... the way you talked. I don't know what it was, but I trusted my instinct..." He looked directly at her. "And I was right."

She pursed her lips and nodded slightly in both agreement and appreciation. She had gotten into the habit of caring for him over the years. At first, she was so grateful for her job and the living wage it afforded, that she protected and nurtured Tommy because she was protecting and nurturing herself. But in the last several years, the nurturing became instinctive, and it was done without thinking — especially for her own welfare. Tommy came to stand for Good, and anything that threatened him became Evil. She assumed the role easily and performed her duties with grace and energy.

Suddenly, the phone rang. It was the garage. Lucy's car would be looked at in few minutes. Tommy looked outside after taking the call and could see that the blowing snow had stopped. A fine mist was blowing over the snow, and it would make traveling worse by midnight. "I'll take you over, Luce. I'm leaving anyway...while the going's good."

The next day the weather was still bad for traveling. The wind blew the snow into hardened ledges of ice that rimmed the streets and hung in shelves along walls and borders of the town. The dampness carried on the wind, even when the snow stopped falling, was chilling and enervating, making anyone caught outside think only of warmth and shelter as they trudged through the heavy snow.

Tommy's head and sinuses ached. The YPD was involved in clearing away the wreckage of the storm that kept howling through the day and sending misery and grief upon the hapless people of Youngstown. All departments helped the traffic division. Vice crimes were few, homicides seemed to be postponed, drugs were not delivered — drops and money were not exchanged.

One of the gas lines in the city had been ruptured and a fire was raging on the South Side. All day, Tommy spelled commanders who had been on the job for more than twelve hours. Food was brought to the people who had been holed up at the station — secretaries, clerks, police aides, and the entire force of police.

There were accidents all over town. Police who had not handled traffic details for years were out in the streets trying awkwardly to manage the disorder. People were stranded, without warm enough clothing to keep them alive, some with injuries, some with small children, all bewildered by the suddenness and ferocity of the storm.

Tommy was at the crisis desk in the lobby giving orders, answering questions, making decisions on personnel. Bumpy and Pete were all over the city, each driving YPD Jeeps, trying to expedite cleanups, bringing coffee and sandwiches. Med was Tommy's personal messenger — troubleshooting when it had to be done.

They worked all day long, handling calls that came from the far corners of the town. Tommy had been in his uniform since four-thirty that morning when he got out of bed, hearing the wind blowing the hard snow against his windows. Now the snow was lessening, and compared to the early afternoon and rush hour, the town was at peace.

More snow would be coming, but the greatest damage, born of surprise, had already been done. Now people would know what lay in store for them when they ventured outside. With most schools and businesses closed, the Valley had settled down. Now there would be waiting — to find out how many people were still stranded, to watch reports of gas company spokesmen asking people to lower their thermostats.

It was as though the weather gave the Valley a chance to catch its breath…a lull in the storm before the second wave hit after midnight. Tommy had sent Bumpy home for some needed rest. Med, whose knees began to ache early on, and who said nothing each time Tommy sent him out to coordinate a fire and police rendezvous at an accident, was also driven home to rest.

With Pete Mencken taking over command of the crisis desk, Tommy finally decided to go upstairs to his office, perhaps to rest his eyes against the pressure and pain of his sinuses around his nose and eyes. In his office, he thought of the bourbon in the cupboard, but this time he knew instinctively that what he needed was sleep, and rest, and peace. He sat in the arm chair by the fireplace, staring at the indistinct shadows cast by the one table lamp he had turned on beside his chair.

It had been so long since he had looked into a mirror, he had no idea what he looked like now. His tie was loosened, his collar open and askew, his hair limp and disheveled, and his new beard a grizzly mask around his face.

Lucy must have gotten a way home, he thought, finally stopping to wonder at the day's events. She had come in early, had helped set up the crisis desk, had called and answered, reminded and remembered, ordered food supplies and coffee, booked rooms at Tommy's bidding at the Ohio Union Hotel across the street for all the staff kept overnight to ride out the storm. She must have gone home, he thought again. Funny, he really never remembered telling her anything, giving her anything to do. She was just there, and ready, and quiet. Things were in progress, or on their way, or already done and working out. She must have gone home already, he thought.

He sat hunched over, with his hoary head in his hands, half asleep, not knowing whether or not he had just dreamed, or had imagined, messages from deep within his soul. Suddenly a door opened in the outside office and steps led deliberately to his room. It was Lucy.

Tommy, looking up at her, having lifted his head from its resting place in his hands, said without being able to see her clearly, "Luce? I thought you went home."

She was taking off her coat as she stood near him. "I was over at the Ohio Union for a few hours."

"You get a room there?" he said.

"Yes. Tina and I, Chief Malatesta's secretary, shared one. I knew I'd be back tonight."

"You didn't have to come back, Luce…What about your son?"

"He's okay. He's staying with his sister."

"But you were here most of the night…all day…"

"So were you," she said calmly.

"But I'm the boss. I had to be."

"And I'm the boss's secretary," she said, walking away to the outer room.

She stopped to watch him for a few seconds from just inside the doorway, where he wasn't aware of being seen. No one, except maybe one of her own children, could look so forlorn and heart-rending as Tommy in his private moments. Here was the chief of police, a fierce fighter, a cunning investigator, a sports legend in the Valley, well-liked, vibrant, self-possessed, yet also haggard and tired. In those quiet times that few people ever saw, there were glints of loneliness, or sadness, or unrequited goodness in Tommy's eyes.

She could hear his heavy breathing as he rested in the chair, his energy spent. "Tired, huh?" she said as she approached him in a roundabout way.

"I'm not as young as I used to be, kid," he said as she stared at the grizzled face and tired eyes mounted on the thick, loosely draped body. He sat forward a little, thinking she would sit across from him as she had done the night before. Instead, he was startled to feel her hands on his neck. For a second, he nearly jumped, but she had already plied some of his shoulder muscles with the first clutch of her hands. "This will make you feel better," she said quietly.

Jesus, Tommy thought, *feel better?* In all the years they had worked together, he never felt her touch except in fleeting instants when she would pass him something, like coffee or a piece of correspondence. But lingering seconds of the warmth within her conveyed to him by her touch were a magical exorcism of the fatigue and soreness and stiffness in his neck and back.

They were both silent as she worked. Tommy groaned in pleasure as she plied his shoulders. Then he was embarrassed for doing it. He caught himself. It didn't seem right to show such a loud response to pleasure. He was careful. He didn't want her to know how much he enjoyed her touch, didn't want her to know that his dreams could be only one thought removed from what she was doing to his neck to what he would do to her wondrous body. He was afraid she'd get the wrong idea, so he sat still and silent. "You're really stiff," she said. "Do you have a lot of soreness?"

He shook his head. "Just old age," he said without looking at her. She kneaded a little more roughly in response to his personal jest, to let him know she didn't agree. After a few more minutes, she stopped just about the time it seemed right to do it.

"Thanks, kid. It really felt good. I appreciate it," Tommy said, looking at her as she walked around from the back of his chair to the one opposite him. As she sat, she folded one leg under her and stayed watching him quietly for a few minutes. He looked down at the floor, resting his elbows on his knees.

"You can go home now, Chief," she said in a smooth, intimate tone, different from what she used during the work day. This was a tone of involvement, what she would use on a child, or someone close, someone she cared about. "Chief Mencken's rested; he can handle the desk. If you're worried, I can call you if something happens."

"If I go, you go," he said emphatically. "Whatever you do here can wait till tomorrow. Why are you here anyway? Did you go home?"

She shook her head. "I slept at the Union, remember?" she reminded him.

"Two hours isn't enough. You don't get paid enough to do this around-the-clock stuff."

She didn't say anything more. Tommy stood up and went to the bay window and peered out into the night: around street lights and high lit places. The snow was still coming, in smaller bursts, but the street crews were finally beginning to get ahead of the weather. Eight more inches tonight some time...but if the storm would go through Columbus and come south of Youngstown into Pennsylvania, they might get only half the predicted snow. He turned to her. "Think I'm worrying too much?"

She smiled. "You've got good people here. You don't even know how much snow we're going to get...And you're dead on your feet."

He nodded, appreciating her logic. "Let's go."

———◦⊷◦———

Youngstown got a break. The storm did what everyone hoped — went through Salem, south of Youngstown, and into Pennsylvania. The Valley caught a swipe of snow, three inches more, and settled into quiet waiting, slowly piling snow aside, and watchful of the new soft snow still flowing through the town in intermittent bursts.

The next morning, Tommy came to work, early as usual, having rested for seven hours during the night — long for him. Lucy was not there when he walked into the office, so he left the door to the outer office open behind him. Schools were still closed, and many cars were buried in the snow that was being plowed by street crews. All meetings of public agencies were cancelled. Many businesses and plants were closed or open only for the second shift.

Lucy came in about a half-hour after Tommy, still sooner than she was scheduled to work. But she knew that Tommy would be there, so her place, she felt, was in the outer office. She came in and, upon seeing a clean-shaven and rested Tommy, smiled and said hello. "Do you still want the crisis desk set up today?"

"No," he said, "I've already given Captain Laney orders to take it down."

"So back to normal, huh?"

"Yep," said Tommy. "And tonight, we leave on time."

The day went well. Crime that normally occurred outside, was driven inside, and more domestic quarrels became fights, and some of the fights became bloody. But none of it was new or unexpected, so by the end of the day the snow had stopped, and the police were doing their work as usual.

At quitting time, Tommy and Lucy parted, and Tommy went home to shower and shave again the stubble that had grown during the day. After supper and a little rest, Tommy groaned and brought himself erect. It was time to see Smokey.

The streets weren't in such bad shape as Tommy drove through Youngstown to St. Rita's Hospital. He had gone there too much lately, he thought, had gone to too many wakes, had listened to too many funeral homilies, had sat too often listening while people talked about the passing of friends, young and old. And now Smokey. Here he was, keeping watch on an old friend, a part of his life, and hoping in the same old helpless way that death would wait, would give this good man another chance to be with the people who cared about him and needed him.

He had, by now, learned the quick route to the Oncology Unit. And the nurses knew him too. They felt sorry for him as much as for Smokey. Tommy seemed so forlorn and lonely that he touched the hearts of the nurses who saw him come up so many nights and sit beside his old friend.

The charge nurse greeted him as he came up to the desk. Most of the visitors were gone, with the exception of Tommy and some few unfortunates who were watching the life evaporate out of the body of a loved one. "Does Chief Smolenski have any visitors?" Tommy asked.

"No," the nurse said. "Mrs. Smolenski was here all afternoon, but she left after supper."

"How's he doing?" Tommy asked.

"Real uncomfortable…nauseated all the time from the treatments. It comes and goes; one minute he's fine and the next it's vomiting and chills. It should pass when the therapy is done."

She led Tommy down to Smokey's room and ushered him in, checking to see that the IV was flowing properly. Smokey was sleeping, so Tommy sat in the chair beside his bed. The nurse looked at him watching Smokey, checking his face out, touching the hand nearest him for a moment and marveled at his concern. Would her boss ever visit her almost every night, and stay long into the evening, just out of compassion and caring?

When she left, Smokey stirred and became aware of Tommy sitting right beside him. "Tommy? You been here long?"

"Just got here, kid."

"What are you doing out on a night like this? You must be tired as hell."

"I got some rest. It wasn't that bad. That second storm dipped under us, so we lucked out."

"You have a crisis desk set up?"

"Yeah."

"Damn," Smokey muttered, "I should have been there to handle it."

"Since when can't I handle a crisis desk? You were just where you should be — here."

"You know what I mean," Smokey said. "That was my job."

"All the crooks stayed home, Smoke. It was one traffic detail after another. All we did was dispatch cars and call in street cleaners and tow trucks."

Smokey nodded. The scene was so familiar over all those years. He remembered them from the fifties and sixties all the way up to three winters ago.

"You handle the one next year. I'm gonna bail out and give the whole thing over to you."

Smokey chuckled. There were times during Tommy's visits that the two men sat silently near each other, thinking their own thoughts, sorting out their own lives. The nurses even talked about it: Tommy reading the paper and from time-to-time bringing up a topic for them to analyze.

Sometimes they gave it short shrift, and sometimes they talked long and deeply about it. "Here's a quote from Captain Christopher Laney," Tommy said with a slight smirk.

"Let me guess," said Smokey wearily. "He saved Youngstown all by himself…calmed the storm, drove crime off the streets."

Both men chuckled. "Got it right, kid," Tommy said.

Again, there was silence between them for a while. Then, Smokey talked. "Tommy, I really appreciate your coming all these nights."

Tommy didn't answer for a moment, then he said, "I know, kid. It just helps pass the time."

"But you must have other things..."

"It's you or the Silver Bridge, Smoke," Tommy said, interrupting him. "These visits keep me on the wagon."

Smokey smiled to himself, knowing that his friend was making the visits seem therapeutic when he knew the chief better. He decided to change the subject. "Anything more come up about that coke in Danny Bellino's car?"

"Nah," Tommy answered. "I talked to Danny. It doesn't look like those kids were into drugs. Did you know Danny and his old lady were separated once?"

"Yeah. I knew after they got back together. You don't think that had anything to do with it, do you?"

"I don't know. Maybe for once it was just a mistake."

For a while longer they talked. Then, after a few minutes of silence, Smokey started getting restless and his breathing became heavy and rapid. He put the nurse's button on and looked at his friend. "Tommy, I'm gonna have an accident here."

Tommy bolted upright from his seat just as the nurse hurried through the door. "Take it easy, kid. I'll be outside waiting."

As Tommy waited outside, another nurse went down to Smokey's room to help out. He could hear the retching noises that Smokey made, seeming to resonate from his thorax through his throat. He could also hear the cool and patient voices of the nurses trying to soothe him, trying to help him through the ordeal.

The charge nurse came up to Tommy. "Chief McCarrie, if you

want to wait in the lounge, I'll call you when everything's all right. These things don't last too long. But you might want to let him rest after it's over."

"Yeah..." said Tommy. "I'll just stick around to see he's okay. Then I'll go."

She nodded approvingly. "He should be okay in a while."

Tommy walked down the long corridor to the visitor's lounge at the far end. It was a place where windows enabled visitors to see the many hills of the city and to watch the patterns of streetlights cross each other in sparkling ribbons, trailing over hills and across flat areas. The downtown Dollar Bank sign was lit up, a landmark that identified the town for years.

Tommy sat grimly in the dark silence of the lounge, the sounds of Smokey's pain muffled by the distance, the darkness seeming to envelope even the hospital floor which now had dimmed all its lights. Except for pitiful folks like Smokey, the night was a time for rest.

Tommy passed a half hour, looking outside from time-to-time, then sitting back down in the darkest corner of the lounge in a big, soft chair. He tried to sort out his day, but it wouldn't happen. Then he tried to determine what he would do in the next eighteen months to take care of his friends and stay out of Carly's way. He'd go see Elly and that would help. Then he'd try to decide what to do with the rest of his life. He'd try to decide if he could help becoming an easy drunk as soon as he turned in his badge.

He heard some steps in the distance but didn't look around. Strange how the one sharp sound resounded through the quiet hallway. Smokey was silent now. Tommy knew the nurses were washing his face and giving him a new nightgown and fresh bedding. One of the nurses left Smokey's room; he was sure of it. Without seeing, the sharpness of all sounds in the quiet of the floor enabled him to guess what was going on.

Then, the other sharp sounds began again. Hurried steps full of purpose. One footfall heavier than another making rhythmic irregular hits on the marble floors. They were a man's steps, Tommy realized, and they were coming toward him. Finally, he sat forward as the steps came into the lounge. He was in shadows, but in the dim light, he could make out the tall, angular body of Med Williams.

"Tommy," Med said, calling out into the room, not seeing the chief.

"Yeah, Med, what is it?"

Med advanced toward him and stopped a few feet away. "Bumpy sent me to get you…"

"What's wrong?"

"Pete just took the call. Danny Bellino's kid… They found him and that girlfriend of his…. Jesus, Tommy, they're gone. Somebody done killed them both."

Part II

Elly

A S HE DROVE THROUGH the mist, he could already see several squad cars, with no lights flashing, and fire trucks with crews spraying water and chemicals on the fire. What a terrible thing to investigate, the killing of a cop's children. Tommy slowed his car to a stop, waiting a second behind the wheel before getting outside. He looked out into the night. All the onlookers had been driven home — by the rain, the cold, and the late hour. And now it was the police and the ambulance that waited.

Outside, he strode past the first few officers that he met. Med was there already, giving orders to his men about how he wanted the Bellino car collected. Tommy looked at him for a moment, but didn't interrupt. Then he walked up to Pete Mencken and stood beside him in horrified silence waiting for Pete to fill him in with information.

"It was set on fire," Pete said to the Chief, "probably to hide something. My guess is the kid was killed before the fire. We'll have to see if Jacko Horowitz can find out how he died."

"What about Danny?" said the Chief.

"He's back home. Bumpy's there with him. A doctor and a priest are on the way."

"What about the girl?" Tommy asked.

"She's over there..." He pointed into the woods. Tommy took a deep breath. "God, why does somebody have to do this?" Pete said.

Tommy shook his head. "I want this fucker, Pete. Whoever did this is gonna bleed through the eyes."

———— ⬦•⬦⬦•⬦ ————

As Tommy walked, the cloudy sky seemed to give a murky feel to the night, barely permitting sight. Some figures seem to move in silence as some others just stood, waiting grimly for more orders. The ominous yellow tape engirded the crime scene. Tommy made his way into the glowing commotion deep within the woods. A young sergeant immediately started talking to him. "Young woman, Chief...from the college, someone said. Anyway, she's back over there." He pointed to a recession of flat land further into the woods. Tommy started in the direction he pointed. "You knew this girl, Chief?" said the sergeant, having heard the whispers of the crews on the scene.

"Yeah, a little," said Tommy slowly. "She was engaged to Danny's kid."

"You may not want to see it, then, sir. It's pretty bad."

Tommy nodded appreciation for his solicitude. "It's okay, Sergeant. I'll check it out."

How many times had he seen this, Tommy thought as he stepped forward. A lovely young girl turned into a lifeless mass of gray flesh? How does being a cop do this to you? That you can see the body of someone who touched your heart, and yet examine her corpse clinically, as though she were an unknown cadaver? Maybe for a cop there's a certain anesthesia for the soul that keeps you from being revolted by the carnage you see. Somehow, your soul is inured to the blood of innocents, the screams of families, the prodigal waste of life. Somehow, you see glazed, sightless, open eyes and only imagine what they saw in their hour of death, and never what they saw in halcyon days.

But whatever was in his heart had to be kept there for another day. The sickening sights he'd see, the fear of discovering new horrors, the emptiness in his stomach, all had to be banished. Now there was a killer out there who had every advantage, whose work was done, who will get up tomorrow and read the paper, hear the news, have breakfast, drink coffee, and plan his day.

As Tommy trudged through the wood, he could see the flood lights from the laboratory crew. In a few moments, he was there with them. And there was the body of the girl who used to be Neva, who served him coffee, who hugged him when he left her, who called him Tommy the Quarterback.

There was blood everywhere. Her eyes were closed. She was naked, and covered with blood, on her neck, on her groin, beneath her breasts. The men all nodded to the chief as he approached them. And suddenly they knew that this case had become special.

Tommy stared grimly at the horrible sight before him. What was once so full of promise, so special, so lovely, had been butchered. "Any blunt blows or gunshots?" he said suddenly.

"Just those cuts that we can see, Chief."

Tommy noticed her hair and her body, facing upward. It didn't seem like rape. But then to take all her clothes off and never touch her? To kill her as she stood before him naked and terrified? If this wasn't a maniac, it was a man who enjoyed humiliating women. It was someone who needed to punish them, someone who could face a woman and slaughter her as she watched.

He stooped over the girl's body as the men worked. Then he stood erect and wrote something into a small notebook that he had in his pocket. "Anybody know why she was taken to this place?" Tommy said.

The sergeant, who had followed him and was observing Tommy from behind, answered. "We got a call, Chief. Some kids found them… as they were playing in the woods."

What a strange place, Tommy thought as he looked around. *A remote piece of scrub woodland on the East Side? Why here?* "Check this place out, Sergeant. Are you gonna be around till daylight? Matuszak, right?"

"Yes, sir, I'll be around. We'll see if we can find anything."

Tommy turned to the assistant coroner. "Why isn't she covered?"

"I have to do some…"

"Cover her, goddammit," he snarled.

The young doctor blanched. "Okay, Chief, okay," he said.

Tommy took one last look at the girl. Then he turned back to Matuszak. "Don't let anyone but our people back here, understand?" he said.

Now he had to forget that Neva was one of the few fresh visions that had come into his life in many years, and brought him memories of Anita, the sweet Italian girl who he had given up, who might have made his life so different.

Now he has to think of this girl as a victim, a case. There might be another day when he could sort this awful memory from the joyful thought of what she might have been, of how easily she had touched the stony heart of a burnt-out alcoholic gargoyle and make him sense warmth again.

Sergeant Matuszak returned to him. "You're Joe, right?" Tommy said. The sergeant nodded. "All right," said Tommy in a reassuring tone, "let's treat this just as though one of our officers was killed. These are our people in those body bags, Joe. So, do your goddamned best to make this a good case, okay?" Joe nodded again. "Be professionals… Work hard, keep it quiet, and nail this son of a bitch. Understand?"

Late in the afternoon of the next day, Bumpy walked through his door and sat down in a slump in front of Tommy's desk. "So, how's it feel to be boss?" Tommy said grimly, with a smirk. Bumpy huffed his displeasure. "So, what have we got on those two kids?" Tommy said.

"The lab said she wasn't raped. Pete called me a little bit ago," Bumpy answered.

"No drugs... any money, any equipment?"

"Nothing. Just like the last time. I put Joe Matuszak on both cases."

"So, what do you make of this, Bump? Those kids weren't drug pushers. Why are they down at the morgue? You think this was a drug hit?"

"No way, Tom. For one thing, I know Danny... and I've watched that kid of his grow up. He wasn't into drugs. Second, both you and Smokey talked to those kids... and there just wasn't anything there."

"So, why are they dead?"

"I don't know, kid. Maybe it's some crazy screw-up and they just got caught up in it."

The next few days were ones filled with the grief of two families. Tommy paid his respects at the funeral home where both bodies were kept — in the same room. He expressed condolences to both parents, and then waited for Danny later, when the visiting lines began to thin. During a few hours of standing and watching, Tommy greeted policemen old and new, politicians, friends, neighbors, and people he didn't know but who just wanted to talk. Most didn't complain. All they really wanted were reassurance that the murderer would be caught and punished. But these were promises he couldn't make. He had seen too many crimes go unpunished in the legal wonderland of our justice system.

Once, when he found Danny in the outer hall on his way to the men's room, he beckoned him to come forward. "How's the family holding up? How's your wife?"

Danny shook his head. "Not too good," he said worriedly, looking back into the viewing room.

"You have a doctor handy?"

"Yeah…she's on medication now," he said.

"Mothers are different from fathers, Danny. And God knows she's new to this. She has to find her own way of dealing with this grief. As long as you're there, you're helping."

Danny seemed only a little consoled, and Tommy knew it. The grief and pain were there as they would be on any father's face in this circumstance. But there was something else, a kind of bewilderment that Tommy sensed when looking into his eyes, something like the dumb fear you'd see in a hunted animal's eyes who didn't understand the pain being inflicted upon it. "Danny, if there's anything you need, any way we can help, just let me know. Everyone wants to help."

"How's the investigation going?" he said abruptly to Tommy.

"Still getting it all together…lab reports, questioning people, file work. You know we're going to have to talk to your family…and the girl's family?"

"Yeah, I know. I just hope we can help somehow."

"We'll see. Take as much time as you need for yourself or your family. We'll get your checks out to your house. Just try to handle this the best you can."

"I'll be back. I want to see how the case…"

"You know you're not going to be on this case, Danny."

"Chief, that's my kid in there," said Danny, gesturing over his shoulder. "How do you expect me to handle everyday details when I know his killer's case is being handled?"

"Because you're not a rookie cop, Boyo; that's why. And any lieutenant knows that you don't ever put someone so closely tied to the victim on his case. Now, Joe Matuszack is a good cop, and he'll handle the case because he knows how important it is to you and to all of us."

Danny shut his eyes and took a deep breath. He knew the chief was right, but he felt he had to try. Tears ran down Danny's cheeks. He quickly went for a handkerchief. "You see, Danny," said the chief, "there's so much more for you to handle now. Let someone who has some detachment move it along."

In their exchange, they lost the sense of where they were. The words between the chief and Danny Bellino seemed to sequester them from the other people in the funeral home. Though the caskets were closed, and placed side-by-side, there were two seating areas, chairs for the families, and then chairs behind them for their visitors.

Just as Tommy and Danny were finishing their talk, Danny's brother suddenly walked up to them, looking frightened and worried. "Excuse me...Danny, you'd better come back in; it's Kaye."

Danny turned immediately away, heading toward the room where now, suddenly, Tommy could hear hysterical cries, and other voices calling in fear and confusion. Some of the voices were from Danny's two remaining children, imploring their mother to stop screaming the strange, incoherent words that seemed to rasp from her throat.

Suddenly, the atmosphere changed. Instead of quiet grief, there was now chaos, showing how tormented and stricken the family was. Tommy, though he had seen them a few hours before, had not had a chance to talk much with Bumpy or Med. But now he saw them standing together quietly watching Danny Bellino's family come unraveled by the outbursts of Kaye, the mother, who, earlier in the night, had seemed remote and self-possessed.

Tommy walked up behind Med and Bumpy and stood quietly watching the turmoil. After a few moments, they saw a well-dressed man of medium height shake Danny's brother's hand, and kiss Danny's mother, the small, attractive, gray-haired woman who had sat quietly all night long, and then leave the room hurriedly.

Bumpy sensed that Tommy was curious about who the man was. "That's Jack Pagliaro. He's was some kind of cousin to Danny's father," he said under his breath. By then, the man had gone. Tommy noticed that he was treated with some deference by some of the other men in the Bellino family, one of them holding his coat while he put it on.

Meadows turned back to Tommy but, like Bumpy, spoke softly without taking his eyes off the troubled couple seated in front of the caskets. "I think they're businessmen. Pretty flush. This guy is Mose Pagliaro's younger brother, the family lawyer."

"Mose Pagliaro? Isn't he the guy that was trying to buy Barber Park a few years ago. And then the Carling Tower downtown?" Tommy said aloud.

"That's the guy," said Med.

Just then Kaye fainted, and the doctor who was a family friend held some smelling salts to her nose. They propped her backward in the Queen Anne chairs and revived her, the doctor talking softly while Danny held her hand. The shrieks of the women relatives, the mournful exclamations of the grandmothers, the crying of the young girl who was the sister of the dead boy, the sobbing of the girl's mother and aunts...all this happened during Kaye Bellino's demonstration. Tommy had seen such funerals before, with mind-numbing tragedy written so large across the lives of so many good and unexpecting people.

"What made her start carrying on like this?" Tommy said in a voice so soft it was barely above a whisper.

"It was when she saw that Pagliaro guy," said Med.

———◆·•◆•·◆———

The next few days were dreary ones. Everyone's heart went out to the poor young couple who had lost their eldest son and the beautiful young girl who was to be the bearer of the grandchildren now lost to them forever. And no one could also forget the sight of the frail, desolate, tired-looking woman who was Neva's mother, sitting stoically among her children, staring at the casket that held her daughter.

Finally, after a seemingly endless mourning period, the young couple was laid to rest. And it was decided by both families that the two would lie side-by-side with a single gravestone that would say, *Neva, Novia de Danny Bellino, and Danny, Novio de Neva Molinero.*

———◆·•◆•·◆———

In days thereafter, Tommy often sat brooding in his office, thinking about the young couple. Who would murder two children who held such promise of bringing love and goodness into the world? Bumpy would come up to see him if there ever was breaking news about anything important...and if Bumpy didn't come, he'd send Med. This afternoon was Med's turn.

"Hi, Chief," Med said as Lucy ushered him into Tommy's office.

"Sergeant," Tommy said softly in expectation.

Med sat in the chair in front of Tommy, huffing a little as he lowered himself in. He looked nervous and agitated.

"So, what's on your mind, Meadows?" Tommy said, seeing Med's uneasiness.

"Tommy, I think this is gonna happen... Well, I mean, I'm pretty sure..."

"Unload it, Med," Tommy said softly.

Med drew a deep breath. "I got some word today that the mayor's gonna fuck over the department... and you with it."

Tommy grimaced. It did seem too good to be true. All this happening without a move from Carly. Tomorrow would bring a dose of reality. "So, what do we have so far... before Carly screws it all up?"

"The kid's skull showed he was hit with one shot to the head, and then the car was set on fire. The girl wasn't shot or raped, just stabbed... like to cut her to pieces. No drugs in Danny that we could determine, no drugs in the girl, but traces of cocaine in the car. The woods were soaked, and there wasn't anything around the site, no weapons, no prints."

"What about the bullet?"

"That's the strange one. Jacko said he thinks from the bullet shard it was a .32 automatic. How about that?"

"But how sure is he? I haven't seen a .32 automatic in years."

"Somebody said they're starting to make them again," Med said.

"Hell, I don't know. All I know is that Danny's looked like a professional hit... but it was either another guy who did Neva, or the guy snapped — just like any amateur."

Carly Giustino arrived at his office early. Next to winning the election, it was going to be one of his better days. One of his secretaries was there already, an older man who once worked for the Internal Revenue Service and then, later, did creative accounting for Carly's father.

Soon, Mickey came in to get coffee. He looked disgustedly at the secretary. "How come you didn't put some water on?" he growled.

Without looking up, the secretary said, "It's not my job, Mickey."

"You're the goddamn secretary. Why don't you make it if the mayor wants it?"

"If he wants me to make it, he'll tell me," said the older man.

Carly could hear the discussion between the two men. How could he be shackled with such losers? Both of them drove him crazy; one was a stupid oaf, barely able to drive a car and make coffee. The other was lazy and arrogant and effeminate; someone you'd like to punch as soon as you saw him.

But nothing was going to get him today. He had found a way to handle Tommy McCarrie that would make his career take off. It would feel good shoving one up his ass. Just then his secretary entered. She was young, in her mid-twenties, and she wasn't carrying her briefcase. She was the only thing about his office that gave Carly any pleasure. "Hi, Mr. Mayor," she said as she came into his office.

"Hi, Jodi," he said, as he watched her spin on her heels and walk back away from him. Jesus, he thought. How he wished he could turn back the clock and savor that body just one more time. Christmas had always been good to him, and this past Christmas, Jodi had taken him to her bed.

She came into his office again. "I've made some coffee," she said.

"Okay," Carly answered. "You got that press release typed up?"

"Lula's running them off right now."

Carly nodded, drinking some of the coffee that Jodi had brought in. This was the day his administration would launch itself. Today, he'd finally do McCarrie in, and once and for all establish his control

over the Valley. He had been patient and waited for the right time…
something many people thought he would never learn to do.

Jodi came back into the room. "Did Chris Laney call yet?" Carly
asked.

"Just now. He'll be here in a half hour."

"How about the TV stations?"

"They'll be here. I called to remind them."

Carly bided his time as he waited for Chris Laney to come. He
owned Chris now. Soon he'd own the department. With McCarrie
out of the way, Laney would run the show Carly's way. God, it seemed
so easy. Last week it was hopeless, but some good luck and a brain
storm did it. He could make his case that Tommy was showing his age,
that the police department had grown stale and flaccid.

Just then, Chris Laney walked into his office. "Hi, Mayor."

Carly nodded. "You been to the department yet?"

"No, I told them I'd be coming in late today — not why, but when."

"Good. Maybe if we do it fast, we can get some results before they
start fucking things up over there."

Chris Laney was slender and muscular, sandy-haired and handsome. Carly had an instinctive dislike for Laney who seemed a natural
athlete, proud of his body, and confident of its performance. Carly was
everything that Laney wasn't: about five-ten, where Laney was about
six-two. Carly was southern European, and no clothes, however fine,
could give this dark, muscular Italian the agility and natural grace of
the tall and cocksure Laney.

The only things Laney lacked were money and Carly's brains — and
the access to power that they provided. Carly knew it, and so he controlled his envy and quiet animosity toward Laney. Nature may have
given him the cat-like body, so graceful on the playing field, so alluring

to women, but Carly had the things that counted: money and power. And he was the mayor, not Laney. So, Laney was tolerated, and used to Carly's advantage.

"Does anyone know what we're up to?" Carly asked, with a touch of coldness in his voice.

"No one but me, Carly," Laney answered.

"Okay. I don't want some FM rock station blaring the news out before we announce what we're doing."

Just then, Jodi came into Carly's office. "Mr. Mayor, the TV crews are all here."

Carly stood up instantly. "Okay. I'll see them in the communications room...in about fifteen minutes, until they set up their equipment." Then he went into the bathroom adjacent to his office to make sure he looked good for the cameras. Laney sat bemusedly watching Jodi straighten Carly's tie and smooth over his hair. She stood back and beamed at him. "Perfect," she said, smiling.

Carly huffed. He looked okay but would never make them swoon. Hell, they'd probably throw their apartment keys at Laney. But when he looked at himself one more time in the mirror behind one of the closet doors of his office, he was satisfied. *Not bad*, he said to himself. *What more do they want?* He had dark good looks, was rich and promising. Carly sighed...but he still had that look of a guy trying to sell refrigerators.

So, what did Laney have? That something that makes women want to possess him, want to surrender to him. It wasn't just looks, because Carly looked good. It wasn't personality, because Carly was known to be fast on his feet. It wasn't brains, because Carly had the game won on those. But it was the feeling that most men get used to: You go into a room full of women and one or two guys, in a few minutes, have booked the night.

"So, Chris, you have to look like you're strictly business, understand? You're the one I count on to save the department."

"Yeah, I know," Laney said.

"Knowing isn't enough. You have to convince other people."

"I told you I'd be okay, Carly. Believe it."

Carly nodded. He walked through his office and down the back stairs to the conference room. There were quite a few reporters there... they came when called. Carly tried to look as commanding as he could as he stepped up to the podium.

"Ladies and gentlemen, I regret to announce that we have made no progress in the investigation of the brutal murders of the two Spring Common State University students. Almost a month has passed, and as yet there are no leads in tracking down the killer.

"Accordingly, I have, in my capacity as mayor of Youngstown, appointed a special investigative unit, headed by Captain Christopher Laney, who you see beside me here. Captain Laney will answer directly to me and will report to me regularly to keep me updated on progress in solving the case.

"I will then be able to answer the reasonable questions of all citizens of our community who are justifiably concerned by the current lack of direction in the Youngstown Police Department.

"Captain Laney will personally select an elite team of investigators who will finally determine what happened in the case, and will put this terrible event behind us. And then our community can heal itself, thanks to an invigorated, youthful, forward-looking leadership in the YPD."

After the press conference, Carly sat smugly in his office, surrounded by his secretary, Jodi, Mickey, the bodyguard, and another old friend and mentor, Judge East. Chris Laney had just entered the office after finishing his question-and-answer session. "They kept asking me about you," said Laney.

"What'd they want to know?" said Judge East.

"Basically, when he'll clean out the deadwood in the YPD," he said with a smirk.

The following night, Tommy sat moodily in Castorina's Restaurant on the far south side of Youngstown. Suddenly Meadows Williams entered the restaurant, walked up to the bartender, and whispered a question to him. The man gestured toward Tommy's table where he was sitting alone. Med joined Tommy and sat down quickly, heaving a sigh at the comfort he felt when the strain and weight were off his gimpy knees. Tommy eyed him quietly for a few seconds. Med sat morosely staring back at his boss. "So, whenever I see you or Bumpy coming after me in one of these places, I know sure as hell it's bad news."

Med was nodding as Tommy spoke. "The son of a bitch did it, Tommy. Chris Laney's the boss of a special squad that answers only to Carly."

Tommy took a drink before answering. "At least he didn't make him deputy chief, kid. So, we have to make his life as miserable as he makes ours."

"But if the fucker doesn't have to answer to you ... " Tommy touched Med's forearm as his voice rose and he got more excited. Meadows glanced around their table to see if anyone nearby had heard his words. "Sorry, Tommy," Med whispered.

They were quiet for a few minutes, reading the menu and talking to the waitress. "Bumpy said he'd join us a little later if he could," Med said.

"Don't bet on it, Meadows. Let's order."

Just then Med could see a large man coming toward them: Carly's bodyguard and chauffeur, Mickey. "Trouble, Tommy," he muttered as he stared at the man approaching Tommy from the rear.

"Just stay put, Med," Tommy whispered without looking up.

Mickey stopped at their table with a sullen, rough-looking companion standing a few feet behind him. "They let anybody in this place, huh, Murray?" Mickey said, speaking his words back over his shoulder.

"Mickey," Tommy said, "you got the night off, did you?"

"More often, now that you're washed up."

Tommy chuckled. He had a way of maddening Mickey, a kind of special talent for insulting him. "Don't chisel my gravestone yet, kid."

"Come on, Tommy, Carly has you by the balls. You're going down, and you'll take this cripple and those two asshole chiefs with you."

"You never got over not making the cut, did you, Mickey?" said Tommy.

"We just had to make room for your, ah, Afros. I wasn't wired up like you were. Lazarus got you that job just like he got Sergeant Williams here instead of other guys that deserved it better."

"Life's a bitch, huh, Mickey?" Med said. "They just didn't recognize your skill."

"Nah, Med, only a few flaws kept him out," said Tommy. "Like..." Tommy was counting on his fingers. "He was stupid, like he was lazy, like he was a ballless, dishonest jerk. Hell, other than those few things, he'd have been chief."

"Sounds reasonable to me, Tom," said Med, chortling at Tommy's sarcasm.

Now it was Mickey that was growing angry. "I'd have made a better cop than both you two losers. Look at them, Murray." Mickey turned to his dour, vacant-eyed, seedy companion. "A wino police chief and a has-been basketball jock with gimp knees…an affirmative action special."

Tommy put a restraining hand on Med's forearm as Mickey spoke, knowing Med was about to lunge at his tormenter. "How about letting us eat our dinner, Mickey?" Tommy said. "We'll talk some other time. I'll call you when I'm lonely."

"People like you make me sick, Tommy. You get everything through drag. Somebody's always handing you stuff on a silver platter. And then you think you can look down your nose at other people. Ain't this some shit, Murray? A couple of frigging winos acting like they're better than us?"

"Don't take it personal, Mick," said Med. "We look down our noses at all stupid bag men and gophers." The diners who could hear their conversation laughed at Med's taunt.

Mickey was nonplussed for a moment. "Well, let's see just how dumb you think I am, Med. Come on."

Tommy looked around. The restaurant was still, everyone's eyes were on them. John Castorina, the owner, had just walked in the door, and knowing instantly of trouble, he came over to Tommy's table. "Hi, Mickey," he said, laying a hand gently on his shoulder. "Anything I can do to help? I've sent a bottle of my wine to your table, Mick. Please accept."

"Better not send any here," said Mickey, still not looking at John Castorina. "These two winos got enough trouble just driving home without you putting a new buzz on them."

John looked plaintively at Tommy, knowing that the source of the trouble was from Mickey, and sensing a deliberateness about him. This was some kind of plan.

"We'll go, Johnny," said Tommy. "All we did was come in for a quiet supper."

Mickey continued. "Typical dirty cops. Always fade out when trouble starts."

Tommy's face reddened and this time it was Med's hand that was restraining his boss from lunging at Mickey. "This guy isn't taking no for an answer," Med said. "We'd better go, Tommy."

Mickey was somehow convinced that he was playing to a home crowd in the restaurant. His intent was to not let Tommy leave without embroiling him in a fight that would be front page news in tomorrow's Telegram. And now he felt the time was right for a knockout. "I understand that Tommy doesn't take no for an answer, either," said Mickey. "He bangs that Spik secretary every night. Them Afro lips must hum you into heaven, huh, Chief?"

Mickey was right. His words escalated the argument as surely as he wanted. And there would be no parting now without pain. As Murray stepped forward behind Mickey's right shoulder, Tommy's response was low and menacing. "Mickey, I know your instructions are to start a fight, but even you know that this isn't the place. Some night, if you want a shot at me, just let me know."

"So, what do you think, Murray?" Mickey continued aloud. "You think the chief is gonna get a blow job from that Afro-Spik broad tonight?"

"Christ, Mickey, Carly must have a lot on each of you to do this," said Med, holding fast to Tommy's forearm.

"That's it," said John Castorina. "Out, Mickey... and take this guy with you. I don't need your goddamned business. You'll never get in my place again."

Mickey laid a hammy hand on John's chest and roughly shoved him aside. John, not expecting the hit, went sprawling backwards. Med had just a second to see out of the corner of his eye as Murray lunged at his knee, trying to stomp Med's feet out from under him. Med slipped sideways from his chair and fell on his good knee. But Tommy could see Mickey hesitate a second because he hadn't expected Murray to get to Med as quickly as he did.

But his second of hesitation cost him. Tommy, who all through their conversation with Mickey, had managed to get his feet on the rung of an empty chair at their table and quietly position his foot so that he had the best leverage and aim at Mickey's groin. In the second that Mickey blinked, Tommy pushed the chair with all his might into Mickey's groin, catching him low on the belly and driving the back of the chair directly into Mickey's crotch. Mickey let out a woof, an escape of breath that sounded like an elk snorting at a wolf pack.

The tableau was one of Johnny, fallen backwards into a table unoccupied, but laid out with four settings, Med, balanced on one foot and one stiff arm and one buttock still on the floor, and Mickey doubled forward, his eyes and face contorted in pain. In a moment, Tommy stood over him with his foot crushing Mickey's arm before he could pull himself erect.

"Meadows?" Tommy shouted, looking over at his comrade who had caught hold of Murray's jacket and pulled it over his head to bind his arms to his sides. "I'm okay, Tommy," he said as Murray fearfully looked at Mickey who was still on the floor, and in that second took a knee to the groin and went down to the floor himself.

"You son of a bitch," Tommy growled as he drove his knee right into the crook of Mickey's neck near his left shoulder. "Blow job, huh? You miserable bastard. Say it again!" As he spoke, he ground his knee into Mickey's upper back, making him scream in pain.

Then, in the one silent moment amid all the confusion, Tommy could hear Meadows's voice quietly say his name: "Tommy." It was an admonition of an old friend, of one who understood the pain and loneliness in Tommy's life, and who knew that Mickey wasn't the object of Tommy's rage; it was life and the many bad cards drawn to a once-promising hand. But the word reached into the core of Tommy's anger and calmed him. Gradually he let go of Mickey, and waited the few confused seconds until everyone was standing. By then, he was chief again.

"Never again, Mickey," said Castorina softly. It was obvious to everyone who could hear the words of the men that Mickey had provoked the fight. He wanted to get Tommy angry, and to be seen publicly as a brawling drunk. But he did it clumsily, and lost the chance to exploit it in town gossip.

The two men quietly headed for the door as Tommy, Med, and John Castorina watched. "How about a glass of champagne on the house, guys?" said John.

Tommy shook his head. It was time for him to leave and everyone knew it. John waved him off as Tommy turned to pay the bill. After apologies all around, Tommy and Med left the restaurant.

"What d' you make of this, Tommy? Why would Carly give Mickey the green light on something so dumb?"

"I don't know what the fuck's going on lately, Med. Nothing is going by the book... Kids getting killed, Carly not winning the game and still going for the throat... I can't figure it."

"You know his shoulder is gonna ache for a few days. Did it feel that good, Tommy?"

"Nah, Medford, he's just a dummy who picked the wrong time to say some things."

Danny Bellino wasn't feeling much better. As time passed, he grew worse. "I thought time was supposed to ease the pain?" He said to his mother one day. "I think I'm getting worse, Mom."

His mother sighed. "How's Kaye?"

Danny shook his head. "It's been awful since the funeral. She doesn't kiss me, hardly ever talks..."

"Maybe she should go see one of the priests at St. John's," his mother said.

"They've been at the house. She just sits there. When they leave and I try to talk to her, she cries." His mother heard his voice break as he spoke the last few words. As she approached him from across the room, she could see his eyes begin to glisten. "How can I ever get over Danny if she won't talk to me about it, Mom?"

Connie hugged her eldest son, cradling his head in her arms as he sobbed against her. From his throat she heard the same strange wail she had heard from him as he cried at the wake and the funeral. *How alone we are in our grief*, she thought as she remembered the days she cried for her husband, Joe. And now, as she comforted Joe's son, she knew she had to find a way to help Danny bear the pain of the loss of his own son.

Later that night in the dim solitary light cast by a small lamp in her living room, Connie mused quietly about what had happened that day. She worried about Kaye and Danny. Their grief was driving them apart. And somehow, Danny had not only lost his son, but also was losing his wife — again.

———◆◆◆———

First Deputy Chief Liborio Malatesta came into the chief's office and nodded to Lucy. She let him into the inner office as she always did when he didn't walk through by himself. Tommy was sitting at his desk, his chair turned toward the bay window behind him, and he was staring out into the gray afternoon, soon promising somber darkness.

As Bumpy strode toward the desk, Tommy turned to face his old friend — he could tell by the heavy footfalls and no announcement from Lucy. "Hi, Bump, what's up?"

"Not much. Routine stuff. We finally got that wreck cleaned up on Fifth Avenue. Y'know, Tom, we have to get that traffic pattern changed. So far, we've been lucky, but one of these days, a college kid is gonna buy it from one of those cars coming up the freeway ramp."

"How many cars were in this one?" Tommy asked.

"Only five. How about that?...and nobody died. But one of those girls has two broken legs and the other one has a cut going so deep it looked like she might lose her arm."

"I'll write a letter to Carly," Tommy said. "Maybe the asshole can at least handle this one."

Bumpy nodded and thought of something else. "Uh, Tommy..."

"Yeah, bump? Something else?"

"No, not about the case...About me. I can go back to my department any time. I mean...I don't care about being first deputy."

"I know that, Bump," Tommy said, "but you're doing fine...as I knew you would," his voice showing the question he had of his old friend who was acting unusually cautious. "I told you I knew you could do it, right?"

"Well, you know Giustino's gonna try to put Chris Laney in as an acting deputy chief, and already Laney's dick has grown a couple of inches, and he doesn't even start till tomorrow."

"He starts, but he doesn't get near the squads. I don't want him fucking with operations. That's your job, understand? If Carly wants him to head up a special team, that's okay...A waste, but okay. But if he countermands one of your orders, I'll cut his balls off."

"It's gonna be trouble, Tommy. Nothing good can come of this move by Giustino...And I'll kiss your ass if they have a fucking clue on these murders in six months."

Tommy nodded. "And that's when we start shoving this whole idea back up Carly's ass."

———————

Tommy had just gotten out of the shower, his shoulder ache soothed by the hot water splashing on his skin. He sat in his robe on an easy chair, old and shabby and impressed with Tommy's body shape. The news was on and Tommy watched it as he usually did, bourbon in hand, half asleep and waiting for the weather report. When the phone rang, he reached for it reflexively, thinking it would be Pete Mencken, the duty officer that night.

For a second, he could hardly recognize the voice. "It's Elly, Dad."

"Hi, kid. Everything okay?" he said.

"Yeah, it's okay. I just feel like talking, that's all."

"Well, I'm glad you called. How've you been feeling?"

"We're all fine here, Dad...Listen: how would it be if we came to visit you?" She had never done that. But now that she was alone, she seemed to cherish her father more. And suddenly all the estrangement that made it so hard for them to communicate years ago was gone.

"Hell, I'll come up to get you if you want...or let me send you the tickets, El?"

"No, Dad, I'll get it all set up. I'll be in Tuesday night, the twentieth."

Tommy seemed stunned by the prospect of having his daughter with him to take some of the loneliness out of the dark months.

"That'll be great, El. You sure everything's okay?"

"Things are okay as they'll ever be up here, Dad. That's why I'm coming home."

Tommy suddenly seemed to sense something different in her voice, a different tone that made it seem that she had changed her thinking about her life. She had hesitated a few moments. "Dad, I'm going to leave Boston. I've been thinking... Maybe I'll come back to Youngstown... If you don't mind."

"Jesus, do I mind?"

"Well, you know it's been a while since you've had a family member..."

"You come any time you want. I'll be waiting at the airport. Elly, I'm sending you tickets."

"Dad..." she drawled in exasperation.

"Dad nothing. Look, kid, I have a lot of lost time to make up with you... and with the kids. Now, don't try to keep me from helping when I can."

"Okay," she sighed, almost to herself.

Tommy still couldn't comprehend the whole notion of his daughter's change of heart. "You mean it, El? You're really coming back?"

"I've lost my mooring, Daddy. I need an anchor for my life... for me and the kids."

"What kind of anchor?"

"You."

Tommy snorted in appreciation. "I'll try my best, kid, till a better man comes along."

"There aren't any better, Dad," she said. "It just took me a while to realize it."

Never had he heard his daughter take a tone so intimate and heartfelt with him. "Thanks, kid, but you know what I mean. There's a guy out there who's waiting for you, who needs you. You have to hitch your wagon on those kinds of dreams, not on an old war horse whose every birthday is a crap shoot."

"Well, here's to more birthdays," she said, lighter in tone. "It'll be good to see you, Dad."

"You don't know the half of it, kid," he answered. "You're staying with me, right?"

"You or Motel Six," she said, still taunting him.

"I don't mean for a few days. You know that," he said, enjoying his daughter's playfulness.

"We'll see... Are you sure you'd want us there? The kids are noisy and messy... Kind of like me. It would change your life..."

"My life needs changing, El. I pray every night for it to change. Hell, I never dreamed you would ever come back. Now that you are, I'll take noise and a mess anytime. My house seems like a museum, it's so neat."

Later that night, Tommy went to bed weary but with a strange sensation in his stomach that meant he felt good about something someone had done. After their talk, he poured a hot tea and bourbon and drank it slowly as he dreamed of the good his daughter and her kids would bring to his life.

Yet his sleep was fitful. Often, he was awakened by the shuddering of his own body, each time as if in a strange country, not knowing where or who he was. But toward morning, when it was still dark, he dreamed of Neva. He could see her smiling at him as she reached out to touch his hand. She tried to speak, but he couldn't hear. Each time she spoke, he strained to hear her. But her voice just wouldn't come. Finally, in frustration, she began to cry. He tried to comfort her, to hold the hand that she had placed in his, but he couldn't. She began to fade from his sight as he called out to her. And all that he could sense was her voice crying.

Suddenly, he awoke, sweating. For a moment he seemed to hear the echo of her cries in the darkness of the room. But then again there was quiet, only the sound of his own breathing and the frantic beating of his heart.

Finally, he got out of bed, shaved, showered, and dressed. As he had the first of many morning coffees, he stood in his kitchen, quietly thinking of his dream of Neva. How strange it is that these things come to haunt our slumber just when life seems to settle into something good. It was as though happiness was too much to hope for. Happiness had to wait. Neva touched his dreams, and called to him, and he couldn't hear her. But he heard her crying, loud in his ears. As though she was trying to tell him something, to ask him something. *Maybe why nothing had been done,* Tommy thought.

That morning, Tommy was in his office early. Bumpy soon came up to talk about what had gone on through the night. After his report, Bumpy said, "You know Chris Laney has that squad all ready to go?"

"I figured that," said Tommy. "I wonder how long he knew about it before Carly had the press conference?"

"I think since you told Carly where to get off," said Bumpy.

"Anyway, Bump, let 'em go. Give them all the help you can spare. I'd like to catch the killers, too."

Tommy stopped talking for a moment, hearing a noise outside from the street. A screech of tires and a horn blowing. He stared at the sky. "What's the forecast?"

"Snow this afternoon."

In another moment Lucy rang him on the intercom phone. "Yeah?" Tommy said, grabbing the phone on the first ring.

"The hospital called, Chief. Chief Smolenski isn't doing well."

"Jesus," Tommy said, looking at Bumpy who had a concerned look on his face as he listened to Tommy. "Smokey," said Tommy, turning to his friend. Bumpy understood.

———————

Tommy knew this would be his last ride to see Smokey. At the hospital, he nervously rode the elevator, quietly dreading the events that would unfold in the next few days. When the door opened, Tommy walked out and saw Smokey's two sons. He went over to shake hands with the two young men he had known from their infancy. "Mom's in the room with Dad," said the oldest boy softly. "Go on in, Chief."

Inside the room, Tommy could see the slender, tired-looking woman sitting at the side of Smokey's bed. He glanced at Smokey. There was more equipment hooked up to him now... more beeps and movement. He bent over the woman and kissed her gently. "Hello, Trina," he said. She grabbed his hand as he bent toward her and held it to her cheek. "He's in such pain, Tommy."

"I know, kid," Tommy sighed, looking back at his old friend.

"He comes and goes. Sometimes he's lucid and sometimes he babbles."

"Is it any wonder with all this," Tommy said, gesturing at the equipment and monitors that enveloped Smokey.

For several minutes, they sat silently together. The woman still held the chief's hand, seeming to need it for support. Suddenly Smokey coughed and turned his head to the other side of the pillow. His eyes opened and he looked at the two of them sitting there beside him. He snorted and smiled. Tommy stood up. Then Smokey's eyes closed again, and his head rolled toward the center of the pillow. Tommy was about to sit back down when Smokey called him, talking through closed eyes. "Tommy, there was a pile-up on 5th Avenue...Five cars."

"Yeah, Smoke, Bumpy took care of it." Tommy knew he was listening to the confusion of a mind tortured by pain and the anguish at leaving life behind.

"Tommy?"

"What, Smoke?" His eyes were still closed as he spoke, almost as if the effort to open them would be his undoing.

"You know you have to handle that Bellino case?" Suddenly his eyes opened, and he stared right into the chief's. "They aren't gonna find the killer, Tom...not unless you do. It takes an investigator...and you used to be the best. They'll miss something...and you're gonna have to see it."

"I will, Smoke. Relax now. You get some rest."

"I'm gonna get all the rest I need, Tommy," said Smokey. "...Remember, there's something right under our nose. I know it." Tommy didn't answer him. After a few moments of silence, Smokey spoke again. "Take care of yourself, Tommy. Find somebody for yourself... maybe someone right under your nose." He smirked as he said that. "Thanks for being a good friend. I enjoyed it."

Tommy's eyes were full of tears suddenly as he backed away from the side of the bed. He didn't turn toward Smokey's wife who had been witness to the small colloquy between Tommy and her husband. "Trina?" Smokey said suddenly. Just as quickly she was erect and standing over him, her hand instantly drawn toward his cheek. Tommy knew it was time to leave. As he left the room, he gestured to the two boys to go in.

Out in the hall, he mused about all the strange turns his life had taken. We travel so uncertain of who our companions will be, he thought. Friends, just when they're needed most, vanish. And love is snuffed out so easily by death or deceit.

All his life it seemed he'd been lonely. The girl he married, the girl who gave him Elly, had grown distant and aloof and finally false. She left him when he needed her, when he would have given anything to understand her feelings and make things right.

He had never been disrespectful or dishonest. He had been...himself. *He* was all he had to offer: flawed but honest as a man, wise and perceptive as an investigator, and yet blind as a husband. It was he who she rebelled against and fled from. She couldn't say it was his stupidity or cruelty or violence. He never touched her in anger, never was crude or oafish. She fled from him, from what his life had become, from what his future promised.

Suddenly she was gone, and after twenty years, she died, alone and silent, divorced once again, withered, drawn, and yet strangely satisfied. She was so unlike him. He needed people, she didn't; he needed companionship, she didn't. All his life he needed a woman who would share the secrets of his heart, and all her life it never mattered.

And now, he had to give up a dear friend of his youth. He had never known the feeling of a truly loving wife who would cradle his head on her breast against the night. And he grew to accept that turn of fate. But always he had friends. And what he missed and longed for in his marriage had been made easier to bear by the friendships that he had.

And yet, tonight he had to step back and watch an old friend say goodbye to the wife and children he loved, and then to die.

The next few weeks were ones of great sadness for Tommy. The death and burial of Smokey had affected him more than he ever thought it could. He sat morosely in his office, distant, preoccupied, and introspective. Lucy would look in on him from time to time, but there was really not much for him to do. Bumpy had organized the departments under his command and had seen to it that the units remained responsive and efficient.

Chris Laney, after the initial splash of publicity about his special squad, settled into the casual enjoyment of his authority and independence. But he made no progress on the case. The murderers of the young couple were free, and by all reckoning, unmolested by discovery or light.

For the few months following Smokey's death, Tommy was given to more introspection than usual — and to more drink. He made some visits to the Silver Bridge but was much less belligerent when the squad car ordered by Chief Malatesta showed up to take him home.

Through his loneliness, he thought of Elly and Danny Bellino and Danny and Neva. Those few last words of Smokey's were strange: "There's something everybody's missing..." It was instinct, Tommy knew. From his hospital bed, from the confines of his modest office at the YPD, Smokey had been watching and thinking. And he knew that there was something over Laney's head, even if he really wanted to see it. But what? All those months since the murders and the special squad was still secretive, aloof, and smug. And yet no murderers have been found. "...Something everybody's missing."

But slowly, Tommy's juices began to flow again. He had only gone on one real bender in the weeks since Smokey died. Other than that, he was solemn and preoccupied. One night Bumpy had come in to the station to talk to a night officer and afterward, noting that the third-floor office facing outward showed a lighted window, he came upstairs to talk to his boss and old friend.

"How ya doing, Bump?"

Bumpy sat down in the chair opposite Tommy. "Better yet, how're you doing, kid?"

Tommy shrugged and was silent for a moment. Then he said, "Has Laney come up with anything on the Bellino case?"

"What do you think?" said Bumpy sarcastically.

"What the fuck's going on, Bump?"

"I ask him every day, Tommy. They're always closing in on some lead or questioning a suspect."

"You know it's been almost six months since they started this investigation?"

"Yeah... You know, Tommy, there's not a good cop among them. Hell, they trip over their own feet. Let a nice young ass walk by and they'll piss all over any evidence they have."

"It's a deadly combination, kid... arrogance and incompetence."

Danny Bellino slowly drove the car into the garage, and sat for a few seconds after turning off the ignition. He could hardly believe the turn his life had taken. Suddenly, being good, doing your best, being honest, being faithful... all those things didn't matter in his life. He had done them all, and yet, in a stroke, his whole life had changed. Danny's death had changed his future. All the memories now had one fateful ending. There was a finality about dreaming. And the grandchildren he hoped for, the little boy who could carry on his name, the little girl who would sweeten his life all his days, they would never be born.

He wearily pulled himself erect as he opened the back door and reached for his briefcase. *What would she be like tonight?* he thought as he walked through the back door of his house. He dreaded seeing her, dreaded seeing the pain, the unraveling of a once-vibrant personality.

She was standing in the kitchen when he entered. "Hi," she said, looking up at him with a wan smile as she tended the food that she was cooking.

"Hi," he answered. As he passed her, he bent toward her to give a kiss of greeting. But she had sensed his move and placed herself in a position where he would have to almost impose himself upon her. He snorted softly and walked away, not pursuing her. She was relieved that she didn't have to deal with his intimacy.

Later, when Danny had changed his clothes and come downstairs, he went back into the kitchen. "Where are the kids?" he said.

"You mean Carla and Joe, don't you?"

"Yes, who did you think I meant?" he snapped.

"One of 'the kids' is gone. You didn't mean him, did you?"

Danny was hurt and angry instantly. "Don't start with that, okay? I lost him, too." He paused for a few seconds. "What a lousy thing to say…"

"I just wish I could handle losing a child as easily as you," she said.

"Jesus, handle it? Is that what I'm doing? We *do* have two other kids, and other family, and a life. If I don't fall apart then I'm cold-hearted, right? And you're the only one who feels pain, and grieves, and misses Danny."

"You're not a mother. You don't know what it's like."

"But I'm a father," Danny said. "And he was our first-born son… named after me." His voice was softer, less argumentative, and he moved toward her. She stiffened, and he could see it, but she didn't move away. He stopped moving toward her. "Kaye, this isn't supposed to drive us apart. If anything, we're supposed to be..."

"Closer?" she interrupted. "Losing Danny is supposed to help our marriage, is it?"

"You know I didn't mean it that way, Kaye. I mean..."

"I never know what you mean."

He was silent for a minute, staring at her, trying to fathom her anger. "You're just trying to start a fight, aren't you? You don't want to heal things between us?"

"Heal? How can you heal the wound left by the death of your son?"

"I mean heal the breach between us," he said softly.

"I don't know if we can," she said.

"If you can cause a split, you can heal it."

"I didn't cause the split, Danny," she said, her voice rising. "You say you didn't, and I say I didn't," she said. "But you just can't face reality."

"The reality I see is simple. I don't want this marriage to break up...I didn't want it before, and I don't want it now."

"Your version of reality is always simplistic."

Danny gestured with his fist, not as a menace, but as though he was trying to grab a solution out of the air. "Why can't we make it right between us, Kaye? This has nothing to do with Danny's death...it's the same old thing...you and me. Why can't you let us have peace?"

"I'm the one who needs peace," she screamed suddenly. "I'm the one who's lost a son — and what do I have for it?" He looked at her, startled to hear her say those words. "I can't stand this, Danny," she said quietly.

His voice grew louder now. "What you can't stand is me; face it. It's always just me."

She was silent. "Well, say it, Kaye, goddammit!" He was goading her, and he knew it, almost daring her to say what she otherwise wouldn't. "Admit it. It's not Danny's death that's done this. It's between us. That's why you can't even look at me... or let me touch you."

"I just can't go back to the life you want, Danny... the family you want... I never will."

He hesitated, seeming not to know who she was. Then he said, "This investigation's going on, and sooner or later they'll come up with something. After that, there's no sense lying to ourselves... Then you do what you have to do. But at least honor Danny's memory enough to wait until his killers are caught."

"Damn you, don't talk to me about honoring Danny's memory. I'm his mother; I brought him into the world..."

"And you were willing to break up the family that he was born into, right?"

"There was nothing to break up."

"If there was nothing to break up, it was because you can't stand the sight of me or my family," Danny muttered, bewildered and hurt. But she made no move to help him. Once, that look would have melted her heart. But now, there was such a gulf between them that she couldn't go back to being the dutiful, loving wife again. She had contaminated the love that they once had.

Pete Mencken came into Tommy's office as he usually did... quietly. He was the opposite of Bumpy... slender and reserved, with a whimsical sense of dark humor. "You wanted to see me, Chief?"

Tommy waved to a chair as Pete sat down opposite him. "So what the hell's going on, Peter?" Tommy asked.

"I don't know, Tom. Every time I ask Laney about the case, he blows smoke up my ass. Tell you the truth, I don't think they know what they're doing. There's not one idea man in that whole bunch."

"So this special squad's a complete waste, right?"

"It's a waste if you want to catch crooks," Pete said sardonically. "Looks good in the paper, though…and on TV sound bites."

Just then the door opened and Bumpy strode into the office. "Pete, you know we're missing a car?"

"What?" said Tommy. "How the fuck can we lose a car?"

"Special squad's too busy holding meetings," said Pete. "They can't even figure out who has all the cars."

Suddenly Bumpy stood up and walked around behind Tommy's desk to look out the window. He surprised both the other men, though they were used to Bumpy's nervous ramblings. "He's getting a free ride… too free…"

"What are you saying, Bump?" Tommy said, knowing what he was thinking.

"I mean he doesn't know shit about being an investigator and yet Carly's covering him. They haven't turned up one fucking piece of good evidence. Every time I ask…" He looked at Pete who finished his sentence. "…They blow smoke up your ass."

Then, Pete turned to Tommy. "He's a pretty boy, Tom. And he doesn't have the instinct or the investigative experience. All he's got is that goddamned law degree."

"He's right on the money, Tommy," said Bumpy. "I've seen you piece things together out of spider webs and moonbeams and catch a crook. This fucker couldn't find a clue if it was wrapped in gold foil."

Tommy stood up and walked over to the fireplace. He was quiet for a few moments. So were the others. Then he said, "So you think I've been letting him get away with too much?"

Pete looked over to Bumpy, giving him in the quick glance, the cue to speak for them both.

"Chief," said Bumpy, surprising Tommy with a title he seldom used to his old friend, "It's time. I know you've been missing Smokey, but..."

"But I haven't been doing my job, right?" The two other men hesitated for a few seconds, giving swift reinforcement to each other in sideways glances. Bumpy spoke again. "Not if want to catch the murderer of that girl, Tom."

Tommy snorted and smiled slightly in grudging assent. *The girl. Jesus, was it that obvious? That a young girl could get such a hold on the heart of a jaded, old, leathery chief of police... and everyone in the world would know it?* They were all silent for what seemed several minutes. Then Tommy spoke, shrugging as he talked, "You're both right... What can I say?" He turned back to face them. "I just kept feeling sorry for myself."

Bumpy walked over to Tommy, facing him in front of the fireplace. "So are we gonna catch this murdering bastard or not?" he said softly.

Tommy smirked and Pete breathed a sigh of relief. "If we don't do it, who's gonna do it?" Tommy said.

"We might as well discount anything they have, Tommy," Pete said. "A rookie, the first week, could have found everything they've come up with so far."

"Okay. Let's do it right, then. I want Laney's squad in this office on Friday morning... everybody, and no excuses — but I mean everybody. And Laney better be there with bells on or I'm gonna tear him a new asshole."

"You know he's gonna run to Carly soon as he hears about it, don't you?" said Pete.

"Bet your next pay on it," growled Bumpy.

That night, Tommy listened to music on his stereo. As the old songs came and went on the CDs, he would think back to happier days when music was in his heart as well as in his ears. *We have to start at the beginning,* he thought. *Those two kids weren't drug dealers; there was no coke dust in the car anywhere. So what do we have? Two kids slaughtered. But why? If it wasn't dope money, then what? And to kill them both? And to be so vicious? Smokey sensed it. What we see isn't what we get.*

Who would kill Neva? And why? All Neva would do for Danny would be to have his children and make a man of him. All Danny would do for Neva would be to love her, have kids by her, and become a solid citizen. But who does that bother or offend? Only a psychopath. But how does a psycho know those two kids?

Tommy shook his head. *Whoever killed them didn't know them. No. It would have to be someone who didn't see their own kids in Danny or Neva, someone who couldn't get a warm feeling from seeing that young couple so fresh and clean and full of promise. But that is someone without soul or conscience, someone who can hate and kill without remorse.*

Or could it be to punish someone else? Neva's mother maybe? A cook and waitress, barely fluent in English? No... never. She would never be part of anything that would incite someone to do such violence.

Then Danny and his wife? No... if Tommy's intuitions were ever right, if he ever knew an honest cop, a good father, and a good husband, it was Danny. What company could he keep that would visit such hell upon his life?

But what about his wife? Beautiful, non-ethnic... a porcelain, red-haired antithesis of Danny, who was born into a strong Italian family. Tommy knew Danny's uncles, Rino and Lou, and his mother, Connie. He had been to their houses for weddings and mercy feasts, baptisms, and graduations.

And it was a family full of life, warm and all-embracing. But to a porcelain doll who had strayed into this cauldron of noisy vitality, love and respect, honor codes and private family business, all-embracing might be all smothering.

Tommy had only seen her a few times, most recently when he returned young Danny home after his night in custody with Neva. And she was relieved to see her son. The terrible worry that had afflicted her mother's heart was relieved. And yet? And yet there was still pain in her eyes... not from the fear of harm to her son, but from the fear of something else she could not deal with. No matter what Danny said about their marriage enduring, the pain was hers alone. And Danny couldn't see it and wasn't part of it.

Tommy stood up and poured two big fingers of bourbon. As it came to his lips, he smelled the pleasant, soothing balm to all his lonely nights, but at his lips, he hesitated. This would taste too good. This would become more important than his reason. This would dull his instincts. And he needed them all, vibrant and unrestrained.

These terrible nights when he dreamed of Neva dying, of screams he couldn't stifle or escape... They had to end. Soon his life would change again. Elly would be back; Carly would be waiting for him to stumble every day. Soon he would not be Tommy the Quarterback.

He put the glass down. It had to end, and if Smokey had sensed something strange, Tommy had to find it. He had to live up to Smokey's faith in him.

───◆───

The next morning, Tommy didn't go into his office until almost nine o'clock. Med Williams showed up first, then Pete, then some of the special squad. Only Danny Bellino wasn't told to be there. The chief sat morosely behind his desk, nodding to each as the men slowly filed into his office. Finally Bumpy came in and sat in one of the large Queen Anne chairs in Tommy's office, near the fireplace.

Bumpy began to lead the discussion according to orders from Tommy. "Captain Laney, you know why we're all here. Give us a report on your progress in solving the Bellino murders."

Laney sat quietly for a few seconds, looking bemused and condescending. Finally, he spoke, "I've been keeping the mayor's office informed on a daily basis...and he seems satisfied. We're tracking down several leads that might develop into a conviction. I'm sure you understand: these procedures take time to work out."

There was some coughing and palpable nervousness as Laney spoke. Bumpy went on: "But tell me, Captain, what's different now? What has changed since this investigation started so many months ago?"

Even Laney was beginning to respond to the nervousness of the other men in the room. It was dawning upon him that this might be a set-up. It occurred to the others in the squad, too. And many of them were not as smug and secure as Laney. And Laney's voice grew a pitch higher, his mouth a little dryer.

Bumpy persisted: "What about DNA reports? Any confirmation?"

"None that we could use," Laney answered.

"No fingerprints?"

"No."

"No leads on the crack? Who the hell's making the stuff out there? Are they doing it all over town? So why don't we know?"

"We couldn't trace this to any of the known dealers in Youngstown. We think it was from an out-of-town source."

"What source?"

"Pittsburgh."

Pete countered Laney with an audible snort. "Pittsburgh?" he said. "So why is this suddenly a mob operation? Stuff some weirdos can make in their goddamned garages? And tell me why in hell somebody's gonna knock off two kids and waste almost a quarter pound of Pittsburgh crack...to what end?"

Laney was getting angry. He viewed Mencken as his intellectual inferior who had achieved rank above Laney only by being a long-time insider. "We've been through all this before, Chief. There are no leads in the Valley. We can't trace the connection those kids had with a dealer here. It had to come from outside. And the lab guys said it looks like the chemicals they use in Pittsburgh." Then, he turned back to Bumpy. "What the hell is this? Why are we being interrogated as though we're rookie cops? I give regular reports to the mayor and that's all I'm required to do...I don't have to take this."

Just as Laney was finishing, everyone in the room heard the crash of glass and pens and bookends and pencils hitting the floor and scattering. Tommy had swept his desk clean with his right arm as he sat behind his desk. Suddenly, he stood up, and before the eyes of the startled lawmen he smashed his radio against the fireplace.

They sat in silence, stunned by the strange outburst of their old boss. They knew he had a temper; they had heard all the stories about his rages. It was the stuff of legends. They stared into the wide-eyed face of the chief, nervously unsure of what he would do next.

"Listen to me, Officers. I want some action on this case. I want..." He paused looking at all of them in an exaggerated gesture, his neck forward, veins protruding, staring into each man's eyes. They stared back at him, nervous now, wondering what he would do next.

Lucy almost crashed through the door, startled by the noise and the sound of glass breaking. Pete put his hand to his lips in a gesture of silence. She surveyed the room for a moment, then when Pete nodded, she closed the door.

"Clues, goddammit…evidence!" Tommy stalked them as a snarling lion would stalk a herd of zebras. Laney's men sat in silence as the chief passed through them from the front and the rear. "Where the fuck did the crack come from?"

"I told you: Pittsburgh," Laney said angrily, yet with some timidity.

"You swear it wasn't Scranton, or Harrisburg…or Philadelphia? You might as well say it came from the moon. Listen, Officers, I want some fucking clues, and I know this is asking a lot, but ideas, too. Find the weapons, find the motive, find some goddamned evidence. And if that crack's from Pittsburgh I'll kiss your ass."

"Chief, why don't you calm down and let us do —" said Laney.

"Your job, right? That's the last thing I expect, Boyo. It's been almost eight months since those murders, and we still don't know one damn thing about the case that we didn't know a half year ago. I mean…am I the only one here who notices something strange? Two young kids from good families get snuffed as though they were a couple of torpedoes from a New York Mafia family…and that doesn't strike any of you as strange?" As he spoke, he stomped the radio that had bounced onto the carpet. "You have nothing! Not a fucking thing that a good cop wouldn't have landed on day one."

Laney was angry now. Some of his team were beginning to agree with Tommy and were sympathetic. Danny Bellino was well liked in the YPD, and some even realized they would be hereafter be known as members of a sham investigation that might somehow taint their futures in the YPD. "Chief, this is bar talk," said Laney, "and we don't have to take this. I report to…"

Tommy grabbed Laney by the lapel of his suit and brought his face down to his. "You smell any whiskey on my breath, Captain?" Pete had maneuvered his way behind Tommy and very calmly laid his hand on Tommy's back. The touch had an almost magical way of getting Tommy's attention, and Tommy let loose of the younger man. But he was still angry, and it was invigorating and cathartic, and he wasn't about to lose the feeling. "Clues, Men!" he thundered. "Hair, buttons, dirt...anything. And I know this seems like a long shot with you guys, but we need imagination."

"Chief," Laney said, flustered and angry, "I'm not going to subject my men to this kind of haranguing ever again. I report to the mayor and he's all that I'm going to deal with from now on."

Tommy's voice grew calm and cold and soft. "You report to *me* you son-of-a-bitch. I'm the chief of police, and I don't give a rat's ass about the mayor. But I care about the YPD, and I care about Danny, and I care about those two innocent kids that were killed on our fucking watch. Hear that?" he said to the whole room, turning to view them in a panoramic sweep. "...Our watch! Now you do what you have to do, but in two months, if you don't have something to go on, you men are all going to be reassigned. And this game has changed, Captain. From now on, I want your ass in Chief Malatesta's office every morning with a full report. You are a subordinate officer and you're also Chief Mencken's subordinate, and you better start acting like one or I'm gonna cut your balls off. You got that, Captain? I want goddamned results." Tommy stopped for a few seconds and surveyed the room, looking hard at the men on Laney's squad. "And now, Captain Laney, you can take these inept, unprofessional pretty boys and get the hell out of here." He stopped and stared as he watched Laney's men head toward the door, a suddenly vanquished little army.

Lucy had not had breakfast that morning, so she decided to have lunch out alone because most of the other secretaries had gone to a birthday luncheon for an old colleague she didn't know. She ate in solitude, having coffee after her meal as she read the Telegram.

She heard voices of some men behind her that she couldn't see. It was casual conversation that had grown louder during their table talk. She knew they were cops, and suddenly the conversation turned toward something she was interested in.

"All I heard is what Lissner said," said one voice.

"So? What'd he say?"

"He said they went up there for that special squad meeting…up in the old man's office. Everybody was sitting there. The chief wasn't saying a goddamn word and Malatesta and Mencken were trying to get something out of Laney."

"And Laney was blowing smoke up their asses, right?" said one of the talkers.

"Yeah. They said the old man was so quiet, everybody thought he was just smashed. Then when Laney wasn't giving Malatesta the straight scoop, Tommy lost it."

"Yeah," said another narrator, "they said he cleared his fucking desk…papers, pens, lighters, blotters, everything…just kept sweeping till it was all gone."

"Then he tore Laney a new asshole," this other speaker interrupted. "He said he wanted clues…DNA, fingerprints, soil analysis…and of course Laney didn't have a damned thing. So, Laney comes back with something about Tommy's drinking and the chief damned near strangled him. Then he started throwing things again."

"Jesus," said another voice, "He must be losing his mind."

"Nah, some of the old-timers said he used to do that once a month. They said they were always buying stuff that he kept breaking."

Lucy left. She had never seen Tommy do anything like she just heard from those men. She knew he had a temper, but she never saw him wreck an office.

Later that afternoon, Bumpy came upstairs to talk to Tommy as he usually did. "Chief," Lucy asked Bumpy, "is Chief Tommy all right?"

"You mean because of all the commotion?"

She nodded, looking intently at him. "You never saw him the old days, Luce. He was a perfectionist...and he used to mess things up about two, three times a year. The old secretary used to just buy new stuff every time. But I'll tell you, he kept things on the up-and-up. A crooked or incompetent cop was damned near good for a whole new set of furniture."

Lucy smiled, and Bumpy went into the chief's office. A few moments later Tommy walked in as Lucy and Bumpy were waiting for him. She studied him in the few seconds he stood before her. It seemed strange to imagine him younger...and so intense. She had only known him in calmer days, when his legend was intact, and when he drank more, and ate more, and worried more, and had become a pale shadow of his sterner self.

But suddenly he was smashing things again, and in a way, it was exciting: He wasn't going out quietly. And if he smashed things when he was a good cop, maybe being a good cop was at the bottom of this whole change.

"So, Liborio, what's the story?" Tommy said.

"Zippissimo," Bumpy growled. "I told you, Tom: nobody knows what the fuck to do."

"Let's give them another month. I've got some things to take care of. Then we'll do our own investigation."

"Things, Tommy?"

"Elly's coming, Bump."

"Yeah? How long she staying? Wasn't she just here last month?"

"Forever, kid. Since her divorce, Boston doesn't seem to be the place for her and the kids. They're all going to live with me. How 'bout that? A house full of people?" He was smiling grimly, as though he doubted his own ability to handle it all.

"You gonna be up to all this, kid?" Bumpy asked.

"It'll be messy and noisy I suppose. But I think I'll love it. I need those kids around here."

Bumpy stared at him a few seconds. "Yeah, I think you will like it. But first remember you're a cranky old bastard and those kids'll test you every inch of the way."

Tommy chuckled. "I guess I can't bust up any furniture, huh?"

"Well, hell, if that's all you need, you can come over and do my place. Jesse's been trying to think up and excuse to get a new living room."

It was getting dark at Port Youngstown. Elly's flight would be in at 6:30 and already Tommy was there at five. In the bar, he drank bourbon over ice and nursed it. It seemed strange knowing she was coming home. If only he could be sure she really wanted it. They'll have to talk. He has to understand what she's thinking — how long she's going to stay without running again. Jesus, what if she hates my life? What if she's bored? The kids are bored? They'd have to talk. What would make her change her mind? What metamorphosis occurred in her life that made her lonely for her father? For the life surrounding him?

He waited impatiently as passengers filed out of the gateway. Then, suddenly, she stood there, poised, yet uneasy, looking right at him. And then he was aware of her eyes, that gray, bright part of her face. She had become a mature woman. And whatever may once have made her features too sharp, whatever confidence, and pride, and assurances of life, there was a softness now about her, about her eyes, that made her face more attractive than it ever was. *God*, he thought as he watched her coming toward him; *she's beautiful.* Amazing what pain can do. Of all the damage it can cause, all the heartfelt consequences, all the time it haunted lonely hours, all the destruction of spirit, this time it had worked some unintended magic. It had softened her features and brought wisdom to her middle years. And a gentleness that came from knowing how fragile life and happiness could be. She had become a lovely woman.

She embraced him and he held her tightly against him almost as though he feared that a passing fancy would make her leave him soon again. Without a word between them, he stepped away and grabbed each of the kids and held them to him. In only weeks they seemed to grow more and seemed to be strangers to him each time they met again. Mike was slender and slight, two years younger than his sister who had just turned fifteen. And Carrie was more like her mother, a fuller figure who was approaching womanhood fast, and like her mother had become beautiful.

In the car, Elly was subdued, and they listened in silence at the chattering of the kids in the back seat. When they got home, each of the kids began to rearrange what now were to be their new rooms.

Tommy and Elly went out into the kitchen and Tommy made coffee. They talked a little, but didn't really say much. "Tired?" he said.

She nodded. "I'm tired just thinking of what I have to do yet." She took a sip of coffee. Suddenly, without looking at him she said, "Are you going to be up to this, Dad?"

Tommy shook his head, and she seemed startled. "Jesus," he muttered. "That's what this is all about isn't it? No wonder you hardly talked to me!" He paused and walked over to her, staring down at her as she looked uneasily up at him. "Kid, I look at this as one of the true blessings of my life. Here I am hoping against hope that you won't get bored with me and want to go back to Boston. And I think...what if Dave would call you and ask you to come back?"

She was shaking her head as he spoke. "Dave's been married for about three months...I've only known for a few weeks. So Boston's the last place I could find any peace." She stood up and put her hands on his shoulders. "I need this, Dad. I need you in my life. The kids need you. I'll stay as long as you'll have me."

Tommy was gradually getting back to work. Elly had been back a week, and things were beginning to settle down. Tommy had been quietly watching the progress on "the Bellino case," as everyone now called it. Pete Mencken, Med, and Bumpy kept him posted on the lack of progress on the Bellino murders.

One day, soon after Tommy went back to work, Lucy admitted Med into the chief's office. "Chief," said Med, sitting down as Tommy motioned to the chair opposite his desk.

"How's it hanging, Med?" asked Tommy cheerfully. But as he spoke, he realized that Med had some new information for him. And then he grew serious and quiet, with an alert, concerned look on his face. He nodded his sudden understanding of Med's mission to his office.

"Tommy, remember when we talked about that guy by the name of Mose Pagliaro?"

Tommy stared momentarily, and Med knew he had brought the chief some good information. "Meadows, that's the second time I've heard that name in a couple of weeks. Who the hell is he? What's he all about?"

"We were down at the Pig Iron drinking a few and one of the patrolmen on Traffic said that he worked a private party the other night. You know? When that woman totaled that Lincoln...and herself?"

"And this was Mose Pagliaro's party?" Tommy said.

Med nodded. "And her husband wasn't there, Tom...Anyway, Pagliaro's a high roller, and a ladies' man. And you know what? He and Carly have a thing going."

"So, this has nothing to do with the Bellino case?" said Tommy.

"Nah," said Med; "But watch yourself. If this guy's a behind-the-scenes kind of guy, and a friend of Carly's, then you don't want him on your Christmas list."

Tommy nodded appreciatively. "Anything else on the Bellino case?"

"We won't have anything until we do it ourselves. You know that."

"Med, you keep yourself loose. I'm gonna need you from time to time to help me out."

Med nodded, puzzled about what the chief had meant. "You goin' back in the saddle, Tommy?"

"Hell, Med, it's been so long since I've been a cop, I might have to learn the drill all over again. But, with Bumpy and Pete running things...and Laney keeping the mayor happy, I don't have a hell of a lot to do. So I figure I'll take a shot at it."

Carly was in his office sitting quietly alone, trying to avoid reading a report from City Council on traffic flow in rush hour near Spring Common College. His door was open, and Judge East walked in as he usually did on Thursday afternoons after he met with his referees from common pleas court.

"How are you, Mr. Mayor," East said in his usual tone that was a combination, learned long ago in dealing with his young protégé, of cheerleading and patronizing.

"Judge," said Carly, not too brightly.

"How's the day going?" asked the Judge, knowing from the tone of the mayor's voice, and from long experience in dealing with his pupil whose career he molded masterfully, that things were not going well.

"What's going on, Carly?" Carly shrugged. "You and Ginny again?"

The mayor nodded. Things had not gone well for Carly and his wife the last few years. When once she would look away from Carly's affairs, suddenly now she looked directly at them. And Carly wasn't able to figure out why the affairs now suddenly mattered more than they once did.

Judge East sighed. Then, he said with some exasperation in his voice, "Carly, you can't keep doing this. If she walks, you can kiss the governor's job goodbye."

"I'm tired of it all, Judge. I just don't care if she walks. Others have been divorced and made it. Hell, Reagan became President."

"Reagan divorced a movie star, and no one cares about that. Besides, he was married to his second wife for more than thirty years. You aren't the same."

Carly fidgeted in his seat. He knew the judge was right...he was always right. But this is more than he could stand. Hell, those broads didn't mean anything to him. They were fast conquests. And they kept him feeling like he still had it. She had to know he really loved her. And why now? Why was she suddenly so hard to deal with?

The phone rang...the mayor's personal line. It was his wife, Ginny. "Can I count on you to be home tonight?" she said without any greeting.

"Yes, I told you I'd be home, didn't I?" he answered curtly.

"You tell me a lot of things that you know aren't true," she said. "But Lisa asked me if you'd be here."

He hesitated for a minute of silence, glancing over at Judge East who was listening but seeming to be disinterested and reading a newspaper. "What'd we get her?" he asked his wife suddenly.

"We got her a clutch purse, some underclothes, and a stereo," his wife sighed. "It was my money you used, goddammit. Don't start with me."

There was total silence on the other line. Carly waited a few seconds, then glancing at Judge East, he spoke, this time in a softer tone. "Look...I'll be home around five-thirty. Anything else I can bring home?"

"No," said his wife softly.

When he hung up the receiver, East looked at him for a moment, then abruptly stood up. "I'll see you tomorrow night, Mayor," he said.

Carly watched him leave his office. As the old man walked away, the mayor knew that he had just been silently rebuked.

<hr>

Tommy was having a bad night, although he slept nearly six hours. But they were fitful hours, and he was tired because he would awaken often, as though a voice were calling him awake. His house was a large four-bedroom colonial with a staircase leading upstairs into an open area around which were three regular bedrooms, two bathrooms, and one large master bedroom in front of the house.

Tommy had a habit of leaving his bedroom door ajar so that air could circulate better. He didn't change his custom when Elly and the kids moved in. So, if his night was lonely and troubled, someone out in the upstairs hall could easily hear his coughing and tossing and turning.

At six-thirty that morning, Tommy was downstairs in the kitchen, quietly making coffee. He had heard Elly's alarm go off a few minutes earlier and could hear her stirring in the bathroom and then back in her bedroom. He could hear her awaken Carrie and Mike and then come downstairs. "Good morning," she said as she entered the kitchen. The darkness outside had created a strange ambiance in the house. Only the kitchen, of all the downstairs rooms, was lit up.

"Good morning, kid," Tommy said, not brightly.

Immediately Elly went to the cupboard for peanut butter, and then she put bread in the toaster. Tommy stood silently watching her as she walked around the kitchen, setting the table, buttering toast, getting cereal and milk and jelly. Both were aware of the other as Elly went about her business and Tommy pondered what he was about to do at the station.

For a moment, Elly left the kitchen and went to the foot of the stairs to call up to the kids. When she returned, Tommy said, "I've poured you a cup of coffee," as he pointed to the steaming cup on the table. She went over to it and raised the cup to her lips. Then she turned abruptly back to Tommy and said, "So, who's Neva?"

Tommy frowned inquisitively as he stared at her. "Where did you hear that name?"

"From you," she answered, taking another sip and acting nonchalant.

"Me?" he said

"Do you have a girlfriend, Dad?" she said, smiling.

He snorted and shook his head slightly. "So where did you hear about her, El?" he said seriously, surprising Elly by his tone.

"The whole house would have heard you if they were in the upstairs hall last night," she said.

"Me? You mean I talked in my sleep?"

"It was more than talk, Dad. There was some...anguish in your voice."

He nodded silently in agreement and marveled at his own betrayal of his private thoughts. "She's not a girlfriend," he said, looking away from his daughter. "She's, uh...she's dead." Elly's expression changed from whimsy to concern.

Tommy could see that she didn't understand and that suddenly she could be worried about him. "She's a case, El. She and her boyfriend were killed about a year ago and we haven't been able to get anywhere with it."

"Did you know them?"

Tommy was appearing to be nervous, and Elly sensed his discomfort. "The boy's father is Danny Bellino, my best lieutenant."

"Oh, my God! Danny? His son was killed?"

"Do you know him?"

"I graduated a couple years after him at St. Mark's. She was..."

"You knew his wife, too?"

"Everybody knew her. She was the senior prom queen, beautiful enough to be a model...and he was captain of our football team."

"Were you friends?"

"No," she sighed. "He was friendly and nice. But she didn't talk to people like me."

"Like you?" Tommy said a note of skepticism in his voice.

"She was gorgeous. And I was a 'brain' and she was a 'social'...and a rich one at that. How did such a horrible thing happen, Dad?"

"Young Danny and this girl, Neva, were a nice young couple. The Spring Common police caught them with a bag of crack cocaine in their car, but when we — I — investigated it, I knew it wasn't theirs." Tommy stopped for a few seconds and then looked back at his daughter. "I liked them, El, especially that girl, Neva. They were beautiful together...and a few weeks later, we found them both dead."

"How awful. Poor Danny."

"Yeah. One of the most senseless things I've ever seen. Those two kids wouldn't hurt a fly. They had everything going for them: They were in love..."

Elly was shaking her head in sympathy with Tommy's mood as if to confirm that his anguish was right. But as she listened, and during their pauses, she suddenly thought of the reason why they had begun their dialogue. And since it was such a strange side of her father that she was not used to, she was curious. "So, Neva was the girl?" she said finally to Tommy who had been with his own thoughts.

"What? Yeah, that was her name."

"Was she a friend?"

"No. I didn't even meet her until a few weeks before she died. It was the damnedest thing. Smokey came into my office one day and said they had caught those two kids with a lot of crack in their car... Danny and Neva. But, hell, they were no more pushers than you or I."

"But you got to know her?"

Elly was trying to understand her father without knowing all the thoughts that haunted him. Tommy nodded, as much to organize himself as to agree with his daughter. "I talked to them both shortly after they were brought into the station. She was gentle and intelligent..."

"And beautiful?" Elly interrupted.

He smiled slightly. "Like you," he said.

She snorted. "But this girl was special, right?" Elly said.

Suddenly, Tommy was seized by a revelation. Here was his daughter, boring in on him with questions. Questions of a kind that stripped away layers of obscurity and uncovered the truth; questions like the ones he would have asked in olden days when he called himself an investigator. And Elly was doing it instinctively and unerringly, all on a few words she had heard him mumble in the night. She was his daughter all right. He smiled to himself, and she noticed that it had come from a sudden thought, a revelation. "Yeah," sighed Tommy.

Elly was staring at him, and he glanced back at her for a moment before taking a sip of coffee. "But she reminded you of someone, right?"

"Right again, Inspector," Tommy said, this time making her smile slightly. "You want a job in the YPD? You'd get more done than those assholes that are supposed to be handling the case."

"Not my line of work," she said.

Just then, the two kids came into the kitchen and began chattering about school and their new friends and teachers. Tommy let himself be enveloped in the fog of noise and energy and movement, toast and milk and books and lunch money and keys and kisses and time growing short until the bus comes. And then in a moment they were gone, and all was quiet.

And then came Elly again. "What did she look like, Dad?"

"Who?"

"You know who" Elly said firmly. "I can't be polite about this now, Daddy. I have to know."

Tommy had not heard her call him Daddy in years. Dad was always more formal and more respectful but less intimate — at least the way Elly said it. "She looked Hispanic. I don't know…maybe Mexican…or more likely Puerto Rican around here."

"Not like Mom did…or me?"

"No," he said, shaking his head.

"She was strange. When you think of her you see colors. Everything on her was bright. Her skin, and a yellow ribbon in her hair…browns and yellows…white blouse. Somehow the colors mixed well and were stark and vivid, the way only a young girl could look, the way Carrie looks. I don't think I ever saw a grown woman with that kind —"

Suddenly he stopped talking, listening to the words he had just said, as though he had seen something in his mind's eye that had never occurred to him before. He stared ahead away from Elly. And she watched him, as he further raised her suspicions about what he was going through.

Then, Elly suddenly backed away. There would be another time to find out about this mysterious girl. And there would be time to find out what she had done to him that changed him so. "Are you going to work today?" she said.

"Yeah," he said. "My vacation isn't over until Monday, but maybe I'll go in for a little while."

<hr />

Kaye was quiet as Danny dressed. "I'll be gone a long time today, remember. Chief Malatesta and I are going to Cleveland for some meetings with the FBI," Danny said.

"Okay," she said, showing hardly any emotion.

"Kaye?"

"What?"

"I know you don't think there's much left between us, but... Well, it doesn't have to end... at least not on my account."

She didn't respond. Then he made his way toward her and stood facing her. She looked up at him, this time speaking plaintively. "I don't think I can do it, Danny."

He leaned forward without a word and kissed her. It was a soft, lingering kiss, on her cheek near her mouth. He let his cheek remain on hers for a few seconds longer than usual. Then as he pulled away, he said, "I still love you."

When she heard Danny's car backing out of the driveway, the tears that she had been trying to control welled up in her eyes, and suddenly overflowed upon her cheeks. He was such a good man, so much better than the others she had known. If only he were lazy, or stupid, or oafish, or insensitive. But he was none of those things. All he was, was predictable. He had given himself over to their love completely. He was so comfortable with life, with her, the kids, his mother, his brother, with police work.

Nothing was forbidden to Danny. Everything that surrounded him looked like it was always meant to fit into his life. And yet Kaye had given all that up. From Danny where nothing was forbidden to Mose where everything was forbidden: forbidden talk, forbidden meetings, forbidden touches, forbidden sex.

Kaye began to prepare the shower water, testing it against her wrist to set it right. She soaked her hair and washed it thoroughly, rinsing it many times until it squeaked between her fingers. She soaped her breasts, her buttocks, her legs, her groin. She knew she looked good even in this beginning of middle age. She knew her firm legs and flat belly were what all men desired. She knew the thrill of touching her that had gone to two new men in her recent life.

She stopped, turned off the water, and stepped out of the shower. Even in the steam heat of the room, she shivered. She began to dry herself and sought her image behind the steam against the mirror, but it didn't come. Why was Mose the one? He wasn't better looking than Danny, though he dressed better, was more elegant. But why? She shook her head. She didn't want to think that it was because of the elegance of his lifestyle, the money, the cars, the sophistication, the world travel, the house. And yet, all of it came together in him. And what she got from him was not the promise of success that Danny offered, but rather the actuality of success, the smell and feel of it.

Mose had an ease about himself, a quiet confidence that Danny lacked. But it was more than that. Mose had a sense of menace about him, the easy air of command, the sense that dire consequences were the result of his disobeyed orders.

All of these things brought out in her a thrill that she never got from Danny. The lovemaking wasn't as comforting with Mose as it was with Danny, but it was more thrilling, more exciting.

In a sense, all the difference between them was in her. In the way she was transported into a world of fantasy when she and Mose made love.

In was the way Danny was so earnest, so loving, so unmysterious. Chris was even different from the others... tall, lean, physical in a way that Mose and Danny were not. Danny was gentle, afraid to hurt her. Mose was deliberate and aloof. Chris was rough, and careless. Chris wanted pleasure and gave only pleasure. Mose gave nothing. Danny gave his heart.

She wanted sex to be thrilling, and for fleeting moments in the beginning it was. In the beginning before she began to think. Within one year, she had sex with three men. Yet making love was never different. When she was with Mose, she wanted the attention that Danny gave her. When she was with Danny, she wanted the animal pleasure that Chris gave her. And when she was with Chris she longed for the loving touch, the tenderness, the sense of belonging that only Danny could give her.

And yet Danny slept beside her at night full of hope that their love could be salvaged and made whole. His faith tortured her because some day she would have to tell him.

And, also, through those nights, her dreams were haunted by the loss of her son who was growing into manhood so surely and steadily. He had the same simple longing for love that Danny had, the same capacity to love that Danny had, yet the same impulsiveness and quick temper that she had. His promise for the future was secure. He had the intellect, the looks, the personality to have a successful life. And he had Neva.

Kaye shuddered, unable to control the impact of grief and jealousy and anger that Neva always brought to her heart. Damn Neva. Kaye had always known, and always feared, that Neva would be different, that she would weave golden threads of love around all the days of Danny's life. She would never hurt him the way Kaye had hurt his father. She would be content with their life just as Danny was content with what he and Kaye had made. And Danny would never have to ask for love in return for his own, or doubt it the way his father did. Neva would always give the love that Danny could never get from Kaye, pure and untainted. Untainted.

Kaye shook her head to her own thoughts. She had hurt Danny too much. He had lost a son and had been betrayed and lied to by his wife...with one man he barely knew, and another that he did know but detested.

How could she tell him he had lost his wife to two different men, none of whom were his equal as men or fathers yet were his better in their capacity to inflict secret pain upon the honest grief that he bore in his heart. Oh God. If she could ever do one last bit of good, she could never tell Danny, who she could never match in his capacity to love, but who, she knew in her own imperfect heart, was the best thing that had ever happened in her life. Oh, Danny.

Tommy was in Columbus for a state chief's conference for three days. On Friday morning he made the long drive back to Youngstown, up I71 to Akron and then on I76, through the rolling hills, east to Youngstown. He listened to music as he pondered what he would do. He couldn't free up Bumpy or Pete, but Meadows would do just fine.

Lucy had gotten the Bellino file and photocopied all of it for him while he was away. As he drove through the darkness, the road wound through patches of fog, then haze and mist, and then clear night. He decided to drive into downtown Youngstown. Sometimes, his office was his refuge against the world. He would go to the YPD station, read his mail, have a drink, and call Elly and tell her to put on some tea.

Elly, in her own quiet way, had taken over the house and become its mistress. When Tommy went home each day, he found it brighter, cleaner, more organized. Often as not there was the wonderful aroma of food cooking that set a warm tone for all the time spent there. And Elly and the kids were delightful. She was so mature, so much the best of Tommy and Janet that she had turned the kids into gentle, noisy, loving images of herself. She wasn't working yet. In her divorce settlement, David had to provide her three years of alimony and child support until Carrie was eighteen. But next September, Elly would be working, Tommy knew.

Tommy parked in one of the temporary spots in front of the station because they were clear in the evening. He waved to the night desk officer, spoke briefly to Pete — no news on Bellino — and headed upstairs. As he reached the top of the stairs he could see down the short corridor to his office, and there were lights on.

He turned the knob and found the door was locked. With his key he opened it quietly. As he entered the office, he noticed that all the lights in the waiting room were not lit. And then he turned abruptly toward Lucy's desk and was startled to find her standing a foot away. "Lucy? What are you doing here? Is everything okay?" She just looked at him and nodded. It was then that he noticed that she wore jeans and a sweater.

She shrugged. "Once in a while I come back down at night. Since my son's almost always gone lately, I have time to do work with no interruptions. Is everything okay with you, Chief?"

"Yeah. I just got back from Columbus. Haven't been home yet. Came in to look at some things."

She hesitated for a minute, fretful because Tommy was seeing her in jeans. Then she said, "The Bellino file copies are in the top drawer of your desk."

"Thanks, kid. I'll check it out." He walked into his office and sat behind the desk in the light provided by his desk lamp. Immediately he took out the file and began to read through it. Lucy busied herself in the outer office as he read.

For several minutes, both were silent. Then, Tommy stopped reading for a moment and looked away from the file. Just then he saw Lucy walk past the door opening, then walk back again. The image of her seemed to linger in his mind's eye even after she disappeared from sight. Jesus. She was more than a man could stand. If there was any woman who looked better in a pair of jeans, he'd never seen her. He shook his head, chiding himself for his thoughts. He had to tell her something more important than that he'd like to take her to bed in his impossible dreams.

He called to her, and she entered the room. Tommy had come from behind the big desk and was busy turning on a few more small lights. "Have a seat," he said, gesturing toward one of the two chairs in front of the fireplace. She looked at him curiously.

"You know I've just been treading water almost the last year — since Carly was elected?" She half nodded, seemingly reluctant to agree with him. "But I've decided to change some things."

She smiled. "New desktops?" she said, trying to break some of the tension that she felt.

He chuckled. "More than that," he said. Then he paused a long time. "Lucy, you know how much trouble this Bellino case is in, don't you?"

"I know it bothers you very much," she said.

"Yeah."

"You thought that girl was special, didn't you?"

He nodded. "It was such a waste, Luce."

Suddenly she stood up. "I'll be right back," she said. She walked out into her office and stayed a few minutes. Then she came back with two cups of tea and handed him one. He nodded and took a sip, setting his cup on an end table as soon as he drank.

"Lucy, girl, I'm gonna become a cop again."

She arched her eyebrows as he spoke. "You're quitting?" she said anxiously.

"No, kid, nothing like that." He hunched over in his chair, drawing his face a few inches closer between them. She sat still in the chair looking at him apprehensively as he spoke, her feet together and still on the floor, with her body twisted slightly to hold her torso erect.

From time to time, he would take quick glances at her, as was his custom. He never touched her, only looked. It always pleased him to watch her when she didn't know he was. She was so relaxed, so natural, so unhurried in her movements. And he enjoyed the natural play of her hands as she worked, and the beauty of her face as she concentrated on things, unaware of his attentions.

Suddenly, a thought came back to him, recalled from what he had said to Elly about Neva a few days before. The contrasts in Lucy were stark and beautiful. She had that lovely tan skin and flawless complexion, a yellow band in her hair and white blouse and yellow sweater. Her hair was pulled back tight, tied behind by a ribbon. Her hairline was perfect, her eyes dark and enticing. She was the same, flawless, clean mélange of stark contrasts that some beautiful young girls have – like Neva had. Graceful hands, wide full mouth, dark hair and eyes, burnt golden skin, full, shapely body. This was cleanliness, a natural flow of colors. This was music to the eyes.

And yet, as she sat before him, uncertain of what he would say, she was still vulnerable, and that vulnerability was her magic. Other women, far less gifted, would flaunt what they had. Others would be proud, and unapproachable. But Lucy did not have the hard and proud eyes. Hers were gentle, and uncertain, and bespoke pain in a life now past. In her eyes one could see the richness of wisdom, the understanding that life was unpredictable, and sometimes hurtful.

"I'm going to make the Bellino case my own," he said.

"But Captain Laney..." She let her voice trail off.

"Captain Laney is playacting, and you know it. That group'll never find the killers of those kids. Meanwhile Danny's heart is breaking."

She was beginning to feel a little better. "But you'll still be chief?"

"I'll still be chief, and you'll still be my secretary."

She sighed, relieved to hear him. "But what will I do? If you're not doing what you do now, will I have any work to do?"

"You'll have plenty to do. You can help me keep an eye on this place — you'll be my eyes and ears. You can tell me what's going on and if I have to do anything then I'll do it. Understand?"

She shook her head. "Chief, I'm just a secretary. I —"

"Lucy, do you want to help me?" She just looked at him without answering. "Do you?"

"You know better than to ask me that," she said, suddenly annoyed and disappointed.

Tommy sighed. He could easily sense her mood. "I'm sorry, kid. But I trust you. And there's no one else who can do your job. You fit me like a glove, Luce."

She was still doubtful, but his words had a strange affect upon her. Fit him like a glove? Could he be so careless with his language to say things that would mean so much to an ordinary person like her, and yet not mean anything at all to him? Maybe he's just tired and overloaded with cares and worries. Maybe he doesn't mean a thing by it. "Can you do this investigation all by yourself? With no help?"

"I did it before you were out of diapers, kid."

Finally, she smiled. "I don't think so," she said calmly.

"It's not like anything'll change very much. I'll see you every day and I'll still act the chief...It's just that I have to get back to being a cop. Meadows is gonna help me, and Bumpy and Pete will give me some slack around here."

She nodded, unconvinced. Things would not be the same and she dreaded it. Her years with Tommy had been the happiest of her life. She actually became somebody as she worked with him. All her life before, she had been a loser.

She had married Ed Searles because she was pregnant. She was young and poor and impressionable. He was a Youngstown baseball phenom with major league potential who drove a Mercedes. She got pregnant again three years later. Meanwhile, Ed had several tryouts with major league teams but was always sent back to the minors. And each time he was, he became more bitter and abusive, and found it satisfying to beat her up.

She had learned the secretarial skills once in high school and then forgot them during her years of following Ed around the National League. But after one bad beating when she realized how paunchy Ed was getting and how easily he had migrated from booze to cocaine, she knew her days were numbered. Ed was going to be gone someday, and she, if she were still alive, would be alone with two small children.

In all, she stayed married to him for seven years. And in those years, she knew no peace, no affection, and no caring. She was tied to his ambitions, cursed by her naivete and by her dependency. She realized too late how incurable his affliction was. Ed was like so many local phenoms, so far outclassing his teammates with his strength and grace and speed as to seem angelic in his gifts. He reveled in the adulation of the local fans, sensing their awe of his abilities, inflated by the adoration of local groupies, sexy, pliable, resilient young woman.

He would tell a constant stream of stories to his bar pals of women like the blonde divorcee with the hard, thirty-something body who fucked his brains out for three straight days of non-stop sex, and long after he could respond to her, she rode him and stroked him and sucked him and massaged him and oiled him until he became a legend.

Lucy heard the snickers; she lived with the humiliation because he was her husband, and she was poor and lucky to be paid attention by such a young man so full of promise. And she really wanted him to succeed. She knew if he could make a pro team, then the demons within him could be exorcised and she could then give him a life she knew he would want.

But he never made a pro team. Once the Chicago Cubs gave him a six-week tryout, but then they let him go because bigger, faster, more powerful players began to beat him out. And in later times, there were phenoms who beat him out only because they were younger. And then there were times when the younger groupies looked right past him to the younger phenoms. And suddenly the thirty-something divorcees didn't seem to have that final perfection that was the stuff of legends.

And he no longer spent three days any more getting worked over by haunted women looking, themselves, for fulfillment that never came… even after three desperate days of effort, days of sweat, days of cocaine, days of intimacy easily given and easily forgotten.

And, meanwhile Lucy was home… in a seedy apartment, being a good wife, raising the two kids, and trying to not notice the blond hairs on his clothes, the telltale reddish monthly stains that rubbed on to the shorts that she bleached white and washed, folded and put back into his drawer.

But the great curse, age, began to possess him, and the crushing realization that as good as he was on the field, there were others who were better. His talent just wasn't big enough. And the skills that he had honed in these later years, skills that he desperately wanted to maintain in his early thirties were fading. And the half-steps he lost to the younger players became measurable. And he suddenly found himself in a category beyond what he once was in — beyond promise.

And in time it all blurred into a cocaine haze, peopled with strange women and preying men. The one face he saw clearly was Lucy's. And in her eyes, he saw the pain, the sense of lost opportunity, the quiet, unstated longing for relief. And it was that face and those lovely dark eyes that tortured him. She never complained, but she looked at him through eyes that saw beneath his promise and knew the sudden fear that had invaded his soul, fear of not being good enough, fear of not living up to expectations, fear of humiliation for having to be ordinary, to go to work, to earn a living. And to earn it not by his athletic skills, but by his mind, never used to potential...and be just like everyone else. And suddenly he realized he could never live like that before the eyes of those who knew him. Especially before Lucy, who had once seemed a perfect match to him: her exquisite body and his, her sensual attractiveness, his imposing, athletic grace.

But now she looked better than he did. Every man who ever saw her dreamed of taking her to bed. And now he was getting a shock of prematurely gray hair and a stiff shoulder and a slight paunch, low in his groin. And he played for lesser teams in the minors, teams where, as days passed, he was not the best athlete. And after a while not even one of the best.

And Lucy still watched him, always with that same look, always with pain and resignation. And one night after a bad bout in a bar, when he consciously settled for a hit on a woman long past her prime, and when the woman rejected him with a knowing smile and a toss of her head, he had enough. And so, he went home drunk and met Lucy, and saw that look.

Hitting her was something he once never imagined he would do.

She never played around, never blew his money, never neglected her kids, never turned him down for sex. But even so, sex for her was now a duty, something she never enjoyed. And all of a sudden it was easy. When he sent her sprawling, her mouth bloodied, he liked the feeling. Her look had changed from resignation to fear. So, he hit her again. And suddenly the puffy, cracked lip, the swollen cheek, the red eye had made her grotesque, and not desirable. And they were even.

Yet...even in the beatings she was different. She never cried, or screamed, or cursed him. She quietly suffered the blows while softly pleading for him to stop. But there was never anger, never hatred, only hurt. And he began to realize how extraordinary she really was, not just in the way she looked, but in the way she acted. And, strangely, all of it seemed to repel him. He couldn't face her, so he'd hit her. And it became something of a relief. After the bars, after the coke sniffing, after the women, after the booze, he'd go home and hit her.

She had tolerated the other women, the constant travel, the loneliness she felt during the interminable baseball season, the drinking, the feast or famine income, and the drunken rages. But then one day, he mauled her so bad that she almost died, and he ended up on the road again, never to return to the warrant that was posted on him in Youngstown. And later, after a fight in a bar in Rhode Island, he drove a car away from the bar with a local woman. No one could ever figure out what he had tried to do at the crossing, but a high-speed passenger train cut the car in two, instantly killing Ed Searles and his lady friend.

And Lucy became a real person after he was gone. A new widow, she was determined to fight to keep her little family together. She wanted them to make something of themselves. But she knew she first had to make something of herself. She became a secretary and had one job after another. Sooner or later, every boss wanted her to barter her body for her job. And every time she left.

And after all the other jobs, she met Tommy. One day she found out about the chief of police hiring a secretary. She almost didn't go for an interview. She was too old, she told herself. She had kids and home worries. She was full-bodied, good-looking enough for a proposition from a dirty old middle-aged guy, but she didn't have the youthful, slender body and carefree insouciance that men like so much. But when she went for her interview, this middle-aged guy treated her with respect. And that day Tommy changed her life.

And over the nine years she worked for this complex, private man who drank too much, she became whole, and she became good at her job, the perfect secretary. She anticipated his needs. He was the chief, Tommy the Quarterback, who treated her with respect. He paid her well and inquired after her kids, her health, her family, her welfare — polite, non-probing, respectful inquiries.

In his own way, Tommy was in awe of her beauty, her quiet poise, her honesty, her thoughtfulness. Never a false moment in her existence. To him it always seemed that she was beyond the reach of mortal men. She was only available to millionaires and sports stars and politicians, men with youthful bodies the match to her own.

And Tommy never let himself dream of her because he had learned that being good wasn't enough in life. You had to be lucky, too. And smart. Smart enough not to marry the wrong woman, smart enough to know that balding old drunks in the twilight of their careers could never hope to attract women who looked like Lucy. And so, he spared himself the heartache of rejection. But just touching her, just holding her in his arms, still seemed like the dream of a lifetime.

All his life he had never made love to a woman whose heart belonged to him alone. And in his age, he had given up dreaming of the chance. If there were dreams to be had, they revolved around work. Around Neva. Around vengeance.

Lucy studied him in the long few moments that they sat opposite each other saying nothing. He was a strange man, so much in command, so used to it. And yet as he sat opposite her, he seemed nervous. But then, when he was something other than Tommy the Quarterback, when he talked to her, when he was close to her, he was always nervous.

She often wondered why he never tried to hit on her as every other employer she ever had did. Maybe he had a superior caste of WASP and affluent Irish friends, and they just didn't get involved with secretaries. The kind of women he would love were pure white, educated, politically connected, beautiful, confident and rich.

So, Lucy was shy and deferential. She knew she was not of his world, yet she was thankful over the years as she came to respect him and care about him, as he became the focus of so much of her day, as she saw him put upon and hurt, as she saw the vulnerable and grateful heart beneath the gruff exterior. And over the years, as her children thrived in the tranquil life she was able to afford them, thanks to Tommy, he became more than just the focus of her day, he became the essence of her day, the reason why she organized her life. And when she thought of the changes his retirement would make in her life, she was heartsick. Suddenly her world seemed spiritless and gray, and she would contemplate her waning years unfulfilled by the one element that would give them meaning...the one element she needed as roses needed rain, the elusive element she was always afraid to dream of as if wishing it could make it vanish: the complex heart, the animating voice, the nourishing spirit of the man who drew from the inner core of her a love she never knew she was capable of giving, a love fettered against the reality of a world that would not ever let it happen.

"I'll do whatever you want, Chief," she said quietly to him.

"Does the mayor know?" Mose asked his brother.

"Nah. I don't think so. He's too busy 'running' things," Nick Pagliaro said with a smirk.

"The game was supposed to be with married women. This kid's what? Eighteen? Twenty?"

"You know, Mose, I've always been nervous about Laney."

"Yeah, he thinks that law degree makes him special."

"We have to keep that asshole from fucking up a good thing. This Giustino kid's a spoiled little bitch, and she could go off on him any minute. Then where would we be?"

"Tell him I said to leave her alone. There's no need to go after her. I thought he was banging that Bellino broad anyway."

"She's another one…got some screws loose in the head. Chris said she's been hanging up on him when he calls."

"Tell him to go back to her. She's good-looking…not a great fuck, but she tries hard."

"Man, his dick must have grown an extra three inches when he was laying her. Especially when he was around her husband."

"I don't give a damn who he's banging. Just tell him to leave the mayor's daughter alone."

"You know, Laney really should win a bonus prize with this one," said Nick. "Those two broads are beautiful — light and dark. Bellino's wife looks like Miss America, and Carly's daughter looks like she could fuck a rattlesnake."

Chris Laney was fed up with the whole police scene. Maybe he should take the bar exam, finally after all these years, and work in the prosecutor's office. Police work was all boring and full of politics. And he had to deal with assholes like Tommy McCarrie and Bumpy Malatesta and Pete Mencken. Even Danny Bellino still irritated him. He acted like an Eagle Scout, ambitious without seeming to be. He was probably going to make captain next year. It bothered Laney that even with his law degree he couldn't lord it over Bellino. Danny had a master's degree in police science and somehow that was more impressive to the YPD than Laney's degree. Bellino had become one of them easily; he seemed to be a natural, following on the heels of Laney who was always a rank above him.

Laney remembered Bellino as a rookie cop, two years younger than he. Within a year, he had quit being a foot patrolman and started on his way to being a detective, making sergeant early, making lieutenant early.

Bellino tried to show that he was one of the boys...but superstraight. He was likable and naive, but typical of all the command officers surrounding McCarrie, unimaginative and plodding, with no style or panache.

Laney drank from his pilsner glass and snorted as he swallowed. Jesus, if only Bellino knew he was fucking his wife. And when he saw Danny, so earnest in his approach to work, so open in his affections, he would smile inwardly. He had the ultimate revenge against another man: he stole his wife's faith, and he stole his wife's body. God, it felt good. And the poor bastard didn't even know what was going on. He just lived his life, never knowing what hit him.

Suddenly, he changed his thoughts. Bumpy Malatesta was going to be asking him for another report, another ball-twisting session. He was really fed up with that asshole. It was harassment...only that.

As he drank another sip, he looked at the telephone. Time to call Kaye. Soon he was up and in the dim corner of the bar, under the Coke sign, in an old phone booth with no light on when the door was closed. "Kaye?"

There was silence on the line at first. Then, she said, "I can't talk to you anymore, Chris."

"I have to see you, Kaye. Meet me at my place tomorrow night." There was silence on the line. "Kaye?"

She was shaking her head as she spoke. "I don't think so," she said.

"I know Danny's working tomorrow. You can come...or do you want me to come to you?"

"No...No. I'll try to get there," she said softly.

He knew she would come. He smiled to himself after he hung up the receiver. This would be good. But now it was almost too easy. Now she had become too predictable. And the thrill of the first encounters was gone. He had seen Danny, talked to him, watched and listened to him, and all the while he was fucking Danny's wife. That flush of conquest, of stolen pleasure, heightened whenever he saw Danny, was beginning to pale.

Carley was angry at his wife for letting things get out of hand. "How in the fuck can I run this city if I have to worry about the police — my police — picking up my daughter some night!" Ginny didn't answer. "So where is she now?"

"I don't know," she said.

"What?"

"She said she wasn't coming back."

"Jesus Christ! And you let her go?"

"How was I supposed to stop her? Tie her up?"

"She's your daughter. Don't you have any more control over her than that?"

"She's twenty, and you don't keep twenty-year-olds grounded in their bedrooms at night...and she's also *your* daughter..."

"Who is this guy?"

"I don't know. She won't tell me."

"Jesus," said Carly, shaking his head at what his wife had told him. "My name will be splattered all over the Valley."

"Your name already is," his wife said coldly.

He nodded in agreement, thinking of what his political opponents had done to him during the long campaign. "She's done her best to screw up our reputation."

"That wasn't what I meant," his wife snapped.

Then he knew what she was saying. He took a deep breath. "How long are you gonna hammer me with that? Are you going to punish me every time someone sees me take someone to lunch?"

"The other one started out with your 'going to lunch,'" she said.

"Ginny, I'm sorry. I told you that. I've stopped it all. I want to be a good mayor, a good father..."

"In that order," she said, coldly.

"Not in that order! Jesus! Do I have to watch everything I ever say now? I told you: I'm sorry. I haven't done it again. She's gone. I want to be good to Lisa...and to you."

She was quiet for a few seconds. "I guess I just find your overnight reformation hard to believe."

"Please, Ginny, all I want is some peace."

"And you'll always be honest with me, will you?" she said skeptically. "No more lies?"

"What lies? I've told you; she's gone. It's over and I'm out of it. Isn't that enough?"

"No, Carly, it's not enough."

He turned toward back to her. "Why the hell not?

"Because you haven't told me all about your affairs."

"What haven't I told you?"

"Did you sleep with Jodi?" He hesitated. She surprised him. Jodi? What in God's name would make her bring that up? As he hesitated in silence, she grew more animated, more vocal, less careful about being overheard. "Did you?"

"Yes…" he said softly. "But it was before…"

"Before?"

"Before I realized how much you and Lisa mean to me."

She paused and sighed, shaking her head as she spoke. "I'm not really sure I can do this, Carly."

"Jodi was the last. I swear to God."

"And you never thought of getting rid of Jodi? You slept with her and then kept her around…to answer the phone when I called, to say hello to me when I came to the office. God, Carly, how could you?"

He walked toward her and stood in front of her, their faces a few inches apart, but he did not touch her. "Ginny, I was a dammed fool. I don't know what I was trying to prove with all that chasing. Now when I look back on it, it seems that I hated you…but I never did. I never wanted to hurt you. As for Jodi, she's a good secretary and a nice kid. And it was my fault, not hers."

"She knew you were married. She knew me. She knew I liked her.

And still she went to bed with you. It was more than just your fault, Carly."

Carly was silent. He stepped away from her and watched her. She stared back at him expectantly, not knowing what her next thoughts or words would be in reaction. "I didn't know how much I needed you to make my life work," he said, softly.

"As a hostess for your parties?" she said.

"No. You must know it's not that."

She stared at him. He had never been very demonstrative toward her, toward anyone. And yet now for the first time in years he seemed honest and genuine. Maybe his father's illness had made him think differently lately. Whatever it was, it was unexpected, and welcome. Suddenly the man who had hurt and humiliated her so many times was standing before her talking softly, asking for forgiveness. She lowered her head and tears began to flow from her eyes.

He lowered his head to hers and kissed her on the cheek and she clung to him, throwing her arms around his neck and sobbing.

The exhilaration Tommy felt was tempered by the thoughts of Neva and Danny Bellino. This was all serious business, not a game for some old guy to swagger around flashing a badge and playing investigator. This was about the murder of a girl who had shed brief light on his existence.

But it had been so long. Where would he start? He wasn't even up on all the new crime detection techniques, all the science and electronic stuff, microchips and microscopes. He'd have to learn, but it would come slowly. Being a politician-cop drains the vital instincts right out of you. But how can you get them back except to remember the old ways, the ways that always worked?

He sat, drinking coffee in his office, hearing Lucy quietly stirring in the outer room. All his instincts drew him toward the Bellinos. That night, a few weeks ago, when he tried to parse the events that surrounded the killing of those kids, he had been ruminating about Danny and his wife. He had a feeling that the secrets behind these events were known to someone in that house. Maybe Danny, if Tommy's instinct had not completely failed him. But, then again, maybe Danny's wife, if his instincts were still good. She seemed to be the only mystery, the only one who was a closed book in a family full of open faces and easy social intercourse.

This would have to be his own style, his own case, and he would do it alone. And the first step would be the Bellino house, to see if his rusty mind could stumble on things to think about that might be easily obvious to a better cop. But he wanted to find out something else, too. He wanted to see if the old instincts could be reincarnated, or if they were atrophied to extinction from lack of use.

He rose from his chair and walked to the outer room. "Luce, will you find out if Danny Bellino's on duty tonight? Quiet like." She nodded, and he went back inside to put on his coat.

Tommy parked his car on the street and walked up the driveway to the house. When he rang the bell, the door was opened by Kaye Bellino. She seemed shocked to see him, knowing that no good could ever come from a visit from this man. Without a word, she stepped aside, letting Tommy walk into their house.

She escorted him into the living room where Danny was reading quietly by himself in a large, stuffed chair near an old fireplace glowing with hot coals from wood spent by an hour's burning.

"Danny," she said in a quizzical tone, "Chief McCarrie's here."

Danny, too, was surprised to see his boss. "Chief?" he said after staring at Tommy a few seconds. "Sit down…please."

As Tommy sat down, so did Danny, with Kaye sitting opposite the chief, but still more than arm's length from her husband. She glanced at Danny and then looked away, back to Tommy.

"What have you been told so far?" Tommy said abruptly, wasting no time on pleasantries.

"Not much, Chief," said Danny, looking at Kaye nervously. "They haven't come up with much…no prints, nothing from a DNA test."

"Do you have anything to tell us?" said Kaye somberly.

"No," Tommy said, choosing not to elaborate on a list of non-leads and failures of imagination.

"So as each day passes the job gets harder," Kaye said. "And Danny's killers are safer, and we're one day less likely to find them."

"Let me find them, Chief," Danny said.

"No, Danny. You know that's not right."

"It'd be better than what you're doing," said Kaye. "He'd be working on this instead of just sitting around here doing nothing," Kaye said.

Tommy sensed the double edge in her tone: the first was frustration at not being comforted by the apprehension and the punishment of the killers, but the other was resentment, somehow directed at Danny for the position they were in.

"I shouldn't have to tell you two, of all people, that someone as emotionally involved with this case as Danny, shouldn't be on it."

"Hell, Chief, what's the difference? Those guys wouldn't know a clue if they stubbed their toes on it," Danny said.

"So you've heard nothing?" Tommy said. Danny shook his head, and his wife sat stoically, staring at the chief.

Tommy had been watching closely in the last few minutes. There was something wrong between them. He could see it from the beginning; Kaye could have sat nearer to Danny, but instead she sat apart from him. And they never looked at each other, never spoke in tandem, even about their anguish, which involved them both so much.

He could sense the strain. And he could also sense the harshness of their feelings. Danny was wounded and confused; Kaye was bitter and angry.

"And how are things between you?" Tommy asked, catching them off guard.

"Things?" Kaye answered.

"You know what I mean," Tommy said pointedly. "We're getting by," sighed Danny.

"What business is it of yours?" said Kaye. "I thought Captain Laney was the chief investigator."

"I've decided to do a bit of investigating myself," Tommy said.

"A bit of investigating? You alone?" said Kaye angrily. "What good can you do if a whole team can't find anything?"

"Kaye," Danny said softly, admonishing her to give Tommy a little breathing room. "You, Chief? When did you start this?"

"Just now, Danny. You see, I don't like way things are going either," he said, looking at Danny's wife. "And this is my first step. Right here."

"And what did you expect to find here?" Kaye asked. "We're not the killers."

Tommy took a deep breath then spoke very deliberately. "I came here because I want to begin again. I want to learn how to see those kids through your eyes."

"But why do it all alone?" Danny asked.

"Because for now it's best. Later I may get others involved, particularly Med Williams."

"Med Williams? He's not a homicide man!" Danny said. Kaye just threw up her hands in disgust and stood up out of her chair.

Tommy was uneasy being in this house that had known such anguish and had waited so long for any faint glow of hope. He could see two fretful people pained almost beyond endurance by the loss of a son and his lovely young girl.

But they were turning toward each other in anger also. Tommy could sense that. There was something in them beneath the agony that most people feel when tragedy strikes down two beloved children. And it was there before the loss of Danny and Neva.

"Med Williams is a good cop, Danny...with better instincts than any of those guys on that new squad. And he knows the streets and alleys of Youngstown. Besides, I can trust him, and I need somebody I can trust."

"But you can trust me, for Christ's sake! Let me help."

"Med Williams didn't lose a son to a murderer, Danny. He doesn't carry the pain that you do. And you know his judgement won't be clouded by the memories and agonies of what he's lost. Look at me Danny." Danny and Kaye both turned toward him. And Tommy spoke very deliberately, "You can't do this. You have to let us try to catch these killers."

Danny turned and walked a few steps away. "There's got to be something I can do. From the station. There's got to be something I can do."

He spoke with his back to Tommy, but the older man knew what he was asking and couldn't deny it. "If I need some help, I'll come looking for you."

Danny had turned back toward him, and nodded assent after Tommy spoke. Then Tommy turned toward Kaye. "And I don't know what's going on between you two, but whatever it is won't bring those kids back. Remember that."

Later that night, as he sipped the tea Elly had made him before she went up to bed, Tommy mused about Danny and Kaye. She didn't acknowledge his last admonition about their troubles not bringing Danny and Neva back. Instead, her eyes were cold and vacant. He couldn't fathom the pain in those eyes either. It was not what he saw in Neva's mother's eyes: the desolation of a mother who had lost a child, the bewilderment, the sense of grief that innocents can't bear. Could it have been remorse?

Is that what the strange pain in her eyes bespoke? Something she had done that had brought about a grief so different from that of Neva's mother? Something she had done? Or something she couldn't face with Danny? No, something she couldn't face with herself. That's why the half-tones of resentment along with the remorse.

Who knows, Tommy wondered. Maybe it's been such a long time that he's lost his instinct. Maybe it's just old age keeping him from seeing the ordinariness of what he saw. Maybe he was trying too hard.

"What's going on?" Carly said to his secretary as he quickly worked through his mail without looking up at her.

"Nothing new. Chris Laney called...said he'd be over later today."

Finally, he looked up at her. "Okay," he said in a dismissive tone.

She turned on one heel and walked into the outer office. Something had happened to Carly that was beyond her control. And there was nothing she could do. She realized that what they had was a passing fancy. Carly was a playboy. And yet, she believed he liked her and seemed gentle enough and decent enough.

Suddenly she returned to the mayor's office, closing the door behind her. Carly looked up at her this time, knowing there was trouble ahead.

"Carly?" she said looking down at him from the front of his desk. "What's happened? Why am I being treated like a stranger, like a Kelly girl?"

Carly looked down away from her gaze. "I haven't mistreated you, have I?"

"Mistreated me? No, not as a boss, but as someone who was in my bed making love to me a few weeks ago, it's mistreatment."

Carly stood up and walked around his desk to confront her. "Come on over here," he said softly, touching her shoulder to guide her toward the chairs in his office.

The phone rang and she hesitated, then answered. "Mayor's office. Oh, hi, Judge East…" She glanced at Carly who shook his head. "He's not here now, Judge. He'll probably call in soon. At home? Okay. I'll tell him you called."

Carly signed in relief as she hung up the phone. They both then sat on a couch near the bookcase along the wall.

It was strange how so many offices in Youngstown resembled each other, as though they were all designed by the same architect. No one seemed to expect anything different. The boss's office had a wide view, a desk, a fireplace, a conference table and a couch and chairs. In his way, Carly's office was like his father's, like Judge East's, and like Tommy McCarrie's.

"Jodi, I've been trying to find a way to talk to you..."

"Why didn't you just talk?" she said.

"Because I wasn't sure what to say to you."

"Because you're going to dump me?"

"You knew it couldn't go anywhere. My career would be gone in the Valley if I had a messy divorce."

"Shit," Jodi muttered.

"But that's not it," he said, touching her arm as if to restrain her from leaving. "But you knew that I was married, right? And I never told you that I'd leave my wife... What we had was nice... fun. Can't we let it go at that?"

"You weren't acting like it was just a fling. You made it seem like... You told me I wasn't like your wife... that we were good together that you could talk to me."

"But I never said I'd leave my wife, did I?"

"When we were in bed and you said so many things, it sounded like you would."

"I can't help what it sounded like," Carly said impatiently.

She stood up and started toward the door. "Damn you and your wife," she said throwing the telephone onto the couch. But in a few steps Carly caught up to her.

"Jodi, don't do this. Come back and talk to me."

"Let me go, Carly," she said shaking her head as he spoke closing her eyes so as not to look at him.

He held her by the arms until she quit struggling. "Come on," he said softly, urging her toward the couch.

When she sat down again, he pulled a chair opposite her and sat down face-to-face with her. "You deserve a better deal than I can give you, kid," he said.

Jodi was surprised at the tone of his voice. It had a fatherly quality that she had never heard from the brash young mayor. Carly shrugged. "My dad's gonna die…I've hurt my wife…I've hurt my daughter…" He looked up at her. "And I hurt you."

Jodi was crying as she looked at him. For the first time since she had ever known him, she felt sorry for him. And she didn't know how to deal with this new mayor.

"Here's me, Mayor of Youngstown, and my dad doesn't even know that I am anymore. Hell, he doesn't even know *who* I am when he sees me." Carly shrugged again, his voice cracking and his eyes suddenly glazed with tears. "My life's falling apart, Jodi. I think I may have lost Ginny. She doesn't trust me or believe in me. Hell, Lisa doesn't even *like* me. And I promised you things I couldn't deliver and it…" He looked directly at her. "It never even entered my mind how much I was hurting you. I never gave it a thought. Hell, I just used you. I wanted to be a big shot…to let the whole world know that I could get all the women I wanted…young, beautiful ones like you. I never cared about anyone…not Ginny, not my daughter, not my dad…not you.

"But now all of a sudden, I do care. I have to help you out of this mess. I don't want my life and all my problems to ruin your chances to be happy."

———◆◆◆———

Kaye Bellino knew that if Chris Laney persisted, she would finally give in, and finally meet him. God, she hated her life. She was drawn toward Laney, but not for the reason she was drawn toward Pagliaro. Laney had that animal attraction that so captivated her. And he was just so much more exciting than Danny: more vain, more dishonest, more violent, more cruel. He was also more unfeeling, less sensitive.

And for him sex wasn't making love as it was for Danny. To Chris, sex was only for pleasure, only for those who looked as good as he did. She knew she would meet him.

At his apartment, he said, smiling, "It's been a long time, Kaye... too long."

"I shouldn't have come," she said nervously as he took her coat. "I have to leave soon. Danny gets off early tonight."

"You say that all the time," he sighed.

"I'm just telling you so you don't wonder why I just get up and leave," she said.

"You can leave any time you want," he said.

Kaye looked at him as he walked toward the closet with her coat. He wasn't looking at her. But he knew, as did she, that she wasn't going before they had sex.

He walked back toward her and stood a few inches away. For a few seconds they didn't speak, never moved. She could feel his breath upon her face, warm and excited. And she breathed in the aroma of him.

Suddenly she pushed her body into him and raised her lips to his, drawing hungrily. He was pulling at her dress just as she was trying to undo his shirt and his belt. She was helpless, she knew. She also knew that she had no control over her feelings, that there would never come a day when she would be able to stop what she was doing. In a few moments, without words, she was on the floor with him naked and moaning and enraptured as he entered her. They didn't take too long — not much foreplay. And yet somehow with Chris she didn't want foreplay, didn't need it. She was wet and ready, hot and breathless when he touched her. With Danny she needed foreplay; with Chris she only needed to breath in the musk of him, to respond to his lips.

When they were done, he got up quickly and put on his briefs. "Where are you going?" she said.

"Nowhere," he answered abruptly.

"Why so quickly? What do you...?"

He looked back over his shoulder at her but said nothing. He continued to dress.

"Can't you just stay and hold me for once?"

"I held you before."

"But you didn't mean it. All you wanted to do was get your rocks off," she said disgustedly.

"You'd better go. Maybe you were right after all...you shouldn't have come. I shouldn't have asked you."

"Why didn't all this occur to you before you fucked me? Or are you just trying to confirm that the thrill was gone...that you were tired of me?"

"Don't be so melodramatic. I'm just getting ready to go. I'll be getting a call later."

"Who is she?"

"It's a call from work, Kaye."

"I've been married to a cop for a long time, Chris," she said. "And don't ever remember his getting any midnight calls."

"Maybe if he was a better cop, he would have."

"You bastard!" she hissed. "Bad enough you're fucking his wife, then you have to lie about the thing he does best."

"If I fucked his wife, it was because she came to me willingly and laid it all out for me. And I can't help it if a guy can't please his wife..."

She stared at him for a few seconds, as if really seeing him for the first time. Her face contorted in horror, and she placed both palms of her hands one over each temple.

He looked at her as she stood before him in silence. He seemed puzzled but indifferent, almost aloof. Suddenly he was curious about what she'd do next.

"It never was right, was it?" she said softly.

"Why are you doing all this now, Kaye? For Christ's sake. We had something going and we both enjoyed it. Why do we —"

"You enjoyed it because you were fucking another man's wife."

"I enjoyed it because you and I are good for each other."

"And now we're not," she said.

"We're not only because you say so. Why don't we just forget this and go out and have a drink?"

"I don't want a drink. I want to know that you need me."

"I need you. I've told you that. What's gotten into you? Just tell me what I've done that's set you off like this."

"That's just it. I'll always have to tell you. God, what have I done!"

He was getting angry. "What you did was shack up with a guy who knew how to push your buttons. And now you can't deal with the guilt." He paused for a few moments. "Just remember one thing: I didn't ever twist your arm. You came to me because you were hot for some action... for a piece of strange."

His words seemed to strike her across the face. "You've never given a damn about any of this, did you? For you it was just a roll in the hay."

"It was just a roll in the hay that you liked, too. Remember how you screamed the first time? Remember how you wanted me to fuck you all night long?"

"I remember that, in the end, it was always unfulfilling, Chris. Never what I wanted it to be. And I kept thinking that just one more time would be... and it never was."

"Well, maybe what you wanted was something your husband couldn't give you, or Mose...or me. Maybe that ought to tell you something."

"It tells me that I'm stupid...that I've thrown away my life for a bastard like you who can't feel anything."

"Well, since we're calling names, what do you call a woman who cheats on her husband by fucking two other guys?"

"You knew about Mose?" she asked, her voice cracking. "All this time?"

"Mose and I are friends, Kaye. He introduced us, remember?"

Kaye had gone limp. She braced herself against the wall. Finally, she whispered the words, "He passed me on to you. Oh, God!" as though she finally could see what the whole world would see if they only knew.

All the sympathy and shared heartache everyone gave her when she lost Danny and Neva would be gone. And this sudden tragedy, this disruption in their life stream, would now be looked upon as her punishment for violating the one law of God they all understood.

And Danny? What would she do now? She had hurt him, and he didn't even know it. God, what had she become? Someone no one could ever satisfy? Someone for whom no man could make her life exciting?

She stared at Laney as he took a bottle of beer from the refrigerator. That rush that warmed her low in the belly when she needed excitement, the rush that from Danny had long since vanished, had also vanished from Laney as she watched him, moving about oblivious of her pain.

Suddenly, she beheld all the evil that she had brought upon her life. She started to speak to Laney but hesitated. He looked back at her, quizzically and yet unmoved, almost unfeeling. She knew from the look that he would never be the man she fled from Danny to find. And Mose was just Laney, only with more polish. They were both cold inside, and nothing she could do would make them different. And nothing she could do would bring Danny back to her if he found out about Mose and Chris…especially with the memories of Danny and Neva haunting him.

Her thoughts of Danny were unbearable. She couldn't face him, even in her mind's eye. For any other woman, he would be a dream come true. None of her friends had known husbands who really made love when they were having sex. None had known the tenderness of their relationship. None had known a clean, trusting, honest man capable of total devotion to his wife. And none had betrayed such honor to two different men…and borne the punishment of God for the defilement of their love.

She put on her coat, and Laney was surprised by her quick movement. All she did was stare back at him as he watched her. He doesn't have a clue, she thought. Not a bit of feeling about her. For a few long seconds they studied each other, she hoping that he would show some spark of affection or commitment, and he wondering why the affair they had put together was unraveling.

They parted silently, Laney never realizing that he had to convince her to stay, and never dreaming that she wouldn't come when he called her again.

Outside, Kaye sat in her car quietly. She could feel her heart thumping in her chest as she breathed. She surveyed in her thoughts the wreckage of her life, her betrayal of Danny.

She couldn't go to him now to make amends. She wanted to. She wanted to say how sorry she was. She wanted him to understand, to forgive. But what she wanted could never be. Once would have been a mistake, but twice was a violation of every happy memory they held between them. And both were sins against the memory of Danny and Neva.

She started to cry. It seemed that within a moment of her life, her marriage had collapsed, her son had died, and she had become the whore of two men not able to tie the shoes of the man she knew loved her more than anyone else in the world. And yet she had sought them out to give in to the strange urges she held deep within her.

But now she saw in Danny the honest love that she had so long taken for granted. And that her sin was worse than adultery because it was also a sin of prodigality, further corrupted by the sin of untruth. And no amount of remorse would erase what she had done to Danny and to the memory of her son. She knew that she had degraded herself so far that Danny could never touch her again and not feel the twinge of regret for what she had done to him and to their children. And not to face him would mean not to go home again.

She started the car and rode toward downtown. She thought of the Mahoning and the many roads leading to the river's edge. As she headed east, the car ran faster.

———◆◆◆◆◆———

Tommy was getting used to his new home life. And it was a relief, because somehow, he grew more relaxed around the noise and bustle of the house. Elly had settled in easily as the mistress of the house and seemed content. The kids had found new friends already, and Boston was a fading memory for all.

"El, you ever gonna have a social life?" he said one morning after breakfast.

She turned to him inquisitively. "So, what brought this one on?"

He shrugged. "I don't know. I think about you staying here and not having friends."

"I'll have friends, Dad. I've already found a couple girls at church."

"What about men friends? You can't stay here cooped up in this house forever."

She sighed. "I don't meet many men, Dad. I'm not a socialite; I don't go to bars. I'm thirty-eight years old. Maybe there'll come a time. I just can't force it to happen."

"Do you think you could fall for someone else, El?"

She nodded thoughtfully. "I think so, Dad. There must be some nice guys out there... some guys like you." She was smiling. "And if one of them asks me out, I might say yes."

Tommy spent the morning tending to his work as chief. Lucy had made up her mind to settle into the new-style job. The strange emptiness of the office the first few days seemed disturbing. But she was getting used to it. As usual, she eyed Tommy from a distance, looking at him from time to time. She felt so much better when he was around, just like in the old days. He seemed to be the rock upon which the force rested. As long as he was in the office things were okay.

She brought him coffee and he stayed in his office doing things that had to be done but were not urgent. And the gray afternoon passed slowly. He and been trying to piece together the Bellino case, trying to at least know where he stood. But his instincts weren't enough. He needed the experience to bring the instincts to life.

Finally, he sat in his office drinking Lucy's warm coffee... and doubting his own abilities in solving the case. After an hour of lazy reverie, he was about to go home when he heard the door in the outer office slam. He heard footsteps — more than one set — and the heavy stride thumping against the floor as the steps grew closer to him.

The leader could be only one man who entered unannounced, and strode through the office, as he did through the YPD, as a squat giant who feared no one in his sight. Bumpy Maletesta suddenly appeared in Tommy's office followed by Pete Mencken. Bumpy stood silent for a moment, uncharacteristically hesitant to speak. Yet his face was flushed and strange looking. Pete looked shaken and quietly troubled. Finally, Bumpy spoke: "Jesus Christ, Tommy, Danny Bellino's wife was just killed in a car wreck...a few miles from here."

Tommy had to visit the scene before he saw Danny. Jesus, he thought, how could all this be happening to that poor kid? Tommy dreaded what he was going to see...as he did when he approached the scene of Danny and Neva's deaths. But this one was different. Now he had gotten over the horror. Now he was an investigator, and now he had to let his senses in on the full awfulness of what he beheld.

"What's going on?" he said to the first officer he saw.

"Look's like she just lost it, Chief. Somehow, she got over that guardrail and must have slipped down that ravine into the water."

Tommy nodded as he walked closer to the action. He could see a large YPD tow truck, a "jaws of life" truck, and an intensive care ambulance. Med was there already directing the drivers of the trucks to get the car up as whole as they could. Med nodded as Tommy approached.

"How's Danny?" he asked the chief.

"Bumpy and Pete went out to see him," Tommy said grimly.

"I can't figure this one, Tommy," said Med. "I don't know what she could have hit coming down here. She had to be going faster than hell."

"Could it be some malfunction like bad brakes?"

"Maybe," Med said. "But this doesn't look like your basic accident."

"Yeah?"

"This car was going too fast for this place. Look at those tracks. Look at the trees and brush…a straight shot into the river…no skid marks."

"You think she might have been running from someone?"

"Hell, I don't know, Tommy. All I know is that this is weird."

He walked away as an officer came toward him, asking him about how to handle the car. Tommy watched the wreckers move the car onto a platform rig so it could be towed intact back to the YPD garage.

He approached the coroner who had been watching also from a distance and had examined the body and the site briefly before turning it over to the people from the YPD lab.

Dr. Jack Horowitz saw Tommy approach from a corner of his eye. "Jacko," Tommy acknowledged.

"What a deal, huh?" the coroner said turning toward Tommy who was slightly taller than he.

"Yeah," said Tommy. "That kid sure didn't need this."

"You mean Danny?"

Tommy looked at him quizzically. "Yeah," he said.

"He might not like what he hears, Tom," said Jack.

"What're you talking about, Jack?"

"You have no idea, do you?"

"Jack, for Christ's sake, I'm in no mood for riddles!"

"Tommy, I'll bet my next pay that this was a suicide."

"And how the fuck do you know that?"

"I don't 'know' anything...not yet. But I've seen a lot of these things, and it sure as hell has a certain look to it."

"Well before you decide on the 'certain look,' how about if you call me before you release your report?"

"Why are you in on this, Tommy? What's the deal with my report?"

"Because Danny's one of my cops, and I just want to know what you're gonna say beforehand."

Horowitz huffed in annoyance. "Okay, I'll call you...probably late tomorrow afternoon."

———————

At four o'clock the next day, Lucy transferred a call from Jack Horowitz into Tommy's office. "You want to hear what I'm gonna report on the Bellino woman, Tommy."

"No, Jacko, I don't want anything over the phone. I'll be right over."

"But I can read it verbatim and FAX you a copy."

"I said I'll be right over, Jack," Tommy said gruffly.

A few minutes later, Tommy was ushered into the County Coroner's office. Jack Horowitz eyed him apprehensively as he came forward and sat down in front of his desk.

"Since when does the chief of police become so personally involved in a suicide?" Horowitz asked coolly.

"Since what you say about this accident can drive a stake into the heart of a good, young lieutenant of mine that he'll never recover from."

"I have to be honest, Tommy. Right?"

"Yeah, right. Old Honest Jack."

"What the hell's that supposed to mean!"

"It means that we both know that your verdicts in the past have saved special people a lot of trouble and grief..."

"Damn, you, Tommy. Don't you start that with me. I'm a good coroner...and an honest one, even if you don't believe it."

"I do believe it, Jack. Or else I would have made your life hell these last thirteen years."

"So what do you want?"

"I want some answers...honest answers."

"So ask your questions. I called you like I said I would."

"Do you remember any those cases that I helped you with when you were a greenhorn?" Tommy said testily. "You remember a few times when I saved your ass in court because you fucked something up?"

"This is payback time, huh?"

"Only if you want it to be, Jacko. I don't have a gun to your head."

"Shit, Tommy..." Jack drawled. "So, what do you want?"

"How solid is the evidence of suicide?"

"Solid enough."

"But what I'm asking is...given the evidence..."

"Could I be reading this evidence another way?"

Tommy looked at him. "Is there any doubt, Jack? Are you sure?"

"Hell, Tommy. I just make my best judgment call. But why the hell are you so hooked on this case?"

"Because Danny Bellino lost a son and now a wife. And in the ashes has to raise two other kids without a mother."

Jack nodded, acknowledging Tommy's motives. "So what do you want, an accident?"

"If you can spare it, Jack. Unless you have it cold, and unless there's no possibility you could be wrong."

He stood silently for several long seconds. Then he nodded. "Okay, I think I could say this was accidental. I'm just weighing my doubts more than I usually do."

Tommy sighed in relief, and patted Jack on his shoulder as he turned to leave. "I owe you a dinner, Jacko."

Horowitz smiled. Tommy was a good man. And this move didn't compromise his integrity. If Tommy would have said he owed him something more, he might have felt that Tommy was trying to muscle him. But for a dinner? Tommy was acknowledging that it was an intellectual decision rather than a moral one. The rest was easy.

"One more thing, Tommy," he said as the chief was nearing the door out of the office. Tommy turned back to him, curious about what Jack would say. "She had intercourse not too long before she died."

Tommy was surprised. "Any sign of struggle or violence?"

"No."

"So, you think it was normal?"

"Yeah, I do. By the way, was she with her husband tonight? You know? The guy whose sensibilities you're trying so hard to spare?" Tommy looked at him, knowing what he was suggesting. "But I forgot. You're the investigator. I'm just a coroner."

"And not a bad one at that. Thanks, Jacko"

"Yeah," Jack said as Tommy closed the door behind him. "But I still think she drove that car over that fence deliberately," he muttered to himself.

<hr />

Mose Pagliaro was shaken when he heard of Kaye's death. Suddenly things were happening beyond his control, and it bothered him. She was good for him while it lasted. She was enthusiastic but not gifted.

She tried, but Mose realized that she could never like sex. She wanted sex to give her fulfillment for some desperate longings in her life that never came. And now she was gone.

Nick Pagliaro, Mose's brother and right-hand man, came in the door to his office. "You hear about Kaye Bellino?" Mose asked him.

"Yeah. Word's out all over downtown," said Nick.

"Has Laney been banging her lately?"

"I'm not sure…I know he always has a few other ones on the hook."

"What about the mayor's daughter? He still getting into her pants?"

Nick sighed. "I don't know, Mose. He's not smart enough to listen about things like that."

"You just tell him straight. Lay off the mayor's daughter."

"There's something else you may not have heard, Mose…"

"What?"

"Word is that Tommy McCarrie has been asking questions all over town."

"I thought the mayor took care of it with Laney and that special squad?"

"Yeah, but they can't handle McCarrie. Hell, he's acting like a detective."

"That son of a bitch Irish drunk. We can't let him start meddling with things. He'll fuck up all we've got going, Nick."

"So what if he finds the killer? What do we care?"

Pagliaro looked at him strangely. "Care? You think Laney is gonna go down in flames without dragging us down with him?"

"Hell, Mose, hardly anybody knows us. We lie so close to the ground."

"And I want it to stay that way," Mose said. "And you tell that fucking Laney that he has to shape up."

"What if he won't listen?"

"Then we call Philadelphia or New York. I'm tired of trying to talk sense to him." Nick nodded. He knew what his brother meant. And it was frightening to think of what could happen to their lives. All these years they slowly built up strength and contacts with hardly any muscle. Only a few times did they have to make those calls to Philadelphia for some torpedo to come west to do a job.

Life was good. Good money, good food, easy living, and good-looking, pliant women. Both he and Mose had too much at stake to let a jackrabbit like Chris Laney end it. "You know, I should have seen this coming a long time ago. I must have been crazy to screw around with someone we couldn't control. He already gave us a close call with those Bellino kids."

"But as long as he's heading up the investigation, we know it's going nowhere, right?" said Nick.

"Yeah, but what if McCarrie starts on this?"

———————

Tommy forced himself to go to the funeral of Kaye Bellino. At the funeral mass, and later at the cemetery, Tommy's thoughts were morbid and remorseful. The memories of Neva haunted him as he stood silently at the grave side. Pete and Med and Bumpy stood beside him, but not really with him, sensing instinctively that Tommy felt alone in this crowd.

From time to time, he'd look at Danny, who clung to his daughter and his son. Poor guy. Who would have ever thought, seeing him grow up, that the onset of his middle years would bring him such sorrow? Tommy shook his head silently to himself, answering his own dreamlike thoughts with waking gestures. And he never deserved any of it...a good father, a loving husband, a loving son, a good cop. Why should this tragedy be visited upon such a family?

Suddenly, as he pondered what was before him, he felt a presence beside him. He turned to look; it was Elly. She nodded slightly and quickly looked away. But of all the people in the world who could have eased Tommy's anguish that day, the best of them was Elly.

After the ceremony, the undertaker announced that a mercy feast would be held in the reception room of St. Ann's Church. They filed back to their cars and Tommy turned back to his daughter. "Nice to see you," he said.

"You too... I just thought you might like some company." He smiled slightly, but she caught it. He was amazed at her. It was as though an angel had come into his life to light every dreary moment in it. She seemed to know what to say to him, when to talk, when to play, when he needed her beside him. And Tommy loved every minute of it.

They drove separately to the mercy feast. In the hall, Tommy spoke briefly to Pete, Bumpy, and Med and asked them to join him and Elly at a table. Elly had not seen the men for several years, yet she spoke easily and warmly to them. She liked Bumpy very much and enjoyed teasing him in the old days. But now she was polite and somewhat reserved.

It was strange, Tommy mused, how dinners after funeral masses were hardly distinguishable from retirement parties or graduation parties. There was much noise and laughter and clanking of plates. Even Danny and his children seemed more animated, if slightly glassy eyed.

As everyone made table talk, Tommy moved about the hall, seeing old friends — Connie, Danny's mother, Rino and Lou, Danny's uncles — working the room. Subconsciously, he seemed to be avoiding Danny, but he did talk to Rino and Lou. "How're the card games down at the Tre-sette?"

"We miss you, Tommy," Rino said. "It's just like church. I pay my dues and my brother collects." They all laughed.

"Listen, I'd like to talk to you guys soon, okay? Maybe we can have dinner before a game?"

Rino and Lou glanced at each other quickly. "This is about Danny, right?"

Tommy nodded. "I'm worried about him. I'm not sure how much more of this he can take."

"We're playing this Friday night. Why don't you sit in with us? The gang would like to see you. It's been a while."

"You know my daughter and her kids are living with me now, right? I might pass on the late-night stuff...but I will buy you some dinner. I'll call you, okay?"

"See you Friday, Chief," Lou said.

Just as Tommy was turning to go back to his table, he saw Elly coming toward him. "Would you like me to come with you when you talk to Danny?" she asked.

"Yeah," he sighed as he urged her toward Danny.

Danny saw the chief out of the corner of his eye as he was talking to someone else, but he didn't see Elly. Finally, he was able to turn toward Tommy. "Hi, Chief," he said softly.

"I'm sorry, Danny. Let me know if there's anything I can do for you. You take as much time off as you need. You're on the clock."

Tears welled in Danny's eyes as Tommy hugged him. It was then that he saw Elly. But before Tommy could introduce them, Elly said, "Hello, Danny. I'm very sorry."

"Elly?" Danny said. "I hardly recognized you."

"I'm living back in Youngstown. My children and I...with Dad."

"Thank you for coming," he said.

They stood together awkwardly, the three of them, and passed a few more polite comments among themselves. Then they said goodbye.

———•◆•———

Tommy sat in his office later that night thinking of the funeral... and Danny. He thought again of Jack Horowitz's comment: Kaye Bellino had intercourse shortly before she died. Shortly before. He called Jack Horowitz in his office. "Jacko, in the case of the Bellino woman... you said she had had intercourse shortly before she died, remember?"

"Yeah, Tommy, I remember," said Jack, still mystified by Tommy's interest in the case.

"So how long could it have been? I mean, she could have had intercourse with her husband that morning, right?"

"No, Tommy, it was more recent than that."

"Not that morning?"

"No... within a couple hours. There was still a substantial amount of semen in her vagina."

Tommy was silent on the other end of the line. After several moments Jack said, "Tommy? Are you okay?"

Tommy stirred from his thoughts suddenly. "Yeah, Jacko, I'm fine. Look, I appreciate your being square with me on this. Uh... the intercourse isn't going to be anywhere in your report, right?"

"No, Tommy, now that you've convinced me it was accidental," the coroner said sardonically. "So how much longer am I gonna be in your debt, Chief?"

"Only till hell freezes over, Boyo. Some debts are eternal."

Horowitz chuckled. "Okay, Tom, since I can't ever square my debts, I'll just keep on asking favors."

"See you, Jacko," Tommy said.

———◦✦◦———

Tommy couldn't understand what troubled him about Jack's information. A few minutes later, he ambled past Lucy. "I'm going downstairs."

Down on the second floor were the detective offices, the data room, some interrogation rooms, everything that was the control center of investigations. Bumpy was in his office, and seemed surprised to see Tommy enter without his secretary announcing him. "How's it hanging, Liborio?" said Tommy nonchalantly.

"Smooth and running, kid." Bumpy looked at his old friend quizzically. "So, what's going on, *paesan?*"

"Social visit. Got anything to drink, Bump?"

"Pop for you, kid, or some chrome-stripping coffee."

Tommy chuckled. Only one man alive would talk to him like Bumpy. "I want you to check a logbook for me, Bump."

"Okay, which one?"

"Detectives…on the 27th."

"What're you looking for?"

"What was Danny doing all day?"

Bumpy glanced at Tommy but responded to him quickly, "He was here all day."

"What time did he go to supper?"

"About six o'clock."

"How do you know?"

"Pete and I were with him."

"Then, did he come back with you?"

"Yeah, we were here all night…at least until the call came in about Danny's wife. What the hell's going on, Tom?"

"So, he never was out of the station that day?"

"No. I told you. Now what the fuck's happening?"

Tommy came further into Bumpy's office and closed the door behind them. "Jesus Christ," muttered Bumpy, knowing he was going to hear something he didn't like.

"Jack Horowitz told me that Kaye Bellino had intercourse within a few hours of her death."

Bumpy stared at him silently, never moving, showing no emotion. Then he put his head down, letting his chin rest against his chest. He blew outward through his lips as he raised his head back up toward Tommy. "And Danny was with me all day long..."

"Jacko told me something else, too, Bump. He said that that accident was a suicide."

"Jesus Christ," muttered Bumpy. "They gonna say that in the coroner's report?"

Tommy shook his head. "I think I convinced him that, if he wasn't that certain, a bad report would ruin Danny and those kids. The whole family's too good for that."

"So now what?" Bumpy said.

"So now there's another ring on the pole. And I'll kiss your ass if this doesn't fit around the deaths of those two kids, Bump."

"What?"

"I'm doing this one alone. No one knows what I'm about... except you, Med, and Pete. That's it, and Danny doesn't know anything about this forever, *capeesh*?"

Bumpy nodded. "I'll see what I can find out. Just keep me posted."

"Every once in a while, I might need a good stakeout crew, so keep one handy — and quiet, okay?"

"Yeah."

Laney was upset yet relieved by Kaye's death. He had found out that Horowitz had ruled it accidental, so he was home free in her case. And yet she was easy to miss. She was beautiful and had a great body. Her belly was flat, and her legs were firm and muscular, but not hard and angular. She looked like a model in a *Sports Illustrated* layout. And she tried to please even though she didn't have the talent. He wasn't sure if she ever had an orgasm, but she faked a good one, and she kept coming back.

He would call Lisa Guistino in a few weeks — maybe a couple — and get her back on the string. Lisa was so unlike Kaye; she wasn't as beautiful, but she was twice as sexy. She was black-haired and olive-skinned, tanned dark in the summer and smoothed and glossed by the creams and oils she put on her body. And she was talented. She could fuck a man's brains out and still keep trying. If Kaye never had an orgasm, Lisa had dozens all through the night. She loved sex, and she didn't have to fake a thing. And to Laney she was as captivating as any woman had ever been. She had a face that told the world she was made for fucking. And the face and eyes didn't lie; she was gifted. Maybe it was because she was so much younger than he. Whatever it was, it had hold of him and he couldn't get loose.

Every man who saw her would leave home just to spend a night with her. And as beautiful as Kaye was, she was no match for Lisa. Lisa looked so different naked, than Kaye did. Kaye was proud of her looks in the cool and distant way a model presented herself as someone inaccessible. Lisa was arrogant about hers. She learned when she was a barely out of childhood that the sight of her in a bathing suit would make men go quiet and dreamy. Pagliaro had warned him to stay away, but he couldn't. She was the first one he thought of when he needed sex. And she was always ready.

But he had to be careful; she was the mayor's daughter, a spoiled bitch, almost as volatile as her father. And he had to stay on the right side of Carly. Hell, he had to stay on the right side of too many people – Mose, Carly, and now Tommy McCarrie. This was going to be something he would have to take care of, Mose or not.

———◆◆◆◆———

Tommy finally read the coroner's report. Accidental, no mention of semen in her vagina, no mention of alcohol in her blood. He knew that Danny would be coming back to work soon. And when he came back, he and Tommy would have to talk.

As Tommy read, Med walked into his office, ushered in by Lucy. Tommy looked up from his reading. "Accidental," he said. Med nodded knowingly.

"What else does it say?"

Tommy took a deep breath. "Not much…but there's something he didn't say. Kaye Bellino had intercourse shortly before she died."

"And Danny was on duty here at the station all day, right?" Tommy nodded. "So now what?"

"So, now I think I find this guy…because now I think he's tied to the murders of those two kids."

"You think she knew anything about that?"

"No. She wouldn't be part of anything like that."

"So?"

"So, I don't know. I don't know who she was cheating with…or if I'm wrong about the murder of those kids. There's just something weird going on."

Med thought for a few moments. "You have to talk to Danny."

"Yeah," Tommy said. "But I have to wait. That kid's had enough for the rest of his life."

Med nodded. "What now?"

"I'm gonna talk to Danny's uncles. I've been friends with them all my life."

Later that day, Tommy called Danny's uncles, Rino and Lou, and set up a dinner date that Friday night. "Meet us at the Berlin Roadhouse...if we go to Castorina's or the Tre-Sette, we won't be able to talk," said Lou.

He had known the two men since they played on the same football team together. Lou was a year ahead of them in school. They were good friends who warmed to the occasion whenever they and Tommy met. Dinner was at six o'clock. Tommy argued with them about the bill, insisting that he pick up the tab against their huffing and protesting. Finally, they relented, and then they settled down to talk over coffee and Sambuca.

"So what's up, Tommy?" said Rino, sipping from the glass of clear liqueur.

"I have to find out some things about Danny and Kaye, but I don't want to ask him. So, you two are the next best thing."

They nodded in agreement. "Okay. So, what do you want to know?"

"Well, I know that they were having some troubles. Did they have any trouble with young Danny?"

"Nah, he was a nice kid. Sometimes a little mouthy, but anybody that's Connie's grandkid is gonna have a mouth."

Rino chuckled. "Did you know anything about young Danny's girlfriend?"

"You mean Neva," Lou said.

"Yeah."

"Well, she was wonderful. Everyone in the family liked her."

"Did Kaye like her?"

Rino shrugged. "She wasn't as beautiful as Kaye, but I think most guys would like her more. Besides, she had a nice way about her. She talked to everyone, acted respectful. Kaye would have had a tough time getting used to her."

"Let's get back to Danny and Kaye. What do you think? How bad was their life together?"

"Bad enough so that Connie thought they'd be getting a divorce. Danny's death held the split off a little."

"What about now? What do you think their chances were?"

"All we know is second hand, Tommy. We get all of it from Connie."

"You could tell it wasn't going well. She never was with him, and when she was, she stayed across the room from him," said Lou.

"I never saw her touch him. Never…in years," said Rino.

"Was it that bad, that he never touched her?" Tommy asked.

"They were barely making a go of it, Tom…holding it together with spit and paper."

"Could you guys be wrong about all this?"

"Both of us?" said Rino.

"You think she could have been cheating on Danny? Or he was cheating on her?"

"I believed it from the start," said Rino. "But Lou didn't."

"Only I've come around on that one. I think there was someone else, too," said Lou.

"How about Danny?"

Both brothers shook their heads together. "Not Danny," said Lou.

"It just wasn't his style."

"Tommy," Lou said, glancing at his brother as he spoke. "Somehow the killers of these kids and Kaye dying are hooked up. You know that." Rino nodded as Lou spoke. They obviously had been talking about what Lou had said.

"Yeah, and I have to find out what it's all about, right?"

"Yeah."

"Listen, don't tell Danny about this, huh? I have to watch myself."

"Are you taking over the investigation, Tommy?" said Rino. "I thought that asshole Chris Laney was doing it for Carly?"

"They don't know what the fuck's going on. Not a one of them is a good cop. But I want to sneak up on them. Before Carly can find anything out about me, I might make some headway on the case."

"If we can help you, let us know, Tommy."

"Thanks, kid." Tommy turned to Lou then back to Rino. "Son of a bitch looks good for an old man, huh, Rino?"

"Hell, if you never worked, had money, and a nice girlfriend, you'd look good, too. Every once in a while, our sister tears him a new asshole, and I just sit back and enjoy it. He needs that so he won't get so damned arrogant."

"How's Connie taking this thing? What a time for her, huh? First her grandson, now a daughter-in-law?"

"She'll help pull Danny through...and those two kids. She's made for putting people back together," said Lou. Rino nodded.

"Tell her I'm thinking about her," Tommy said.

⸺◆⬥◆⸺

A few mornings later, Tommy was having his usual breakfast of toast and coffee when Elly came into the kitchen. "Hi, Daddy," she said. Tommy reflected as usual about her near presence in his life. She was calling him the more familiar "Daddy" nowadays. It was as though she had discovered something new about Tommy, about his loneliness, and about the need for femaleness in his life. And she fell into it so easily; suddenly the house was hers, her curtains, her towels, her furniture arrangements, her shelves. Tommy would come home and find that the kitchen towels were in another drawer, or the glasses were on another shelf, or the living room furniture was rearranged. And he never said a word in protest about any changes that she made, changes that revoked decisions her mother had made thirty years before. When Tommy lived alone, he just lived there — as though it were an apartment. Whatever the cleaning lady proposed, he did. It never occurred to him to change any drawers or shelves around. His wife had made those decisions long ago. It all worked, and he adapted to it. And after his wife was gone, he saw no reason to change. He just lived there.

But in his secret heart he felt pleasure with the way Elly so quietly and confidently made her imprint on his house. Just as her fine mind and mature spirit made their imprint upon his life.

"What's on the agenda today?" he said as he poured her a cup of coffee. He noticed that she put milk into her coffee and seemed puzzled; she used to drink it black.

"Irish style," she said, anticipating his question. "Boston, remember?"

He smiled to himself. Strange how in the midst of his lonely life of unfulfilled dreams something magic happened. When once he wanted a large family, he had only one child; when once he wanted sons to carry on the McCarrie promise, he got a daughter; when once he thought his personal life was over, he got a lovely girl who brought two noisy, messy, wonderful kids into his house. Strange.

"So, what are you doing today?" Tommy insisted.

"You know what I'm doing. I've got an interview," she said.

"Yeah, I know…Listen, if you get out early enough, stop down at the station. I'll buy you lunch."

She seemed surprised but nodded right away. She too marveled at the way their lives had meshed so soon into a family. She would sometimes think of what her life might have been if David had been a better man. But it wasn't meant to be. So suddenly, in the midst of all the turmoil of her middle years, she found a home. And all the warmth that was lacking in her house in Boston, she found in this unlikely place. And now she was looking for a job, a new career.

———◆◆◆◆◆———

Tommy spent the morning with Bumpy and Pete, the two deputy chiefs. The station was in good hands. A new police class was turning out okay…not too many duds. Some would make fine cops.

Then he went back to his office and wrote some letters and made some phone calls.

As Tommy was preoccupied with his work, Lucy was typing one of the letters he had written, hand scribbled, indecipherable except to her. She patiently did all that came her way flawlessly and quickly, and, in a short time, pristine copies would be back on Tommy's desk shortly after he produced them.

Suddenly, as Lucy typed, a rather tall, sandy-blonde woman walked into the office. She knew immediately that the young woman was related to Tommy. She had his gray eyes and pale skin. And she had that look, the look of spirit, of intelligence, of grace.

Elly was startled as she came into Tommy's office. She had been there many times as a young girl and not much had changed externally, the hallway, the imposing wood facade to the chief's office. Yet this time as she entered, she encountered a strikingly beautiful woman. Hispanic, she thought, and sexy in a quiet way. *And never mentioned once by my dad.* "Hi," she said to Lucy, who had stood up as Elly approached. "I'm Elly, Chief McCarrie's daughter."

"Hi," she responded. "I'm Lucy, the chief's secretary."

Both women sized each other up quickly. It happened in a few glances, and words, and gestures. Both liked what they saw, Lucy was smiling and calm and seemed very gentle. Elly was smiling and self-possessed, quietly confident, but warm and friendly.

Finally, Lucy broke the silence. "Uh, you can go in," she said almost as a question, facing Elly, but gesturing back over her shoulder at Tommy's door.

The awkward new moments were dissipating. "My father told me about his wonderful secretary," Elly said brightly. "He just never said how beautiful you were."

"And he always told me about his brilliant daughter. He just never said that she was lovely, too."

Both women smiled. They liked each other. And it would mean that they would see each other again and talk again.

Just then Tommy opened the door and came upon the two of them. He seemed awkward. "Hi, Dad," Elly said reflexively.

Tommy didn't answer. He looked back and forth from Elly to Lucy. "So, you two have finally met," he said, recovering.

"Yes," Elly said, "And we're going to talk soon about all your faults and shortcomings." Tommy snorted and Lucy smiled, enjoying the gentle teasing of her boss.

For a few seconds, none of them spoke. Then suddenly, Tommy

handed Lucy a paper. "More work," he said to her. She took the paper and held it for a moment, glanced at it and said, "I'll have it after lunch."

"I told you, you didn't have to rush..."

"It's okay; I can do it," she said softly. He nodded, looking at her face which he had been avoiding, and then looking at Elly.

The brief colloquy between her father and the beautiful, almond-skinned secretary gave Elly a chance to see Tommy in a new light. She saw what only another woman would see who watched others she cared about. This was not just a boss and a secretary. There was something more here. But whatever it was, it was obvious only to people who had eyes to see such things. Her father acting more than his usual polite? More than his usual deferential? And yet he seemed unaware of his behavior. And Lucy, so enthralled by the presence of the chief, so open and vulnerable?

Elly also noted in that moment the absence of a ring on her finger. Unmarried, such beautiful shades of color, the olive skin, the dark hair, the simple dress. *Stark colors*, she thought. Stark colors! And she remembered Tommy's use of those words when he was talking about Neva. This was the face that made him stop in mid-sentence that day. This was the voice that soothed him and calmed him and made his day complete.

This woman was the grownup version of Neva. She was the only chance Tommy the Quarterback had to find the kind of love that had been denied him all his days, to be awakened in love and kissed good-night in love, at once well within his grasp and yet, in his timid dreams, far beyond his fingertips.

Mose was suddenly nervous. The more he thought of Laney and the mayor's daughter, the more uneasy he became. This is something that could fuck up a good thing, he thought. All his best laid plans, his careful existence, all the power he had gathered unto himself — all of it could be lost in a foolish, thoughtless moment. The mayor's daughter, for Christ's sake!

He had been lucky so far. Kaye Bellino was out of the picture at just the right time. With Carley in the mayor's office, things were going fine. He would be the conduit for the Pittsburgh gang to get itself into all the business of Youngstown, legit or not. And those Cleveland bastards would be out in the cold. Serves them right…a bunch of fucking thumb-breakers and knee-cappers with not a brain in one of their heads.

And his money was flowing in…eight million last year and probably ten million next. All of it quiet. Nobody even knew his name.

Mose stirred a little as his secretary brought a drink in to him. "Where's Nick?" he asked her.

"I'm not sure. He just said he was going out."

"Send him in when he comes back," he said absently.

When Nick came into Mose's office, Mose gestured for him to shut the door. "What's up?" Nick said.

"I'm worried about Laney," Mose answered.

"You hear something?"

"No, but he's like a time bomb. He fucked up that crack deal and then tried to finger Bellino. He fuck's his wife and kills his two kids when they catch him loading the car again…with almost a half fucking pound. And then he can barely cover his ass until we get Carly, who hates him, to put him in charge of the investigation. Then when he's in charge, he starts fucking Carly's daughter."

"You know, Mose, I've been checking on that investigation. Some of our guys are watching it all. They say Laney doesn't know jack shit about being a cop."

"Well, we said we wanted a dummy heading the investigation, right?"

"Not if the dummy is stupid enough to get the chief of police involved, we don't."

"What are you talking about?"

"Word has it that McCarrie's out asking questions about those two kids."

"Jesus Christ," Mose muttered. "Let's get Carly over her fast."

"Mose, all of a sudden everything is changing. Two weeks ago, I thought we had everything in hand. Today it's like we're walking through a goddammed mine field."

"Maybe we should do away with Laney?" Mose said almost to himself.

"What? Knock off a cop who's chief investigator and get McCarrie involved for sure? You know what would happen if this thing got any bigger? The FBI, Mose."

"Well then, Carly has to get us out of this mess. But whatever we do, we can't let him know what's going on."

———◆·◆·◆———

"Danny's back to work today," Bumpy told Tommy in his office early one morning.

"How is he?"

"Seems okay — about as good as could be expected. He doesn't say much."

"How about his other two kids?"

"I think Connie's going to move in with them for a while."

"That should relieve Danny a little bit, huh? Connie's a good lady."

"Yeah. But neither one of them banked on this. I wonder how it'll work out?"

"I don't know. Listen, I'm gonna want to talk to Danny today, Bump."

"You got something in your craw, kid?"

"Tell me why Kaye Bellino would try to kill herself."

"You don't know she did, Tom. That's Jack Horowitz's best guess. You know he's been wrong before."

"I'll bet the house he's not wrong on this one, Bump."

Bumpy sighed. "Yeah, I saw the accident."

Later Elly called Tommy in his office. "So, what's up?"

"They offered me the job," she said.

"Well?"

"What do you think?" she said.

"I told you what I think. I know you don't want it, so why take it?"

She sighed. "El, you're more qualified than that job. You have enough money to live on. You know dammed well I'd be happy to give you whatever you need."

"No way, Dad," she said. "It's just that I want something that's a little more interesting."

"Keep looking, kid," Tommy said dismissively. "Uh, I won't be home for supper. I have a meeting here with Danny Bellino. It's his first day back to work."

She was silent for a few seconds. "How is he?"

"I guess he's doing the best he can. He has those other two kids to worry about."

Late that afternoon, Danny Bellino entered the chief's office. "Good to have you back, Danny," Tommy said as he motioned for

Danny to sit across from him in one of the Queen Anne chairs by the fireplace. He studied Danny as he moved across from him. He looked tired. "How did the day go, son?"

Danny nodded. "Better than I expected, Chief."

"You did some thinking about coming back, right? You know if you're not up to it you can go home any time? You'll always be on the clock."

"I really appreciate that, Chief. You don't have to do it. I've got some comp —"

"I know I don't have to do it. But it's done."

Danny looked like he wanted to leave. He cast glances from side to side, as if expecting to find recording machines taking in his answers.

"I won't keep you hanging, Danny," Tommy said softly.

Danny nodded once in appreciation. "Danny, you know that this investigation is going nowhere." Danny snorted.

"So, I'm gonna promise you something. I'm gonna have my own little squad — much smaller than Laney's — and we're going to solve this case."

"But... Hell, Chief, with all due respect, you haven't been on a case in years." Danny's voice was strained. "How am I supposed to get any solace from that news? We have a whole squad of incompetents who haven't found a clue in more than a year." Danny stopped talking for a few moments. Then, he started again, this time more agitated, and his voice more shrill. "And so, to make up for that, there's a new team composed of the traffic sergeant and the chief of police — neither of which have been on a murder detail in years."

"I wasn't such a bad cop in my day, Danny. And Med knows the streets and has a good eye for trouble. We might be better than you think." Danny didn't answer, so Tommy started talking again. "You know that it doesn't take a whole squad to ask the right questions and look in the right places."

"If a whole squad can't do it, how can two men who both have other jobs? How in the hell can the chief of police take time off to investigate a murder? Jesus, Chief, you make it hard to take."

"I know, kid, I know. But I'll tell you something. I won't ever rest until I find out who killed Danny and Neva. I pledge that to you."

"And you won't let me help?"

"I told you. You're too close to this. But I never said you couldn't help. I just don't know what I'll find, so I don't know what to ask you to do yet."

"Chief, I've been thinking about maybe quitting. I can't handle this. Every day I come to work and see Chris Laney not doing a fucking thing...blowing this investigation. And I think, I can sure as hell do better by myself. Even if I were emotionally involved, I'd be doing more than those guys."

"Danny, you have to take care of those two kids. They're depending on you. If you quit, you sure as hell won't be able to do for them what you could on a lieutenant's salary."

"But I might find Danny and Neva's killers," he said.

"I'll find them Danny. I know how to run an investigation. Just get yourself whole again. And look after your mother and your two kids."

Danny didn't answer, but Tommy knew that he had calmed him down. Danny sat back in his chair.

"I have some questions for you," Tommy said.

Danny looked surprised. "Well?" Danny said.

"How did your wife and Danny get along?"

"She was his mother for Christ's sake, Chief. How do you think they got along?"

"I don't know. I'm asking."

"They get along fine. He was a little hard to handle, but he was crazy about her. He was never mean or nasty to her."

"How did Kaye get along with Neva?"

"Chief, what the hell does Kaye have to do with the murders of the two kids. You see why I'm worried about the case?"

"Let me ask the questions, Danny," Tommy said, calmly reminding himself that he was dealing with a man profoundly pained by loss. He imagined himself in Danny's place and marveled as the younger man's composure. All he showed was irritation, and Tommy knew he, himself, would have done at least that.

"Did you and Kaye argue the last few months before she died?"

Danny grimaced in exasperation. "Kaye again? Just let her rest in peace, okay, Chief?"

"Please, Danny," Tommy said softly. "Answer my questions so I can help you."

Danny was quiet for a few minutes. Then he said, "Yes."

"How bad was it?"

"It wasn't vicious or mean. It was usually about..."

"About what?"

He hesitated. "About us."

"So?"

"We always seemed to have a wall between us. We didn't communicate much. Then, it seemed we gave up trying."

"And you were separated for a while, right?"

"Yeah."

"Did you know the guy she was seeing?"

"No."

"I asked you once; now I'll ask you again. Did she have an affair with this guy?"

"She said she didn't," Danny said deliberately.

Tommy stared for a few seconds at his lieutenant. Danny eyed him nervously. "I know this was hard for you, Danny. And I appreciate you talking to me." Danny nodded. "I'll find them, kid." Danny stood up, shook Tommy's hand, eyeing him skeptically and walked through the door.

———✦———

Carly walked into Mose's office after being announced by his secretary.

"Mr. Mayor," Mose said cheerfully, shaking the younger man's hand.

"How's it going, Mose?" Carly said.

"Not bad...how about you?"

Carly grimaced, indicating that things could be better. "How about some coffee?"

"Yeah, thanks, I could use a cup."

"How's your dad?"

Carly shook his head. "He doesn't even know me when he first sees me. I have to tell him who I am. Then, half the time he thinks I'm my brother."

"I'm sorry to hear that, Carly. Is there anything I can do to help?"

"No, Mose. There's not much anyone can do."

Carly hesitated for a few moments, suddenly wondering why Mose had asked him to stop by his office. "So, what's up?"

"Well, I wanted to talk to you about Tommy McCarrie."

Carly snorted. "You don't have to talk long about him before I get an ear full."

"I understand he's checking around — doing a little private investigating," said Mose.

"Well, I'm not surprised. Chris Laney's crew just doesn't seem to have a clue about the case."

"But I've heard that Laney is being hindered by McCarrie. I thought you told him that the special squad was in charge?"

"Well, I did. But it's hard to tell the chief of police that he couldn't ask any questions about the case...especially if the case isn't going anywhere."

"But a meddling old boozer can screw up the chances of finding the killer. This thing could make you look bad, and I'm interested in your future. I want to see you in the governor's office someday."

Carly nodded. "Thanks, Mose. I'll talk to McCarrie. Maybe I can get him to back off. The thing is, he's so damned independent. He knows he's going to retire so he doesn't give a shit about what he says or does."

"How's everything else going?" Mose said, deliberately changing the subject.

"Okay," Carly said unconvincingly.

Mose let Carly's words pass. "Remember, Carly, you have to be squeaky clean when we make a run for the governor's office."

"I know. I know," Carly said wearily. It seemed that he was always getting the same advice from Judge East.

"Remember, I want to help, Carly. It'd be nice to have a *paesan* make it big. Those Ku-Kluxers out there would hate to see it. They're more worried about Blacks and Jews and women making it. People don't realize that a Black made it to the Supreme Court before a Catholic dago did."

"That's because we're all Mafia, right?"

"You know McCarrie's one of those people."

"Yeah," Carly muttered thoughtfully, "I think he is. That bastard hated my dad all his life and now he hates me."

"He can hate all he wants, Carly, as long as he doesn't fuck up our lives for us. You have to keep him from doing that."

"I'll talk to him," Carly said.

"What're you doing here so late?" Tommy said to Lucy as he walked into his office after a late meeting of City Council.

"My son is going to pick me up. We're going out to dinner."

Tommy smiled. "It seems funny now that Eddie's grown up. I remember him as a little boy. How's his work coming along?"

"It's really nice. They allow him to schedule around his classes. And it's not too far from Spring Common, so he can get back to work right away."

"It's nice to see these kids starting to earn some money," said Tommy. Lucy nodded in agreement. "Well, I'll see you tomorrow. What restaurant are you going to?"

"Castorina's. He loves Italian food."

"Do you know Johnny?"

"The owner? No."

"He and I are old friends. He's a nice guy. Talks too much, but you can't help but love him."

Tommy seemed to have a worm afterglow as he walked to his car. It was nice thinking of her as more than a secretary. But it seemed strange now that they had never broken bread despite all their years of working together.

Elly greeted him warmly as he walked into the house. "We're

ready," she said.

"Smells good."

"Just meat loaf and mashed potatoes. But it does smell good, huh? Shows you how long we go without decent meals around here."

"I'm eating better now than I ever did. You're gonna get me fat... fatter."

"We'll work it out of you."

They sat at the table, Elly's children talkative and noisy, funny and delightful. After the meal the children cleared the table and then went upstairs to do their homework. And Tommy and Elly sat contentedly drinking coffee and not talking. Then, Elly spoke first. "How long has she worked for you?"

"Who?" Tommy said reflexively.

"You know who I'm talking about, Dad," Elly said.

"If you mean Lucy. It's been about nine years. Why?"

"No reason, just curious. She's lovely, isn't she?"

Here we go again, Tommy thought to himself. He was proud of his daughter's insight and instincts, but he often squirmed as she bore in on things that she was curious about. "Yeah, I guess so."

"You guess so? Is there a man that comes into your office that isn't stunned by her?"

"What's your point, counselor?"

"No point. Just making an observation." Tommy nodded, not believing a word of what she said. "So, she's not married, is she?"

"No, she's not married. She's divorced...and then her husband died. I don't know what you'd call her now."

"Oh," Elly said and grew quiet.

After a few seconds, Tommy said, "So, what's this all about, El?"

"She's in love with you," she said calmly.

There had been few times in his life that Tommy was at a loss for words, but this was one of them. Elly looked at him and coolly sipped her coffee from the cup that she held above her elbows resting on the table. She nodded to his questioning look, reaffirming what she had just said. "That's nonsense, El."

"I'll bet you the whole first paycheck I make when I go back to work."

"What the hell do you know, daughter? You've seen her for a few minutes and all of a sudden you know something that no one else knows?"

"I know, Dad. Besides, who do you see every day that notices anything? A bunch of middle-aged male policemen?"

"Why are you doing this, Ellen?"

"I'm not trying to make mischief, Daddy. I'm being honest about what I saw."

Tommy sighed. "First of all, you're wrong. Second, she…I never gave her…I never came on to her. I always treated her with respect."

"Don't you see, Dad? That's what started it all. If you would have come on to her, it wouldn't have worked."

"Nothing did work, Ellen. She's out of my league. There are guys with money and position who would love to take her out. Guys with class…and flat bellies who look good in suits, and who dance like Fred Astaire."

"And does she go out with these men?"

"Hell, I don't know. I don't think so. I just don't know much about her private life."

"Why not?"

"Well…because it's something I don't feel comfortable asking about."

"Oh," she said. Just then, Carrie came downstairs to ask her mother something. As Elly talked to her daughter, Tommy saw his chance to escape. He patted his daughter's hand and motioned to the upstairs. She smiled, nodding as Carrie talked.

———— ✦ ————

Chris Laney was getting nervous. Soon she would be there, daring him not to be captivated by what she looked like. A knock on the door let him know she was there.

"Hi," she said, walking in as soon as he opened the door.

He had known many women in his life, but never one who turned him on like this one. She was dark and sexy and full lipped, with sleepy eyes, even when she was wide awake. She always looked like she was ready for bed, like she was ready to be fucked. And she was so young.

He closed the door behind him, as he watched her take off her coat and kicked off her shoes and then turn back toward him. He came toward her, and she stood still, waiting, smiling slightly. He caught the arrogance of her and wanted to stifle it while still getting her into his bed. He kissed her roughly, crushing her lips with his, and then suddenly he broke away from her gently and stepped back, trying to collect his thoughts.

He couldn't let her think that she controlled him. She was too much of a bitch to let her get such a hold of his life. Besides, there were other women, all books on the shelf of his memories, their faces blending into a fog of images that he could barely recall. He used them and gave them over — to other boyfriends, other husbands, to other men. He got over them, he would get over this one.

And he liked the sudden look of doubt that crept into her face, despite the hauteur that was her trademark. Could he be growing tired of her? Could there be someone else? And at that moment, he knew how to play his hand. She could be controlled by doubt and uncertainty. If she were uncertain, she would try harder.

She also liked the cocaine. It made her an animal in bed. She sucked his cock as though she were trying to prove something, as though she were getting even with Daddy. Laney smiled inwardly at his achievement. When they first met, she was just a spoiled bitch who looked good. After his tutelage, she was a bitch who could fuck and suck a man into heaven.

They didn't talk much, they never did. They drew a few lines of coke and began to fuck. It was a ritual almost like a Japanese tea ceremony, but soon they were rolling on the floor and the bed, straining against each other, sweating, gasping, huffing for breath against the heat they both generated.

Lisa lay contented and tired in the bed beside Laney. Meeting him had been such a departure in her life. She had never blown coke, had fucked only a few times before, and had never sucked a cock. She was a little girl. And now she had become a woman, and she liked it.

But she was worried about Chris even though she tried not to show it. He acted like he didn't need her. She knew she could turn him on, and he liked it. But she also knew that she couldn't communicate with him. He was strange…so distant, so guarded. She was closer to her father than she was to this man she had been so intimate with. She could read her father, could speak to his inner self. But with Chris there was no inner self ~ at least none that she had discovered. "Chris?"

"What?" He was facing away from her, but she knew he was awake.

"How long are we going to do this? Keep hiding like this?"

He lay on his back, turning his face toward her. He stared at her for a few seconds. "You haven't figured it out, huh?"

"But why? Why can't we be proud of...I love you, Chris...Why can't I let people know that? Why aren't we proud? Why do we have to sneak around?"

"We've been through this before, Lisa. Do you know what would happen if everybody out there knew about us?"

"I don't think anybody gives a damn. And the ones that do can't stop it."

"Lisa, I'm almost old enough to be your father."

"Oh, God, why do we have to go through this again. Why does it matter so much to them if it doesn't matter to us?"

"Do you realize that if I would have fucked you a little more than a year ago, I could have been in jail?"

"But you didn't, did you? And you're in charge of a special squad, handpicked by my father. He'd like us to be together."

"God, are you naive! Your dad wants you to marry some brain surgeon or corporate lawyer, somebody's kid your age so he can forge a coalition to run for Governor, then President. He'd sell your mother to crack dealers if he could get the nomination for Governor. Do you think he wants to see a story about his daughter getting involved with a guy almost his own age? A guy who works for him?"

"But you'll be chief someday."

"Not as long as Danny Bellino is wired up for the job," he muttered.

She sat upright and held her head in her hands. "I can't stand this, Chris. I'm going to tell them."

"Like hell you will," he said angrily. "You say a word about it and I'll walk on you. You'll never see me again."

"Well, maybe that is what we both need."

"Go for it, baby," he said softly, getting out of bed and going to the bathroom. After a few minutes, he came out again. She was looking at him doubtfully, worried that she had pushed him too far. He walked into the kitchen naked, opened the refrigerator and took out a cold beer. He leaned against the kitchen counter, looking out into the raining night and drinking slow draughts from the bottle.

In a few minutes Lisa, also naked, came into the kitchen. She stood away from him. "I just think it's time we let everyone know how we feel about each other. I love you, Chris," she said, softly.

"I told you all the trouble it would cause. What's wrong with being together here? We have good times, don't we? When the right time comes, then we'll tell the whole world."

"Will there ever be a right time, Chris?"

"I told you there would. I love you, too, you know." He listened to his own words. *Amazing what a man has to do for some good ass*, he thought.

She came into his arms, and they kissed. "I don't like to fight with you," she said.

"Me neither," he said.

She was young, and loved as a child, and pampered. It was almost impossible for her to believe that someone could look her in the face and still lie to her. So, she never pushed him past denying once. She didn't want to hear him say he was through with her.

Carly walked into the Youngstown Police Station and into the elevator. Soon he was walking down the corridor to Tommy's office. Mickey was following closely so he could open the door when Carly would enter. But this time after he entered the outer office, he waited for Lucy to admit him to Tommy's inner sanctum.

"Mayor," Tommy said warily.

"Chief. I've come to talk to you about a problem I keep hearing about."

"What's that, Mayor?" Tommy said, gesturing toward the chair opposite him. Mickey sat on the couch that was parallel to the chairs.

"I understand you're doing some private investigating."

"In what sense?"

"I'm told that you're asking a lot of questions about the Bellino case. Chris Laney tells me your meddling is hindering his investigation."

Tommy's chuckle belied his anger, but he held his composure. He started speaking softly and slowly. "Uh...Carly, I am the chief of police. And I was checking into the progress of an investigation under my charge."

"You don't worry about that investigation. Captain Laney is quite capable of handling it. And he reports directly to me. So, there's no need for you to be involved at all."

"First of all, what Laney knows about murder investigations can fit into a thimble and leave more room for what you know about being mayor."

"I'm not the problem, Chief, you are."

"You know, Carly, whenever we talk, the conversation always revolves around the same thing. You don't want me to do my job...and I do."

"Your job is to stay out of the way and let this investigation continue."

"You don't want an investigation; you want it to go away before the next campaign. If that were your kid in the ground at Calvary you'd be screaming bloody murder."

Carly was silent for a moment thinking about what Tommy had said. The thought of his own child lying dead made him chill, the hair on his scalp tingle. "I'll tell you something, Carly," Tommy continued, noticing that Carly had been affected by the image of death he had conjured. "Laney, your boy, is fucking up this investigation beyond belief. And if you let it go on, I'm gonna dump all this shit in your lap — publicly."

"You threatening me, Tommy?" Carly said, now barely in control of his anger. Mickey was sitting nervously at the edge of his seat. Tommy glanced over at the driver quickly, instinctively sizing up the threatening forces arranged against him. Mickey grew even more nervous, catching Tommy's glance.

"Fucking A, Carly, it's a threat. If you don't get out of here and leave me alone, I'll call a press conference and start bitching about how you're tying the hands of the YPD. I'll just let Laney drag you down with him."

"You bastard. Why don't you just drink your fifth of bourbon a day and let us run things? I'm giving you time to retire. Somebody smart would have gone out quietly."

"I told you before, Carly, I'm not that smart. I just keep thinking about how Danny Bellino feels when he goes to bed at night. How do you feel, Carly? Safe? Your kid okay? Your wife next to you, asleep?"

"You think I don't want to catch this guy? I have a daughter. I know how Bellino must feel."

"No, you don't, boyo. Neither do I. All I know is that it would hurt more than anything I can imagine. And that poor kid has lost a wife and a son — and a girl that would have been a wonderful daughter-in-law."

Carly took a deep breath, staring at the carpet on the floor at his feet. Suddenly, he stood up. Mickey watched him move, then quickly brought himself erect. "Tommy, if you know what's good for you, you'll do as I said. Leave it alone and ride out your time till retirement."

"No fucking way, Carly. I want to nail the killers as my final act of being a cop, and I don't give a damn if you like it or not. I want to fry some son of a bitch for what he did to Danny."

"Tommy, if you fuck anything up, I'm gonna hang you out to dry. I'll nail you."

Mose Pagliaro drove into the garage of his modest office on the South Side. He was masterful at concealing himself from public scrutiny, although some who knew him thought it was less masterful and more paranoid. Some thought it was just fear of being caught in a Cleveland/Pittsburgh mob crossfire. But Mose learned early on to trust that God-given instinct for secrecy, and it served him well.

In a way he was a showoff. The secrecy was a showoff. Women he had known were fascinated by the stealth he had managed to acquire, the strange sense of sinister confidence he exuded. They were often stunned by the relatively modest appearance of his possessions. He didn't drive a Cadillac or a Lincoln; he drove Buicks, loaded with all the comforts and features as the other cars, but not as attention-getting. His home office was in a quiet, genteelly shabby part of town, and was drab and dated outside.

It was only on the inside that one could see his taste for finer things. The inside had been decorated by a professional. The furniture was lavish and expensive. The walls were hung with original paintings and expensive limited-edition prints. The bar stocked with whiskey and liquors from small, exclusive distilleries from Europe, limited vintage, proprietary brands, specialties of the house. The carpets were lush and beautiful, the ambiance light yet not garish. Soft music playing, indirect lighting, open windows on the sides where panoramas of the city could be seen day and night, where looking out was easy and looking in was hard.

Mose was the master of his little world. Pittsburgh and Cleveland were each an hour and a half away by car. And he had delivered both mobs more than he had promised them. Everyone was happy. And when they were happy, they left him alone.

He remembered once, when he was a young man, meeting Carlo Gambino in New York. He walked around like the owner of a neighborhood grocery store and dressed the part. It was hard to believe that he ran a billion-dollar industry, a soft-spoken, reserved little gentleman. Mose studied him and his life, and he knew that it was the kind of life that suited him. Gambino showed him that you didn't have to be flashy or loud. All you had to have was money and influence. And Mose was a willing pupil.

Now things had begun to happen that threatened the tranquility of his secure little world. "Nick here?" he said to his secretary.

"He's in his office."

"Tell him I want a meeting tonight... Laney, him, and me."

That night, the men assembled nervously in Mose's inner office. Mose came in and sat down in one of the easy chairs at the head of a small, closely-set, square array of chairs and couches.

"We have a problem," he began as soon as he sat down.

They looked at each other. Nick was silent. "Nobody knows?" said Mose disgustedly. "Well, I'll tell you. You..." Mose said, pointing to Laney. "You are fucking Carly's daughter. And me? I got Tommy the Quarterback conducting his own private investigation into the Bellino case. Both these things are in your hands, Chris..."

"Listen, the mayor's daughter will be out fucking some other guy the day after she and I are finished," said Laney, interrupting Mose. "She likes to fuck. Besides what the hell are we worried about anyway? You have Carly in your pocket."

"Don't ever say that again," Mose hissed. "What I have going with the mayor is some influence. The last thing I want him to hear is that I have him in my pocket. What the fuck is wrong with you?"

"But what are you afraid of? He knows he needs us in the elections."

"He needs us only if our support can do him some good. If we come off on the front page like a bunch of hoods, he'll tell us to go to hell and find someone else who wants to buy in."

"It has to stop, Chris," said Nick. "If we let her get out of hand, the publicity might kill us."

"I never complained to you about the broads you were fucking, Mose."

"Listen to me, you…" Pagliaro caught himself. "This one could cost us money and fuck up something it's taken years to build. It could queer all our futures."

"I like this girl, Mose," Laney said.

"Jesus Christ? You hear that, Nick?" Mose growled. "The kid's in love…and he doesn't give a shit what all this will do to us."

"Chris, we always talked about fucking married women…so they couldn't give us trouble," said Nick. "Now you're banging a single broad that's barely twenty years old, half your age, for Christ's sake."

"I'm telling you once more, I want this thing with Carly's daughter to stop. Find someone else to be in love with," said Mose. "Hear me, Chris?"

The room was silent. Finally, Laney nodded his head and said,

"Okay," under his breath.

"Good," said Mose. "Now let's talk about something else. What's going on with Tommy McCarrie?"

"Word's out that he's asking questions about the Bellino kid," said Laney.

"What about, Carly?" Mose asked Nick.

"No dice," said Nick. "McCarrie told him to get fucked."

"Jesus. The mayor can't control the police chief. What a hell of a way to run a city."

"This guy's different, Mose," said Laney. "He was a big football star in the fifties, was a decorated Marine in Korea. He's tough to control. It would be too much bad publicity if Carly fired him."

"You think he'd find something, Nick?" Mose said. "I heard he used to be pretty good."

"Not if Chris does what he's supposed to be doing."

"But hell, Mose, he hasn't investigated a case in twenty years. I say let him go," said Laney. "He won't find anything. I've seen to that."

"Can we get to him?" Mose asked his brother.

"I don't know," said Nick. "He's just an old boozer. He doesn't have any family, any broads…"

"No family?" said Mose.

"Uh…his daughter's moved in with him from out of town with her two kids," said Laney. "I don't know how long she's staying."

"We need some way to undercut him. Can we get to someone in his office?"

"He has only one secretary. She's been with him for years," Laney said.

"So what's her story? Can we reach her?"

"I don't know if we can, Mose. She's loyal to Tommy. You ever see her?"

"No."

"She'll knock your eyes out," said Laney.

"What do you mean? Good looking?"

"Yeah. A little bit."

"Is McCarrie banging her?"

Laney shook his head. "I don't think so. I've never seen the two of them together out of the office."

"She married?"

"No, I heard she's divorced. She's some kid of mixed-race Puerto Rican, Chinese, Indian, White. Probably has some Black blood in her, too. But she would be a real A-1 fuck."

"How old are her kids?"

"She has a daughter who's a teacher and a son at Spring Common."

"I'll have to think about this," Mose said, flashing a glance at Nick. "Chris, you keep an eye on McCarrie. I want to know every move that bastard makes." Then he paused again. "And I sure as hell don't want any fuckups like what happened to that Bellino kid and his girl. Understand, Chris? You do that again and you're finished."

The Mill Creek Mall was crowded. Everyone seemed to be out buying something for Easter. Elly was tired of walking around, so she sat on one of the benches in the concourse, waiting for her two children to meet her when they were done shopping.

It was amazing how much life there was at the mall: old people walking the concourses, young parents with small children, teenagers meeting each other in the beginning rites of spring, and some few people alone, as she was, trying to sort out the cards that life had dealt them. She had bought a cup of coffee from the shop in the mall that launched its seductive smell into the air beguiling all the coffee-drinkers who passed by.

She shook her head slightly as if to admonish herself for the thoughts that intruded upon her consciousness. She was lonely in the midst of the most happy and secure times she'd ever lived. The kids, once reluctant travelers, were now thrilled with Youngstown. They liked the friends they had encountered, the schools, the beauty of the Valley, the harsh winters, the ethnic mixture, the culture of the town. It was a small version of Boston without the water. And they were crazy about Tommy. He was more of a father to them than David had ever been — his quiet sense of authority, his wit and gentle play, the warmth and love they felt in his house.

The noise of people passing by was muted by her thoughts. She was troubled by what the future would hold. She was happy now, and she thought Tommy and the kids were happy. But would she ever get to the point where she would feel stuck in a life that was too secure, too predictable? She shook her head again. *God*, she thought, *how soon we forget. Remember Boston? Remember the coldness between her and David? Remember the feeling of being in bed with an alien who recoiled at her touch, who was false to her, who she could not believe even when her heart desperately wanted her to? Remember the pain of seeing the kids growing up in the same house with a father who was a stranger to them...and didn't care that he was?*

And now none of that was in her life anymore. They had gone from one strange, hostile island to a land of warmth and quiet and caring. Only one thing was the same: the empty bed, the sense that she had never in her life enjoyed the wonder of being loved by a man that also loved her, that believed that she was the greatest blessing in his life. She would miss that, she thought. As happy as her life now was, of all the good things she could tally up, she would have to be content with that part of her life left unfulfilled. It was not meant to be.

"Elly?" someone said, off to her side. She was startled for a brief moment and turned to the embodiment of the voice.

For a split second she could only see a frame, and not distinguish the face that owned the voice. But then, in a moment, she could. "Danny," she said.

"Are you resting between trips?" he said.

"Easter shopping...Uh, but I'm waiting for my kids to join me. This corner is our rendezvous spot at five o'clock."

"Oh," he said. "I'm waiting for my mother. I took her Easter shopping, too."

Elly instinctively moved over, allowing room for Danny to sit beside her. He sat down easily. "How are you, Danny?" she said. He knew what everyone meant who asked the same question.

"I'll be okay, Elly," he said sincerely.

"Good. You've been back to work a while, huh?"

"Yeah. It was good to be back, to keep my..." He paused for moment, looked at her, and then said, "I'm pretty busy now. We're computerizing practically everything in the YPD that doesn't walk and talk." She laughed softly. "How about you, Elly? You're back in town for good?"

She nodded. There was something unnerving about him. When she had known him years back, he was an upperclassman, a football star, and president of the National Honor Society. He was nice enough, and somewhat aloof, and not nicer than he had to be. Sometimes his manner came across as smugness, though not of the disdainful kind. He was tall for an Italian, nice-looking, middle-class, intelligent, and civil if not warm toward his social inferiors.

But that was then. Now the smugness had long since been erased by adversity. Now his other qualities were more becoming, because they were there in spite of the pain in his life, the pain that everyone, especially women, could always see in his eyes. And now, to women, he was sympathetic. Every woman that knew him felt motherly toward him. And they all wondered what it would be like to be loved by a man as honest and sincere as this one.

But Elly felt uncomfortable around him still...as though she were back in high school again, an underclassman and a social second-stringer. Her intellect told her that what she felt was nonsense. She had come to know many men in her adult years who were of a superior caste to Danny.

"Do you work now?" he said.

"Uh, no, I may go back to work. But I'm in no hurry."

"What kind of work do you do?"

"I'm a librarian. I have a BA in communication and a master's in library science."

He nodded appreciatively. "Where do your children go to school?"

"St. Mark's."

"Really? Mine both go there..." Just as he was talking, he was distracted by the sight of his mother walking toward him. She was an attractive woman in her mid-sixties, short and slightly built, with black hair streaked with gray. She wore glasses and walked with a quick gait. Both Danny and Elly stood up as the older woman approached.

"Hi," said Connie, brightly. "Were you waiting long?"

"Nah, I've just been here a few minutes and I've been talking..."

The two women looked at each other and seemed pleased by the other's inviting expression. Connie Bellino was a shrewd observer of people she encountered, especially women, especially women she encountered with her son. She liked what she saw: a tall, slender woman with a pretty face, with beautiful, intelligent eyes, and a gentle expression. It was strange. There was something about her that struck a pleasant note in Connie's mind. Maybe it was the fine straw-blonde hair and the way she dressed, clean and unpretentious.

"Mom, this is Ellen." Danny hesitated for a moment. "I'm sorry, Elly, I..."

"Konstanty," Elly said, finishing for him.

Connie smiled and said hello. But there was still a question in her eyes. She didn't know how the two should have known each other. Elly could read the questioning look. "My maiden name was McCarrie," she said to Connie.

"We went to St. Mark's together, Mom. She was a couple years behind me," Danny said, sensing his mother's need for more information.

"You're Tommy's daughter." Connie blurted out brightly.

"Yes," Elly answered.

"God, I've known him all my life. I knew you when you were a little girl. And now you're a lovely young woman."

"Thank you," Elly said, blushing slightly.

They talked a little more. Connie learned that Elly was divorced and lived with Tommy, and that she had two children at St. Mark's — almost the ages of Danny's children.

They laughed often as though they had known each other for a long time. As they talked, Connie studied the fair young woman, and her curiosity increased with each word that Elly spoke. And a sense of admiration swept over her. The younger woman was so poised, so intelligent, so warm and gracious, that Connie could not take her eyes off the girl's face.

Danny seemed to have known her a long time and was very much at ease talking to her. It was pleasant and light, and he forgot the heaviness of his life in talking with these two charming women.

Soon, Elly's children approached, and after introductions all around they said goodbye. Danny spoke a soft goodbye to Elly. But his mother added to what her son said: "It was nice to have met you, Elly. Please say hello to your father for us."

Part III

Lucy

L UCY'S SON, EDDIE, LIKED the food at Castorina's. They tried to go to different places on Thursday nights, but Eddie, whenever he was in doubt, would always think of the wonderful Italian food that John Castorina served at his place.

One night, John was talking to Rino and Lou Bellanca and their sister, Connie Bellino, when all three men noticed the striking woman who entered the restaurant with her young son. "So who is that, Johnny? Tell us so my brothers can put their tongues back in their mouths."

They all laughed. "I don't know who she is, Connie," John said. "I know that's her son, and they've been in here a few times lately."

"I think I know who she is," said Lou. "She's Tommy McCarrie's secretary."

"Really, Lou?" said John, still looking at Lucy.

"Yeah. When I was up in Tommy's office...I think I remember her."

Rino chuckled. "He thinks he remembers her."

"Quiet, you," Connie hissed at her youngest brother. Just then John was called away by a waiter. As they watched him walk away, Rino said, "Watch. In a few minutes he'll be over there talking to her, and he'll have a book on her before the night's over."

"Is there anyone who likes the restaurant business more than Johnny? It's like he makes money off his hobby," said Lou.

"You know, I saw Tommy McCarrie's daughter last week," Connie said, changing the subject.

"Yeah? Where?" said Rino.

"At the Mall. I was with Danny, and I left him for a while. When I came back to the food court, he was talking to her. They went to St. Mark's together."

Connie took a sip of coffee and seemed to be reflective. "So?" said Lou. "What about her?"

"She's lovely…very nice," Connie answered, not looking at either of her brothers as they watched John Castorina make his way toward Lucy's table.

"Good evening, I'm John Castorina. How is your meal?"

Lucy smiled. "Very good. We love Italian food."

"Any Italian food?" he said brightly. "From any place?"

She beamed at his teasing. "No, Mr. Castorina, not any place. This is my son, Eddie, and your restaurant is his favorite place in all the world."

"I've seen you in here before," said John.

"My boss recommended it a few months ago. Then after the first time, we couldn't stay away."

"Your boss? And who is this wise man?"

"Chief Tommy McCarrie."

"I knew I'd seen you before! Your Tommy's secretary, right?"

"Yes. I have been for a long time. My name is Lucy Searles, and this is my son, Ed."

"Searles? Searles? There was an excellent baseball player from the East Side…"

"That was my late husband," she said.

"A sad loss," John said. "Would you please accept a complimentary desert? Any friend of Tommy's is always welcome here."

"Thank you, sir," Eddie said.

They chatted a while longer. John was his charming self, and Lucy was her usual soft-spoken and reserved self. Finally, they parted, with John sending Tommy his regards through Lucy.

None of them was aware that there was someone watching Lucy from one of the booths in the long alcove that held the more secluded eating places. Mose Pagliaro was sizing up his quarry. He never had much trouble finding a way to meet women. He was smooth and nice-looking and well-tailored. But he liked to be ahead of the game. He just had to pick the right time. And Lucy would be easy.

———◦✦◦———

Tommy was in his office early one morning. Spring was coming to the Valley, and it was going to be a beautiful day, the first of many before the hot summer months.

Lucy patched in a phone call, but before Tommy answered, she stepped into his office. "The President of Spring Common," she said.

Tommy knew no good would come from a call from Miles Wingrave. He sat down at his desk and lifted the receiver. "Dr. Wingrave?"

"Chief McCarrie, nice to talk to you."

"Can I help you?" Tommy said.

"Well, Chief, I'm calling to inquire about the Bellino incident. Some of our people within the university have been concerned that no progress has been made."

"Well, as you know, Dr. Wingrave, the Mayor appointed a special squad to investigate those murders."

"But we've heard nothing in months, and more than a year has passed... The Board of Trustees wants to know..."

"If we publicly report our progress in the investigation, we'll soon stop making progress, Dr. Wingrave," Tommy said.

"Well, I'm disappointed, Chief. When two members of the university community are killed, I would think... Besides, I have to report to the State Board about safety at our college and I still have these crimes on our record."

"When we find the murderer, we'll let the community know right away. In the meantime, maybe the mayor can give you some consolation. This is really his investigation."

Wingrave was quiet for a moment on the line. "His investigation? But you're the chief of police."

"It's the mayor's task force — a special squad charged with the investigation of the Bellino murders." The President was quiet for a moment. "I'm sure he wouldn't mind," Tommy continued. "In fact, I think he'd appreciate your concern," Tommy said, smiling to himself at the thought of this pompous man harassing Carly.

Just as Tommy was finishing his talk with Wingrave, Bumpy walked into his office. Tommy motioned him forward when he hesitated and pointed to a chair. In a moment, the chief was off the phone. He chuckled when he looked at his old friend. "That was Wingrave from Spring Common. I just sicced him onto Carly. I told him the Bellino case was the mayor's investigation."

Bumpy chuckled. "I never knew you had that mean streak in you, kid."

"You gotta play the game the way it's played," Tommy said. "So, what's up, boyo?"

"Nothing. The Bellino case is still nowhere."

"Bump, doesn't it seem strange to you that there was nothing found on those bodies? The DNA tests are useless; no clues; no evidence. What d'you make of that?"

"First, Laney's team has probably passed over hundreds of clues that are now lost for good. And second..." Bumpy hesitated.

"And second?" said Tommy.

"And second, it seems that the only way those hits could be this clean is if they were done by a real pro."

"So, somebody hired a torpedo?"

"It's not too hard to imagine it, Tom."

"But why? What is there about those two kids that made some nut want to waste them? What could they have done?"

"Well, Tom, you either have to entertain the notion that they were pushers and damned good liars who came from families as good as the ones they had. Or..."

"Or?"

"You first, you're the chief," Bumpy said lightly to his friend.

Tommy took a deep breath. "Or it had to have been an out-of-town job with a hired gun and had to cost a hell of a lot...all to waste two kids. And with a .32 Winchester Silvertip slug! Hell, I don't even think I know anyone who has a .32 automatic. Do you?" Tommy looked at Bumpy. "You buy any of that so far?"

"I'll buy the part about the hit. But what I can't figure is why...why did he cut that girl to pieces? That's not mob style."

"Do you think Laney has any idea that there's something strange behind the murders of those two kids?" Tommy said.

"All he cares about is getting laid...chasing anything that walks. Must have a cock like a horse." Tommy nodded, looking away from his old friend. "How're Elly and the kids?" Bumpy said.

"Huh? Oh, they're fine. Things are crazy, you know. Those kids have taken over the house."

"And Elly?"

"She's taking over, too, Bump. The place looks so nice…bright, clean. Bookbags, CDs, video tapes, cases of pop, coats, food…it's all over."

"But you like it, right?"

"Yeah, kid. With the kind of life I was looking forward to, this was a nice change."

Carly was tired as he drove into his garage. He hadn't been feeling so good lately. Jesus, it was like being an old man at the age of forty-four.

When he entered the kitchen, he couldn't hear anything in the house. *I wonder if Dad's okay,* he thought. As he entered the living room, he saw Ginny sitting on a sofa. It was dark in the room, with only one light burning in a far corner behind her, making her face hard to see. "Ginny? What's wrong?" She shook her head. "Is Dad okay?" said Carly anxiously as he moved toward her.

"Dad's okay," she said softly.

As he drew near her, he could see her face was puffy and her eyes were red from crying. He touched her tentatively, not knowing if somehow, he himself had been the cause of her anguish. "What's happened?" he said softly.

"We're losing her," she said.

"Who? Lisa?"

"She wants to move out…and…" She began to cry, and he moved forward to hold her. As he did, she clutched him and began to cry more.

Suddenly she pulled away to look face-to-face with her husband, who she thought she had lost, who was suddenly trying to convince her that he still loved her. "I think she's taking something, Carly."

"Lisa? Don't be silly, Gin. She might move out, but I don't think she's into drugs."

"She's my daughter, Carly. I know there's something wrong."

"Who does she want to move in with?"

"A 'friend.' And she won't tell me who it is."

"She won't tell you who it is, for Christ's sake? Who does she think will pay for all that?"

"She says she makes enough now to do it...especially if her room-mate splits the cost."

"What about the drugs? How do you know?"

"Her eyes, Carly. The way she acts...and once I found something in her blouse pocket when I was washing clothes. I can also tell that she's seeing someone by her panties..."

"Jesus Christ," Carly whispered as he held his wife to him. "What have I done?"

She pulled back away from him. "What you've done is between you and me. You have always been a loving father to her."

"Is she in her room?"

"Yes...What are you going to do?" she said as Carly moved away from her and stood upright.

"I'm gonna find out what the hell's going on once and for all. And I want to know who she's banging, for Christ's sake."

"Carly, please. Don't go up there now. She'll leave for sure."

"If she's going to leave, let her leave. I'm tired of this. You've been a wreck for dammed near a year because of..." He stopped. He didn't want to finish his sentence because he knew that he was the real reason for her anguish.

Suddenly, he started upstairs. His daughter was in her room with the door closed. He opened it and walked in. She was packing clothes into a suitcase. "Where are you going?"

"Away from here," she answered coldly.

"Where?"

"To a friend's apartment?"

"Who? What friend?"

"You wouldn't know her," she said, still packing and never looking at her father.

"What's her name, Lisa?" Carly said.

"I said you wouldn't know her," she said again.

Carly grabbed his daughter and spun her toward him so they could look at each other. He shook her as he held her by both shoulders. "Who the fuck do you think you are?" she screamed, throwing a blouse that she was holding in her hand at him. It was then that Carly struck her, hitting her with the full palm of his hand across her face. He held back the force of the blow, almost as an afterthought in mid-swing, but he did hit her and the blow was sharp, and the sound was sharp, and the pain shocked her more than it hurt.

"You bastard," she said, holding the cheek that he had just slapped. "If you don't get out of here, I'll call the police," she said.

"I own the police," Carly said. "Call them if you want."

She turned around suddenly. "I'm just getting out of here," she said, throwing some other clothes in the suitcase.

"If you go, you're never coming back," Carly said as she walked past him.

"Come back to what? Another beating? There's nothing to come back to."

"You know what this will do to your mother, don't you?"

"I'm sorry for her. But she married you. I can't help that."

"Lisa..." Carly called helplessly to his daughter as she ran down the stairs. He could hear his wife sobbing as she called her daughter's name. In a few moments, he heard the door slam and a car start. She was gone.

———

"So how are you fixed for funds?" Tommy asked his daughter as she started to clear the dinner dishes from the table.

"I'm okay. Why?"

"I put some money into your checking account this morning."

"You did? Why? How could you do that?"

"I'm the chief of police, remember? I can do a lot of things."

"So, they let you put money into any old account just because you want to." Her voice was getting louder, about as close to being shrill as Elly's could get.

"No...not anyone's, just my one and only daughter's," Tommy said calmly, sensing her irritation.

"I told you I didn't need money," she said.

"And I told you I have money I don't know what to do with...look, we've been over all this before. When are you gonna let me help? Why do you force me to do underhanded stuff."

"I didn't force you," she said angrily. His bemused smugness at something he had done irritated her even more. "You shouldn't have done that, Dad. I..."

Tommy held up his hand palm forward toward the remonstrances he didn't want to hear. "I'm going to put more in every so often. And face it: You can't stop me."

"I'll...I'll move out."

She was sorry the moment she said it. His expression changed and she knew she had hurt him. She began shaking her head before he even asked her: "You don't mean that, do you?"

She had tears in her eyes as she spoke. "I'm sorry, Daddy. You know I didn't mean that."

He stood up and hugged her. Then he sat back down as she turned away. "Please let me help, El. You're all I've got. And I don't want you cutting corners just 'cause Dave's not paying you enough."

"I'll be okay, Dad. You know if I ever needed money I'd ask."

"Like hell you would. Besides, I'm just saving you the trouble of asking."

"You can't keep doing this, Daddy," she said.

"Look, someday everything I have'll be yours anyway. What's the difference?"

"That's not something I want to discuss." She said as she left the room.

He sat just drinking his coffee, thinking instinctively that she would be back. In a moment she returned and sat down. "How's the Bellino case going?" she said to his surprise, seeming deliberately calm about it.

"It's not going at all. I haven't had the time to do the legwork... It's hard getting leads."

She smiled faintly to herself, and Tommy began to get nervous. He had gotten used to his daughter's Socratic style and yet was always surprised at her skill at cozening her father. He squinted at her across the table. "What do you want, daughter?"

"Why should I want anything? I'm not here to receive, but to give."

"Give, huh? Give what?"

"Give time... help."

"To me?"

"Yes, to you…on the Bellino case."

"Oh, no! No way," Tommy said, standing up and pacing to the sink and back.

"But, Dad, you just said you don't have enough time to…"

"I'll have enough time. I'll make the time."

"But I can really help you, Dad."

Tommy stared back at his daughter for a few seconds. She reminded him of her look when she was a little girl. "Kid," he sighed, fearing that her penetrating look would wither his resistance and lead him to do something foolish. "Number one, you're not a cop and I'm dealing with something strange here. Number two, and this is the big one — you're talking about a vicious murder with guns and slashing and drugs involved…and I don't have a clue about what or who it is. I can't let you do it."

She looked up at him, those lovely eyes piercing his soul. She knew he was right. It was a crazy dream. Yet…"I can help you behind the scenes. I'm a librarian, don't forget. I know how to chase down information."

Tommy, who had been shaking his head, was suddenly seized by her idea. Maybe she could. She was smart as anybody he'd ever known, and if he were running a secret operation, it would be wise to have good help…that he could trust.

Elly noticed the change in his expression immediately, and she moved in on her father. "You know I can do a lot of things, Dad."

Tommy shook his head, chuckling to himself. "Maybe," he sighed, finally. "…if I can find something for you to do."

———•◦✦◦•———

"What did she say?" Judge East said to Carly.

"She's not coming home," Carly muttered. "She's staying with a friend."

"Who?"

"Some girl from work."

"The one who looked like she's been around the world four times?"

"That's the one."

Judge East sighed. "Carly, we can't let this thing blow up in our faces. I want you on that State Central Committee next year, and we have to go into this quietly."

"Yeah, I know, Judge," Carly sighed. "I just don't know what she's gonna do from one day to the next." Then, he stopped and looked back toward his mentor. "And we've spoiled her all her life."

The judge just nodded quietly. He had been present at Carly's father's wedding, Carly's wedding, and every important family event for fifty years. Carly was a son to him and Carly's advancement would be the fulfillment of his dreams. He also enjoyed the vicarious thrill of seeing the young man wield power in the Valley, as though he himself were doing it.

"How're you and Ginny getting along?"

"Okay, Judge."

"You settled things, then?"

"Yeah, I think we know what we have to do to make it work."

"That's good news, Carly. It won't be so hard to get your name up now."

"Yeah," Carly said softly. "Do you really think we should try it this time, Kel? Not two years down the road?"

"You have to move now. Gierman's already got his people out. You know how much leverage those Cleveland people can exert."

"Jesus, I'm tired, Judge. My dad's getting worse…Lisa's driving me nuts."

The judge was getting impatient and spoke with an unusual edge in his voice. "Carly, either you want this, or you don't. If you don't go after it now, who knows what it might be like in two years. You might be…" He stopped, but Carly instantly read his meaning.

"Be beaten, right?"

"It damned well can happen," said the Judge.

"I need time. I have to get this goddamned wino McCarrie the hell out of this investigation…"

"Carly, I've told you before, forget McCarrie. One of the dumbest things you ever did was to put that investigation under one command. Now if the thing's a failure, it'll be your failure because they report to you."

"Judge, that son of a bitch put my dad in jail two times. You ever go to school when your father's jail term was all over the front page? I swore then that I would get him if it was the last thing I do."

The judge was silent, but he stared ahead, the tips of the fingers of both hands joined together almost a gesture of prayer and meditation. Finally, he spoke softly, almost cooing the words in exasperation. "Carly, there's one thing you'd better get straight right away. Are you after McCarrie because of what he did to your father or what he does to you? It makes a hell of a difference…to you and to me."

"What d'you mean?"

"I mean that your dad is beyond revenge, and I don't want any part of a crusade to avenge your dad because of what happened to you in grade school thirty years ago."

"Yeah, but he's not your father, Judge," Carly snapped.

The judge suddenly flared in anger. "Now listen to me, you little…"

He caught himself and regained his composure. "Don't tell me about doing good things for your dad. I was with him since before you were born, and I'm with him now. And I don't need any lectures on loyalty from a spoiled kid who has a chance in life his father never got, and now wants to go on a suicide mission to shoot down a respected police chief. Remember that Tommy's not your future; he's the past. Let him go."

Carly wasn't listening to his mentor. He hated McCarrie, and he wanted to wipe that goddamned smug look off his face... and he wanted his dad to know that he did it before he died.

Tommy addressed a class of criminal justice majors at Spring Common. As usual, he begged off the coffee klatch afterward, putting in a perfunctory appearance and finally leaving quietly. On his way back to the station, he stopped at Ruby's restaurant and had a cup of coffee with her. Then, he stopped to see Lou Bellanca about playing a game of poker with them Saturday night. He even thought of stopping at the Silver Bridge, but he knew he couldn't get away with it, not unless he wanted to give up the whole rest of the day. When he left Lou's shoemaker shop, he did what he always did: step outside, stop for a second, let his senses vibrate to any passing danger.

Some old colleagues from the force used to taunt him when he said that was what he did. They were non-believers, but they were often dumbfounded when Tommy would be attuned to things that the rest of them had missed.

And this time he sensed it again. Maybe not danger, yet not the absence of danger. There was something wrong. He took a deep breath and paused another second. Then he walked deliberately toward his car, got into it, and drove away, seeming not to act differently than ever. But this time, he waited and watched.

Abruptly he changed lanes on the freeway, deciding to get off on the Market Street exit heading south into the uptown. Slowly he came to rest at the Market Street light, watching to see who was behind him, who had made the lane change to follow him. But he didn't recognize anything...nothing familiar. A dirty Lincoln, rusted and yellowed by years of street salt, two Black men driving, conversing easily with each other, laughing and talking with animation. No, they weren't the ones. Another Chevrolet sedan driven by a woman with recently set hair, elderly and preoccupied with her own thoughts, staring stoically ahead. Behind them a green car, clean for this time of year, and two male figures sitting quietly. He couldn't see them well, but he would watch to see what would happen next.

As he drove uphill on Market Street, he slowed his car down to a deliberate, steady pace. He was coming near Hugo Malatesta's garage. He pulled into the lot and quickly got out of his car, walking directly into the mechanic's shop. As he entered, he quickly looked backward out the window now that he couldn't be seen...and waited. A green Buick passed slowly, with the passengers craning their necks to find Tommy's car.

They weren't a couple of old torpedoes, Tommy thought, as Hugo walked through the door from the body shop. "Hey, Tommy, how you been?" said the owner. He was a half-foot taller than his brother, Bumpy, and a year older. But he still had the tank-like physique and gruff delivery of his brother.

"Got any coffee, Hugo?" Tommy said.

"Sure, I'll get some." As Hugo walked away, Tommy studied outside again. Nothing. Hugo brought back a steaming cup of legendary strong coffee. "Everything okay, Tom?"

"Yeah, kid. I was wondering if you guys were playing poker this week."

"Yeah. You think you can make it?"

"Yeah. I have the strong urge to fleece some wealthy dago brothers."

Hugo chuckled. "My brother giving you a hard time lately?"

"Yeah, he doesn't show me any respect," Tommy said, chuckling as he sipped his coffee, raising the cup toward Hugo in a half toast.

"Hell, he never shows any respect for anybody, especially for friends or family."

Tommy nodded, smiling, and occasionally looking outside. "I don't know what I'd do without him, Hugo," Tommy said. "Since he pulled me out of the ditch in Korea, all he's been doing is saving my ass."

"He feels the same about you, too, Kid. You got him Jesse, you saved his life in the Maranzano War, you got him through college. I'd say you're a match made in heaven."

"I figure he still owes me for Jesse," Tommy growled as he turned, once more, toward the window.

"You waiting for someone, Tom? You need a ride...I can have Luke take you..."

As Hugo was speaking, Tommy saw the green Buick again...the third time. He made no move, but slowly turned back to Hugo. "No, kid. It's alright. I just have to get back or your brother's gonna raise hell with me about being gone all morning."

"Tell Bump I'll bring Jesse's car over tonight. We're almost done."

<hr />

Later that night, at home, Tommy thought more about the green

Buick. They were both younger men, both white, but not really good about being seen. There was something strange. All they were doing were following and watching, casing every move he made. Nobody from the mob would send two young guys, like these, to tail someone. They'd send someone experienced…and a lot better than these guys.

But who could be watching him…local people? And why? What was he doing that would endanger someone enough to put a tail on him? This couldn't be a Pittsburgh or Cleveland operation; it had to be local. Somebody local wants to nail him.

Just then Elly came into the room and sat beside him, handing him a cup of late-evening tea. "So, how'd your day go?"

"Okay," Tommy said perfunctorily.

"Just okay?" she said.

"Yeah, nothing special. Why do you ask, daughter?"

"Because you've been preoccupied since you got home. And now I find you out here all alone, not watching TV, not reading the paper."

"You know," he said, playfully striking her knee in a brush-like manner, "you never used to be this much trouble when you were a little girl."

"I've been saving it all up till now — honing my skills. Now, come on, tell me what this is about. The Bellino case?"

"The Bellino case? Where'd you hear that?"

"From you. I heard you talking to Uncle Bumpy."

"Well, we're nowhere."

"Why would somebody hurt two kids who had never done anything wrong in their lives?"

"That's the big question, counselor."

"Do you have ideas about it?" she asked earnestly.

"No."

"What are you going to do?"

"Keep..." he hesitated for a moment. Should he tell her about being tailed? If he did, she'd be all over him with a million questions. But she'd be asking them anyway. And every night when he comes home, she's there. Even if she doesn't ask, she looks curious, and it drives him crazy because he's never sure just when she'll serve him that tea or coffee and something good to eat... like now... and then sit near him and start boring in. And it's not just because she's a busybody. She never has been. It's just that damned curiosity and the exhilaration at unraveling a complex case as though it were a puzzle. And, God, he admired that in her. Bumpy and Pete and Med can't deal with the speculative side of this investigation; they all have departments to run. So now he's going it alone, without a partner to bounce off small ideas, quiet thoughts, fleeting intuitions that might be keys to the case. "You know what?"

"What?" she said breathlessly.

"Somebody was tailing me today."

It was as though a dam had burst. Just that little secret had brought her into it. This was the McCarrie case now. No one could stop them. "So, what did you do? Are you going to be in danger now? Did you tell Chief Malatesta? How are you going to know if you're in danger?"

"Easy now, kid. Look. If I start telling you stuff there are three conditions, understand?"

He waited for her response. "What are the conditions? I don't trust you," she said.

He smiled. "First, everything is between you and me, right? Second, you have to let me be an investigator, a cop. Third, you have to do exactly what I tell you... no freelancing, okay?"

"Sure, those are fine, Daddy. Now tell me what..."

"Ellen, I'm serious. It's one thing to be a sounding board for my ideas, but quite another to get involved in the case. I don't want any of that, you hear? I can't deal with this case if you're in harm's way. Your kids don't have a father now. They need their mother, understand?"

"I understand. And I'll just help in any way you want."

"Good," he said, satisfied with himself. Maybe it was just the realization that he couldn't keep her from asking questions anyway. It cleared his head.

"So, are you in harm's way, Dad?" she said.

"I don't think so. But somebody must be worried enough to tail me... Maybe I'll let them catch up to me someday."

⸺◆⸺

Mose Pagliaro walked quickly to his car. He had to make sure he met the Puerto Rican woman at the right time. He knew that on Thursday nights she had supper with her son, most of the time at Castorina's. But occasionally they would go elsewhere, and he was waiting for his chance to meet her somewhere else.

She wasn't going to Castorina's tonight, having turned away. He decided to follow her, being as distant and discreet as he could without losing her. She turned up Market Street, heading into the uptown shopping area... maybe even toward Boardman and the outskirts of the city.

Mose thought about what he would say to her, about how to get her alone, without her son. All of a sudden what usually was easy, seemed hard. She drove past the uptown and headed for Boardman, and suddenly she turned into the Heidelberg parking lot. Mose waited as she left her car and entered the restaurant. If he was lucky, her son wouldn't be there yet.

Mose entered hurriedly and followed her to the captain's desk. She said she wanted a table for two, non-smoking. She was led away by a young woman and seated by a window overlooking part of the Valley from the high viewpoint of the dining room.

Mose said he wanted a table for two, non-smoking, but said he wanted to choose his table. He slipped the young man ten dollars, and the captain said, "Just go in and pick one. I'll send the waitress to wherever you are."

Mose went into the far dining room and found his place, exactly opposite, but at an angle to Lucy. He could look at her easily, and they could talk without anyone overhearing them... a perfect spot... and her son was nowhere in sight.

Mose ordered coffee. She was waiting, occasionally looking at her watch and looking outside into the weather that had grown colder and rainier. Mose acted preoccupied, but until she looked in his direction after looking at her watch, he made no move. But there came the right moment, and he spoke. "Looks like this might turn to snow," he said. At first, she seemed surprised that he spoke to her.

"If it gets a little colder," she said cordially.

"It's a little late in the season for this. I think we've paid our dues already this year, don't you?" She nodded, smiling. "Have you ever eaten here before?"

"Yes," she said. "Several times."

"This is my first time. Is the food good?"

"It is. Especially their chicken and veal dishes."

The waitress came up to Mose and asked him for a drink order. Mose ordered white wine. As he and the waitress talked, he could see Lucy looking outside and then at her watch.

When the waitress went away, he waited a moment, sipping some wine, then spoke, "Excuse me, but are you going to be eating alone?"

"No," she said calmly, "I'm waiting for my son. He said he might be a little late, but I hope he's being careful in this weather."

"Yes, young people are too confident in their reflexes." He paused for a few seconds. "Do I sound that parental?"

She smiled again, this time seeming to be less reserved with this attractive, friendly man with such easy manners. "I guess once you are, you can't help it."

"He wouldn't happen to have a phone in his car, would he?" Mose asked.

"No," she said wistfully. "I wish he did...now."

As the rain and wind struck violently, the first sweep of the storm tore through the Valley. "I'm sure he'll have sense enough to pull over until the heavy weather stops," Mose said.

She nodded slightly but didn't answer him. After a few more minutes, he spoke again. "Listen, would you care to join me...until your son comes? Then you can decide if the two of you will want to stay or eat separately."

She didn't answer, avoiding the decision and the commitment her response might make. "How about it?" he persisted. "I don't bite."

She took a deep breath and nodded slightly. He instantly stood up and held a chair for her as she walked toward his table. "Storms are not supposed to be sat through alone," he said.

Lucy felt strange the moment she sat at his table. He was a handsome man with an easy, unthreatening manner. Yet she wished her son would come soon. She always wanted the future to unravel her way, not this haphazard way, over which she had no control.

"Would you like more wine?" he said.

"No," she said. "Listen, I think I should move back to my table. I shouldn't..."

"He'll be here soon...as soon as the storm is over," he interrupted. She didn't respond, but also didn't move. For a few seconds, they sat in silence. "My name's Mose Pagliaro, what's yours?" he said.

"Lucy Searles," she answered.

Mose tilted his glass of wine slightly toward her and said, "I'm honored, Lucy Searles."

Lucy couldn't help being captivated by this charming man with Mediterranean manners, who seemed to have an instinct about when to push himself forward and when to leave off. "So, this young man who will be joining you soon...are there others?"

"I have a daughter two years older. She's twenty-two."

"And what does the girl do? In fact, what do they both do?"

"She's a teacher at Thorn Hill...Spanish, and he's a senior at Spring Common."

"And what's his field?"

"He wants to be a chemical engineer."

Mose pursed his lips and made a facial gesture of admiration. "A smart one, huh?"

"I like to think so...How about you? Do you have any kids?"

"Two girls who grew up with their mother in California...and who I see about once a year. They're both working out there."

"Are you divorced?"

"Sixteen years," he answered without looking at her, sipping his wine.

"What do you do for a living?" she asked, surprising him.

"I'm in real estate investments," he said. "What do you do?"

"I'm secretary to the chief of police."

Mose nodded admiringly. "Looks like it's letting up out there, your son'll be here soon."

"I just hope he's okay," she said.

"He'll be okay," Mose said. "I know it." She smiled. "So, is it exciting to be a secretary to the chief of police?"

"Not very. Things are usually quiet."

"You mean he's not where the action is?"

"I guess so...not directly. He does get around the station a lot."

Mose changed the subject. At first, he stared at her for a few seconds. Then he said, "You know, you look very familiar. I must have seen you before around Youngstown."

"I don't know; I don't get around much," she said.

"Well, if I haven't seen you, I should have seen you." She seemed puzzled, so he clarified his words. "Women as attractive as you should be seen. Roses are not meant to be hidden from the light."

She smiled again, blushing a little. Just as she did, her son walked in, soaked and disheveled. "Are you alright, honey?" she said.

"Now I am, Mom. What a mess out there! The power is out on the North Side, and parts of the town are flooded, especially toward Struthers."

The young man finally realized that his mother was seated with someone. They waited for him to stop talking and then said, "Ed, this is Mr...." But she hesitated, having forgotten his name.

"Pagliaro," Mose said extending his hand. The boy grabbed it. "I hope you're okay. Your mother was very worried about you."

"I'm okay," Ed said.

"Please sit down," Mose said, standing up. The young man hesitated for a moment. "Mrs. Searles," Mose said, turning toward Lucy, "my office is near Struthers. If you'll excuse me, I think I'd better go check to see if it's intact. A flood there would really spoil what has been a very nice day." She accepted the compliment, nodding appreciatively. "Ed, it was very nice to meet you. Your mother said you're a connoisseur of fine restaurants. So am I. Perhaps we'll see each other again and compare notes."

Ed smiled. He was affected by this warm man who had just, once again, extended his hand in friendship. His mother was smiling, so he knew that all things were right. "I'd like that, Mr. Pagliaro," he said, shaking Mose's hand.

"Have a nice evening," Mose said, turning back to Lucy, and then turning away toward the door.

Bumpy came into Tommy's office later than usual. He sat down heavily in his chair, knowing that he would soon be leaving. "You playing poker Friday night?"

"Maybe," said Tommy. "How about you?"

"I don't know. Jesse has to help out down at the church. I think she's gonna hit me up to help also."

Tommy smiled, as if telling himself a new private joke. "How's Jesse doing? I don't get a chance to see her much anymore."

"Hell, you keep turning down our dinner invitations."

"Only one time, and that was because I had to help Elly at school with the kids."

"Now Jesse's offended. She thinks you've gotten too dammed snooty…don't hang around with your old friends anymore."

"Jesse couldn't be offended if she tried. I can't help it if she wants me more than she wants you."

Bumpy chuckled. "She does seem to cook better meals when

you come around."

"Guilt! You keep poisoning her mind about me, and then she feels guilty. So she treats me like a king to make up for it."

"I can't seem to break her of all those bad habits."

"I suppose she still looks as good in a bathing suit as she ever did. Jesus, I must have been crazy to introduce her to you. Goddamn, what lousy luck."

The two old friends enjoyed their byplay, as they always did. There was more than a ring of truth to the talk whenever they mentioned Jesse. Bumpy was the envy of all the guys in his circle because of her. Not only did she have a great body, but she was attractive and clean. And she was crazy about Bumpy. He was her whole life, and the life she gave him was sweet and full of hope. She was an excellent cook, a fine mother, and a natural leader with a keen intellect. And Tommy introduced her to Bumpy a long time ago. And from the moment the two unlikely people met, it was a fairy story that unraveled before the awed eyes of those who could only marvel at the magic between them. That elusive magic that never erupted between Jesse and any one of the eligible and willing young men in their circle, not Rino, or Lou, or Hugo, or Smokey, or Tommy...only Bumpy. And none of them understood it; they only marveled at it and wistfully envied their dear friend for his lifelong stroke of luck.

"So, what's the scoop, *paesan?*" Bumpy said.

Tommy knew that he was asking a personal question. The YPD was running fine with Bumpy as deputy chief, so in the absence of crisis, the police were doing a good job. But Bumpy wanted to know only about his friend's private life.

Tommy took a deep breath. "I'm being tailed, Bump."

It caught Bumpy by surprise, and he wasn't sure he heard Tommy right. "A tail? Who?"

"I don't know," said Tommy. "They don't look like choir boys, but they don't look like torpedoes, either. And I made them without their knowing it."

"You think they're mob, or reporters, or…"

"Or what?"

"Or some of Carly's boys?"

"I don't think so, kid. These guys just didn't look that good."

"What makes you think Carly has anybody good?"

"Still, Bump, this doesn't fit."

Bumpy was quiet for a few moments. "Where's your piece?"

"Right here. Why?"

"Still the Smith .45, right?"

"How long have you known me, Bump?"

"I want you to carry this, also," said Bumpy, reaching across to Tommy, handing him a small flat package, a pocket holster.

Tommy took the holster and removed a small Beretta .25 automatic from it. "What's this? Your gun?"

"Yeah, but I want you to keep it. I have other ones."

"Bump, you've had one of these for twenty years. I can't take this."

"You never know where something might happen…or when that .45'll run out of rounds. And when a little extra fire power might come in handy." Tommy was shaking his head. "I've got this one," Bumpy said, pointing to his nine-millimeter Glock strapped to his waist. "I'm not leaving here unless you take it, Tom."

"Hell, I haven't been shot at for years. It would be a waste of a good gun. These Berettas deserve more use than I'll give them."

"Tommy, are you gonna take the fucking thing or not?"

"Okay," Tommy sighed. "Now go home."

"Pack double. And watch those tails. I'll check with you tomorrow."

Tommy spent the evening at a high school basketball game with Elly. Mike was playing in his first game at St. Mark's. As Tommy entered the crowd, he said hello to so many old friends that it seemed the whole East Side was there. St. Mark's lost, but Mike played two quarters, and Tommy and Elly were nearly hoarse from yelling.

The next morning, Tommy drove to work, carefully watching his rear-view mirror to see if the tail was back. It wasn't.

After a morning at work, Tommy decided to check the bank records of Kaye Bellino. There was still something troubling about her death, and he couldn't help thinking that her death was connected to the deaths of young Danny and Neva.

In the YPD garage Tommy walked purposefully, nodding to an old garage attendant he had known since his rookie days in the YPD. He awkwardly fumbled for his keys since he now carried them in a different pocket because of the Bumpy's little Beretta.

It was only when he was a few feet from his car that he stopped and looked upon a vacant space.

"Where the fuck's my car, Liebowitz?" he growled to the old man.

"Uh...Med Williams took it," said the attendant.

"What for? Where'd he go?"

"Uh...Chief Malatesta was supposed to tell you...You have to use his car for a while." Liebowitz was holding out a set of keys to Bumpy's light blue Pontiac. Tommy grabbed the keys and turned toward Bumpy's car.

At the bank he checked into Kaye Bellino's finances. Nothing. She and Danny shared the same account. At the Credit Bureau, he checked their debts. Nothing again. They had a Visa bill of a few hundred dollars. Other than that, they were clean.

So, either one of them had a secret stash, or they were both on the level. So why was he still troubled about Kaye Bellino? Maybe because it didn't add up. She killed herself, he was sure. But why? Being married to Danny? With kids as nice and well-scrubbed as they had?

Every normal woman in the world wants a husband like Danny. Why didn't she? Why did she play around? And who did she play around with?

On the way back to the station, Tommy passed Spring Common. He decided to find out about Kaye Bellino's college career. He went to the records office and asked the clerk at the window to admit him to her boss. In a moment, Tommy was admitted to the Office of the Registrar.

"What can I do for you, sir?" a woman behind the counter said.

"I'd like to see the transcript of a Kaye Bellino," Tommy said.

"Are you related to her?" she said officiously.

"No, I..."

"Well, if you're not a relative, I'm afraid I can't let you see her transcript. Our privacy policy is..." Tommy discreetly laid his shield and card on the counter as they talked. "Get it," he said coldly.

In a few moments, she returned, personally carrying the transcript. As she handed it to Tommy, her phone rang again. She answered it. Tommy was studying Kaye Bellino's history at the school, especially her recent history, when suddenly, he heard the woman plead in a strained voice, "But I was only trying to uphold university policy." More angry words on the other end of the line made her sorry she surreptitiously called the president. She then quietly let down the receiver and looked at Tommy with a shell-shocked look on her face. "I, uh...didn't mean to insult you. I assure you I had no intention of hindering your investigation. I just didn't know you were the chief of police. Please...take the transcript. We'll send someone out to get it when you're done with it."

Tommy took the transcript and headed back to the police station. He felt strange driving Bumpy's car. He always felt strange driving any car but his own. But it was a nice day, and he enjoyed the sun and the music on the radio. Bumpy had opera tapes in the car. *Must be genetic with dagos*, he thought, chuckling to himself. As he pulled into the YPD garage, he noticed that his car was not in his place again.

He was annoyed at seeing the empty parking place. He went up the elevator to his office on the third floor. He nodded to Lucy, who was on the phone talking to Pete Mencken, jotting down information about a report on the Traffic Division.

Tommy went inside and sat behind his desk. Lucy came in to ask if he wanted coffee, and she returned in a few minutes and set the cup on his desk.

There was nothing unusual about Kaye's transcript. It listed cryptic names of courses, abbreviated in codes that university people would easily understand. The names of professors were listed beside each course. He recalled words Danny had said when Tommy asked him about the man his wife was seeing: "He's the kind of guy that always makes someone like me look bad."

That had always been one of Tommy's talents as a cop. He could file, instinctively, words or phrases, images and sensations, in far parts of his memory. Then, in future investigations, those stored snapshots could be called forward to give substance to an idea. There might come a day, as in completing a jigsaw puzzle, that one momentary mental fragment remembered would make a whole picture emerge.

But this girl took courses in the liberal arts, required mathematics, language, science, English, history. Her last English course was taken two years ago…Poetic processes. It had to be that guy that she got involved with. Besides, she took two courses from him, according to the transcript.

Just then, Lucy opened his door and announced a caller. "Sergeant Williams," she said.

Med walked in somewhat gingerly, as though the old sports injuries were acting up. But he was also acting jaunty and bright. As he sat down in one of the chairs in front of Tommy's desk, he threw a strange key onto Tommy's blotter.

"What's this?" grumbled the chief.

"Your new car keys," he said.

"What'd you guys do?"

"Fixed it up."

"So, what's the new key for?"

"That's a remote starter and a lock."

"Remote starter? Who the hell told you to do that?"

"Deputy Chief Liborio Malatesta. Your old friend, Bump."

"But what the hell for?"

"Protection. You're being tailed, aren't you?"

"Who the fuck told you that, goddamn it?"

"We have your office bugged," Med said, smiling.

"That little bastard wasn't supposed to talk about that."

"He only told me, Tommy. None of my guys knew anything about why they were doing it. I just told them you needed one."

"I'm gonna quit telling you guys things anymore. No matter who I tell, all three of you always know."

"All for one, one for all. That's our agreement."

"So does this thing work?"

"Come on. Let's go down and try it."

———— ❖❖❖ ————

Mose was sitting at his usual table at Castorina's, quietly eating a light supper. This might be the night; they often ate here on Thursday nights. Just then, Lucy and her son, Ed, walked into the restaurant. Mose pursed his lips. God, she was a sexy woman. But she had more than just good looks. She had substance; she had a calm, unaffected manner that made every man that saw her think that she would be warm and lovely in his bed.

But one of the secrets of Mose's success was that he never mixed pleasure with business. He watched as they sat down, not noticing him. He bided his time and then made his move. Lucy and Eddie had ordered and were waiting for their meal, making idle exchanges, talking lightly.

He approached them quietly. "Good evening, Mrs. Searles," he said as he reached his hand toward her son for a shake. The boy responded warmly. Lucy was polite and smiling.

"Have you eaten already?" Lucy asked.

"No, I just got here in a few minutes before you. Sometimes I stop here on my way home, especially if I have a lot of homework."

"Would you like to join us?" Ed said.

Mose was a good actor. At first, for a split second, he feigned surprise. Then he looked at Lucy. "Would you mind?" he asked politely, knowing she would be unable to resist.

"Oh, no. Please join us," she said softly, trying to smile through some slight discomfort.

Mose nodded to a waitress and sat down at the table. "Have you ordered yet?" he asked, knowing they had not.

"No," Lucy said, "we were just about to."

"What do you like best?" Mose asked the boy.

"Lasagna," he answered. "How about you?"

"I like the pasta with olive oil sauce. And you?" Mose asked Lucy.

"I like the veal piccata," she said.

"Well, I guess we know what we want. Will you both be my guests this evening?"

"Oh, no..." Lucy said, but Mose interrupted her.

"You can reciprocate some other time. And I'll take it graciously. It's just that I'm sort of excited about seeing you here."

"You must like the same food that we do," Ed said.

"It seems that way, doesn't it? As I grew up, my family always took food quality seriously...even if it was simple, peasant food."

Lucy said nothing. Ed's comment seemed to raise a flag in her memory. She began to wonder, at least for a moment, how this charming man could have met them twice while she and her son were dining out. And yet...he was so gracious, so natural and easy in his manner that it was hard to mistrust his motives.

She studied him as he talked to Ed. He seemed like a genuinely nice man. He was impeccably dressed, European looking, and clean. It made him look better as a package than the sum of his parts. He was balding, but looked distinguished, smiling, but not presumptuous. Elegant, but not arrogant. And as he and her son talked, she began to admire his demeanor, and she began to loosen her reserve and warm up to this stranger.

The meal was a great success. Mose was a good listener and asked good questions without seeming to intrude into their private lives. Lucy even found herself laughing softly at a few of his remarks about Italians. She found his self-deprecating humor engaging. She began calling him

"Mose" at his insistence, and he responded with "Ed" and "Lucy."

When the waitress came with their checks, they silently slipped the money into paper envelopes. "Are you sure I can't buy?" he said to Lucy. She shook her head.

Then, Ed said, "Well, Mom, I have to go back to school. I have to run a program tonight, and the computer's probably free now."

"Don't be late," she said.

Ed shook hands with Mose and said goodbye. When he was gone, Mose was silent and Lucy became uncomfortable. Finally, she said, "Look, Mose. You're very nice..."

"But you don't date," he said, finishing for her. She stopped for a moment, staring at his face, but she said nothing. "I don't date, either. How's that?" he said, looking directly back at her. She smiled slightly, hating the way she succumbed to his charm, hating the way he disarmed her. "But do you think that two people who don't date could ever have dinner together...on a non-date? Just dinner?"

She smiled again, looking away from him as if needing to think and not being able to if their eyes met. "I pay my taxes, and I'm not a child molester or a mass murderer."

She laughed softly. "That still leaves a lot of room for bad things," she said.

"I think you're right," he said, looking away from her, pouring some wine into his glass. But then he turned to look at her. "So why not have dinner with me, so I can spend the evening telling you all the other bad things I don't do?"

She didn't want to laugh, and he knew it. But he also could see that she couldn't suppress it. Finally, she shook her head, in that way surrendering to his blandishments. "You might enjoy the evening," he said. "How about it?"

"All right, just dinner. But you have to know it can never lead any-where."

"I know. We'll just have a nice dinner, and we'll talk, and then just so I don't get any crazy ideas about another non-date, I'll take you home and then throw myself into the Mahoning and drown. How's that?"

She was frustrated because she couldn't find a way to dislike this man. In fact, she liked him very much. He was…perfect, and she laughed. "You are crazy!" she said lightly.

"Yeah. But I know one crazy guy who's gonna have dinner with you, right?"

———————

Tommy could see the car in his rear-view mirror again. Who in the hell were they? Who did they work for? This time he was ready for them. He had told Med to station two of the motor pool heaps in dif-ferent parts of the South Side.

As he drove, Tommy could see that they were following him. He was puzzled. When would they make their move? What did they want? Soon he had to do something. When he accelerated his car, he caught them off guard and they lost him. In a moment he turned into an al-ley and parked his car behind a garage so it couldn't be seen from the alley way. Then he ran to an old Ford that was stationed on the street perpendicular to the alley. The key fit perfectly and the car started. Tommy backtracked. Somehow, he had to come up behind them. If they were as inept as they seemed, it would be easy. All he needed was a little bit of luck.

But for a moment, he thought his luck had run out. He cursed softly and whirled the car around a corner. He still couldn't find them on the new street. He turned another corner. Still no green Buick. And he turned another corner. No sign of them. He took a deep breath. Then, as he drove, he suddenly saw the green Buick. *Jesus,* he thought, *they were in McDonald's.* They blew their jobs and a few minutes later they were drinking coffee and eating.

Tommy waited, slouched down low in his seat far enough away from the two men so as not to be noticed. They ate, seeming not to talk much. After several minutes they went out to their car and drove out of the parking lot. Tommy started his clunker and followed them. They turned down Market Street and headed downtown. They were going into rush-hour traffic. Tommy cursed as he was stalled behind a line of cars waiting for the light to change at the bottom of the bridge.

Up ahead, he saw them turn down Front Street. In a few minutes he turned, too. And for a second he thought he had lost them, but then he saw the green Buick in the distance, pulling into a parking lot.

Where were they going? They walked across the street, and suddenly Tommy was going in the opposite direction. He cursed again, trying to find a place to turn, but the traffic flow prevented him from turning back. In a few frantic minutes he turned around and headed back toward them, but they were gone. He pounded the steering wheel in frustration.

Finally, he headed back to the station. Liebowitz would be there to park the clunker, and Tommy would have his Oldsmobile again. But as he turned into the garage he had a strange sensation, as though he had suddenly became conscious of a mirage. He saw one of the men. These guys had to be cops!

Liebowitz came over to his car the moment he recognized the chief. He had learned never to ask questions, and Tommy ventured no explanations. He told Liebowitz to take the car down to the motor pool and tell Med that it worked fine. Liebowitz nodded.

Upstairs, Lucy smiled as he entered, and she could sense that he was preoccupied. He said a few words and walked into his office. Inside, he sat in his desk chair and swiveled it toward the window. He moved closer, as he often did, staring at the moving humanity outside. They were cops. What the hell? Cops tailing him? This thing was taking on more facets than he expected.

Of all the people who would want him tailed, it would have to be Carly. And if Carly wanted it, he couldn't have a dummy like Mickey do the job. So, he had cops do it. Cops. And which cops would he use to do it? The ones that belonged to Chris Laney.

So now the game had changed. He was watching Laney and Laney was watching him. But his guys weren't even good at it. Suddenly he told Lucy to call Bumpy. A few minutes later the burly figure walked into the office, unannounced, as usual. "So, what's up, kid?" he said as he settled into a chair opposite Tommy.

"The guys tailing me are on the job," Tommy said grimly.

"Who are they?"

"I don't know. I'm not even sure if I could pick them out of a lineup."

"Then keep your eyes open. We first have to find out who's the tail…then who's the *padrone*."

"Yeah," said Tommy pausing to think, "but suppose it's Carly, what do I do?"

"Let's see who makes the next move. Hell, they can't tail you forever, right?"

"Yeah," Tommy said, pensively.

"Remember, Tom, we don't know if this is just one of Laney's lame ideas…or Carly trying to put some nails in your coffin. So be dammed fucking careful."

"Yeah, I will, Bump. It's just a puzzle. I don't even know if these guys are all together...or if we're fighting some kind of two front war."

"Yeah...Where's your cannon?"

"It's in my jacket over there," Tommy said, pointing to the .45 automatic in his shoulder harness.

"And where's that little Beretta?"

"I have it here. I've been keeping it in my pocket."

Lucy lay awake thinking. She had agreed to go out with him, but now she wasn't sure why. It was something she never wanted or needed, and yet this man got her to do it.

She shook her head on the pillow. Maybe she should tell him it's a bad idea. Maybe she should tell him...What? That she's loved Tommy for nine years and that she just can't imagine getting involved with someone else? And that chances are that Tommy won't ever take her out to dinner much less get involved romantically with her?

But Mose said he just wanted dinner. He didn't seem like the type to do all this just to get her into bed. He just didn't seem the type. But what was his type? He's so nice to Eddie, and relaxed and comfortable with her. If he wants to take her to his bed, he hasn't really come on to her the way so many other men have in the past.

And what would it be like to be in bed with a nice man? Since Ed left, she had never done it. Maybe there was something wrong with her. Maybe that's why Ed went astray. She could never seem to give him all wanted. Maybe she can't give *any* man the excitement that he wants. She can give love, and warmth, and care, and comfort. But can she give them the thrill they want, what they think her body promises?

Could it be that Tommy McCarrie felt that way, too? Maybe something told him that she didn't have that mysterious essence that would transform all the days of his life. Maybe it was something that they all felt but couldn't articulate. Maybe it was instinctive, as an animal knows what mate is good for it and what is not.

All the times she had been hit on by other men since she and Ed separated, it was done by men she either didn't like, or men she was unsure of... but never by the one man whose love would have made her remaining days on earth a song. So now this stranger comes along... at a time when she had resolved to just take what life had to offer. To be content to grow old alone and watch her grandchildren grow up.

Strange that she was troubled by a man who seemed polished and relaxed, and with no demons to torment him. Where Tommy was gruff and moody, Mose was friendly and easy, and showed no sign of the alcoholism that lurked in Tommy's life like a dark angel that followed every step he took.

Suddenly, it felt good to have the rapt attention of a man, even if he might only want her body. But then maybe he could want her just for what she is? And maybe she should settle for that in life, and not sit by with idle hopes that lightening would strike someday between her and Tommy. Maybe she should take the choice that life has set before her. Maybe Mose wasn't like all the rest. Maybe he'll be just as good as he seems.

———— ✦ ————

"So, how was your day?" Elly said to Tommy who had slouched into his favorite chair. He seemed tired.

"Lousy. I'm not making any headway."

"How much time are you able to spend on it?"

"Not as much as I need."

"Are you still being followed?" she asked.

"Yeah," Tommy said pensively. "You know, El, I think those guys were cops." Tommy suddenly gave up all pretense of keeping her out of it. She was too curious, too engaged. She was irresistible.

"Oh? Did you see him? Who is he?"

"Now take it easy. I just think it's a cop because I think I saw him go into the YPD station."

"But where were you?"

"I was following them. And I got turned around on Commerce Street and they gave me the slip. Then I think I saw one of the guys going into the station. At least he looked like the guy."

"So, what does that mean... if they're cops?"

"It means that somebody is trying to get something on me."

"What do they expect, do you think?"

"I'm not sure. I'm not even sure who's behind it. Maybe the mayor... I'm just not sure."

She was quiet for a moment, then she said, "What are you going to do now?"

"Gonna talk to all the Buick dealers in town to see how many of them sold green ones during the last few years."

"Good. That's what I'd do, too," she said.

"Well, thanks, daughter. You have any other advice?"

"As a matter of fact, I do."

"Yeah?"

"Let me do it."

"How can you do it?"

"Either you come with me, or I'll go alone... I know you're going to be busy this week with the FBI conference."

"So how do you know all this stuff? Who the hell have you been talking to?" said Tommy testily.

"Oh, I just keep a tape recorder in your room, so when you talk in your sleep, I know all about it."

Tommy looked at her, staring at the beautiful, clear, gray eyes. He shook his head slightly and laughed at his daughter's taunts. "I hear you talking over the phone, Dad, to Uncle Bumpy. And you tell me a lot of this yourself," she said, trying to reassure him.

"What makes you think that those dealers will talk with you?"

"You can make me a special investigator...an administrative assistant of sorts."

Tommy looked at her. "You really think you can find this out?"

"I know I can, Dad. I can handle this just fine...maybe without leaving the YPD station."

Tommy didn't respond for several minutes, all the time wrestling with the mental picture of Elly coming to harm after trying to help. "Okay, you can do it — just 'cause you won't bug me anymore. Can you use the computer?"

"Maybe," she said, beaming, knowing that this was only beginning for her. "I'll start tomorrow, okay?"

———◆••◆———

Carly was sitting in his office brooding over the turn his fortunes had taken. He had vanquished all his enemies except one, McCarrie. He had bright political prospects. Some of the people in Columbus were talking to him about running for state auditor or maybe even lieutenant governor. Not bad for a dago kid from Youngstown.

If only his family could believe it. Lisa was on her own, working as a waitress while going to school, suddenly a stranger to him. And his wife. She was still a stranger, as though she couldn't believe he still loved or cared for her. No matter what he tried, he couldn't take away from her that constant doubt, that constant mistrust born of her pain at finding out that he had cheated on her. Even when he thought he had her convinced, even after they made love more passionately than they had ever done, she still had her doubts. She didn't trust him.

And his father…dying slowly, half-conscious all the time, seldom recognizing his children, frightened, child-like, and pathetic.

What a life. Maybe he should chuck it all and just be a business-man. That'd be the easy route. Join the country club, attend the Jay-cee's dinner every year, maybe get appointed to the Board of Spring Common. It would be an easy life: all those administrators sucking up to him, sitting at meetings having tea and crumpets with all those solid citizens.

And wouldn't it be nice not to have to take any shit from every crybaby and hustler in the Valley. Let somebody else deal with all those assholes on the take. What he wouldn't give to just be free, to have the phone ring and not dread answering it.

And who the hell said he could ever be governor or senator? All the WASPs were hurdles in his way. And who's to say that some superstar with red hair and perfect teeth, another Robert Redford, wouldn't sweep all those party hacks off their feet? They really don't go for dagos that much; unless they're convinced, he can win beyond a shadow of a doubt.

And now, without his dad, how was he going to keep all those people in line? Hell, they've been on the take all their lives, why wouldn't they just go to someone else now and see what kind of deal they could make? Judge East could help, but he's getting old, and isn't well. So, who was he going to turn to? Mose? Mose would sell him out in a minute if he thought he could get a better deal. Mose looks for people he can control, people who are on the take. He sure doesn't want someone who won't snap-to every time he wants something done.

And his dad never trusted Mose. Even though Mose was closer to the Mafia, he wasn't one of their best men. Hell, they don't trust him either. And Laney would sell his own mother into white slavery if he thought it could get him somewhere. So now he's all alone, except for Judge East.

Jesus, what a mess. He picked up the phone and called his wife. "Did you hear anything about her?" he said without a greeting.

"No," his wife answered. "What are we going to do?"

"We're going to live our lives, goddamn it. I'm tired of worrying about her."

"Carly, most of this is our fault; you know that."

"Don't give me that," he snapped. "She's had the best of everything...schools, medical care, clothes, travel. What more does she want?"

"She hasn't had the best of us," she said. "We were always fighting; you were..."

He looked at her. "Cheating on you, right?"

"I wasn't going to say that."

"Bullshit."

She didn't answer him, and he regretted talking to her as he did. "I'm sorry, Gin," he said. She nodded acceptance. There would have been a time when he would have said worse and made no apologies, but lately he was changing, thinking things that he had never thought before, and death colored most of those thoughts.

He thought of Lisa, so bitter, so prone to torture him and herself.

She was self-destructive just to spite him, throwing all he was back in his face...to make him pay for hurting her mother, for his temper tantrums, for his cheating, for his swagger, for his style.

God, he used to hold her in his arms when she was a little girl. She used to touch his face and look into his eyes as though she were trying to imagine why this man would love her so. And yet today, the child that used to giggle at the way his beard stubble tickled the palms of her hands has been struck in her own lovely face by the father she had caressed so many times as a baby.

How could a life that seemed so filled with promise as his and Ginny's end up like this, he thought, *like nothing else they ever wanted?* It was more than he could bear, and it wasn't over yet. Soon his father would die, a shadow of his former self, weighing almost a hundred pounds less than he did in his prime. Soon he would go through that ordeal. The father he had so long admired and loved would be gone.

The record room was a musty smelling place. Elly would blow her nose from time to time and study her handkerchief to see dark dust she had expelled from her nostrils. *It would be a miracle if they ever got all this stuff on computers,* she thought. Yet at the computer she was suddenly at home. Let's see...all the green Buicks sold in Mahoning County in the last five years. It didn't take her long to figure out how to retrieve the data. She soon had a list of all the green Buicks sold. She smiled smugly.

On her way out of the deserted room, she walked through a double door and on the other side she was suddenly face-to-face with Danny Bellino.

"Elly? What are you doing down here?" he said, strangely surprised to see her.

"I was tracking down some data for my dad," she said, always nervously when she was in his presence.

"Is he working on…?" Danny stopped for a moment. "I heard he was working on Danny and Neva's case."

"Yes… I'm pretty good at information retrieval, being a librarian."

"Can I help?"

"Uh, no. I'm almost done."

He knew she wasn't. And she knew he didn't believe her.

"Danny… you… I can't get you involved with this. Uh… my father thinks —"

"Elly, I'm going crazy because I don't see anything being done."

She shook her head. "I can't imagine the pain you must feel, Danny. I wish I could, but I agree with Dad. You shouldn't be involved in this."

"Hell, Elly, how could I not be involved? How could I not? It's so easy for all of you to say so, but none…" He turned and walked away.

She had hurt him, and she knew it. As he went away, she was suddenly torn between what she knew her father wanted and what she knew would help Danny in his anguish. She ran after him. When she caught up with him, he turned toward her, seeming so genuine and honest that she felt ashamed for not being truthful with him.

"We're both pretty good at computers. Maybe my dad might not mind that kind of involvement."

He sighed and closed his eyes for a moment. "Thanks, Elly. Thanks a lot."

"Danny, I'm going to be here a while. If you want to help, you can join me."

He nodded. "I'll be back down in a little while."

Elly walked back to the table where she had been working. She had to get the information she had promised her father she could retrieve.

In a short while, she heard someone coming in her direction. When she took her eyes from the computer screen and looked over her shoulder, she saw Danny.

"So, what are we looking for?" he said as he drew a chair near hers.

"Cars."

"Cars? What kind of cars?"

"Buicks...green ones."

"So what do these green Buicks have to do about the case?"

"We don't know..." She looked at him sheepishly. It was obvious that she was going to allow Danny into her part of the investigation. She was still much the schoolgirl in his presence. She shook her head to herself as though frustrated by her lack of control. He was just so... so attractive, so appealing. And she was being naughty by not doing what her father wanted, keeping Danny out of the case that had such ties to his heart. But she also knew that as long as Danny was completely involved in her part of the case, she would also be as honest and open with him as she could be. She was never any good at lying. "My dad's being followed by two men in a green Buick," she said finally.

"Really?" he said. She could sense his wheels turning. As soon as she said the words, Danny began to think like a policeman. "You think it's related to my case?"

"We're not sure. It just might be Carly trying to get him for being off the job...Or it could be someone who's worried about what Dad would find out."

"What has he found out?"

"I don't know. I've just talked him into letting me help him. He didn't want me anywhere near this case." She stopped and looked at Danny. "And he was right, wasn't he? Here I am doing the very thing he didn't want: getting you involved."

"I know what you're thinking, Elly. But it's not you. I would have been involved all along. I just wouldn't let anyone know."

"But now I know," Elly said. "And now I'll..."

"Please, Elly. I have to try to find their killers. I'll never rest a day in my life if I didn't try to help. Hell, no one else except your dad is even looking."

"I hate deceiving my dad, Danny. Especially when he's worried about you."

"Elly, will you do this for me? I know it's against your dad's wishes, and I know he means well for me, but he's only one man, and that's not enough. I have to be involved, understand? I see those kids every night when I close my eyes. Every night."

"Danny..."

"Please, Elly." She closed her eyes, as though trying to banish the sight of him importuning her. "I'll help you do the research, Elly. We'll do the legwork that your dad can't do."

This was all so new to Elly. Her husband had never been one to ask her earnestly for anything. It wasn't David's style. He would use deception and stealth and leverage. He would lie. Now this man with a broken heart was asking to help her, which really meant he was asking for her help.

"Okay, Danny. But you have to trust me, and you have to let me work with my father without trying to change anything. I still don't want to hurt him by being false to him. He means nothing but the best for me... and for you, too."

"I don't want you to be false to the chief, Elly. I just want to do what I can... just if you'll let me help you." Then he looked downward, away from her. "And if you think you can't do it, or you think this compromises your relationship with your dad, you can just tell me and that'll be the end of it... our working together."

"But you'd still work on your own then?"

He looked back up to her and just stared at her face for a few seconds, enthralled by her beauty, the sincerity in her eyes, and by the way she was listening to his pleas. "I can't stop — not until they're caught. Not until I know."

<hr />

She sounded friendly on the phone, Mose thought. Maybe he'd get lucky, in more ways than one. This one was so very different: She was dark and quiet, had lovely eyes, and wonderful tanned skin. She was a combination of worldliness and naivete, laughed quietly but often, was playful but not familiar... always on her guard. Half the time when he talked to her, he felt that she'd heard it all before, a hundred times.

She was a challenge all right. But he needed a spy in McCarrie's office. And he couldn't trust Laney to get a network going. But besides all that, he liked her.

He just had to be careful not to let her know what was on his mind. Somehow, he had to turn her into a mole in McCarrie's office. He had to find out what the old man was up to that would damage his operation. He had to be able to ask her things without her getting suspicious. And the best way to do that was in the afterglow of lovemaking that made it all seem right.

<hr />

"How're you doing, kid?" Bumpy said as he settled down into his favorite chair opposite Tommy. "Pete says you look tired... and Med said you were here till ten o'clock last night."

"How does he know? Why was he here late last night? And screw Pete; he doesn't look so chipper either."

"Just calling 'em as we see 'em."

"You bastards all have walkie-talkies on you? Or better yet, are you always out at Ruby's drinking coffee and chitchatting about how old the boss is looking?"

Bumpy chuckled. "Well, that was interfering with our social life, so we decided to bug your office — someplace in here." He waved his arm around the room. "It's a hell of a lot easier with the bug."

Tommy laughed. He was tired, and the laugh felt good. "This FBI conference is driving me crazy, Bump. Remember when we decided to bid on it three years ago...seemed like the right thing to do at the time?"

"So, what happened?"

"So, the hotel dining room can't handle all the conventioneers at one time. And there aren't enough downtown hotel rooms to handle all the people coming. There might be an employee strike with picket lines...which we can't cross. Little things like that."

"Jesus. Smokey used to make it all look easy...and you're in there now taking up the slack for me."

"Better you should run the YPD like you're doing. Hell, I'd feed the FBI in a tent just to keep you chugging along."

Bumpy nodded in appreciation of the compliment. "Nothing new on the Bellino case. All we're doing is paying a whole squad of dummies to sit around doing paperwork...I'd like to have those bastards doing regular duty. I'd show 'em what real police work is like."

"I haven't done much on the case this week," Tommy said as if to himself. "And yet I never get any good news. This is the biggest goddamned fiasco I can imagine."

"So what's Elly doing around here?"

"She's been driving me crazy wanting to help me on the Bellino case — she didn't know about Danny's tragedy. So I told her to get me a list of the green Buicks that were sold in the Valley during the past five years."

"So they're running down cars through the BMV?"

"Yeah. She knows a lot about information retrieval on computers. Wait a minute. Did you say 'they'? Who's they?"

"Elly and Danny. Who else did you put to work?"

"Not Danny, I didn't. What the hell's he getting involved for? Jesus Christ, doesn't..."

"Tommy?"

"What?"

"I know what you're thinking. And I feel the same. But now that I think of it, maybe it's best to give him *something* to do with the case. Information retrieval sounds okay if it'll keep him out of harm's way."

Tommy was silent for a minute, thinking about what his friend had said. "Bump, if anything ever happens to that kid, I'll never be able to live with myself. And Elly? Jesus."

"I know, I know, Tommy. But hell, at least they're here where we can keep an eye on them...and Danny's not out there breathing heavy and stalking the streets with a .45."

"Not all the information we need is at this station, kid," said Tommy. "What do we do if someone's out there waiting on them to blow their cover?"

"I don't know, Tom. But I do know that Danny's either going to be working with us or on his own, and if you didn't have your mind on Elly's safety, and that kid's troubles, you'd go for this in a minute."

Tommy took a deep breath and settled back in his chair. "Yeah, you're right, Bump. Jesus, I'm acting like a father, huh? And I'm afraid of losing Elly or him…he's already been through so much."

"Yeah," Bumpy muttered.

"When did you last see Elly?"

"I think she's down in the stacks."

"So, where's Danny?" Tommy asked knowingly.

"Where do you think? You know, Tom, Elly's a very attractive girl."

"Don't start with me, Malatesta. You go down there and send them both up to this office pronto. I'm gonna whip some ass."

Bumpy chuckled. "Hell, this is fun, Tommy. We haven't had this kind of stuff going on in ages."

"Don't you have some crooks to catch, Chief?" Tommy said. "And tell your wife I'm still single…and to up your insurance."

Tommy talked to Lucy about the FBI conference after Bumpy left. The two of them alone handled all the arrangements, and she was drawn into it more every day. Finally, Lucy left Tommy alone in his office.

In a few minutes, both Elly and Danny were admitted through the door, looking like two sheepish children. Neither of them sat down until Tommy pointed to the Queen Anne chairs. He was now standing about six feet from them and was not smiling. "So how's the search for the Buick going, Ellen?" he said coldly in the chief's voice.

"Oh, we did a search on —"

"We, huh? When were you going to get around to telling me that you had a partner, El?"

"Oh, Daddy, I wasn't…"

Danny interrupted to speak to Tommy. "It's not her fault, Chief. I was…"

"I was speaking to my daughter, Lieutenant," Tommy said, gruffly.

"I would have told you, Dad," Elly said, almost in tears. "We weren't trying to deceive you."

"You just weren't going to mention a little help from Danny, right?"

She exhaled through her nose softly and closed her eyes, that now had tears in them. "I'm sorry, Daddy."

"Chief, for God's sake, what are you doing? I practically forced her to let me help," Danny said. He stopped for a few seconds, looking at a distraught and defeated Elly. "She felt sorry for me, Chief, and acted out of the goodness of her heart. She doesn't deserve..."

"Don't lecture me on what either one of you deserve, Danny. What you don't deserve is a shot in the back of the head by some torpedo who's going to make a little easy money, somebody who enjoys his work."

Danny took a deep breath. "I was only going to help with information retrieval, Chief. Both of us know computers. I wasn't going out on the street. All I wanted to do was get you as much information as I could. Hell, Chief, you're the only one who's doing enough to need information."

"Tell me, Lieutenant, how do you fit all this into your busy schedule?"

"I don't, Chief. I help out on my off time."

"He's been here all day, Dad," Elly said plaintively. "And he worked last night."

"Now listen to me, you two," Tommy said, suddenly in a more warm and fatherly tone. "You're both going to help me. But no investigating on your own, no freelancing out on the streets...and no more secrets, understand?"

Neither of them answered. "Understand?" Tommy said more forcefully. They both nodded.

"Now what about those Buicks?" Tommy said, watching the two of them suddenly brighten like small children who had been spanked and then forgiven.

"We have a list over the last five years, Dad."

"Twenty-eight green Buicks in the Valley," Danny said as Elly handed Tommy a printout sheet.

Tommy scanned the names of the owners of the sheet. None of them rang a bell. "Did you make a copy of this?" he asked. Elly looked at Danny and smiled slightly. They were computer jocks who suddenly spoke a new language that police chiefs weren't used to.

"We not only have copies, but we have it on disk," Danny said.

Tommy caught their bemused smugness. "Don't get smart, you two," he growled. They finally laughed aloud, releasing the tension that they had felt since being summoned upstairs to Tommy's office.

"Anything, Chief?" Danny said.

"Hell, not that I can notice, Danny. All these dago names must mean that you guys like green Buicks."

Danny smiled. "Sometimes, if we can get more data, you can do a cross check and find out some amazing coincidences…and Elly's a master at pulling that stuff together."

"She is, huh? Just tell her to watch her step around the old man," Tommy said, smirking.

Elly beamed in the admiration of the two men. "Okay," Tommy said, dismissing them. "Let me think about this a little more. By the way, see if you can find out the owners of these companies that bought cars. Also, Elly, I'm going to send you up to Spring Common. I want to know something about Danny and Neva."

Mentioning the two names seemed to displace the banter that existed between the three of them. It was a sound that invoked reality, and the main reason for their mission.

"Can I help, Chief?" Danny said reflexively.

"Later. You're the inside man, remember?"

He nodded.

<hr />

"Chris, do you have any more?" Lisa said as she began to undress. She had just snorted some cocaine that Laney had set out for her. She, in turn, would put it on her nipples and he would snort it from her breasts.

Laney stared at her for a few seconds. "Later," he said. "Come here."

By the time he spoke, she had taken off her blouse and skirt, her panty hose and her shoes. All she wore was a pair of bikini panties.

She came into his arms, smiling as he lowered his mouth to her nipples. She loved the feeling she had when he was overcome with lust for her. They made love as they always did, forcefully, violently, building to a crashing climax.

She could do that to him. She had discovered that she had that magic, the gift of face and body, the attitude of defiance, the careless rejection of authority, that made men crazy for her. Not all women had it. Her mother didn't have it. She wriggled her hips slightly beneath his body, and wrinkled her nose in pleasure as she felt him respond. It would be like this all the time if only they could be married. *No one knows what we have in the bedroom*, she thought. *It's special.*

She slowly pushed herself out from under Laney, who was sleeping, breathing deeply. She studied him as he slept. He was so different from her father. Her father was a volatile Italian, domineering and violent. Chris was cool, yet exciting. He didn't have to play the macho man; he knew he was handsome and fine-skinned and hung. Chris was at ease with his sexuality. He wasn't serious all the time, the way her dad was. Chris liked to have fun. He was just beautiful.

She wanted to marry him. She wanted him to be with her when she was seen around Youngstown. She wanted to wake up beside him every morning, and to feel the warmth of him next to her at night.

"What are you doing?" he said to her suddenly, surprising her.

"Nothing. Just looking at you."

"Come here," he said, reaching out his hand to her. She went willingly, as he pulled her around so that he lay on top of her. "You want to go again?" she said breathlessly.

"No. Christ, give me a few minutes to get my strength back," he said, nuzzling her neck.

"It's been almost an hour," she pleaded.

"We did it twice then," he said, biting one of her nipples. She squealed, pushing him away.

"Chris?"

He knew, when she called his name that way, that she had something serious on her mind, something he probably wouldn't want to talk about. "What?"

"Let's get married."

"Lisa," he drawled, "we've been over all this. You're too young for me and you're the mayor's daughter."

"That shouldn't mean a thing to you, Chris."

"How can you say that? My ass would be bounced out of the force so fast."

"How could you be bounced? I'm twenty years old. You wouldn't be charged with statutory rape."

"Your father would get me. He doesn't trust me to begin with."

"He made you head of that squad."

"He did that because he had to."

"What do you mean?" she said, surprised at his answer.

"Nothing. I was one of the few who wasn't in McCarrie's pocket."

"And for that you got picked?"

"Yeah. For that."

"I want us to be married, Chris. I can't stand sneaking around like this."

"We don't sneak around, goddammit. All we do is act careful."

"All we do is sneak. You never take me anywhere public. We never do anything except come back here and snort and fuck."

"There are worse things you can do," he said.

"I'm serious, Chris. If we can't get married, then I don't want to see you anymore."

"Lisa, we have a good time; we're good for each other. Why should we screw it up?"

"Because I can't go on like this, that's why. I'm sick of what we have to do to keep us a secret. I'm sick of my father. I don't give a damn what all those people out there think. I want us to worry about ourselves... no one else."

"Why should you and I fight when we can be so happy? Let's just wait and see what happens. If we get caught, then we'll deal with it."

"Caught? You mean like 'robbing a bank' caught? God, Chris, what a way to say it."

"No. Not like that. Found out, goddammit, discovered. I didn't say that what we're doing is disgusting or shameful. But it sure as hell is bad politics... and not too good for my career."

"So is that what we're all about? Politics and your career?"

"No, for Christ's sake, Lisa! Listen to me. We take what comes...

only we don't push things into people's faces."

"I don't know. I'm not sure I can do this anymore."

"You have to get your own apartment."

"Why?"

"Because your roommate's always at the other one, that's why."

"But we can meet here."

"But if we always meet here, then someone's bound to find out."

"I told you: I don't care if anyone finds out."

"So now you want marriage, something I already tried once. You want us to join the Rotary Club and play partners golf on Sunday? And visit your dad with the grandkids? Give me a fucking break."

She was hurt more than she was shocked. And she was angry at him for not having any of the dreams her ideal man was supposed to have. "You bastard," she hissed. "You never meant one word you told me. All you ever wanted was fuck the mayor's daughter."

"I never promised you marriage. All I promised was a good time... and I delivered on my promise."

"You delivered nothing, you bastard!" she screamed. "And you're going to be sorry, you lying piece of shit!"

This time he was up on his feet, and he lunged at her, grabbing her mouth in his hand and squeezing her cheeks together. "What did you say?" He shook her head with his hand. "Don't fuck with me, lady. I don't like someone screwing around with my future. And remember, I didn't force you into my bed."

She was frightened now because he still hadn't released her. As he squeezed her mouth there were tears in her eyes. She couldn't believe he was so unfeeling, so unaware of what he meant to her.

For a few seconds, they stared at each other. She could feel his breath upon her face, could see the coldness in his eyes. Finally, he released her and backed away, pointing a finger at her from his out-stretched arm. "I'm warning you, Lisa. Just watch what you say...because I'm not gonna let you or anybody else fuck up my life. Understand?"

She was shocked at the violence of his response. "You son of a bitch," she said, brushing past him. "I'm getting out of here." She grabbed her clothes that were strewn in a path leading toward the bed, and went into the bathroom, slamming the door behind her.

Laney stood, as though in shock, wondering what he was going to do now with this spoiled, volatile little bitch, twenty years younger than he, who relished being a pouty, spoiled child with a woman's body and an animalistic attitude toward sex.

She stormed out of the bathroom, still gathering some of her things. "I'll come and get my other stuff when you're gone."

"Lisa, don't do this."

"What are you going to do, Chris? Hit me like my dad did? You're no different than he is. I'm a fool for thinking you were."

"Lisa, let's not spoil this just because you're mad. It's not you. I'm just not ready to get married to anyone."

"Then all you need is a whore who'll give you a suck and a fuck on call."

———

Tommy was going over the list of green Buick owners. Pete came into his office and sat down opposite his boss. "Here's a list of all the green Buicks sold in the Valley in the last five years," Tommy said. "Any of those names mean anything? Any kind of bell?"

Pete scanned the list for several minutes, then finally looked up at Tommy. "Pick out just one name, Pete," the chief said, studying his friend, waiting for him to pick out the name Tommy had settled on.

"Pagliaro," Pete said, handing the list back to Tommy.

"Yeah," said Tommy, nodding in agreement. The few people whose instincts he trusted all said the same name. "So why does this name jump off this sheet at us, huh?"

"We could all be flat wrong," Pete said. He was a younger version of Smokey, careful, prudent, always on his guard, always on Tommy's side, ever since their days in college when he was a freshman and they were juniors.

"Right. That's why we're gonna be real quiet about this thing."

"Tommy, if he's involved in tailing you, then he's dangerous. You have to be careful."

"I will, Pete. I think I'm gonna see if we can get Danny and Elly to find out more about this guy. How is it that his name has been men-tioned so much recently…when none of us have ever heard of him before…and we know everybody?"

"The only one I've seen is named Nick. Remember? He was at Danny's kid's funeral?"

"Yeah, a small guy, dressed to the teeth."

"He's a lawyer, I think. His brother's named Ambrose, but he goes by Mose."

"Maybe Bumpy or the Bellanca brothers would know," Pete mused. "You playing poker this Friday? Ask Rino or Lou."

"I'll check Friday. You playing?"

"I don't think so. May's mother's coming into town. I'll be busy."

———————

That Friday night at the Tre-Sette, Agee Mancuso's bar on the East Side, Tommy arrived a little early. He and Agee were old friends who had known each other since they were in grade school. Tommy was devouring on of Agee's famous steak sandwiches and listening while the normally laconic owner talked.

"How're you doing, Tommy?"

"I'm okay, Ag. How about you? How's your wife feeling?"

"The doctor said that she's gonna be okay. After the surgery and chemo, they think they got it all."

Tommy nodded. "That's good to hear, kid."

"So how come you're here so early... not just to eat one of my sandwiches, right?"

"I was hoping to see Rino or Lou before we started. I'd like to talk to them."

Agee chuckled. "Tell 'em you're gonna throw them in jail. I'd like to see their faces when you show them the cuffs."

"Hell, after all they win from me in poker, I'd like to see them in jail myself." Tommy chuckled, enjoying the image of the two brothers in a cell.

Shortly, Rino and his brother walked in the door, talking to a few patrons at the bar as they made their way back toward Tommy, whom they had seen after a nod from Agee that the chief was there.

"How're you doing, Chief?" Rino said as he sat in Tommy's booth, moving in so Lou could sit down also. "Tommy," said Lou.

"Hi, guys. How's it going?"

"Not bad, kid," said Lou, glancing at Rino who had also sensed that Tommy had other business to talk to them about. "So, what's up, Tommy?"

"I need a little information," said Tommy.

"So ask, kid," said Rino.

"What do you guys know about the Pagliaro brothers?"

They glanced quickly at each other. "Not a hell of a lot," said Lou. "They're not Youngstowners; they moved into town about fifteen-twenty years ago. They used to be hooked up with Jack Mannaseri before he died. Then they went out on their own. They buy property and own apartment buildings. The older brother's named Mose and I think he runs the outfit. The younger brother's Nick, a lawyer. I think he had something to do with the Mahoning Valley Sanitary District, and you know the reputation that has."

Lou glanced at Rino and hesitated. "Go ahead. Say it," Rino chided.

"Okay," said Lou to himself as if to unleash his hesitation. "We think they're wired. We've always thought so."

Tommy was suddenly very interested. "How do you guys know so much about them? No one else seems to have ever heard of them?"

"They lie low," said Rino. "But they're some kind of distant relative to our late brother-in-law, Danny's dad. We've seen Mose a few times; he's real quiet. Nick does the weddings and funerals. He likes to let people know that he's a lawyer."

"Who're they close to? Pittsburgh or Cleveland?"

"Why can't it be both?" Rino said.

"That's living too dangerously," said Tommy.

"It's both, Tommy," said Lou. "Mose is good at covering his tracks. Word has always been that he could handle them both. And he sure as hell looks like he does okay."

"How does he operate? Out of where?"

"At some little place on the South Side. I forget their company name, but it's near Indianola, by the old dairy."

Tommy thanked his old friends for all the information they had given him. He was going to have to smoke the Pagliaros out.

As they were starting to head into the back room to play poker, Rino put a hand on Tommy's shoulder to speak softly to him. "I don't think Danny knows much about the Pagliaros. If he did, he wouldn't like them."

"What're you doing up so early and all dolled up?" Tommy said to his daughter as she walked into the kitchen.

"Job interview," she said as she drank the coffee Tommy had poured for her.

"Job interview? Where?" Tommy said, trying to keep the anxiety out of his voice.

"A library. Where else?"

"What library?" he said, showing even more concern.

"I don't know. They didn't say," she said as she stood against the counter across the room.

"Do they interview on Saturdays now? And what if it's far away? And in a bad area?"

"Don't try to conceal your disapproval, Daddy. You really should give vent to your feelings more," she said, smiling.

"This isn't funny, daughter. What's the big hurry for the job?"

"It's only a part-time job, Dad…twenty hours."

"But what if you can't do it? I mean…here you're taking care of the house and the kids. And me…how are you gonna help me now?"

"Help you? I thought I was supposed to be on piecework, not on full-time duty? I didn't know we were a team."

"Haven't I been letting you help me?"

"'Letting me help' isn't exactly job security, Dad."

"But it can't be for the money! You have plenty now that you never use. I know."

"That's your money," she said, calmly.

"Don't start with me, Ellen. I've settled that with you."

"What about helping you? We haven't settled that."

"Look, kid. Whenever I need help, I ask...I can't do the case twenty-four hours a day, and sometimes I just don't know where to turn, or how you can help."

She nodded in acceptance of his point. "Even if I get the job, which I'm not sure of, I'll still have plenty of time to do things for you."

"Not if you're at some damned library when I need you," he growled.

"So all of a sudden I'm indispensable, right? And the mighty Tommy the Quarterback can't handle an investigation without his daughter around to help?" she said sardonically.

Tommy laughed softly. He had never been called that name by a member of his family. "Watch your tongue, daughter. And learn more respect for your elders."

"You bring out the worst in me sometimes," she said, still smiling. Then, looking at the clock, she said, "Oh, I'm late. Here I am arguing with an old crank, and I might end up being late for my first job interview. Wish me luck?"

He nodded, a slight smirk on his lips. Then he gave her a hug, and she left.

———◆———

Elly had read Kaye Bellino's transcript over and over before making her first visit to Spring Common. In the library, she searched the computer for the names of all the professors Kaye had had while she was a graduate student. Tommy had told Elly to look for someone early middle aged, charismatic, and attractive to women.

As she searched, she found out that two of the men had retired and were elderly. Another had died. One had gone on to teach at another college. She decided to go to the department where the remaining male resided.

She approached the secretary to ask her if the professors were in. Most were either in their offices or teaching class. She introduced herself as a special investigative researcher for the Youngstown Police. "I've heard you were coming," said the woman coolly.

"Are you going to be taking a break any time soon?" Elly said. "I'd like to talk to you."

"I can take one in a few minutes," she said pleasantly, responding to Elly's courteous tone. "Why don't you wait for me over there," she said, pointing to a chair.

Elly felt a rush. She tingled with excitement. Here she was, actually investigating a case. She was being trusted by the chief of police to find out information that might be hidden in the obscure precincts of a large bureaucratic university.

"Okay, we can go now," the secretary said, urging Elly toward the cafeteria where they could talk over coffee.

"Would you look at the names of these professors," Elly said, handing her the list. "Do you recognize any of them?"

"All of them. There are two that were only here a short time — one or two years — then they left."

"I'd like you to tell me a little about each one. Just what you really thought of them."

The secretary suddenly looked skeptical and a bit apprehensive. "I don't understand," she said.

"I'm trying to find out a little about them ... but this is just between you and me. No one around here will know anything of what we're talking about." The woman seemed convinced, but still hesitant. Finally, Elly said, "For example, were any of them nice looking?"

She laughed softly. "Not many. You don't know much about college professors, do you?"

"Just from my own school experience," Elly said. "But why don't we start with that. As I go through the list, would you tell me who most women around here think is handsome, or alluring, or appealing?" She nodded. "How about him?" Elly said, pointing to the first name, trying to get the secretary involved before she had time to hesitate.

The secretary shook her head. "He's an old man," she said.

"Him?" Elly continued.

"Uh, he's ... well ... he's ... " She shook her head. "I'm not sure."

"He's homosexual?" said Elly. The secretary nodded, relieved.

They went on, one-by-one, examining, through the eyes of the secretary, all the professors who had taught Kaye Bellino. None of them seemed to be the type to lure an attractive woman like Kaye from a good marriage with Danny.

Later that night, Elly and her father sat in the living room alone, drinking tea. "None?" said Tommy.

"It didn't seem like it, Dad, unless one of them is secretly irresistible."

"In other words, we'd have to go out of our way to imagine one of these guys sweeping anybody off their feet, right?"

"Right ... even the ones who have gone on to other schools."

Tommy was quiet for a few minutes, sipping his tea and looking thoughtful. Elly studied him expectantly as Tommy stared into nothingness while in his mind roiling the ideas over into a coherent statement. "So..."

"So, what?" Elly said.

"So, she could have lied to Danny," said Tommy aloud to himself. "But why? If not a professor, who?"

"You mean she could have been lying to Danny about some phantom professor? Just to keep him from suspecting the real one?"

"She had Danny completely convinced that she had never slept with this guy."

"Did Danny really believe that?"

"You know Danny," Tommy said. "Is he the kind of guy who would not believe the woman that he loved when she tells him, looking right into his eyes, that she never was unfaithful to him?"

Elly was suddenly shaken by the intrusion of Danny into the conversation. It had all been such a clinical discussion until he was brought into it, until the appreciation of his virtues made the whole thing something personal. Would a man like Danny not believe his wife? No. She knew. He was too trusting, too unwilling to believe in love being returned with betrayal.

Suddenly, Elly was quiet. This time it was she who stared into space trying to understand her own thoughts. "Elly?" Tommy said.

"But maybe she was lying?" Elly responded. "I mean about having an affair at all. Maybe she was just telling Danny that?"

Tommy sighed. "I think Kaye Bellino was a suicide, El. There was just enough doubt about it for me to convince the coroner that he should rule it accidental...for Danny's sake. Even Med Williams thought she did it deliberately."

"My God," Elly said under her breath. "Does Danny know it was a suicide?"

"No," Tommy muttered, looking away. "He doesn't have to know."

"But what if it comes out as part of this investigation?"

"Then it comes out. But we shouldn't be the ones to tell him...
And there was some doubt about it, remember?"

She nodded her head to affirm reality. "God, Dad, what must it
have been like for him to be hurt so much by Kaye and then lose his
son...and then her?"

Tommy shook his head. "He wanted to believe her, El."

Both of them sat quietly with their own thoughts for several minutes. Then Elly asked the question Tommy dreaded hearing even
though he knew he would have to answer it for himself. "So, what do
we do now?" said Elly.

Tommy looked at her for a moment. "What do you think?"

She took a deep breath and closed her eyes. "I think I don't like
this investigating business."

"We have to know if she was carrying on with someone else," said
Tommy.

More silence between them. Tommy, despite his circumspection, had
become personally involved in this case, more so than any other in his
career. Neva, Danny, Kaye Bellino. This case showed that he was vulnerable to fears of fading abilities, and blunted instincts, and lost insights.
All he saw were pieces. All he longed for was a vision of the whole.

"Dad?"

"What?"

"Can I talk to Danny about his wife?"

"I don't know."

"Either you have to do it, or I do. And maybe this time it should
be with a friend rather than with a boss?"

Tommy nodded. "Yeah...maybe."

Once again, there were many eyes on the big black Oldsmobile as it came slowly down the narrow street. Tommy drove close to the house and parked, and then got out quickly, looked around, sensing eyes watching him, and walked up on the porch. He rang the bell, and could hear noise within the house, a human voice calling as he waited. Finally, the door opened, and a grizzled, white-haired, white-bearded Black man stared out from a crooked stance.

"How're you doing, Coach?" Tommy said.

"Tommy? Land sakes, come on in here!" The old man stepped aside, pointing with his cane to the hallway where he wanted Tommy to go. "It's good to see you, son," said the old man.

"Good to see you, too, Laz. How've you been feeling?"

"I'm okay, Tommy. Ruby takes good care of me. Don't tell her I said that."

"Ruby's a saint to take care of a cantankerous old goat like you."

"Yeah, she's a good girl, Tom."

They sat down in facing chairs in the little den where Lazarus spent most of his day. Football trophies and pennants and pictures and books lined the walls. His cane leaned across the back of the table in front of them. Laz studied his protégé and knew instinctively that the younger man had not come merely on a social visit. "So, what's up, Chief of Police?" he said to Tommy softly.

"I need some info, Laz."

Lazarus brightened, and his heart beat faster. He needed this to make his day. "If I can get it, you know it's yours. What's this all about, kid?"

"I've been working on the Bellino case for a couple of months... quietly."

"I know."

Tommy chuckled, shaking his head. "Is there anything about me you don't know?"

"Not much. When are you gonna wise up and marry that secretary?"

"Jesus Christ, Laz," Tommy said, never ceasing to be astounded by how much gossip the old man knew.

"Okay, okay, let's get on with it. Tell me what you want," Laz said eagerly.

"I want to know about two brothers named Pagliaro." Tommy handed him a note with the two names on it.

"These guys in the mob?"

"Could be. They just keep to themselves and cover their tracks real well."

"You think these two guys are tied to the Bellino case?"

"I don't know, Laz. Maybe, maybe not…but something else. I've been tailed lately by a couple of bruisers in a green Buick. So, we ran a check on all the locals who bought green Buicks in the last five years. That name was on the list."

"So why'd you pick this name out?" Laz was relishing his role in the discussion.

"I don't know. But in the last year or so I hear this name, Pagliaro, several times…somebody I don't know, somebody who has money, and somebody whose brother went to young Danny's funeral. Then, when I show the list, cold, to Pete and to Bumpy, guess what name they pick out? Of all the dago names they see on the list?"

"And you don't know if it's just Carly's out to get you, or if it's something to do with the Bellino case, or both?"

"I'll tell you, Laz, I've been thinking this through for weeks. I just can't see a connection. But then maybe I've lost my vision. I haven't been a cop for a long time. Maybe my instincts are gone."

"Don't do this, Tommy. I know you. They ain't gone. They're just a little rusty. Remember one thing: if you don't crack this case, no one will. All them other bastards want is enough time to pass so's everyone'll forget."

"Thanks, Laz," said Tommy. "Will you let me know if you find out something?"

"I sure will, Chief," said Laz, suddenly enlivened by his assignment by the chief of police.

"You be careful, huh, Laz?"

"Sure, kid, you know what I always told you. Always watch your back. Well, I do too."

<hr />

It was quiet in the stacks of the YPD. Elly had been there a little more than an hour trying to find more information for her father. Suddenly she heard a door open and steps coming into the room. It was Danny. She had gotten to know the cadence of his steps, the sound of his entrance into the room.

"Hi," he said simply as he sat down in a chair he drew near to her. He hardly looked at her, looking instead at the screen she was studying. "What're you up to?"

"How did you know I was down here?" she said.

He stopped for a moment, not answering her, then he said, "I didn't. If you want to work by yourself, I —"

"I didn't mean it like that," she said softly, looking at him as he avoided her gaze.

"Why do we have to go through this all the time, El?" he said plaintively, as he turned toward her. "Why do you make me feel like I'm trying to con you out of the family jewels?"

She lowered her gaze into her lap. "Danny, if this were anything other than 'the Bellino case,' do you think I'd be so torn by what we do here?"

His expression showed that he didn't understand what she had said. She continued again. "Do you think this would be any problem if there weren't a chance that you'd get hurt?"

"I can get hurt any day, Elly. I'm a cop."

"But you're different, Danny; don't you see that? You're a cop who has lost a wife and a son and a daughter-in-law. And you're someone that my dad cares about very much."

"Elly, look...I can't just let this go. Every moment of my experience, my education, has trained me to solve these kinds of cases. And, Elly, those were my kids." His voice was rising. "And I can't stand it unless I do something."

There was silence for several seconds, then Danny said, "Could you go for a cup of coffee? Away from here?"

She nodded. "Where?"

"At the little diner on Wick Avenue, near the college. It's nice and quiet this time of day."

"All right," she said, turning off the computer.

"I'll drive, okay?"

"Maybe we should both drive. I'm not coming back here tonight," Elly responded.

At the diner, when they ordered coffee and hamburgers, Danny drummed the tabletop with his fingers for a few seconds. Elly was feeling awkward and nervous. She still couldn't get over the feeling that she had in his presence. He always made her flush, made her pulse quicken, made her eyes and hands move restlessly.

"Elly, I'm sorry about pressuring you. I know it puts you in a spot... and I sure don't want to come between you and your dad."

"I'm sorry too, Danny. I can't imagine all that you've been through. And then when all you ask is to be involved, to help out, I make it hard."

They sat for a few moments, sipping coffee and talking to the waitress. Then when the waitress went away, they began to eat their food in awkward silence. Suddenly, Elly stopped and looked at him. "Danny, I know you had some troubled times during your marriage..." Danny looked back at her, surprised at the change in their conversation.

"How do you know about that?"

"I know it because it might have something to do with your case."

"Jesus Christ," he muttered. "What could it possibly have to do with the deaths of those two kids? How in the hell can you say that?"

"I wasn't the first to say it, Danny. And it doesn't have to be true. But it could be that..."

"That what, Elly? Finish."

"No."

"Damn you, Elly. You can't do this. Finish what you started."

"I can't. We shouldn't have come here, Danny." She got up and gathered her bookbag and her coat. He grabbed her forearm just enough to make her feel his restraining force.

"I'm sorry, Elly. Don't go," he said softly.

She looked down at him. Their eyes met for several seconds, each trying to read the other's face. How strange it all seemed. Here she was, arguing with a man she hardly knew except in tinted, girlhood memories. Yet in the times she had been with him recently, she felt more alive than she ever had been with David. And in those moments, his anguish, his frustration, and his disappointment had touched her heart more, without any contrivance, than ever David had done in all the years of their marriage. Not once did her husband's words or feelings touch her heart. Never. Yet this man could reach far into her soul. And then they communicate. They argue. They feel.

"Please, Elly."

She sat down, and quickly glanced out into the diner. To the customers, they were a couple having a romantic spat, so almost all of them quickly lost interest.

"Don't go like this," he said.

"I don't want to hurt you, Danny. Yet every move I make seems to cut at you. I hate this. I never should have gotten involved in this case."

"You're the only person I get upset with," he said. "And all you're trying to do is help."

His hand was still resting on her arm until he and she both became conscious of it. Slowly he released his grip. After a few seconds, she said, "Danny? We can only work together if we're completely honest; I know that. And if my dad can't let that happen, then I don't want to do this anymore."

He nodded. "Thanks, Elly. But you don't have to do this. I guess…" He stammered. "I guess your dad's right. All I do is ladle emotion in where science and deduction alone should count."

She sighed. "Can you do this without emotion, Danny?"

He shook his head. "I don't think so."

"I have to ask you something," she said.

He seemed surprised. "What about?"

"About the case…about you."

"Are you doing this for your father?"

"We talked about it, and he agreed to let me try, if I could."

"What do you want to know?"

"Well, what I...Please don't get mad..."

"Elly, for God's sake, what is it?"

She took a deep breath. "Could Kaye have been not telling you the truth about having an affair with a professor?"

He sat back in his chair and pushed himself away from the table, looking at her all the while. He stared at her for a few seconds, studying her face. He could see tears welling in her eyes as she waited for him to speak.

This was all so strange. All the years he had been married to Kaye, he never experienced what he did now with this slender, beautiful girl with gray eyes, crying because she thinks she hurt him. This girl had some kind of tether against his heart.

"What part?" he sighed. "About the affair or the professor?"

"Either," said Elly.

He broke his gaze and looked out the window as he thought. "Yeah, I suppose she could have, Elly."

"Well, if she —"

"Lied?" he interjected.

"Could it have been someone else? Someone not a professor? Maybe another student?"

"What makes you think that?" he said, now more interested in her reasoning than he was with his own anguish.

She waited a few seconds before answering. "I've seen her course transcript. There just wasn't any professor she could have been involved with. Some were older, some were gay, most were married, several were women...and none of them had ever been known to have affairs, especially with students. We can't be sure, Danny, but it could well be that she never had an affair with a professor...if she ever had an affair at all."

"You think she might not have had an affair? Is that right?"

"I just don't know, Danny."

He looked out the window again and was quiet for a long time. Then he nodded slightly, affirming his reasoning with himself. He turned back to her. "All that time after it happened, I believed her. She had never gone to bed with him; it was just candlelight and wine and poetry. I made myself believe her because I was afraid of being so hurt that I'd start hating her for what she did to me."

Spontaneously she reached for his hand and touched it, simply laying her hand over his. "I'm so sorry, Danny. I wish I were never part of this — of hurting you."

He stared down at her hand without looking up. He wrestled with the two sensations he felt: first, the pain of admitting to himself — and to someone else — that Kaye had been unfaithful; second, the strange feeling that had been lost on him since he was little boy, the sense of compassion he once felt from his mother and his grandmother and his aunts when he was pained by the outside world, the sense of compassion he now felt from Elly, and never felt from Kaye.

Finally, he looked up at her and nodded. In the few seconds that their eyes met, they communicated something that neither one of them understood, but that went from her heart to his and from his to hers. "We'd better go," she said, and they both stood up as Danny laid money on the table for the uneaten hamburgers and half-drunk coffee.

Outside, they walked in silence until they came to her car. "Don't quit on this case, Elly. Your dad needs your help."

She was surprised at his blessing for her involvement. "Can you work on this case, Danny?" He was shaking his head as she asked the question. "...If we both need your help? No secrets, no lies?"

He looked at her face. "Do you want me to?"

"Yes."

"What about your dad?"

"I'll talk to him. I'm sure he'll feel as I do."

————— ❖ —————

Lucy was tired. The strain of getting the FBI conference organized burdened her days and left her exhausted at night. But it was more than work that tired her. It was the strange turn her life had taken. She was being drawn into a relationship with Mose, and she didn't know how to cope with it. Sooner or later Mose would expect her to go to bed with him. It was only natural, she knew.

But she also knew that look of disappointment, slow in coming, but inevitable, when she would be unable to give of herself the life, the vitality, the joy of being with him, that only comes from love. She felt it all closing in on her. Soon Mose would be less a gentleman and more a man. It could not go on this way.

But what would she say? She hated seeming to be a tease, using him just to have some interesting companionship. She knew instinctively she would not love him. He was too tailored, too manicured, too scripted, too rich. No matter how hard she tried, she couldn't talk herself into it. But she also knew there was something about him that was pleasing, and warm...something fascinating and mysterious. So why not go to bed with him? Why not try, and see what happens? Maybe Mose would give her one night that brought her more than excitement...maybe warmth, or even passion. She longed for that touch in the afterglow, the soft whisper that stirred her heart, that night that held no secrets, that night that made her know what God always meant by love.

But will the night ever come? Will she ever find a man who would return the love she so willingly gave and so desperately wanted? Will she ever find that soul that would so bond with hers so that all days were lonely until she was with him again, until she heard his voice, until she touched him? God, will she ever find anyone but Tommy?

It was Friday, and the weather was warm and inviting. Tommy was going through the reports of the chiefs of divisions, sitting quietly in his office. He wanted a drink. It had been a while since he had tied one on, and he missed it. But anymore there were few places he could go to enjoy a good drink. He was always in the wrong place at the wrong time: home, with Elly and the kids, in his office, with Lucy outside to see him if he got sloshed, at the Tre-Sette with Agee and the guys from the East Side to watch him. Only at the Silver Bridge could he drink alone.

Just then the door opened, and Lucy walked in. She seemed strangely uneasy as she approached his desk. He watched her come toward him and for a few seconds lost his train of thought. He had gotten to know the smell of her, that strange bouquet that he never experienced with any other woman. The sight of her brightened his experience; the sound of her made the day have music; the unexpected touch of her made the rest of the day glow with her remembrance.

"Chief..." She seemed to hesitate. "You think I could take the rest of the afternoon off? I have all the work done and..."

"Why do you have to ask? Take it. You deserve it."

"Well, I wouldn't, but I have to be at a restaurant early. We're going to see *La Traviata*. I've never been to an opera."

"Does Eddie like that stuff?" he said, curious now about who she was going with.

"Oh, no, he'd sooner die than go. I'm going with a friend."

"Go ahead. I told you, you don't have to ask. Just let me know if you liked it."

"Thank you, Chief," she said, turning to walk away. Then she said back over her shoulder toward him. "Have a nice weekend. I'll see you Monday morning."

Tommy was disturbed by the thought of her leaving, but more disturbed by the thought that maybe she would go out with someone other than her son. Jesus, what if she's going out with another guy? In his consternation, he did something he never did. He said, "An opera, huh? Must be a heavy date."

She was startled by his comment. There seemed to be no humor in what he said; it was almost a note of disapproval. "Just a date," she said, unsmiling and hurt.

After she left, Tommy tried to concentrate and couldn't. Finally, he closed the reports and put them away. He called down to Liebowitz to tell him he was coming. Then he went to get his coat from the closet. But before he did, he stopped, went to the cupboard and poured two fingers of bourbon and downed it quickly.

He got home just in time for supper. Throughout supper he said very little, but instead listened to the children talk about school and sports and social life. Elly at first sensed a strangeness about her father, but didn't say anything while they ate. After the children cleared the table and brought coffee to their mother and grandfather, Elly realized what part of the strangeness was. With all the odors of food and cooking and the combination of pop and coffee smells there was another, something she seldom sensed, the smell of whiskey.

"So, how was your day today?" she said after the children left the room.

"Okay," he said, "how was yours?"

"You seemed quiet all through supper."

Here we go again, he thought. He could sense her curiosity. He knew she wouldn't give up until she found out what was going on. And yet he himself didn't know what was going on. He was remorseful about drinking. All the resolve he had about quitting had been given up without a moment of hesitation. How little mettle he had. How little. How strange it felt to know that Lucy was seeing another man. *Face it, McCarrie,* he thought, *there's only one reason why this long day seemed so dark.* "I have a lot of things on my mind," he said.

She thought about what he said. What was on his mind that could foster this melancholy? He was never like this when the YPD presented him problems. He wasn't like this when Carly was threatening him. What could make him so morose and unlike himself? Her instincts were unerring...because she was his daughter and because she knew him. Suddenly, she had an inspiration, and she acted on it in the chance she could be right. "So, how's Lucy doing?"

It took a second to know that her question found its mark. He was startled, and his expression and his body posture changed. "Lucy? Okay, I guess. She's been awfully busy on this FBI conference."

"But other than work, how is she?"

He was becoming irritated at her questions and his tone showed it. "How should I know? I told you. I don't meddle in the private life of my secretary," he said sharply.

"It's not just 'your secretary,' Daddy, it's Lucy."

"I don't know, Ellen. Please. Let it rest."

She paused for a moment to drink her coffee which was getting cold. Then she went to the coffee pot to refresh both cups.

"Dad, have you ever taken her to dinner?" she said finally.

"No, of course not."

"Why not? Bosses often take their secretaries out."

"I don't know. She isn't..."

"Just a secretary?"

"Don't start with me, Ellen," he said, standing up to take his coffee to the sink and wanting to fly from the insistent truths that his daughter was telling, or worse, getting him to tell her.

"Daddy, ask her out. It's not some form of assault to take her out to dinner."

"I told you, I'm not in her league, El. She should go out with brain surgeons and heads of big law firms, guys with money and class."

"She'd say yes in a minute, Dad," Elly said, ignoring her father's rationalizations.

"Yeah, well, she said yes to someone else tonight."

"What do you mean?"

"She's going out with some guy."

"And you just let her go?"

"I can't 'let' her do anything except take a few..." He stopped suddenly, staring across the room and looking strange, as though confronting a new vision of life he had never seen. Elly caught it too.

"A few days or hours? Is that it? You gave her some time off early today?"

He didn't answer. Then he said, "She's going to the opera."

"With who?" Her voice was louder than he had ever heard her speak. And the animation she showed was almost as jarring as the change from her normal demeanor.

"I don't know," Tommy said helplessly.

"Oh, for God's sake, Dad, how could you let her go out with some-one? And to the opera?"

"Jesus, do I look like a guy who goes to operas?"

"That's not the point. What I'm asking is, how could you let her get away like that? Don't you understand? She wants you to ask her. She doesn't want this man." She stopped for a few seconds, suddenly realizing how shrill she must have seemed.

Tommy was dumbfounded by this new, more spirited, more quarrel-some daughter, as aggressive as her father. In a momentary silence, the two children suddenly appeared in the doorway, with worried looks on their faces, unable to speak. These strange argumentative sounds were haunting reminiscences of the desperate, strained confrontations be-tween their mother and their father that later broke up their family. Sud-denly they remembered the tears and loneliness of Boston, things that they thought that they had forgotten in Youngstown, in Tommy's house.

In an instant, the looks on their faces told both Elly and Tommy what was on their minds. She looked at her father and tried to find something to say but couldn't. Tommy looked back at her and then the kids. He cocked his head slightly and said to the children, "I've been a bad boy, and your mom is scolding me for it," he said, smirking.

Elly smiled and closed her eyes in relief. "Maybe you and I can have a talk, and you can give me some pointers on how to handle her when she gets like this," Tommy said. "You must be used to it, huh?" He was smiling still and finally they were relieved.

"Are you arguing?" Carrie said, still not convinced that all was well.

"We argue all the time," Elly said. "I was just a little louder this time."

"All the time?" said her son.

Tommy came to the rescue again. "This is good arguing, kids — a debate. Nothing bad comes from this. Did we scare you?"

"You're not fighting then?" the girl asked.

"No, honey, we're not fighting," said Elly.

"I didn't do anything bad," Tommy said.

"…Only dumb," said Elly with a grin. Tommy laughed and looked at the kids. "It's okay…really."

―――――◆►◉◄◆―――――

"So, how's the secretary?" Nick Pagliaro asked his brother.

"She's okay…nice."

"You making any headway?"

"Soon. I should get her in bed this Friday, after the opera."

"So, operas heat 'em up, huh? I'll have to try that," said Nick.

"What's going on with the mayor?" Mose said, changing the subject.

"He's not doing a damned thing. His old man's dying and his daughter's busy fucking Chris Laney."

"I thought Laney was gonna quit seeing her?"

"Well, he hasn't, and he's gonna be trouble. Mose, that Laney's a crazy fucker; he has more loose screws than a cheap Erector Set."

"I know. But we can't move on him yet. After McCarrie gets out of this investigation, I'll put in a call to Pittsburgh. Then he'll be gone."

"Jesus Christ, every time I think of what he almost cost us, killing those two kids, I get the chills. You realize what would have happened if we'd been implicated in that hit?"

"You don't have to tell me, Nick. I was there, too, remember? All I know is the guy's about outlived his usefulness, and he's gonna be wacked before he drags us down with him."

"See, he thinks he's equal to us, that he can tell us to go fuck ourselves."

"I know, I know," said Mose. "Remember what I told you: with him, it's not if, but when."

"I hope we can stay out of jail until we finish him," said Nick.

"I'll have a talk with him. Damn, I wish he and Carly got along better."

"Yeah, only thing, they hate each other...and that's without Carly knowing he's fucking his daughter." He paused for a moment. "Course, I'd give my left nut to fuck her myself."

"Yeah, she sure grew up in a hurry, didn't she?" said Mose.

"Hell, Mose, you aren't doing so bad. McCarrie's secretary puts 'em all to shame. You ever fucked a Puerto Rican before?"

"Not yet...until I do this one. You know, she's got all kinds of mixed races in her, and I'm gonna enjoy it. She's the kind of broad that believes in love...like giving you her ass should make you marry her."

"Well, enjoy it while you can," Nick said. "Just remember she has to be willing to spy for us. You think you can get her to do that?"

"I'll have her giving us blow jobs in McCarrie's office," Mose said. "Then we nail Laney, and we make Carly governor. Jesus, what a nice thought: to have the whole Valley in our pockets."

"What about McCarrie?"

"This Lucy will help us, I know it. As long as we keep throwing him off, he'll never find anything on us until we're gone. If he gets to be too much trouble, maybe we can have Laney do us one last favor."

"Do a hit on the chief of police?" Nick said skeptically. "How can we get him to do it?"

"I'll make the bomb, and he'll help me wire the chief's car."

"You still remember how to do that? You haven't done one in years?"

"It's like riding a bike."

Nick snorted. "It better work the first time," he said.

———◆———

It was Friday afternoon, and Lucy came into Tommy's office with someone hanging on the phone. "Agee Mancuso," she said. "He said he's a friend."

"He is," said Tommy. "Put him through." She turned to go back outside to her desk. The office seemed a bizarre wonderland of late. All the talk between Tommy and Lucy seemed perfunctory and cordial but strained and too polite.

Suddenly, Tommy's phone rang. "McCarrie," he said, picking up the receiver.

"How're you doing, Tommy?" said Agee. "You playing poker tonight?"

"I was thinking about it, why?"

"Rino and Lou want to buy your dinner, so come early. They said they have some things to tell you."

Tommy hung up the receiver and thought about his friends. What winners they were...honest, full of integrity, warm, friendly. People to cherish. Yet they cope with life. Lou lost Terry just when their lives could have been easier, just when the lifetime of hard work would be paying off. And Rino, he lost his wife, Mary, and then his son Jimmy in the Gulf War...and then there was the mysterious story about the young girl he was going to marry.

And yet they cope, playing all the cards they're dealt. *He'll have to reorder his life,* Tommy thought, *to learn from them, to try to find that spark that keeps them going. To find out why his life is so unsettled just when he was happier than he had been in years.*

Later that evening, when he walked into the Tre-Sette, his friends were waiting for him. "How're you doing, Tommy?" they said in unison.

"Mezza mezz," Tommy said, making his companions laugh softly.

"Why should you be half and half? You're a honcho, Tommy. You've always been our hero," said Lou.

"Cut the bullshit, guys. I'm still trying to earn my first mill and you guys are working on ten."

"Money comes easier when you don't give a damn about it," said Rino.

"You really believe that?" said Tommy.

"I sure as hell do," said Rino. "At the worst time in my life, no money in the world would have helped me."

"Me too, kid. No money would have saved Terry for me…or Mary, Jimmy, or Lee for him," said Lou, gesturing toward his brother.

"I think about you guys often," Tommy said thoughtfully. "I know what you've all been through. And Connie, too, losing Danny's kid, and Kaye…and her husband so long ago."

"Maybe you shouldn't think about our family," said Rino. "We seem to lose a lot of people." Tommy raised his eyebrows at what Rino said.

"We have some news for you," Lou said.

"Yeah?"

"Those Pagliaro brothers are really cagey. They don't buy Cadillacs or live in mansions; they dress real well, but not flashy. Mose is the older brother and he's the boss. No one's sure what they do, but they make a lot of real estate deals. Nick has a small office downtown, and Mose has an office that looks like a dump outside…on Maryhill on the South Side. That's also where his lives."

"Does it have a sign out front?"

"No. And you know that's an old neighborhood, Tom. Some of those places are pretty run down."

"So, what's their game? No signs, no big cars…no visible means of support?"

"What did we tell you before?" said Lou. "You know damned well they're wired."

"Yeah. You guys aren't so bad, you know that? I don't care what people say."

"Order your food, Tommy," Rino growled.

Lisa Giustino sat across from her friend, sipping a glass of white wine. "He can be such an asshole sometimes," she said.

"But what are you gonna do, Lis? You said he looked crazy when you threatened him," said Lisa's companion.

"I don't know," she said. "He'll call me again. I know it."

"Are you sure you want to get back with him?"

"You don't know what he's like, Stacy. He's beautiful. He had a body that makes you hot when you see it. The sex is wonderful, and he's so good at it. Most of the time all the other things we do are such fun. Only he doesn't want to get married, and I can't understand it. We're both free."

"Why? Just the age thing? Doesn't he love you?"

"I know he does. You should see him look at me when I take off my clothes…"

"Oh, God, any guy would look like that when *you* take off your clothes."

"But it's different with him. No other guy acted this way — especially after we make love."

"So wait for him to come round...if he's as nuts about you as you say."

"Maybe. I'll see if he calls me."

———◆◆◆◆◆———

Lucy was feeling more resentful now that she had talked to Tommy. But she was also hurt because of what she heard him say. Damn him. He never once showed any interest in her, and yet when she goes out with someone else, he doesn't like it. Maybe he viewed her as his personal possession? Maybe he had a mean streak...to deny anyone else the chance at happiness that he was denied...that he denied himself. She shook her head. She just didn't understand him. Yet he always showed her respect. But maybe it was the same respect he would show to everyone else, to a panhandler, to an old custodian, to Liebowitz? Maybe the kindness that he showed to his inferiors was okay as long as he gave it unrequested, from his lofty position on down.

Well, at least she could work these few final months without illusions that she was special, that someday if they would meet each other on the street and they would be equals.

"I'll see you, Luce. Remember, this Columbus meeting lasts through Saturday morning," Tommy said as he walked past her, their eyes not meeting.

His comment jarred her from her reverie, and her eyes followed him as he put on his coat and left. Still not a hint of warmth in their exchanges. Still fewer exchanges than before. She found herself grimacing against her emotions. How could it have come to this? It had to have been something else, something she did wrong, something she didn't do, something she might have said. God, she couldn't stand this. Maybe it was time to quit.

The phone rang on Saturday morning. Carrie answered it, and in a few seconds came in to Elly as she was making Mike's bed. Tommy had been in Columbus two days and would be home later that afternoon.

"Hello," said Elly.

"Hi, Elly, this is Danny."

"Oh, hi, Danny." She was nervous. It had been a long time since anyone had called her personally. She was always the lady of the house, or the mother of her children, or the divorced ex-wife of Dr. David Konstanty. And no one ever wanted to speak to Ellen Konstanty, librarian. "Is there anything wrong, Danny?"

"No, nothing wrong. But I was thinking…why don't we run more than just the names on those green Buicks; why don't we run down all the business transactions we can find on all of them? Sometimes some commonalities just jump out…What do you think? Can we do it?"

"Yes, I think we can. When?"

"I can't do it until next Wednesday, but if you get a chance, you can start sooner."

"Do you think this might turn up something?"

"Policemen are often more lucky than smart, Elly. Something just might show up when we cross check the names."

"Okay. I'll start it Monday."

"Maybe we'll surprise your dad with our information gathering wizardry."

"Are you on duty this weekend?"

297

"Yeah. Through Tuesday. Wednesday and Thursday are my days off this month."

"Lucky you, huh?"

"Oh, I don't mind it. There's not much to do on the weekends. The kids are usually busy with their friends. I usually sit here or go over to my mother's place for the evening."

"They never told us middle age was going to bring so many quiet weekends, did they?"

"No. That sneaks up on you...Is your dad back from Columbus yet?"

"No. He said there's a business meeting till two. Then he can head back home. I expect him about six."

"Well, I'd better go, Elly. Let me know if you turn up anything, okay?"

"Sure. Goodbye, Danny."

She finished doing the bed. Then she went into the bathroom to brush her hair and wash her face. She looked at herself in the mirror. The sight of her wasn't all that displeasing. So why wasn't she born with dark and sexy looks that draw men to her? Why didn't she look like Lucy?

I wonder what Kaye Bellino looked like? she thought. *Could she have worked beside Danny as I do and not have affected him? Not made him think of her in his private moments? Could she have been like me?*

And why was she even thinking about Danny? God, her dream icon was working beside her as a partner. But a partner who can't imagine thinking of her as someone other than Tommy's daughter.

She stared into the mirror. Her life was nothing like she thought it would be. How little she knew as a young girl about what to expect. David's unfaithfulness, the lies he told her, the embarrassment she endured when she knew the kids heard them argue, the times when he laughed at her tears, the times he no longer cared to hide his unfaithfulness. The times he wanted out.

But was her sin that great? To love a young man full of promise, to bear him children, to keep his house, to offer her body whenever he wanted it, to entertain his social and career superiors, helping him climb the heights? She did it all, and he laughed at her in the end. Better if he would have beaten her. Instead, he laughed at her.

Now, when she could be a perfect wife, a perfect lover, a caring companion, a joy to his middle life, and a promise of love and happy dreams in their old age, there is no one that wants her. She's alone. Even with the warmth and peace and love that exists in Tommy's house, she's alone.

And still she is put in harm's way by working close to Danny, someone she can't have, someone who will never want her. And that great part of her life is a waste, a promise unfulfilled.

———◉◗◖◉———

Mose always tended to take Lucy to places on the outskirts of town, and it never occurred to her why he did. He never once offered her a choice of restaurants because he knew she would probably choose Castorina's. He would come to her door, and she would be ready. When they would get into his car, he always had a small token gift for her, sometimes a single rose, sometimes a few chocolates, sometimes a picture of a beautiful place, sometimes a lace, or pottery, or wooden memento.

Lucy was just unsophisticated enough to think that Mose was acting out of generous, giving, maybe affectionate motives. And Mose was sophisticated enough to know the right time, the right way, the right gift to start the night on the right course.

She seemed subdued tonight. As they talked of mundane things, he drove to the restaurant. Inside, he said, "Something bothering you?"

She shook her head. "No, just feeling a little blue."

"You need a change in your life."

"You think so?"

"Yeah. You need to do something different, something that makes your life have some spark."

"And what would that be?"

Mose grinned. "Maybe just a good-looking guy and going on a cruise with him."

She looked at him in wonder. "You know I couldn't do that."

"Why not?"

"Because I have a job…and a son and a daughter…"

"Wait a minute. Do you ever get vacations on this job?"

"Well, yes, but…"

"But take some vacation time."

"I don't know if the chief will let me."

"Hell, he has to. It's your time. He's only your boss, not a slave master."

"Yes, but there's a lot going on nowadays. We're hosting a regional conference with the FBI at the end of the month, and he's involved in the Bellino case." As soon as she said it, she regretted it. She knew she never should have said anything about Tommy's work. Her heart sank as she thought about what Tommy would say if he knew she had talked about it to Mose.

Mose knew he had struck gold. This was what he was after all along, the internal secrets of Tommy's office. And this was just the beginning, the harbinger of good things to come, what his time and effort was all about. But he was also canny enough not to let her know of the thrill of victory he sensed when she volunteered information he didn't ask for. So, he let the remark pass with stoic disregard and no body language that would betray the excitement of knowing his work with Lucy had shown such promise. "Are all these things that complicated that he can't do them while you're gone?"

Lucy felt relieved. Obviously, her words about Tommy's work had had no impact on Mose. He seemed still intent on getting her consent to go on a cruise.

"I don't know," she said, looking down at her hands that she had placed palms-down on the table.

"Lucy, come with me. It will be a change. It will be relaxing, and I promise you you'll have a good time."

"Let me think about it, Mose. Can't we just talk tonight?"

"Tonight, we talk," he said. "And we drink."

During the evening, they talked as they always did, easy, charming, humorous, and forthright. They stayed a long time. Finally, they left and headed back to Mose's condominium. She looked at him. "Where are we going?"

"Don't get excited. I thought we'd go to my place and have a drink. You've never been there; I'd like to show it to you."

She took a deep breath. "It's okay, Lucy. I won't hurt you...and I won't force myself on you. Come on."

She nodded. At his house, Mose pulled into an old, large, triple-car garage. The whole complex of offices and house above it was made of brick and was behind a front courtyard with bricks along the perimeter of the lot.

The windows needed paint, she thought. It was not what she expected. And the old garage door creaked open as they drove inside. He turned off the ignition but didn't move. Neither did she. After a few silent moments, she looked over at him. "Just a drink, Lucy; that's all," he said quietly.

He walked around the back of the car to open her door. Then she walked ahead of him a few steps to the entry of the house. He reached ahead of her and opened it, pushing it so she could walk through the entrance without hesitation.

They walked through a small corridor with a utility room and a mud room off to the left. Then they came to a kitchen, and he turned on the lights. The kitchen was beautiful: dark wood cabinets, indirect lights, an island with a sink and cutting board, a restaurant-style stove along one wall, refrigerator and freezer with wood paneled front doors, paneled cupboards, and beverage cooler with glass front. The sight was dazzling.

Lucy looked at him without speaking for a moment, as though finally having some insight into his character. "It's beautiful, Mose. I've never seen anything like it."

He took her coat. "Come on. I'll show you the rest of it down here."

He ushered her through the family room, a small library, a living room, an office, and a television viewing room, a small theater. All of it was immaculate; all of it was expensive; all of it designed as though for a movie star. She said very little as they walked through the first floor of the house. He made no attempt to show her the upstairs.

Finally, they were back in the living room, and he asked her to sit where she wanted. She chose a soft leather easy chair and looked out upon the room. "I'll make us a drink," he said. "Gin and tonic for you?" She nodded again.

"So, what do you think?" he said, as he worked at a small wet bar at a far corner of the room. He was asking for a summary appraisal of what she had seen.

"It's wonderful, Mose," she said, studying the furniture and the decorations of the room. All of it had the hallmarks of a fine decorator's touch. It was not modern furniture, but it wasn't early American either. Instead, it looked traditional, but marvelously expensive.

Somehow it matched him. It was stunning in its beauty, something seen in magazines that portray beautiful houses. But it wasn't pretentious or flashy; it was...conservative but elegant. It was Mose.

He returned with the drinks and lit a gas log fire in the fireplace. He sat near her, with a coffee table between them in front. "You're awfully quiet," he said.

She raised her eyebrows. "Just surprised. No, not surprised, but unexpected."

"Why?"

"Because it looks so different inside than it does outside."

"There's no rule a house can't be that way, right?"

"No rule," she said.

"So, let's drink a toast. To the future and to a beautiful woman."

She hesitated for a second, watching him flourish the drink. Then she took a sip of hers. "Thank you," she said.

"You should restrain yourself more, Lucy. Try not to be so passionate..." he said with a smirk.

She laughed softly. "I'm just not used to this kind of thing, Mose. I'm not used to people like you."

"You mean Italians, don't you?"

"No...Yes...I don't know what I mean. All I know is that you're a smooth talker. You're even nice, and I'm afraid."

"You're afraid of me, right? Who could have murdered and assaulted you a thousand times since we've gone out together, but…maybe I'm just waiting for the right time to chop you into little pieces and put you into the freezer. Oh, I forgot, I'm giving a dinner party Sunday, so I won't have room. It looks like you're safe for another weekend."

She laughed again but noticed immediately that he was not smiling. And the words he had just spoken really had a bite to them. "I didn't mean to upset you, Mose. I was just being honest."

"Well, I wasn't," he said. "And if you think you're in danger of being forced to do something here, I'll take you home right now."

"I never said I was in danger. You know what I mean."

"I'm afraid I don't. All I know is that I have been trying to get you to relax and to trust me for almost two months and I haven't been able to do it. I'm beginning to think I'm not up to it."

"Please, Mose, don't take it that way. It's not you…just you. It's all of it — the gifts, the wine, the quiet talk, the car, this house, your wealth. I've never been in this place before, and I just don't know how to handle myself around you. I'm afraid of my emotions. It's too easy to give in to them…I've done that before and it didn't bring me much happiness."

"First of all, I'm not a jock who knocks women around; you should have noticed that by now. And by the way, the gifts and wine and talk are my idea of romance, okay? And some people even think it's a nice thing." As he spoke, he was walking toward the closet. Abruptly, he stopped and took two coats out, hers and his. He walked over to her and handed hers to her. "It's time," he said. As she took it, she stood up and he held on to it so that he could hold it for her as she put it on.

She wasn't sure what to do; he was so different from Ed. Without a word, she walked toward the door, and he followed.

In the garage he said, "Let's go in this one." She looked at him strangely. "I'd like to use different cars from time to time. It keeps them running better." He hesitated for a moment, looking back at her. Then he went to the door of a green Buick and opened the front passenger door for her.

As they drove toward Lucy's apartment, neither of them spoke. Finally, Lucy said, "I'm sorry, Mose. I'm sorry I can't be what you want me to be."

"I never told you what I wanted you to be," Mose muttered, his eyes always on the road as he drove. "What's to be sorry for? All I wanted was for you to be yourself."

"I was myself. And I think that's the problem for you."

"No. You weren't yourself...unless you fidget and worry all the time about whether I'm going to sprout horns and start howling at the moon."

"Did I seem like that?"

He didn't answer. Finally, they pulled up to her condo. Mose opened her door from the outside and walked her up to the door. "I'm sorry, Mose. I didn't mean to spoil your evening."

"It was supposed to be *our* evening, Lucy." He hesitated for a few seconds, then he said, "I've been trying to get you to relax and have a good time since the very start. I've gone about as far as I can go, I think. If you ever want to see me again, call me. If I never hear from you again, have a nice life. You know, it might have been fun." Then he turned around and walked back to the green Buick.

The next day, Mose's brother, Nick, came to the office early. "How'd your date go last night? You get laid?"

"You remember what it was like when we were kids, Nick? How you had to talk bullshit to a broad for days just to get into her pants? That's the way this feels…but I'll tell you something: She'll call me. And if she does, then I got her…her in my bed and McCarrie in my pocket."

———◆◇◆◇◆———

Bumpy walked into Tommy's office and sat down facing his boss, and in the process, throwing a paper on Tommy's desk. Tommy read the sheet. "Who did this?" he asked.

"Your two kids," Bumpy said, smirking, knowing well how to bait his boss.

"And who might they be?"

"Elly and Danny, of course," said Bumpy gleefully, waiting for a reaction from Tommy.

"You're trying to irritate me, aren't you, bastard?"

"Hey, would I do that to you?" said Bumpy, chuckling.

Tommy pushed himself away from his desk and leveled a squinty-eyed gaze at his tormentor, studying the evil, cherubic face that beamed back at him. "You know something I don't know, Bump?"

"Hell, I know things lots of things you don't know," he said. "I even know things *they* don't know."

"Aren't you supposed to be the guy that tells me things, Chief…the guy I count on to keep me informed?"

"Oh, hell, I tell you all the police stuff, but I sure as hell can't always be telling you things you're too dumb to notice."

"Oh, yeah? So suppose you just try…What is there about Elly and Danny that you see that nobody else does?"

"I never said nobody else does. Lots of people know, except for certain dummies."

"Goddammit, where's my .45? I'll show your wise ass!" Tommy pretended to be looking around for his weapon.

"Those two kids are crazy about each other; they just don't know it yet. Connie thinks so, too."

"Oh, you and Connie, the two busiest bodies in Youngstown, have a goddamned secret and you think we're all stupid because we don't share it?"

"Have you ever known Connie to be wrong about anything? Hell, even Rino and Lou are afraid of her because she knows so much."

"No kidding. You think they've got something going?"

"Well, they aren't shacking up together yet, but see, it's all in the family...everybody that watches them can see it. Just watch the way they look at each other...and talk. Kind of the way everybody knows about you and Lucy...except you, Chief."

"You know, Bump, if you didn't save my life in Korea, I'd have killed you a long time ago."

"Twice, kid. Remember that I saved your ass down..."

"...Down the Monkey Club, right? That was Pete, you senile old fuck."

"Both of us. When you fuck up, it usually takes two to get your ass out of a sling."

"Yeah. I've been known to do that," Tommy said.

Bumpy paused a few seconds. "I had Med put one of his guys on a stakeout at Maryhill. Sure as hell...Mose Pagliaro came and went and so did his brother, Nick."

"Rino and Lou told me they're wired."

"Gotta be. No one knows what they really do. Nick's not a real busy lawyer."

"Okay. Suppose I go over there and try to shake the trees a little?"

"On what basis? What would you be investigating? A green Buick?"

"How about the Bellino murder?"

"What the hell would tie him to those two kids?"

"I'm not sure. But tell me, who do you know that would have a quarter pound of cocaine at the ready just to plant in Danny's car? We have to figure this guy as a drug dealer, right?"

"Well, I suppose you don't have to have a very good reason to go over there. But he's sharp, Tommy. He'll be hard to smoke out."

<hr/>

Connie Bellino was sitting quietly in her family room drinking a cup of coffee and half-listening to the news on television. Suddenly, her back door opened, and her son walked in.

"I'm in here, Danny," she called out to him. She knew the sounds he made. Without hearing a word from him she knew it was her son. She also knew her other son who lived in Cleveland, and her grandsons... the beloved Danny, now lost to her, and Joe and Vince who hardly knew her and seldom seemed to want to make the short trip from Cleveland only to see their grandmother. "There's fresh coffee," she called again.

In a moment, he was in the room, seated across from his mother, sipping a cup of coffee. "How'd your day go, Mom?" he said.

"Not bad. I worked at the Cavour Club this morning for the festival. Then I stopped to see Uncle Lou at his shop, and then I had lunch with Jean. How about you?"

"I've been working on that FBI conference. We're supposed to give the delegates a computer demonstration of the YPD's new system. Then I helped Elly do some stuff for her father."

"You seem to work with her quite a bit. What's she like? Is she like her dad?"

"She doesn't have his temper, but she'll tell you straight what she thinks."

"Her dad's like that, at least. And he always looks you in the eyes when he talks. Does she do that?"

He didn't answer for a moment, thinking about his mother's question. "Yeah," he said.

"Do you like her?"

"She's nice. But it doesn't matter whether I like her. She's the chief's daughter."

"Do you like her, Danny?" his mother said, coolly, knowing that her tone would show her notice of his evading her question.

"Yeah," he sighed.

Later that evening, after Danny had gone, Connie sat quietly, thinking about her son. She wondered what he felt in his own quiet moments. How much did Danny's death hurt their already fragile marriage? And how could all this have happened to her son? Somehow, he had chosen a girl for whom love was not enough. Somehow the one man who seemed made for marriage by inclination, by temperament, by his ability to love, was never to find happiness with the tragic Kaye who once seemed to be a perfect match to him.

Connie had known for many years that their union was unhappy — barely tolerable. And she dared not let her intuition loose upon the lives she saw before her. She knew Danny, and she knew he wasn't happy with Kaye. She could see it in the eyes of their children. There was a sense of longing that one could feel in their presence... an unstated longing for what they could never have: a mother and father who loved each other more than anything else in the world, who were bonded together by a love that had given each of them life. Instead, they grew up careful, careful not to make their longing obvious, careful not to be the cause of strain between Danny and Kaye, careful not to let people believe that they were somehow at fault for the lack of love between their parents.

And she saw it in the way Kaye and Danny managed to forge a life together. They were polite, and proper, and careful. They smiled occasionally and were comfortable socially. And yet, their sum was always less than its parts, something less together than they promised as a courting couple, seeming perfectly matched to a future of married life.

She sighed. Could this pale blonde girl of such delicate beauty be the one for Danny? Certainly, she seems far more intelligent than Kaye. And she seems more natural, more genuine, uninterested in putting on airs for strangers. Connie decided to watch her son and this gray-eyed McCarrie girl. Maybe she'd be able to help some day if they needed guidance. Maybe God is playing a strange chess game, using rules that only he could understand.

———◆•◆◆•◆———

Tommy was nervous. This was the time. This was the first day he would be an investigator again. As he walked into the YPD garage, he saw Liebowitz. "Tommy," the old man said, acknowledging his boss of almost fifteen years.

"How're you doing, Liebowitz?" Tommy said warmly.

"Okay, Chief. Gonna retire soon. I can't keep these hours anymore."

"I told you, Josh, there is no fucking way you're gonna retire before I do. Understand? Me first."

"Tommy, there's plenty of people who can do this job. Hell, it ain't much."

"You've been taking care of my car for thirty years and I'm telling you, I ain't breaking in no new attendant. Besides, what're you gonna do with all your money? You own half of Youngstown now."

Both men laughed broadly. They had been friends always. Tommy had saved his job a couple of times when some city councilman wanted to economize in the YPD. And when his wife was sick, Tommy had given Liebowitz time off to tend to the dying woman. They had bonded their friendship over so long a time that each could almost sense discomfort or anxiety in the other just by their brief encounters in the mornings and throughout the day as Tommy came and went.

Somehow a ritual had developed between them. Since Tommy became chief, he never got or parked his own car while Joshua Liebowitz was on duty. Liebowitz insisted on getting it and driving the few feet to turn it over to Tommy. It was a ritual of their friendship that Tommy had grown accustomed to over the years. Sometimes, he would call down to the desk where Liebowitz had been a fixture for so long and tell him to have the car ready. Sometimes he would just show up and ask gruffly where his car was. The gruff, macho talk was part of the ceremony. Liebowitz would take the key that he alone had been trusted with and get the car.

"No kidding, how have you been feeling, Josh?"

"Not so bad for an old guy, Tommy."

"You ever gonna join your sister in Florida?"

"Never permanently...just in winter. Come springtime, I'll be back to call on you."

"Anytime, Boyo, anytime."

In a few minutes, Liebowitz drove the black Lincoln up to Tommy. The chief put his hand on the old man's shoulder and spoke a few more words to his old friend. They both laughed as Tommy settled into the driver's seat. Liebowitz waved as the chief drove off.

What a fishing expedition, Tommy thought. *A has-been detective with not a speck of evidence, going up against a sharpie who has made millions in the past fifteen years right under everybody's nose?*

What would I say I'm after? he thought. *Here's a guy wired to the Mafia, a guy I've never seen in my life. What am I to him?*

Could Carly and this guy be tight, even wired? Carly's old man wasn't wired; he was just a cheap hood who lucked out with a beer franchise around the fringes of the mob, doing business where he could and making a buck here and there. Then with some local muscle and a few good lawyers like Kel East, he was able to become a millionaire and managed to walk the tightrope between Cleveland and Pittsburgh. But his son, Carly, never had the Mafia inclination. Carly looked too good in a suit; Carly had a political dream ahead.

So, what was this all about? Pagliaro had to have a thing going with Carly, that's what. The tail was something Carly would do... inept, half done, poorly conceived. The green Buick has to tie them together.

But what else? The Bellino murders? No. Carly was a pain in the ass, but he wouldn't contract out on two kids. Dagos have a thing about families; they'll waste each other, but not kids or wives. But if Carly wouldn't do it, then why would this Pagliaro guy? So, who and what am I looking for? Carly... the green Buick... Jesus, am I cooking this whole thing up? Maybe after seeing Pagliaro, it'll all fall apart. And then what? No clues, no evidence, no leads, no hope of ever finding the killer of those kids. And what if we have to go back to square one? Where do we start?

Tommy groaned softly as he drove to the South Side. He wouldn't know this guy from Adam. Surprise was his best bet, but if Pagliaro's not there, then where would his surprise get him? All of a sudden Tommy felt sick... as though seeing for the first time that their case is built on gossamer insight, without anything hard to back them up. Intuition, how frail it seems at a time like this.

Soon he was on Maryville, and he knew he had found Pagliaro's place. As usual, he stayed in his car a few minutes. Then he carefully got out, stood surveying the landscape, and rubbed his elbow reflexively against his .45 concealed in a shoulder holster beneath his armpit.

Med's scout had told him that the side door was the one used most often by Pagliaro, so Tommy headed toward the side door. There was no doorbell, so he knocked. No response. He knocked again. Finally, a white-haired woman of about fifty years of age answered the door. She seemed startled to find a stranger confronting her. "Yes?" she said, careful to hold the knob of the door against her hip so that the inside of the building was not visible.

"I would like to see Mr. Pagliaro."

"Uh... he's very busy now. Could I ask your business?"

"My business is with Mr. Pagliaro," Tommy said, holding his shield and license before her at eye level as he spoke.

The woman seemed twice startled, not only at seeing a stranger at the door, but at seeing the stranger identify himself as a policeman. Tommy took a step forward against her indecision to persuade her that he would not be driven off.

Inside, there was a small entry way which opened to a larger room that held a couch and two easy chairs, all done in pale tan leather. The office was beautifully appointed, Tommy noticed: expensive furniture, paintings, drapes, plush rugs. No file cabinets visible. The lighting was soft, and the colors were pastels and soothing designs of blues and greens and yellows. The secretary's desk was the only workaday item at the far corner of the room — and it was a beautifully appointed wooden table. Beside it was a computer and a printer.

The secretary seemed confused. Tommy had seen the type before... nice, gentle ladies very near the middle class, but never quite there. Her parents were probably white-collar workers, bank tellers, insurance salesmen, office workers or accounting clerks. But for reasons unknown, this lady was never able to rise above the entry level of the middle class. And now she seemed nothing more than an aging, dispirited woman trying to work in a microchip age with card catalog mentality, desperate to please a boss whose secret business connections were, at best, sinister.

Tommy felt sorry for her because he knew she was worried about her job, about letting him in to see a boss who never saw anybody. She seemed addled. "Tell him," Tommy said softly. "Let him know I'm here." She nodded, and then opened his door and stepped inside, closing the door behind her. In a few seconds she opened the door and sat down at her desk, ignoring Tommy. Mose Pagliaro appeared in the doorway, looking shaken but controlled. His face was a mask of many emotions that Tommy used to be able to read well and that he began instinctively to recall now as he studied his quarry.

Pagliaro had the pained look of someone trying to gloss over his anger and fear and surprise at seeing Tommy. "What can I do for you, Detective?"

"I have some questions to ask you," Tommy said, nodding to Pagliaro's inner office after glancing at the anguished secretary. Mose understood.

"Why don't we talk in here?" he said. "It'll be more comfortable."

Inside, it was even more beautiful that it was outside. *This guy has class*, Tommy thought. *Decorators must work overtime on this place. But he does everything in the world to hide it. Interesting. He keeps a nondescript and shabby exterior, on an old part of the South Side, and an interior of luxury and matchless beauty.*

Tommy sat in the first chair he saw, without looking at Mose. "Excuse me... I didn't get your name. Are you from the Youngstown Police?" Mose said, taking a seat opposite Tommy. The office was a large room, larger than Tommy's office, but it contained some of the same things: a table and four chairs, indicating that Mose's meetings were smaller than Tommy's, a couch, two easy chairs, a large, beautiful wooden desk, with ornate wood bas-reliefs. It was like Tommy's office, only much nicer...polished wood, soft leather, paintings, and soft rugs. *It could be the office of a Hollywood movie producer*, Tommy thought. And you'd never know it from the outside.

"McCarrie...Are you a native of Youngstown, Mr. Pagliaro?"

"McCarrie? But the chief of...Are you the chief of police?'

"Yes."

Tommy studied the veins in his neck and his breathing as Mose talked. Some few things were coming back to him. Pagliaro was shaken by this visit. Whatever he was into, it was dirty, and Tommy was not a welcome intruder. "Well, what have I done to merit the attention of the chief of police?" Lucy's words rang in his ears. Somehow this McCarrie had tied him to the Bellino murders!

"I trust you haven't done anything, Mr. Pagliaro. I'm just trying to find out some information."

"About what? What information could I possibly have that would be of use to the chief of police?"

"I don't know," Tommy answered. "That's the reason I'm here."

"But with all due respect, Chief McCarrie, you haven't told me any reason why you're here."

"Are you a friend of Mayor Giustino?"

"I wouldn't call him a friend...I know him and have seen him socially a few times."

"So, you and he do not have regular correspondence?"

Mose's stomach was churning, although he masterfully played his practiced role of poised, soft-spoken businessman. "No, we do not. But it would hardly be considered a crime to be a friend of the

Mayor of Youngstown, would it?"

It always bothered Mose to enter a business or personal colloquy with someone he did not know. His old, lawyerly instincts warned him that he should avoid answering any question when he was unsure of the question that would follow.

"How long have you lived in the Valley, Mr. Pagliaro?"

Suddenly, Mose grew irritated and the boiling emotions within him surfaced. "Chief McCarrie, did you come here just to pass the time in idle conversation about my background or did you come, again, for a purpose? I'm extremely busy, and I'll be glad to answer your questions if they have some focus."

Tommy smiled faintly. This guy was sharp, and he knew Tommy was fishing. No wonder he'd made such headway in Youngstown. He knew the honchos and kept out of the limelight, lived the good life and made a ton of money. He was as smooth as silk, and didn't play the ostentatious role of Mafia don, though it seemed to Tommy that he was well on his way.

"Uh, focus...Well, Mr. Pagliaro, do you have any associates in Cleveland or Pittsburgh?"

"No. Why would you think I should?"

"I didn't say you should. I just asked the question."

"Chief...McCarrie — that's Irish, isn't it? — are you trying that old ploy of trying to pin a Mafia connection on every successful Italian businessman you ever see? Because if you are, I resent the implication of your questions."

Mose had settled into his proper stance against McCarrie...indignation at being suspected, but cool and understated.

"Just what is your business, Mr. Pagliaro?" Tommy said, having learned by long experience not to engage in roleplay with someone acting out the part of aggrieved suspect.

"I buy and sell real estate, usually commercial ventures. I also own property in the Valley. What is this, McCarrie? A shakedown? Are you hitting me up for money?"

"Does your company have a name?" Tommy said, ignoring his comments.

"The Lincoln Company," said Mose uneasily and softly.

Tommy had not found a way to penetrate the veneer of comfort that Mose was hiding behind. As in old times, Tommy acted on intuition more often than not, and it paid off by starting him on the way to being chief. His intuition was telling him to ask the question that had preoccupied him for months. "Do you know Lieutenant Dan Bellino of the Youngstown Police?"

"No, but the name's familiar," Mose said. He didn't like the question but tried desperately not to show it. Tommy studied every move he made.

"You have never met him?"

"I don't remember. The Italian community's very large in Youngstown. I may have seen him at one time or another."

"Do you know any member of his family?"

"Well, I don't know, Chief. I mean, if I've met a second or third cousin of his with a different name, it may have escaped me. I might even have met some of your relatives from time to time."

Tommy nodded. Pagliaro was still nervous about the talk of Danny Bellino. But Tommy noticed differences in behavior better than anyone else in the YPD. And Pagliaro moved a little finger, drummed the arm of his chair, and showed a little facial energy, an eyelid shaking, a tightness about the mouth.

"Well, Mr. Pagliaro, I guess it's time for me to go...after one last question. Have you ever been arrested for possession or sale of narcotics?"

Again, energy about the face…jaw muscles flexing, lips tightening. "No, Chief," Pagliaro sighed, "I have not. And, again, I resent the implication."

Tommy stood up and turned toward the door. Then he turned around again to Mose. "Mr. Pagliaro, thanks for your time." Tommy started for the door abruptly.

"Hey, wait a minute, Chief," said Mose, now angered by the smugness of the chief. "What's this all about? You come in here out of the blue and ask me some insulting questions and then you just walk out without a word of explanation? Maybe the mayor would like to know how you treat Italian businessmen. Am I supposed to offer you shakedown money now?"

"I don't need your money, Mr. Pagliaro. I told you: I was just gathering information." Then, Tommy hesitated for a few seconds. Pagliaro watched him.

"How did you get my name anyway, Chief?"

"I'm surprised at you, Mr. Pagliaro, you're a lawyer. You know I'd never give away information like that. It didn't help me in any case, did it? Good day to you."

Suddenly, the door opened, and Mose's brother walked into the secretary's reception room. He was startled to see Tommy standing with his coat on, leaving his brother's office. Tommy noticed the resemblance between the two brothers. "Mr. Pagliaro, I presume," he said, smirking as he spoke, and nodding to Nick Pagliaro. "Good day, gentlemen."

Bumpy came to Tommy's office the next day, in the afternoon. "I'll kiss your ass if that guy doesn't know something about the Bellino murders. He started going all sweaty when I asked him if he knew Danny. He denied it, but his jaw muscles were working overtime," Tommy said.

"You really think this guy knows something about the Bellino murders?"

"Bump, those Bellino killings were a hit, right?"

"Yeah. So?"

"So, if Pagliaro is so wired, how could he not know about the hit on those kids? And how about the coke? Who has the kind of money to plant a quarter pound of dope, at least two different times, just to fuck over a YPD lieutenant?"

"But wouldn't he and Danny have to know each other?" Bumpy said. "And what's Danny got that should exercise this guy so much?"

"I tell you he did know Danny. He got nervous when I asked him about him. Besides, didn't Pagliaro's brother show up at Danny's funeral? He's supposed to be some distant relative, isn't he?"

"So where do we go from here?"

"I don't know. But until I know otherwise, Mose Pagliaro is going to be a suspect in this investigation."

———⁕———

Danny and Elly were scheduled to meet at the computer at noon. Danny was late as usual, hurrying to meet Elly, who had arrived early. Things were changing, he thought as he walked toward the stacks. His mother had elicited from him a comment that he didn't want to make — that he "liked" Elly. But that was an understatement. In fact, he dreaded the day when their work would no longer be needed on the case. It would mean a mixed blessing, that the case was closer to being solved, and that he would no longer have an excuse to see Elly twice a week.

But he was changing, too. During their encounters, his memories haunted him. Strangely, he thought more often of Danny and Neva and how he envied his son for the love that Neva bore him.

Yet, all the vicarious happiness that Danny and Neva promised was never going to be. And he was tormented not just by the loss of his two dream children, but also by the lack of ardor in his memories of Kaye. Now that she was gone, he knew that what they had was so fragile and illusive that it was only a mirage.

Yet now, this slender, blonde girl had suddenly come into his life. And it was hard not to be enchanted by her. She was soft and gentle and vulnerable, so different from the poised and brittle and distant Kaye. Danny enjoyed the aura of her, the faint, almost shy, smell of her perfume, the quiet, but direct way she talked to him, the honest way she said every word she spoke, the depth of character he could see in those gray eyes. Jesus. His feelings were betraying him. It seemed almost disrespectful. She was the mother of two kids, the daughter of the chief, and alone in a new city to raise her kids by herself. God, it seemed awful to be thinking those thoughts about her — as though she were a quarry to all the vultures out in the Valley. He had to keep his mind on business.

"Hi," he said, pulling a chair up beside hers as she looked up at him, away from the computer terminal screen.

"Hi," she said softly, smiling broadly at him.

"You find anything?" he asked, looking at the screen, but caught up in the familiar scent of her that lingered with him from other times before.

"Look at this," she said. "Mose Pagliaro owns about forty properties in the Valley."

"The Lincoln Company?" Danny said. "Are they all filed under that name?"

"Except for one or two that are in Pagliaro's own name."

Danny was quiet for a few moments, staring at the monitor. Elly glanced at him, wondering what he was thinking. "Elly," he said, "see if we can get anything on him in Cleveland."

"You think he has property up there?"

"Why not? If he's in the mob, why wouldn't he have property in Cleveland? It's close."

Just then, a patrolman entered the stacks. "Lieutenant, Chief Mc-Carrie wants to talk to you," he said to Danny.

Danny left Elly after a few words and went directly to the chief's office. "Sit down, Danny. I want to talk to you about the case," Tommy said.

"Uh...I was just down with Elly now and I think we found some good stuff."

"She'll be up later," Tommy said. "Maybe we can talk about it then."

"Okay," said Danny, looking puzzled at the strange treatment he was getting from the chief.

Tommy sighed and sat more erect in his desk chair with the palms of his hands on the surface of his desk. "Danny, tell me what you know about this Mose Pagliaro guy. You ever meet him?"

"I think I've met him once or twice. My mom knows him better. And I've met his brother, Nick, a few times."

"He was at Kaye's wake."

"He was? I don't remember. Nick?"

"Yeah. But nobody seems to know this Mose guy. He keeps a really low profile." Tommy looked away for a minute. "Would you know him if you saw him?"

"I'm not sure. What's this got to do with my case?"

"Maybe nothing. But if Carly's tailing me, and this guy's tight with Carly, then maybe he does have something to do with it. And if he's wired to the Mafia, then he could have a lot to do with it."

"Does he sell drugs?"

Tommy's face wizened slightly. "I don't know, but he sure as hell isn't selling olive oil to Pittsburgh and Cleveland."

Just then, Elly came into Tommy's office. She was smiling and cheerful. "Am I interrupting something?"

"No," Tommy said. "We were finishing…"

"Mose Pagliaro owns four properties in Cleveland — so far. And I've just started the search," Elly said, feeling smug about herself.

Tommy asked Danny. "What're you doing for supper tonight?"

"I hadn't thought of it. The kids are staying at my mother's to-night."

"Would you care to join us?" Tommy asked, winking at Elly when Danny wasn't looking. "We're 'baching it' tonight, too."

"Come on, Danny," Elly said. He hesitated, but she moved toward him to meet his gaze.

"It's on me, and the food'll be good," said Tommy.

"I guess I can," said Danny. "Uh, could one of you drop me off after dinner? I was going to get one of our blues to do it."

"We'll take my car," Elly said brightly.

"No, you take mine, okay?" Tommy said to his daughter. "I'll drop yours over at Hugo's before we eat. He'll take me to the restaurant after I tell him what has to be done." Tommy threw her his spare keys.

"I'll see you in a few minutes," Danny said. "Let me go down and get my stuff."

"We'll stop down to get you. I have to see Chief Mencken anyway."

"Ten minutes," Danny said, now feeling at ease about going out with the McCarries.

Elly and Tommy talked more about what she'd found about Mose Pagliaro. Tommy was in awe of his daughter when she spoke as a librarian. She was so confident of what computers could do, and yet she was enough of a librarian to speak plain language to laymen.

Soon they were on their way down to the second floor to pick up Danny, who was putting on his coat as they entered his office.

"Where are we going?" Danny asked as they all walked down the hallway to the stairs at the back of the building.

"He keeps these things as a surprise if he pays," said Elly gently pulling the crook of her father's arm.

"Castorina's," Tommy said. "How about it, Danny? You in the mood for some dago food?"

"Dad!" Elly chided, not able to suppress a smile.

Danny chuckled. "I can handle it," he said.

"You'll have to forgive my dad, Danny. He's still fighting Celtic wars against Romans."

"I've been called more than that by some of those guys," Tommy said.

"I know you have," said Danny.

Tommy was acting more friendly toward his young lieutenant as his contacts with Elly grew more frequent. She had helped to resolve the thorny issue of how to let Danny be involved in the case, and yet have his involvement be controlled. Danny at least felt that he was contributing to the case, at least moving the investigation forward in spite of the cloud of doubt and confusion that had arisen from the incompetent squad headed by Chris Laney.

As they walked toward the garage, Elly quietly slipped Tommy's keys to Danny and said softly, "You drive."

When they walked through the door into the garage, Liebowitz jumped to his feet and greeted Tommy. "Didn't you go home yet?" Tommy said, faking a punch to the old man's belly.

"Can't go until you do, Chief. How're you doing today?"

"Fine, Josh. How about you?"

"Can't complain, Tommy."

"Have you met my daughter?" Tommy asked, urging Elly forward to meet Joshua. "Elly, this guy's a friend, one of the richest men in Youngstown, and he's been taking care of my cars for about thirty years."

Tommy introduced his daughter to Liebowitz, and they exchanged a few words. "Beautiful, Tommy," he said, still holding Elly's hand and admiring her face.

"Thanks, kid," Tommy said.

"And who's this guy?" Liebowitz said, twinkling as he pointed to Danny.

"Don't forget, when you retire, I want dibs on your job, Josh. Word is, you make more than the chief," Danny said, reaching out a hand toward Josh.

"How're you doing, Danny?" Josh said.

"Okay, Josh. Hanging in."

Tommy turned to Danny and Elly. "You both go on. I'll be over in a few minutes...before you finish your first glass of wine."

"Okay, see you there," Elly said as she and Danny started toward Tommy's black Lincoln. Tommy and Liebowitz watched them walking toward his car.

"Tommy, those two kids mean something to each other?"

"I'm not sure, Josh. But it sure wouldn't bother me if they did."

"That Danny's a nice kid, and I heard all them stories about his wife. He deserves someone as good as Elly."

Just then, Elly stopped, said a few words to Danny, and then both of them turned and headed back toward Tommy. "She forgot her purse in the stacks. We'll probably get to Castorina's the same time you do," Danny said.

"You go ahead, Danny. I'll have it up here waiting when you come back," said Liebowitz.

Danny looked puzzled. "He has his own key," Tommy said in explanation.

Danny nodded and turned toward Elly who was waiting a few steps away from him. Liebowitz was already on his way toward Tommy's car as Tommy was taking backward paces toward Elly's car and speaking to his daughter. "If you want, you can call Castorina's for a reservation," he called. His arm was outstretched, holding Elly's keys as he pointed to the couple. He was standing where he could see Liebowitz out of the corner of his eye.

In an instant, between Liebowitz's turning of the key and the noise of ignition, he heard a strange sound that in an earlier time would have told him to duck for cover. But that noise, in that split second, was already beyond Tommy's ability to react. In a moment, the chief was hit by a shock wave that threw him against another car, about ten feet away and rolled him under the car as though he were a toy.

The flash of the explosion was brilliant and instantaneous, and for several seconds, Tommy was unconscious; then, when he came to, he wondered if he were dead. He felt blood on his head and his arm and his torso, but he could still move all his limbs. He tried to clear his head…his ribs ached as he drew breath. Then he felt for his pistol instinctively and began to urge himself out from under the car. His leg was sore, but didn't seem broken. His arms were strong enough to move him out from under the car so he could pull himself erect. It took a few seconds because the muscles of his legs were weak and cut. He knew that what he felt in his legs were superficial wounds.

Standing, he tried to survey the scene. At one part of the garage was the glow of the fire. Throughout the garage, there was the acrid smoke emanating from the fire that seemed to crawl along the floor then rise to the ceiling. Suddenly, he became conscious of where he was and what had happened. It had taken him a few minutes to understand. Then, in the confusion, he began to fear. His pistol was in his hand, but there didn't seem to be any adversary. But he remembered Elly and Danny. He called out to them, and in that instant, seemed to be aware of a voice calling through the roar of the fire and the confusion. "Elly!" he called in response. "Elly!"

He looked around and turned behind him. There was no one around. Suddenly, he began to hear voices in one direction, from where Elly was calling. Tommy stumbled toward the voice, tripping over some fallen beams and piles of rubble, bricks and wood and parts of cars. The stench of the explosion was strong and nauseating. The smoke and the heat and the chemicals borne on the smoke burned his eyes. He called again and Elly responded.

In a few seconds, he made it into a clearing near the doorway of the YPD station. There he could see a few people enter from the building and stop at the figures that were on the ground. Elly was half sitting on the floor, clutching the limp form of Danny who lay partially across her, face down, with his head on her shoulder.

As Tommy advanced, more and more people poured through the

entry now partially destroyed by the blast. When he got to Elly, Tommy said, "Are you alright?"

"I'm okay, Dad," she said, supporting Danny as she spoke. Tommy touched Danny's back as he knelt down toward Elly.

"Danny?" he said softly, clutching his hair as he knelt.

Danny moved his head slightly. Tommy could feel blood as he touched his young lieutenant. "I think I'm okay, Chief," Danny muttered. "Something's broken and I can't move... my arm or shoulder, I think."

"He threw his body over me to protect me, Dad, and something fell on him," Elly said, still cradling Danny's head on her shoulder, tears streaming down her face.

Suddenly, he could distinguish voices — first Pete's, then Bumpy's. Pete knelt down in front of Danny and Elly, touched Danny's arm and back and shoulder. "I don't know how much is broken, but we can't move him until the life squad gets here." He looked back at Tommy, who was still clutching his .45 automatic as he rested another hand on Elly to support her as she held Danny across her body. Bumpy soon came over and called out to Tommy.

"I'm okay, Bump. Let's get this kid out of here."

"We can't move him yet, Bump," Pete said, still holding Danny to help Elly support him. "Can you feel your legs, Danny?" he said, grabbing the muscled of his back legs.

"Yeah, Chief. It's my shoulder and my back. I don't have enough strength to push myself up."

Pete looked up at Tommy, seeming to breathe a sigh of relief that Danny's back might not be broken. Then Bumpy, who had been giving orders to some other people who began to crowd into the garage, said, "We have to get out of this place or something else may blow here.

Where the hell's the life crew?"

As he spoke, the life squad entered the building and rushed to Pete, who was still holding Danny's arm. "Be damned careful, guys. He has feeling in his legs but can't move his upper body."

Several men expertly moved Danny off Elly and away from her support. Tommy hugged his daughter when they both stood erect. "I'm okay, I'm okay," she said. "Oh, God, where's this blood from, Daddy?" she asked as she touched the back of Tommy's head.

"I'm alright, too, kid," said Tommy.

Just then, she turned as the crew began to lower Danny onto the stretcher. Tommy was still dazed by all that had happened in the few minutes of pain and fear that he felt when he saw Danny and his daughter.

In the chaos and the smoke and the fire and the sirens, he could hear only Bumpy's voice, shouting orders, cautioning people to be careful because of the danger that the building would collapse or some nearby cars would explode.

Suddenly, Tommy was conscious and aware, seeming to fully understand what had happened. He picked up his gun that had fallen beside Elly. "Liebowitz!" he shouted as he ran toward his burning car. "Liebowitz!"

Tommy stumbled as he neared the firemen who were trying to smother the flames. Bumpy suddenly stepped in front of him. Tommy knew his friend would let him go no further. "Liebowitz?" he asked.

"Your car was wired, Tommy. He's gone."

Tommy sank to his knees, holding his temples, wanting to blot out the horrible sounds and smells around him. Then he let out a stream of vomit. The strong, gentle hands of his old friend held his head and went around him in an embrace. "Let's go, Tommy."

The hospital was so quiet at night that the noise of nurses and aides echoed through the hallways in muted whispers. Tommy was in surgery long enough to have stitches in his neck and his legs and to have his ribs set and bandaged. The superficial wounds of his head and shoulder were washed and dressed.

He awoke alone. In the quiet of his hospital room, the pain of the cuts and the bruises from the tumble caused by the shock wave were beginning to tell on his body. His body ached more now than he ever remembered. He stumbled in agony as he walked slowly, dragging his IV stand and quietly opening the door. Elly was dozing on a small couch just outside in the waiting area, her feet curled beside her. Connie and Rino and Lou were talking softly. Lou had just put a light blanket on Elly as Tommy walked out.

"My God, Tommy, you shouldn't be walking around!" Connie said.

"How's Danny?" he said.

"He's right in there," Rino said, pointing to the room next to Tommy's. Elly heard his voice and came awake instantly.

"The nurse was just here," Lou said. "His shoulder is broken... torn rotator cuff...broken clavicle."

"How are you, Tommy?" said Connie.

"Nothing serious, kid," Tommy said. "No injury to his back? No paralysis?"

"They did an MRI. Everything seems okay. He has feeling everywhere," said Rino.

"There was no bleeding in the brain even though he took some kind of hit...no damage to the spinal cord," said Lou.

Tommy hugged Connie. "I think God was looking out for us."

"Especially me," said Elly. "He saved my life."

Tommy nodded, shuddering slightly at the horrible thought of Elly dying. "I guess we wait, huh?"

They all sat down again, and as time passed, they each found a place to sit. Elly and Tommy sat together until the nurse scolded Tommy for being out of his bed. As he walked back to his room, he said, "What about the kids?"

"Aunt Jesse came over to get them. They're going to stay there with Danny's kids until we get all this settled. They'll have a ball."

"Good. If anyone can help to calm them, it's Jesse. At least we're all going to be okay."

"You think Danny's okay, Dad?"

"Yeah, kid. He's young, healthy. Those dagos are tough to beat."

Elly smiled slightly and shook her head, trying unsuccessfully to stop the tears. "I'd be dead today if he didn't protect me from that falling ceiling."

"Those things are something you don't plan, or train for. It was instinct. He wanted to protect you, and he did it without thinking."

"Instinct?" she said, as though doubting the flow of logic from the answer.

Tommy hardly knew what happened the next few days. He was at home, and then he was at the office for a short time. He saw Liebowitz's family. He went to the funeral along with Pete and Bumpy and Med, and all the people who had known the old man since they had been rookie cops. All were in dress blues and formed an honor guard for the old man's body.

Joshua's wife was old and sick, his children middle class and prosperous. There wasn't much he could do for them, and they didn't ask. But still he made a vague, general offer of help in any way he could. They just wanted his killer brought to justice. In parting, Tommy promised them that the killer would be caught and punished.

Lucy had come to the hospital the night Elly and Danny's family had kept a vigil outside the rooms of Tommy and Danny. It was awkward. Suddenly, she and Tommy were estranged, yet neither of them had any understanding of why. She stayed about a half hour and then left. Before she left, she said a few words to Elly, who seemed dazed and fearful, not her real self. Then, she turned to Tommy and stood in front of him awkwardly. She felt that she was out of place. For a few seconds, neither of them spoke. Then, she said, "I'm so sorry this happened. Are you going to be okay?"

He nodded. "Yeah. I'll be fine. I'll be in next week."

"Will you let me help you if I can?"

He nodded.

The Youngstown Telegram made the explosion front page news, despite the reluctance of Tommy and his men to talk freely to the press. They had learned long ago that uncertainty was dangerous. It was against uncertainty that the news purveyors let their imaginations flourish, unbridled by facts, and conjured up strange and shocking news reports, seemingly unrelated to the reality of the event. No. It was always best to talk after the facts were known, after there were four corners on the story.

Carly read the morning paper anxiously, setting down his coffee cup each time he read some increasingly provocative report. He was finishing the article, hoping somehow, he would not be tainted by what the *Telegram* called a "lawless act."

But then, in the final paragraph, the shaft hit home: "Mayor Carlton Giustino, so adept at micromanaging the YPD, appointing special investigative squads that seem to yield no fruits for their efforts, and holding self-aggrandizing press conferences, must bear a large measure of responsibility for this sad state of law enforcement. Under the Giustino administration, Youngstown seems to be mirroring the days of the shootout at Stop 14 and the mob wars of the 1960s where the names of Naples, Aielio, Carrabia, Cavalaro, and Farah were emblazoned across the Valley with lurid stories of turf wars over the numbers game and the fledgling drug racket."

He slammed down his coffee cup. "What's wrong?" said his wife.

"The *Telegram* says I'm partially responsible for the bombing. But nobody around here goes for half measures. The whole Valley's gonna blame it on me."

"Well, you knew they'd be after you the first chance they got."

"Yeah," said Carly absently. "Thanks for all the support, Ginny. I have to go. Is Mickey here?"

"He's in the kitchen," Ginny said. "I didn't mean you had something to do with it, Carly."

"But you didn't say it that way, did you?"

All morning, Carly sat in his office fielding calls from newspaper and television reporters. Later that afternoon he drove to Mose Pagliaro's office. Mose and his brother, Nick, were sitting in his inner office when Carly entered.

"I'm going in," Carly said to the secretary. Before she could protest, he was at the door.

Mose looked up, surprised to see the red-faced mayor in his office.

"Hi, Carly, what can I do for you?"

Carly slammed the door behind him. Nick Pagliaro stood up. "What the fuck's going on here, Mose?" Carly snarled.

"About what?" said Mose calmly.

"One minute you're crying because the chief came to see you, the next minute you blow up his goddamned car."

"Hey!" Mose shouted, interrupting the mayor. "Watch what you say. Who the hell do you think you are?"

"Give me a fucking break, Mose," Carly said. "You guys are crazier than I ever thought. You try to blow up the chief of police because he pays you a visit?"

"What are you talking about, Carly? You're the one who came to us for ideas about how to screw him over. You hate him more than we do," Nick said.

"But I don't want to kill the guy, Nick. You got that? That's the big difference between you and me."

"We didn't try to kill him," said Mose, still sitting at his desk, still talking calmly though he was beginning to become angry at the upstart mayor who he never liked or trusted.

"Bullshit, Mose! You're the bomb expert. That had your name all over it. And if it didn't, you got a torpedo from Cleveland or Pittsburgh to do the job."

"I'm telling you we didn't have anything to do with it," Mose said. "It brings too much publicity."

"But it might have gotten McCarrie off your backs, right? He could be stumbling into all your operations and fuck up your lives, right?"

"What can McCarrie fuck up, Carly? Some real estate deals? Is that what you think I have to fear from him?"

"I don't know what you have to fear, Mose. But his name was on that bomb the minute he left this office. But even I never thought you were crazy enough to kill him. Who the hell's your counselor?" Carly turned toward Mose's sullen brother. "Whoever it was should have his balls cut off."

"You done, Carly? I'm busy."

"Busy, huh? Just don't get your ass in a sling, Mose. I could never help you on something like this."

"Who the fuck do you think you are, anyway? What makes you think I can't take care of myself...so that I'll need you to bail me out?"

"I told you, Mose. I'm through with you. I was wrong. I thought you had some common sense. Instead, you've surrounded yourself with crazy people who never tell you when you're going off the deep end."

Carly started for the door. "You'll need me, Carly...next election," Mose said to his back.

"You aren't worth going to jail for, Mose. It's over. Just watch yourself."

———◆+❈+◆———

Rino, Lou, and Connie were walking slowly down the seventh-floor hallway at St. Rita's Hospital. "You want to get something in the cafeteria?" Rino asked the other two.

They both hesitated, thinking about what to do. "You know," Connie said, "I think I want to go home. I'm tired."

"Me too," Lou said. "Besides, Danny could use a little rest."

Rino nodded in agreement. As they walked farther, they could see a slender figure coming toward them out of the dark far end of the hallway. It was Elly.

Connie glanced quickly at Rino, as if to see if he was thinking what she was. Rino raised his eyebrows and grinned. "Looks like he's not gonna get much rest for a while."

Connie raised her eyebrows in return and huffed softly. "I don't think he minds," she said.

"How about you, kid?" said Lou. "Do you mind?"

She pretended to be annoyed at their teasing, but she couldn't help smiling. "Hell, it couldn't have worked out better if she planned it," Rino said. "Come to think of it, she probably did."

"Our sister's a witch, Rino," Lou said.

Connie cursed them softly but turned a smiling face at Elly as she stopped to talk to them. "How are you feeling, dear?" she said to the younger woman.

"I'm okay, Mrs. Bellino. Thanks." She nodded a greeting to Rino and Lou.

"How're your ear and head, Elly?" said Rino.

"And your chin?" said Lou.

"Not so bad. I've hidden all the stitches under this hat and this scarf. The only thing I can't hide is this," she said, pointing to the small patch on her chin.

"How's your dad?" Connie said.

"He's okay. The cuts are healing; his ribs and neck are pretty sore. But he's getting better."

"Good. I want you and your dad and your kids to come to my house to dinner...as soon as things settle down. I'll call you."

"I'd like that very much. Thank you."

"Tell Danny we'll see him tomorrow. He dozed off while we were in there."

Elly nodded to them as they walked away. Then she turned and walked the long hallway, her heels clicking as she walked. Hesitantly, she peeked into Danny's room. His eyes were closed, but he was not sleeping and could hear her heels tap softly as she walked. Finally, he opened his eyes and brightened when he saw her. "Hi. What are you doing here so late?" he said.

"How are you, Danny?"

"These damned casts are gonna drive me crazy, but I'm fine. I can move my arm…see?" He moved his arm about slightly but stopped abruptly as he winced slightly from the pain of the movement. He relaxed and didn't speak for a few moments. "Don't you get tired coming here all the time? You've been here every day."

"No, I don't get tired. Don't you want me to come?"

He closed his eyes and huffed. "You know I don't mean that," he said. "It's good to see you."

"But you get so many other visitors, I'm afraid…"

He waved her to silence with his right-hand palm down and moving level to the floor, the funny Italian gesture that could also have been used as Indian sign language. "I look forward to your coming," he said.

"Me too," she said, running her hand over his forehead, straightening his hair.

They talked for several minutes about the phone calls he had received, the flowers and cards he was sent. He asked about Tommy and got a full report on his boss. The chief would be back to work by the end of next week.

Elly had been sitting in an easy chair at Danny's bedside. For a few seconds they didn't talk. Then she stood up and came closer to his bed, looking down at him. "Are you leaving?" Danny said.

"No. I have to ask you something."

He stared at her skeptically for a few seconds. Then, he said, "Okay."

"Why did you do it? Throw your body over me to protect me?"

He chuckled softly and snorted. "You ask the damnedest questions, Ellen."

"You're not going to answer me?"

He hesitated, staring ahead to the wall, away from her. "Instinct," he said finally.

"So you would have done that to protect anybody?"

"No, Elly, not everybody... it's instinctive only with people I care about."

"People like me?"

"Like you, okay?" He still wasn't looking at her, but in the few seconds that passed after he spoke, he turned toward her. He stared into her eyes. For a fleeting second, he thought of Kaye. Never had his heart been touched by her then, as it was now by this slender girl. Kaye, who looked so perfect, so much like a retired fashion model, so much like a budding socialite, could never look into his soul the way this girl does so naturally and easily.

She looked away from him for only a second. Then she looked back. "Danny, there's something I have to know," she said, hesitantly. "I —"

"You want to know if I love you," he said quietly.

She was flustered by the matter-of-fact way he said it, and terrified at the answer he might give. She had never felt so vulnerable in her life. All she did was nod, looking down at the IV tube that was in his arm. She touched it absently, with two of her fingers, running them along a few inches of its length.

He shrugged, looking straight ahead. "I think about you all the time... at work, at home. I've never felt like this before, Elly. I'm hopelessly in love with you. I'm just so afraid that all the trouble I've had...

Danny and Neva, Kaye...or maybe your husband."

She laid her hand on his chest to stop him. Tears were rolling down her cheeks. "Why tears?" he asked.

She smiled slightly and shook her head. "I've always dreamed of finding someone like you, and now I have the very one I've dreamed about," she said softly, leaning over to kiss him gently on the lips. He could taste the salt as she drew away. She could see one of her tears on his upper lip.

"This is really you, right?" she said. "Not the medicine talking? You're not going to tell me tomorrow that you don't remember any of this?"

He chuckled. "Don't make me laugh. It hurts when I laugh. I'll only say that if I'm mad at you...or when you don't listen to me when I'm telling you something for your own good."

She was beaming now. "I love you, Danny."

———◆◆◆———

In the days it took Tommy to rest up from the soreness and the medication and to get used to the walking and sitting against the strange stitching patchwork on his ribs, his head, and his legs, he had time to think. He sat in a chair drinking coffee, waiting for Elly or one of the kids to come home.

They would not have to tear down the whole YPD garage. They could reinforce the walls and the ceiling, add a new entrance and fix up the floor. Things would be back to normal in a few months — back to normal without Liebowitz.

Tommy shook his head. How could things be worse? Liebowitz was dead; young Danny and Neva long gone, and Elly and Danny could have turned on that ignition that would have killed them both instantly...with a bomb that was made for Tommy alone. He shivered at the thought of having to bury his daughter...and Danny.

But as the fear of what might have been subsided in the rush of events that followed the death of Liebowitz, another emotion began to well up in his consciousness: anger.

It had to be Pagliaro. But why? What could have prompted him to be afraid of Tommy who was so hesitant and uncertain during their brief meeting? The man who the mayor had undercut? Tommy, who was only asking vague questions? And then after one face-to-face meeting, he had a bomb put in his car? It had to be Pagliaro.

The next day, Tommy went back to work. Lucy knew he was coming, but somehow still was surprised to see him. But he looked different, also. He forced a weak smile when he came through the front door and said very little.

In a few moments, he was in his office with the door closed. Behind his desk, he looked out the bay window. Things had changed. Now he wasn't just looking for the killer of Danny and Neva, he was looking for his own killer, of Danny and Elly's killer. But for a strange twist of fate, they could have all been dead. Instead, Josh Liebowitz redeemed their lives with his own. So now there was mortal danger out there as they walked the streets.

Lucy entered the office, looking uncomfortable. "It's the mayor again. He's called several times wanting to know 'what's going on around here.'"

"I'm going over to see him," Tommy said, "but don't tell him that. Just say I'm not in if he calls."

For several days — ever since the bomb blast — Tommy's anger at Carly had been growing. Now was the time to talk to the mayor. He took his overcoat from his closet and walked out into the front office.

"I'm going over to see the mayor. Don't tell anyone where I've gone," he said to Lucy.

She nodded slightly, trying not to show the look of concern she always had whenever Tommy confronted the mayor. He started toward the door. "Chief?" she said softly.

"Yeah?" he said, turning toward her.

"You don't want me to tell anybody? Not even Chief Malatesta?"

"I don't have to tell…" Tommy started to show some pique as he spoke, but he caught himself. He never talked to her that way. He couldn't start doing it now. He took a deep breath. She looked strange. She didn't know how to work in a situation where the tension between her and her boss was so oppressive. He shook his head, as if to erase the last few words he said. "If he asks you, tell him," he said softly.

She nodded, feeling better that she could now let someone know. "Please be careful, Chief," she said to his back as he went out the door. He never looked back, never answered.

———◦•◦•◦———

He walked into Carly's office and told a secretary who he was. She admitted him to Carly's office immediately after a quick call inside. Carly sat inside, surprised and tense, not knowing what the visit was about.

Without any greeting or smile, Tommy said, "Tomorrow I'm going to disband that special Bellino squad — whether you like it or not."

"You are, huh? Who the hell do you think you are?" Carly said coldly. "I set that squad up, and I'll disband it when I'm good and ready."

"I'm telling you, Carly, either you make it public today or I do it tomorrow."

"Just try it, Chief. And I'll overrule you...and I think I can get Council to back me."

Tommy was angry...and uncontrolled. He lunged at Carly, grabbing him by the lapels and dragging him face to face. Carly was frightened and said nothing as Tommy snarled to him. "Listen to me, you bastard. There was a bomb in my car that almost killed my daughter and a cop. It did kill a friend I've known for thirty years. And it was meant for me, you got that? Now I'm gonna take that squad and try to make them find out who almost wasted the whole fucking police garage. They sure as hell will be doing more good than they would on that Bellino case."

"Take your hands off me, McCarrie. You're through. Turn in your badge!"

Tommy slammed him against the wall and finally hurt him as well as frightened him. "I told you, Carly, that bomb was meant for me and almost killed my daughter. I'll call a press conference and tell the whole Valley that you completely fucked the Bellino case and how you want to set up another incompetent squad on the bomb case." Tommy finally released the mayor and stepped away. "I mean it, Carly. You stay out of my way on this one or I'll fuck up your life so bad, you won't believe it."

"What makes you so sure they'll do any better on the bomb squad than they did on the Bellino case?"

"Because they won't have time to screw around...and they'll be answering to Pete or Bumpy every goddamned night."

Carly walked away, straightening his suit and tie as he walked. "Don't fuck with me on this one, Mayor. I'm right and everybody knows it. I'm gonna get the guy who killed Liebowitz."

Carly was facing away from Tommy across the large room. He was silent for several minutes. Then he turned back to Tommy. "I'll announce the disbanding of the squad this afternoon, and if you don't find the bomber soon, I'm gonna fire your ass for incompetence."

"Just stay out of my way, Carly," Tommy said.

Carly was calming down now, and anger was once again replacing fear of Tommy. "You just remember who's in charge of the police in this town, Tommy."

Tommy glanced at him and then headed for the door. He wasn't going to argue with Carly about who owned the YPD. Everybody in the Valley knew that it was Tommy's department. They also knew that Carly had bought his election. So even though he was the mayor, the money hadn't bought loyalty in Youngstown.

At the door, he was suddenly seized by a strange thought. He turned back to Carly and said, "Carly…do you know anyone named Mose Pagliaro?"

For the first time ever, he saw something new in Carly's behavior: the blanched face and the flush, a prelude to panic. It was an inspired question, because Tommy could see that it struck at Carly as an arrow to his heart.

"No…should I?"

"You never heard of him?"

"I've heard of him. He's the real estate guy, right?"

"Yeah," Tommy said. For another moment, he studied the mayor. Then he turned and left.

Later that night, Tommy sat in his living room drinking a bourbon and tea that Elly had made for him. In his old age, he had settled into a comfortably calm, if noisy, existence. And the routine had grown easy on him. He knew his nights would always be quiet, because the kids would be studying late. They were both busy with soccer and other school activities that they all ate supper relatively late, around seven o'clock. Tommy would often stay later in the office to miss the rush hour traffic.

So, he sat alone, thinking about what had befallen him that day. Carly backed off. Why? There was no love lost between the two of them, so why not stick it to the chief who had jailed his father and who had shown such contempt for him? Why didn't the mayor try to get him when he had a chance? Could it be that Carly understood? That it was one thing to attack an enemy, but quite another to attack his daughter? Maybe Carly felt that this thing was out of hand. Maybe Carly was afraid. If Carly didn't push the buttons and let the torpedoes go, who did?

And what about his answer to the Pagliaro question? Why the ashen face and then the flush? Obviously, he lied about knowing Pagliaro. So, to what extent were they wired? And if Pagliaro was the evil genius behind the bombing, what else was he behind?

He'd have to see how soon he could get all the bomb information together. The FBI lab had analyzed the bomb, but it pointed nowhere. Yet, it was only Pagliaro who haunted Tommy. It was Pagliaro.

But how was he going to deal with this? It's not often that they bring someone in just to plant a bomb. Yet, it had to be somebody good... to get it in there that fast, to wire it just right. How long would the hood be open to get that into the car? And where would Liebowitz be during the time? And who would know that Liebowitz was gone? Who would know? He took a sip of bourbon tea. Suddenly, he sat forward in his seat and stared out into the room. Jesus Christ. It was an inside job.

The next day, after his visit to the doctor for a check-up, Tommy went back to his office. It was raining, dark, and miserable. He took care of business, and asked Lucy to tell Bumpy and Pete to come upstairs after lunch.

After lunch, Tommy worked on reports for City Council, on the next proposal for new garage repairs. At about two o'clock, Lucy came into his office. She seemed strangely uncertain about her presence there.

"Chief?" she said uneasily.

"Yeah?" he answered. "Everything alright?"

She nodded. "Fine," she said, looking away, seeming to be distracted. "Could I ask you something?"

"Yeah. Anything wrong?"

"No," she said uneasily. "It's just that I'd like to take some personal time off... today if I could."

He was nodding assent before she could stop speaking. "Is it okay?"

"It's okay," he said softly. "Is that all?" His comment let her know that the conversation was over.

She just looked at him in a way she had never done before. After a few seconds, she said, "Yes, that's all." She waited still, but the words she hoped for never came. Finally, he looked up from his reading.

"Anything else?" he said. She shook her head and turned to walk out the door. She was hurt again. He also knew she was hurt, but he wouldn't let himself care. Somehow in their estrangement, he had become hardened in the way he treated her. He was never rude, but neither was he friendly, or warm. And it all came from his own anger at himself. Somehow, he had let her get away and he hated himself for it.

When she visited them at the hospital the night the bomb went off, she suddenly felt a stranger among them, and that bothered Tommy more than anything else. But this time he didn't know how to make it better. He was tormented by the thought that he might have driven Lucy into someone else's arms, and yet now haunted by the doubt that Lucy was ever his to lose.

So, in his frustration, he was careful and distant. He was losing her and pretending that it never mattered but hurting to think of her belonging to someone else.

In minutes, Pete and Bumpy walked into the chief's office. "How d'you feel, Chief?" Pete said. Tommy nodded okay. "Hey, Bump, Tommy's lost a little weight," Pete said to Bumpy.

"Yeah, before you know it, he'll be modeling Jockey shorts," Bumpy said sardonically.

They all laughed. Then, Lucy came in with a tray and three cups of coffee. The two deputies thanked her, and she left. "So what's up, kid?" Bumpy said to Tommy.

"I'm disbanding the Bellino squad,"

"When?" said Pete, surprised at his boss.

"Now...before the day's over."

"What're you gonna do about Carly?" asked Bumpy.

"He's gonna announce it tomorrow morning," Tommy said.

"What'd you do, catch him sucking cocks at the Y?"

"It was strange. I went over there and just told him I was doing it."

"Without someone riding shotgun to protect you?" Pete said.

"I did get a little rambunctious," Tommy said.

"You wipe out his desk?" Bumpy said.

"It was easier than I thought. I was just holding him by the neck..."

Bumpy snorted. "You should have brought one of us with you. I'd like some excuse to lay into Mickey."

"You know, I didn't see him. You suppose Carly fired him?"

"Nah. He knows too much. Carly probably has him cutting the lawn," Pete said.

"How do you want me to split that squad up, Tom?"

"What do you think, Bump?"

"Well, Pete needs some people in his division."

"Take them, Pete. You want Laney?"

"Bumpy told me he has dibs on Laney."

"Okay. I don't care how they're deployed. Just make sure they start acting like cops again. And I want all officers to report to each of you daily. If they don't, cut their balls off."

"Jesus, this is a good day, huh?" said Pete.

"Works for me," said Bumpy.

"Leave a little slack in the schedule for some good men. Every once in a while, I might need some help on short notice."

"How's your investigation going?" said Pete.

"Haven't done too much since the bomb...but I asked Carly if he ever heard of Mose Pagliaro, just as I was leaving, and he got all white and wobbly on me."

"He said he knew him?" said Bumpy.

"Knew of him. He said, 'Is he the real estate guy?' Now how do you suppose he knew Pagliaro was in real estate when almost all of the dagos in town never even heard of him?"

"You never know, Tom. Carly's old man might have cut some shady deals with Pagliaro a long time ago," said Pete.

"Yeah," Tommy said thoughtfully. "Still, he did know him, and he lied to me about it. But to answer your question: we're nowhere on the Bellino case."

"What are we gonna do with all the information on that case?" said Bumpy.

"You and Pete talk to everyone on the squad. Find out about leads, suspects...anything they have, which won't be much. Then get it all up here to me."

After a few more minutes of discussion, Tommy said, "Okay, you guys, go down there and kick some ass."

"So what are you gonna do about supper tonight?" Bumpy said.

"Nothing. I'm gonna hang around here until Elly picks me up. She has a parent meeting after school at St. Mark's, so she's going to stop here after she's done."

"I could give you a ride now."

"Thanks, kid. But I want to work on that report to City Council."

———————

Lucy was glad to be home early. It bothered her to think that Tommy had been so cold to her. But she couldn't do anything about it. They were from two different worlds. Tommy was known by everybody; she was known by only a few ordinary friends. He was at home with influential people, and she was at home when she was alone. To him she was a good employee, a nice lady.

It was getting late. Mose would be coming soon. She showered and began to dress. All the while, as she quietly made herself ready for the night, she compared Mose with Tommy. Mose was more polished, was smoother in his speech and manners.

Tommy had a sense of humor, but it was not the wry sense of humor that Mose had. Tommy operated viscerally all the time, in his anger, in his hatred, in his thinking, in his analysis of crimes. Mose was not instinctive; Mose was careful.

And yet, it was nice going out with Mose. His lovemaking was unhurried and gentle. And though she had slept with him only once, it was pleasant, and he was thoughtful. She wasn't sure where their relationship would lead, but she enjoyed his attention, and she enjoyed having another man interested in her for more than a one-night stand.

She checked herself in a mirror and nodded appreciatively. She looked fine. In fact, she was happy. The doorbell rang and she answered it. Mose was thrilled at the way she looked. "You look spectacular," he said sincerely.

"Why, thank you. Should we go now?" She was beaming and slightly flushed in the excitement.

They walked out to his car, and he opened the front passenger door for her. She seemed puzzled. "Did you get a new car?" she said.

"No. My other one's in the garage, so I use this one every once in a while." She glanced at it before she sat down. It was a green Buick.

As they drove, Mose said, "You'll love this place. It's small and they only cook for the guests who have reservations."

"I've never even heard of it," Lucy said.

"You'll like it. Trust me."

The dinner was everything Mose said it was — individual attention from the chef and the owner, with food often prepared at tableside. But in a way, all of it was distracting. They hardly had time to talk at the restaurant. There seemed to be always someone serving them or cooing questions to them about how much they liked the meal.

At one of their quiet moments, Lucy suddenly said, "Oh," almost rhetorically. She grimaced and held her fingers to her lips as many people often do when they become aware of a distraction.

"What's wrong?" Mose said.

"I forgot something at work," she said.

"Something for you?" he said.

"No, something I was supposed to do."

"Do it first thing tomorrow morning."

She shook her head. "It was something I had to take care of. I have to go back tonight."

He took a deep breath. "I thought you might spend the night with me."

"Mose...I think we should slow down a little. I —"

"Let me get this straight: You go to bed with me..."

"Once," she interjected.

He ignored her comment, closing his eyes for a second as if to banish her remark. "...And *now* you tell me we should slow down. Do you have any idea how desirable you look tonight? Why do you look like this if you don't want me to think about making love with you?"

"It's just that I'm...this is all so new to me. I need a little time to get my head straight."

"Jesus," he said, looking down at his drink, "I think you're playing me for a fool, Lucy. I didn't force you into any of this."

She was hurt by his comment. His voice had an edge in it for the first time since she had known him. "Please, Mose, I'm not being a tease." She hesitated for a few seconds. "I've enjoyed our time together."

"How about the other night? Did you enjoy that time together?"

"You know I did. I said it, didn't I?"

"So, what's to decide? Why all the soul searching?"

"Because your life is very different than mine, Mose. Our times together are very nice. I like your company, and I'm happy when we go out."

"So what's the problem?"

"The problem is when I have to leave you and go back to my life alone. Then I'm not certain if I'm doing the right thing."

"Making love to me is the wrong thing? Keeping company is the wrong thing? Have I ever done anything to you that could be considered wrong? Haven't I always treated you with respect?" She nodded quietly, but didn't answer. "So again, what's the problem?"

"The problem is that what we're doing is going to change my life. And that I can get hurt and not just walk away from this. I think you can. I think you are far less vulnerable than I am. So please...let me sort some things out a little, okay? We'll talk about this again."

"When?"

"Soon. I need some time."

He was quiet for a moment, seeming a bit angry. "Just don't take too long. I think a lot of you, Lucy."

She nodded in acknowledgment. "And I of you, Mose. Can you drop me off at the YPD station?"

"How are you gonna get home then? Do you want me to wait for you?"

"My son's home. I'll just call him."

"I can wait," he said.

"I don't know how long I'll be," she said. "I'll be okay...really."

On the ride from the restaurant to the YPD station, they said very little. Lucy was upset with herself. With one foolish oversight, this whole thing started. Their conversation only veered into the direction it did because she had forgotten to put those sensitive papers from the Bellino case in the chief's inner office.

But it was more than that, and she knew it, and it bothered her. She had made love with a man who treated her gently and with respect. The lovemaking was so much better than it was with Ed. It wasn't as energetic, or as physical, but somehow it was better. It was everything she should have wanted. Yet...she felt dishonest, leading Mose to believe that there was not a longing for someone else, not a longing for all of it to be different. She felt cheap for using Mose's attentions when she knew all along that her heart was not ever going to forget the one person she thought about and longed for, the person who never gave her attention as Mose did, who never seemed to want her company... the one person she couldn't live without.

Tommy was tired. He hoped Elly would come soon. It would feel good to get home. It was one of those nights when the pressures of life that seemed to gnaw at his insides would drive him to the Silver Bridge. Strange how his life had changed. He wasn't a boozer as long as his life had some focus. But on days like these, when things seemed so confounded and when he was tired, he would turn to the bottle.

Elly had made the change in him. He wasn't lonely anymore. When he went home after a long day, there was someone there, there was warmth and voices and noise and excitement. There were wonderful, noisy, cantankerous children. There was Elly with her questions, with her beaming face and wide smile. And late at night there was the solitude without loneliness; there were things to care about, things to see and do... so many things that drinking never seemed to fit. His life had lost most of the demons that haunted him... except one.

Tommy stood up and stretched, glancing at the clock, wondering what was keeping Elly so late. His ribs ached and were still not healed yet. But he, as well as everyone else, was on the mend, except Liebowitz. And the killer was loose. But this time, he was going to exact revenge. Youngstown was used to violence, and bomb blasts, and murders. But these were different. These were of two beautiful kids and a gentle, innocent old man.

Tommy started for the liquor cabinet but stopped. He wasn't going to let booze keep his head muddled. He wanted to think clearly, as

351

clearly as he ever had when he was Tommy the Quarterback.

He walked toward the bay window that overlooked the street. He worried about where Elly could be. The soft rain was steady on the streets and fell in flashes as cars passed through the lamplight. He stared, watching cars go by, yearning still for a drink. Suddenly a car drove up to the front of the station, across the street, and stopped, with its motor running. Tommy looked at it carefully; there were two figures in the car talking. The light that reflected other passing cars would shine from time to time against the parked car. He watched as one car passed, then another. The car was green. It was a Buick.

Then, after a few minutes, one of the people got out of the car. And the car started down the street. It was Lucy, coming into the YPD station.

Tommy's breath came in huge gasps as he tried to collect his wits. Lucy? Of all the people in the world, he would least expect to see her get out of the green Buick.

Tommy was paralyzed, his heart seeming to beat in two rhythms, one thumping against his chest and another in his head and neck, making it seem that he was lapsing in and out of consciousness. Something ached, maybe it was his head, or his wounds from his ribs, or his sinuses, but it was painful and disorienting. Instinctively, he turned out the lights in his office and waited, trying to collect the thoughts that seemed to be crashing about in his head. She had something to do with the green Buick! Could she also have something to do with the bomb? Could she be the mole that worked as a spy for them on the investigation?

The moments passed and Tommy was in agony. What was he going to do? What could he do? Could she have something to do with the bomb? With Liebowitz? Oh, God! What would he do? How could she look him in the eyes and betray him? How in the hell did she get hooked up with the green Buick?

He tried to control his breathing so it couldn't be heard. But he couldn't control his heart which he could hear pounding in his chest. Suddenly, the door to the outer office opened. As Lucy walked on the terrazzo lobby, he could hear her heels click against the floor. Suddenly the heels were silent as she stepped onto the rug. She put her coat into the closet. Then, she sat at her desk for a few minutes. Tommy waited in the dark in the inner office, wondering how he could confront her... and when. She got up and walked to the file cabinet. Then she went back to her desk. Finally, she opened the door of Tommy's office and stepped into the dark room, carrying papers and files. She hesitated for a moment at the light switch, then decided to carry her burden a few steps more into the darkness.

Then, Tommy struck. He grabbed one of her arms and spun her back around toward him. She screamed, just as he turned on another, dimmer light at the switch. He grabbed her by the front of her blouse with both hands holding her beneath her neck. The papers had fallen all around them on the floor.

"What are you doing here?" he snarled, still holding her close to his face as he spoke. She was so horrified at the sight of Tommy's anger and the way he spat the words at her, that she couldn't speak. He shook her. "What!" he said angrily.

"I'm...I'm just getting those..." She stopped. She closed her eyes as though trying to wake up from an awful dream. She could feel his warm breath as he held her still.

"Tell me!" he said menacingly.

Never had she seen this kind of fury from the chief. And to think that the worst she had ever seen was being directed at her. She began to cry, tears escaping from under her closed eyes and rolled down her cheeks.

She never cried, not through all the beatings Ed had given her, not through all the loneliness she suffered, not through all the terrible times she had before meeting Tommy. But she cried now. In a minute, this man had done more to hurt her than anyone had ever done. And she couldn't stand it. She wanted to die, but she couldn't. So, she cried.

Tommy saw her tears and watched in silence as he held her near him. Slowly, he let her go, not even realizing he had relaxed his grip. "What are you doing here?" he said again, in a deliberate, almost conversational tone.

She responded this time. "These are the papers from both chiefs... about the Bellino case."

"So why are you back here now? Why not tomorrow morning?" He was growing angry again. "And why at night?"

"I just wanted them to be safe. I knew you needed them..."

"Don't lie to me, damn you!" Tommy said, kicking some of the fallen papers with his foot as he spoke.

She could hardly believe her ears, that this man who had been so gentle and kind for so many years was talking to her with such venom in his voice. "I'm not lying. Why don't you believe me? What do you think I've done?" she said plaintively.

"You have no idea, huh?"

"Please tell me, so I can explain."

"Okay. Explain the green Buick. Explain why you're hooked up with people like that."

"The green Buick? I never saw it until tonight."

"So, the guy you're banging lets you out of the green Buick and you expect me to believe you don't know a thing about it, right?"

Each moment with Tommy was more horrible than the last. She didn't even know the creature before her, who snarled at her like an angry bear, who was totally different that the man who for so many years spoke to her with such kindness. This was not Tommy the Quarterback; this was a monster.

"Why do you talk like that? I ..."

"Do you sleep with him or not? That's all I'm asking."

She closed her eyes again, but didn't answer. She hated what she was, what he had turned into, what he knew she had done. This nightmare was changing her whole life. She would never again trust civility or soft speech. It was all a fantasy, or a cruel deception before this inevitable day when she would be crushed for something she had never done. Suddenly, she lashed out at him, striking him across the chest with both hands, crying and sobbing, but saying nothing. Tommy grabbed both her hands, holding both her wrists in front to him, restraining her.

Just at that moment, Elly walked in the door to the inner office, seeing her father holding Lucy's arms between them, seeing Tommy's scowl and Lucy's tears. "Daddy, for God's sake, what are you doing?"

Tommy ignored his daughter. He finally let Lucy's hands go. "Only once," she said weakly, sobbing then.

"Dad, what are you doing? Stop this!"

Again, both Tommy and Lucy ignored her. "So, who's the lucky guy, Luce?" She stared back at him. "What's his name, goddammit?"

"Mose Pagliaro," she said softly.

Elly suddenly had some idea of what their confrontation was all about. "Jesus Christ!" Tommy muttered softly, stepping back away from them both. "Why didn't you just get a gun and shoot me, Luce?

It would have been easier, and no innocents would have been hurt."

Lucy sank to her knees now, sobbing uncontrollably. Elly went to hold her in her arms. "Get the hell out of here, Lucy. Get out of my sight," Tommy said angrily and coldly as he turned his back to her.

She had stood erect and just looked at Tommy's back. "I would never hurt you. You have to know that."

"I don't have to know anything. All I know is that bombs kill people. And you were shacking up with the guy that had that bomb planted."

"But I didn't know! Don't you understand that?"

Tommy took a deep breath and then turned back around to face them. "Take her home, El. She needs a ride."

"Dad, please. You can't let her go like this."

"Take her home, I said," Tommy snarled, "or I'll call a cab."

Bumpy walked through the backdoor of the Silver Bridge, looking grim and dejected. He had once thought that he wouldn't be making these trips anymore. Sherry pointed quickly to the back table where Tommy sat. He had been there two hours and was very drunk. Bumpy moved a chair and sat down at the table, casting his hat and gloves on a table near them and unbuttoning his coat. Neither man said a word for a few moments. Then, Bumpy turned back to Sherry. "Two coffees, Sherry."

"I don't want any coffee," Tommy said in slurred speech.

"Two coffees, Sherry," Bumpy said again, more deliberately. They sat in silence until Sherry brought the coffee and placed them between the two men.

Tommy raised his head to look at the coffees and stared at them a few seconds. "Don't even think about it," Bumpy warned. Tommy huffed but said nothing else. "Elly called me. She's scared as hell about you."

"I'm not the one she should be scared about," Tommy said.

"You mean Pagliaro?"

"She's been seeing him, Bump. Jesus Christ, when Liebowitz was killed, she was sleeping with Pagliaro."

Bumpy took a deep breath. "Look, I don't know what the hell's going on here, Tom, but if you're telling me that somehow Lucy was part of this Pagliaro deal, then I think you're out of your fucking mind."

"She got out of that green Buick, Bump. She was coming into my office in the dark, screwing around with the papers from the Bellino case."

"Tommy, I know it doesn't look good for her. But you've been a cop long enough to know that very different stories can fit the same set of facts."

"She sleeps with him, Bump."

"Listen, you're the one with the investigative instinct, Tom. And the only reason why it's not working now is…" He stopped.

Tommy looked up to meet his gaze. "Is what?"

"Is that you're in love with her and you can't stand the fact that she could be in someone else's bed." Tommy snorted in disbelief. Bumpy continued. "Tommy, you know damned well that Lucy would never hurt you. Come on, for Christ's sake! She's been in love with you for years."

"If she's in love with me, why is she banging Pagliaro, huh? Elly and Danny almost died because of that bomb, Bump. She couldn't be involved with Mose Pagliaro and not be part of it."

"Tommy…Jesse and Connie and Elly have all told me that Lucy

loves you. That's enough for me, and it's enough to know that she wouldn't hurt you." Tommy shook his head. "Well, then at least find out," Bumpy said. "If she's part of this whole scheme, then prove it and nail her to the wall. But I'll tell you something: she didn't plant that bomb, so there's someone else you have to nail before you get all done."

———————

Elly was awake, curled up with an Afghan on the sofa. She had never seen her father so angry. He didn't care about how much pain he caused; all he wanted was to punish Lucy. Elly had been crying as she paced the floor in the living room, and her breath coming in intermittent shudders because of her crying.

Suddenly, she could see car lights in the driveway. It was a YPD cruiser. A door slammed, and in a moment, Tommy was inside the house. It was only after he hung up his coat in the closet that he saw Elly sitting on the couch. He walked in and stood several feet from her. "Hi," he said.

"Are you alright?" she said calmly. He came closer, so he could see her face better in the dim light. Then, he saw the red, puffy eyes, the disheveled hair, and the dried tear stains on her cheeks. He was overcome with remorse and anguished because of the pain he had caused his daughter. He sat beside her on the opposite end of the couch.

"I'm okay," he said softly.

She could smell the whiskey on his breath. "Where were you?" she said.

"Drinking at the Silver Bridge."

"Did it make you feel better?"

"I thought it would."

"But it didn't?" He shook his head. "Dad?"

"What?"

"Did you hit her?"

He seemed hurt and turned toward her with a frown. "Of course not." He paused, staring at her for several seconds, trying to understand what she was feeling. "Do you think I would do that?"

She shook her head. "I've never seen you so angry. Why didn't you give her a chance to explain?"

"I was afraid of her explanations. I didn't want her to explain all this away."

"Afraid that she might convince you she's telling the truth?"

"Afraid I'd forget about being a cop just because it was Lucy lying to me."

"Dad, I know it looks bad, but I don't think she had any part in that bombing...She just wouldn't."

Tommy huffed in disagreement. "Then why did she —" He stopped, not just from talking about Elly, but not to think of it himself.

"I'll say it again, Dad. She loves you. And somehow you have to do something about this split between the two of you."

He shook his head. "I can't let this keep me from thinking straight, El. I have to look at what happened and see clues and relationships and motives. I can't afford to treat her special and hope to be a good cop. It wouldn't be fair to Neva and Danny."

She stood up and walked to the center of the living room, her face partially obscured in the dim light. "Dad, Uncle Smokey and Uncle Bumpy used to always tell me about you. You were the investigator; you had the instinct. But they always said you had something else. You had a good heart...and that's what made you Tommy the Quarterback." She paused a few seconds. "And you're keeping your heart away from this one."

The next morning, Tommy was in his office early. After a half hour, Bumpy came upstairs to see the chief. When he entered the office, he saw that Lucy wasn't there. He glanced at Tommy and then back to the desk. "Where is she?" he asked Tommy.

"I don't know, Liborio."

"Did you call her?"

"No."

"Why the hell not, Tom?"

"Because I'm not sure if someone who might be guilty of complicity to murder should be my secretary, okay?" Tommy said calmly.

"Jesus Christ," Bumpy muttered. "Can you look me in the face and tell me you think Lucy was in on all that?"

"How do you know she wasn't?"

"Tommy, for Christ's sake, this is Lucy we're talking about. What the hell are you thinking?"

"Just trying to be careful, Bump. The guy she's playing with had something to do with that bomb and you know it…and my gut tells me he had something to do with Danny and Neva."

He was silent for a moment. Then, he said, "You have to talk to her, Tommy. If you want to treat her like a suspect, go ahead. But you have to talk."

Tommy walked back to the bay window and stared outside for a few minutes. "Bump, have you ever questioned someone where you were afraid of the answer you might hear? Because you were afraid they might be guilty?"

"Tommy, I know you've been crazy about this lady for a long time…and it sure as hell must hurt. But if she's part of it, it's best to find out now."

Tommy nodded, but didn't respond. Finally, Bumpy said, "Uh… I'll see you later. I'll get a secretary up here right away."

"Thanks. I have that City Council meeting this morning, and a Safety Committee meeting all afternoon."

In a short time, Bumpy came in the door with a secretary. She was a chubby, pleasant woman with a bright smile. She would be good for a while. But she would never be Lucy.

Tommy worked a few hours on his presentation. No doubt they'd dwell on the bomb and the cost of rehabilitating the YPD garage. Some of the councilmen were up for election in the spring, so they might grandstand a little, but Carly could be burnt on all this, so he'd keep a lid on the most extreme reactions. He had no love for Tommy, but he didn't want extended discussion to get out of hand. Some of the councilmen might not mind seeing Carly in a jam. And some of them might not mind being mayor.

Tommy spent the morning answering questions about the YPD at City Council. For some reason, the councilmen were easy on him, and his testimony caused little discussion beyond a promise to call him back for an update in a month. The first questioner, an old friend who had been on Council many years, led the interview with questions about Tommy's injuries, and Danny's and Elly's. Then he asked about Tommy's long friendship with Liebowitz. At the end of the questioning, there was not much anyone else could ask except perfunctory questions about the cost of renewal of the building.

During the lunch break, Tommy called his temporary secretary, Mrs. Paulsen, for and update on the YPD. Everything was going routinely, she said. "But you did get a phone call from a man named Laz. He wouldn't give me his last name. He said you should meet him."

Tommy was quiet for a moment. "Okay, Mrs. Paulsen. Thanks. I'll call him."

After Tommy's testimony at the Council subcommittee, he left. He was curious about what Laz had found out for him. Slowly he drove his loner car down the narrow residential street where Laz lived. He stopped, looked around, and got out to go up to the porch. After only one ring of the bell, he could hear the halting, bumpy gait of Laz as he made it to the door, shouting for the caller to wait until he got there.

When the old man opened the door, Tommy stood still before him, almost as if to stand for inspection. Tommy had always noted the quick once-overs Laz gave people upon first seeing them. And Tommy had come to know over the years that it was important for Laz to think well of you. In that way, he was no different than he was as a high school football player more than forty years ago. "Hello, Laz," Tommy said simply.

"Why, hello there, Chief of Police. Come on in here."

As they walked back to Laz's kitchen, Laz said, "How're you doing, son? How're them ribs, and what else? Your neck? And how's Elly and that young lieutenant?"

"A lot better now, Coach. And Danny's going to be okay."

"And Elly? She was hurt some, too, right?"

"Not too bad. You know that kid, Danny, threw his body over her and took some hits. Else she'd have been much worse."

"Now why do you suppose he did that, Chief?"

Tommy chuckled. "I don't want to know, Laz. I'm too busy with other things."

"You know already, Tommy. You've always been smart about some things and dumber than hell about others."

Tommy looked around the kitchen into the doorway to the other rooms. "Man, I wish Ruby was here. She'd shush you when you got out of line."

"So, how's that beautiful secretary, kid? You propose to her yet?"

Tommy knew that Laz always let on that he knew much less than he did…and that he often asked questions when he already knew the answers. He did it as a football coach and he never changed throughout his life. It was a lesson Tommy learned early and used throughout his career as a cop.

"You know damned well I haven't," Tommy said.

"Yeah, I know. Look here, son. I found out some things this morning."

Tommy nodded, knowing that his old mentor was going to let him in on some of the things he had found out through the Youngstown grapevine. "I need all the help I can get, Laz. This one's tough. I still have nightmares about Elly and Danny backing away from that car just by the grace of God. And then I think of Liebowitz. Damn, I liked him, Laz. We went back a long time."

"I know, kid, I know. It's just one of them funny things. It was Liebowitz's time. But the Lord wasn't ready yet for Elly and Danny… or you."

"Yeah," Tommy said grimly. "So, what's the story, Laz?"

"Did you know that Chris Laney has been fucking the mayor's daughter?"

Tommy was surprised. "Honest to God?"

"Yep. You know her?"

"Nah. I remember seeing her for a few times when she was a little girl when she was in high school and in the papers when Carly was running for something."

"Well, she's supposed to be a knockout. And by the way, I don't think Carly knows."

Tommy squinted at Laz. "Come on, Coach. You didn't call me over here just to tell me one of my captains was banging Carly's daughter."

"Just hold on, son. Let me tell you the word down at the club. They all knows it, but no one's sayin' why. This Chris Laney? Word is, he's a stone killer…bad as any nigger crack dealer."

Tommy frowned skeptically. "I don't know, Laz. I don't like him, and I'm not sure he's capable of something like that."

"You didn't know he was banging Carly's daughter, either. This is just another piece."

"Okay, okay. What else?"

"He knows your boy, Mose Pagliaro, real well. How about that?"

Tommy stared at Laz a few seconds. The old coach savored these moments when he could tell the chief something he didn't know. "This is all good stuff, Laz. If there's any truth in it, it's gonna help a lot."

"One last piece, Tom. Carly and Pagliaro are a lot better friends than they want anyone to know."

Tommy was quiet for a few minutes, then he said, "Laz, how'd you come by all this?"

"People tell me things, Tommy. Some of the younger guys let me know what they see, what they hear. If they trust you, they talk. And most of the older guys especially knew about Laney. The Black cops that work for you know what's going on among the whites, you know."

Tommy raised his eyebrows in a grimace of appreciation. "This'll do me some good, Lazarus. Just keep your eyes and ears open and let me know if you hear anything else good. See you soon, huh?"

When Tommy left Lazarus, he decided to go home. He had some thinking to do. He had to sort out all the information Laz had served him. He had supper with Elly and the kids. Elly noticed that he was more quiet than usual, so she didn't engage him in weighty discussion. Later, after supper, he sat in the living room drinking coffee. *Somehow, there is a cabal revolving around Pagliaro. Laney's in on it, and so is Giustino. What could they all be doing? Could they be selling drugs? Could they be planting bombs and killing people, for God's sake?*

Suddenly, he stood up, and went to the hall closet to get his coat. "I'm going out for a while. I'll see you later."

Elly watched him leave after she said goodbye. She had been worried about him ever since the confrontation with Lucy. And then Bumpy brought him home drunk. It bothered her that he was aching inside, and she couldn't do anything to help.

Tommy drove through the murky twilight, holding the steering wheel tightly, struggling with the doubts that tormented him since he had caught Lucy in his office. He drove slowly, deliberately, to the North Side. He stopped before a small, neat building made of red brick that sat up from the street about fifteen feet, two flights of brick stairs up.

Tommy took a deep breath. This was going to be tough. He didn't need stairs to make it harder. Wearily, he climbed the steps. At the door he saw her name. He went into the small foyer and took another flight of stairs to the second floor.

Another deep breath. Then he knocked on the door. Somehow, it seemed less intrusive than ringing the bell. In a moment, Lucy opened the door. He was shocked at the sight of her. Her eyes were red, her hair fell loose and long down to her shoulders, and she seemed tired and hurt.

Tommy felt even worse at the sight of her than he ever imagined. How could he have done this?

Neither of them spoke. She still seemed angry despite her ordeal.

She looked back at him coldly, not welcoming him. "What do you want?" she said finally.

Tommy swallowed hard before answering. "Can I come in?" he said softly.

She hesitated for a second, then stood aside to let him in. He seemed to be contrite, so she tempered her anger at seeing him. And, truly, she wanted to see him.

She walked to the center of the room and turned to face him. Again, there was anger in her eyes, and a question about what he was doing there.

"Will you answer some questions for me?" he asked. She started to shake her head and to tell him to leave, but then she caught herself. "May I sit down...please?" he said.

This time she took a deep breath. "Yes."

"How long have you known him?"

She didn't answer right away, but instead closed her eyes and took another deep breath. "Why is it so horrible that I went out with him?"

"Because he's a murderer, that's why."

"He can't be. You just don't know him."

"How long have you known him?" Tommy repeated.

She was getting angry again. She flashed a look at Tommy, her eyes glaring with anger. "Almost two months."

"You've only known this guy for two months and you're convinced he's not a crook?"

"You don't know him at all, and you're convinced he is."

"I know more than you think, and he's a killer."

She shook her head. "You've known me for nine years and you think I'm a killer, too, don't you?"

Tommy was startled by her words. He stared ahead into the room.

He had to decide... Was she involved or not? "I never said that," he said weakly.

"But you think it."

"No, I don't, damn you." Tommy as getting angry too. "All I think is that you were used by a smooth talker to get to me. Do you have any idea what he does for a living?"

"He's in real estate."

Tommy chuckled cynically, shaking his head and muttering "Jesus Christ" softly as he listened. "Have you ever seen his name in the paper? Have you ever seen his name on a for sale sign? He's a goddamned drug dealer, Luce."

"And how do you know that?" she said, angry at his attitude.

"I know."

"Just the way you know about me?"

"Lucy, that green Buick is the one that was tailing me. Those two goons in it were YPD blues on Pagliaro's payroll."

"Then why didn't you say something to me?"

"Why should I involve you in something dangerous? How was I to know that you were seeing him? I don't pry into your personal life."

"You don't care about my personal life, you mean," she said.

"Don't do that. I always showed concern for you."

"Concern the way you did for every panhandler you meet on the street. I never had any reason to think that you cared about who..." She stopped and shook her head to herself, disgusted at her weakness, of how her feelings for him made her so vulnerable. "What other questions do you have?" she sighed, wanting to change the subject.

"Tell me..." He stopped. He was using his investigator's voice, cool and formal. But he wanted to talk naturally, and he couldn't. He tried again. "Luce, I..."

She held up her hand, palm front, as if to block what he said. "Don't tell me you're sorry, because I know you don't mean it."

"I do mean it."

"No, you don't," she said bitterly. "You still don't believe me."

"Would you believe it if our roles were reversed?" he said. As he spoke, she turned her back to him and walked toward a sofa, perpendicular to the love seat that Tommy sat on. "If I told you I had slept with…"

She let out a shriek and sank to her knees on the floor, facing away from him. She started to cry and folded her hands behind her head and clasped her arms tightly against the sides of her head, as though to blot out the world around her that hurt so much.

Tommy had never seen this in all his life. He had never been the cause of personal anguish to a woman, any woman…and never was prepared for the remorse he felt for having caused her torment, hers above all others.

He sprang from his seat and went over to her. At first, he didn't know what to do. He touched her head, but she shrugged away. She was moaning low in her throat and sobbing. He wanted to touch her again but didn't know how. Then he just knelt beside her and put his arms around her. She resisted for only a moment. She settled into his arms, crying loudly and sobbing against his chest.

All of this was new to Tommy. He had never been this personal with a woman, not even with Janet in their best moments. Never had he caused this kind of pain to someone he cared about. "I'm so sorry, Luce," he whispered. "I'm just a dumb fool. I didn't know what I was doing to you."

Suddenly, he did something he never knew he could, as though he never intended it, yet as though he couldn't stop himself. He brought his lips to the crown of her head and kissed her. Then, he kissed her forehead.

They stayed together for several minutes. She made no attempt to break free of the arms that were enfolding her, and he never loosened the arms that held her. "I didn't mean to hurt you," she said softly. "I didn't mean it. I didn't mean it."

What a strange, new sensation: here he was with the woman he loved and desired for years, only now he was not admiring her from a distance where he could look and not touch, dream and imagine. Suddenly, the dreams had all materialized into one shape, the dark brown hair and lovely body of Lucy, who he held in his arms.

After several minutes, they both realized that they had been in an embrace. At what seemed the right time, they came apart. Tommy loosened his arms to move back slightly. She also moved slightly to look at him. "Are you okay?" he asked. She shrugged, looking down away from his gaze. "I knew you couldn't have done those things. It was my ego. I was hurt because you went out with someone else. It wasn't supposed to bother me, but it did. And after the bomb, when I found out it was Pagliaro..." Tommy stopped, looking at her as she sat beside him on the love seat.

She was just looking back at him, her eyes red and her face streaked with tears. Tommy didn't know what to say or how to say it. Finally, he did something that he was good at, something so foreign to the moment, but a change. After a few seconds of eye contact between them, he said, "You look awful."

She was surprised, and let out a soft huff, not smiling, but brightening a little. "These haven't been two of my better days," she said softly. She looked away, afraid that at the memory of her anguish, she would be in tears again.

"Luce?"

"What?"

"I'm really sorry." He started to reach for her hand, but then hesitated. She didn't move hers, and let it rest on her knee. She was sitting on her legs that were folded under her on the couch.

"I know you are," she sighed. "I was just angry."

"I found out a long time ago that people are often cruelest to those they care about the most."

"You care about me? Even though I slept with Mose Pagliaro?"

"I have always cared about you," he said.

"But you never said it."

"I was afraid."

"Of me?"

"Afraid of making a fool of myself. Afraid you might think I was using my position to..."

"I never would have felt that," she interrupted.

"You never made me feel that you would welcome that kind of talk."

"I don't act that way. You were my boss."

"Yeah. And I was not in your league. Hell, look at me and look at you. I was afraid I'd insult you."

"You would never insult me," she said.

He didn't respond. For several minutes they sat on the love seat, close enough to touch easily, but not touching. She wondered what he was thinking. She could sense his grappling with the thoughts he had, and struggling to imagine them spoken. "I didn't want to know that you were somehow involved." He shook his head. "I didn't want to believe that you could be part of it...And I didn't want to imagine him touching you."

He looked at her and saw tears welling up in her eyes again. This time, he reached out and touched her hand. She clutched at his and held it. "I never wanted him to be the one. Since Ed, I've been to bed with one man in twelve years. One time. I was lonely and afraid of growing old without ever having someone, just once before I died, make real love to me." She hesitated. "I'll just never know."

"Hell, Luce, it's easy to love you. You just don't meet anyone but cops and politicians."

"How do you know how easy it is?" she said.

"I just know."

"Have you ever loved anyone?"

He snorted, and looked over at her, but said nothing, looking as though he was incapable of speech. She suddenly realized that of all the dreams she ever had, this one could come true. He was shy and would never speak to her as boss and suitor. If he loved her, he'd kept it in his heart all this time. "Who did you love?" she said softly.

He couldn't answer her. She could see the fear in his eyes. He looked away, and then looked back at her. He shrugged. "Who?" she said again, barely audibly.

"You," he said, his voice weakened by the fear of what she would say to something so improbable.

She moved toward him, sitting closer on the love seat. "How long?" she asked. "As long as I've loved you?"

At first, Tommy thought he had imagined what she said. Then, he turned toward her. "Me? You mean that?" She nodded. "But why didn't you tell me?"

"For the same reason you didn't tell me. I was afraid. You were my boss. I was just a secretary."

He stood up and walked across the room, and stopped, speaking with his back to her. "Luce, this is the best thing that's ever happened to me." He was shaking his head as he talked. He turned around to face her. "But I can't handle this until…until I solve this case."

"I know," she said.

"You mean what you just said? You love me?"

"Yes. Did you mean it when you said you love me?"

He snorted at his good fortune. He had never felt as good in his whole life as he did that moment. "Yeah. How about that?" She smiled finally. "Luce?"

"Yes…Tom?" It was the first time she had ever called him by his first name, and it seemed as strange to her as it sounded wonderful to him.

"I can't go back to that office if you're not there. Will you come back?"

She nodded. "I'll be back."

"Luce?"

"Yes?"

"I'm sorry I ever hurt you." He still stood away from her, talking across the room.

"And I'm sorry about Mose. I wish it never happened."

"It's okay. I'm over it."

"Tom, solve this case soon, please."

"I will, kid." He hesitated for a few seconds. "Lucy, if you ever lie to me, my life will come tumbling down. Nothing else will ever make me happy again."

"I'll never lie to you," she said.

He walked toward her, and she stood up. "I have to go," he said again. She was standing very close to him. "Can I kiss you?" he said.

With that, she smiled and raised her lips to his. The kiss was the most wonderful feeling Tommy ever had. It was gentle and tentative and warm and magical. His arms went around her, and she fit perfectly into his embrace. He had never in his life held anyone so soft in his arms. He had never in his life held anyone who wanted to be there, who really loved him. "I have to go," he said. "See you tomorrow, okay?"

"Tommy the Quarterback," she said softly, smiling as she helped him zip his coat.

Part IV

The Snakes

WHEN TOMMY CAME TO the office the next morning, he smelled the coffee brewing as he opened the door. Lucy was there already, and she beamed as he walked in to see her. "Hi," she said.

"Hi, yourself. You're here early," he said as he entered his office. "Come on in here, will you?"

He hung up his coat in the closet and she waited in the middle of the room near his desk. He walked over to her and kissed her gently and quickly and then walked to his desk. "I think I've forgotten why I asked you in," he said. She laughed.

They both agreed to be discreet about the two of them, at least for a while. There was so much to be done. Tommy was going to look all over the Valley to find the killers. He also knew that Mose Pagliaro was the ringleader. He just had to figure out how.

"I have to know the whole story about Pagliaro. Will you tell me?"

"Yes," she said, "as much as I know."

"What are you going to tell him when he calls you?"

"I'm going to tell him that I can't see him anymore," she said matter-of-factly.

"You know he's going to want to see you."

"I know. I'll tell him it's over."

"But what if he wants to see you face to face?"

"I'll tell him I can't — won't."

Tommy paused a few moments. "I don't trust him," he said.

"He won't hurt me. I don't know anything about his business."

"Lucy... I'll never make it if he does anything to you."

"He won't, Tom. It's not his style."

"But he can pay for someone to do his dirty work for him. He's a killer by remote control, Luce. He just doesn't like to get his own hands dirty."

She wilted slightly at the thought of Mose being a killer, being a man so unlike his persona when he was with her. "How could I be so wrong," she said aloud, but really to herself.

"I know you had feelings for him, Luce."

"But it wasn't love, Tommy. You have to believe that."

"I know. We'll talk, okay? Can you see me tonight?"

She huffed and smiled. "There will never be a time when I can't see you," she reassured him.

She went back out to her desk and began working. Tommy also began working quietly. He was finally going to get a new car, after a few reams of paperwork. He also wrote some letters to City Councilmen. The time passed quickly.

Suddenly, as Bumpy burst into the chief's office, he was startled when he saw Lucy.

"Hi, Chief," Lucy said brightly, smiling. "He's in there," she said, cocking her head in Tommy's direction.

What the hell? Bumpy thought. *What had Tommy done? Lucy's back to work, smiling. What's going on?*

He closed the door behind him into Tommy's office. "Liborio," Tommy acknowledged without looking up from a memo he was writing. Bumpy sat down in front of the desk and stared at his friend. "They're finally going to order my new car, Bump," he said as he put the finishing touches on the memo while his thoughts were organized.

"Fine. Anything you want to tell me, Tommy?"

"Just go out there and catch some crooks, kid."

"Come on, you bastard. How come Lucy's back to work, looking like a million bucks?"

"She always looks like a million bucks, remember?" Tommy said with a smirk. But after a few seconds of smug secrecy, he knew it was time to tell his old friend about Lucy. "We made peace, Bump."

"How much peace did you make, kid?"

"Not that much."

"Jesus. You need lessons or something...or have you forgotten how?"

"She knows how I feel about her. And I know how she feels about me."

"So?"

"So, we let this ride until I get this bombing and the Bellino case settled. I can't do two things so big at the same time...maybe when I was younger, I could have, but not now."

"But that could take forever."

"Not if I nail two people," Tommy said. "I'll bet my next paycheck those two things are related. And Lazarus just told me that Laney and Pagliaro share the same jockstrap."

"You have to figure it that way. But it helps to hear Laz confirm it."

While they were talking, Elly got off the elevator and headed down the wide corridor to Tommy's office. She walked in and saw Lucy with her back to her, looking into a file cabinet. Lucy looked up to Elly and turned to face her. Lucy smiled, a radiant smile that set her whole face aglow. "Hi, Elly," she said to the speechless younger woman.

"Uh...Hi, Lucy," she answered with all the surprise and wonder she felt written on her expression.

"Your dad's in with Chief Malatesta," Lucy said, pointing back over her shoulder. "I'll tell him you're here." She alerted Tommy on the intercom. Then, Lucy escorted her into Tommy's office. Bumpy was just leaving. He winked at Elly, who still had an amazed expression, and left the office silently.

"Interested in lunch?" Elly said to her father.

"Sure, you buying?"

"I'll buy...Dad?"

"Yeah?" Here it comes again, he thought.

"Lucy's back, huh?"

"Yeah," he answered as he went to get his coat. He knew what was in store for him if he didn't level with her. He waited for the onslaught.

"Was she here yesterday?"

"No, this is her first day back."

Elly was unsatisfied, of course. "But she looks...so beautiful."

"She always looks beautiful, El," Tommy said.

"Not like this," she said, turning back to look at the closed door behind her. "The last time I saw her, she was..."

"She's better now. Let's go," Tommy said, walking to the door.

"But..." Elly followed him but stopped her questioning as they entered the outer office. Lucy was at her desk.

"We're going to lunch," Tommy said to Lucy.

She smiled, again a radiant smile. "Enjoy it," she said.

Elly looked at her father the minute Lucy answered him. He was cool...no message in the facial expressions. It was all in the eyes. And he and she had communicated something. Elly's heart began beating faster.

On the way downstairs, Tommy hurried, trying to be a half step ahead of his daughter. "Where's your car?" he said, interrupting a question that was poised on her lips.

"Dad," Elly said, "you know you're going to have to sit still some time. We can't eat on the run."

All through the trip to the restaurant, in the car, Tommy tried to avoid talking about Lucy. But at the restaurant, he was trapped. "So? What's happened that you don't want to talk about with me?"

"Nothing. We made peace."

She studied his face and then took a sip of her coffee. "Peace, huh? Who do you think you're fooling?"

"I'm not trying to fool anybody. I..."

"Dad, she looks like a ray of sunshine in your office. I've never seen her look so happy. And you don't look so bad yourself."

"Well, thank you, daughter." Then he hesitated for a few seconds. "Is it that obvious?"

"It is to the people who are close to you."

"Bumpy noticed."

"So, what happened? Tell me."

"Well, we started arguing about everything... Mose Pagliaro."

"And?"

"It was bad. And she began to cry. And somehow, I found the courage to say I loved her."

"You did? What did she say?"

"That she loves me."

"Wonderful... So that's the reason for the glow," Elly said, almost to herself, answering her own question.

"Listen. We have to keep this quiet. There are killers out there who would try to get to me through her. That was Pagliaro's idea."

"What are you going to do about Pagliaro?"

"I'm gonna hunt down all his hatchet men and then I'm gonna castrate them...especially Pagliaro for using Lucy."

Elly hesitated for a moment. "Dad, could he really be involved in the killings of Danny's kids?"

"You can bet the house on it, kid. That poison's coming from one source."

Judge East walked wearily into the mayor's office. Jodi, the secretary, ushered him in, knowing that he was never to be kept waiting in the outer office. Inside, Carly was finishing a conversation with a city councilman and he motioned to the judge to be seated in his usual chair.

"How are you, Judge?" Carly said when he finished his call.

"Getting by, Carly. What do you hear about the police?"

"Reconstruction started on the YPD garage...and both McCarrie and Danny Bellino have gone back to work."

"That bombing hurts us, Carly. When something like that happens on your watch, it stays with you when you want to move up."

"Goddamned crazy people, Judge."

"Do you have any idea who it was?"

"I think it was Pagliaro, but he denied it."

"What in hell is the matter with them?! Kill the chief of police? They must be out of their minds."

"I don't know what he's up to, but he must have a lot more to hide than we thought," Carly muttered.

The judge was silent for a few minutes. The he changed the subject. "I'm retiring, Carly."

"What?"

"I'm retiring at the end of spring. I sent my letter yesterday to the presiding judge."

"But Kel…"

"We've been over this before, Carly. I don't have the energy anymore. And there are some mornings that my back aches so much that I can barely get out of bed."

Carly sighed. "What am I going to do without you, Kel?"

"I have a telephone, Carly. You know where I live."

"But you always have your hand on the pulse down at the courthouse."

"I'll keep in touch," the judge said. Then he was quiet for a few seconds. Carly could tell that he had something more on his mind. Judge East was strangely reticent, hesitating to deliver his bad news. He started to speak and then stopped. Finally, he spoke, "Carly?"

"What is it, Kel?" Carly said softly, bracing himself to hear something awful.

"I was in the men's room at the courthouse this morning and I heard a couple of attorneys talking. They didn't know I was there… It was about Lisa."

Carly was attentive. "Yeah? What about Lisa?"

"Well, they say she's sleeping with someone."

"Well, who?" Carly said irritably.

"A police officer," the judge said grimly. "You know him, Carly… Captain Christopher Laney."

Carly closed his eyes. Of all the names he could have heard, Laney's was the one he dreaded hearing most. He fell back into his chair and looked helplessly at his mentor.

"Could you be wrong?" he said.

"Maybe… but I don't think so."

"Jesus Christ," Carly muttered under his breath. If there were any man in the world he would not want his daughter involved with, it was Chris Laney. His head fell forward as though he had become unconscious. Finally, he looked up at the judge in despair. "What am I going to do?"

"Well, just how bad is this guy?"

Carly snorted. "About as bad as you can get. He looks like a movie star. He can lie and look you right in the eyes as he does it. I swear he could kill someone without missing a heartbeat. I don't think he has a conscience."

"How in the hell does a guy like that become a policeman? And what in God's name made you appoint him to head that special unit on the Bellino case?"

"I wanted to screw Tommy McCarrie over," Carly said, not telling the judge that the special squad was Mose Pagliaro's idea.

"Carly, you have to understand something: You can't always give vent to your feelings and then jump into these dumb decisions. Sometimes you have to let things pass."

Carly nodded, as he always did when the judge lectured him about his life and career. "He put my dad in jail twice, Kel."

"That's no excuse for self-destructive behavior, Carly. That time's passed. And if you're not careful, you'll be in jail, too," the judge said irritably. "Stop going out of your way to make new enemies out of your dad's old enemies."

"It's not your dad who's been fucked over."

"Don't lecture me about your father. I've known him longer than you have. He wasn't some wallflower who McCarrie kept harassing for no reason. He did some shady things you didn't know about...and the fact is, he got caught."

Carly didn't answer the judge. Instead, he was quietly thoughtful for several minutes. Then, he said, "What am I going to do about Lisa?"

"Can you talk to her? Will she listen to you?"

"No," he sighed.

"Then call Laney in and tell him to let her go or —"

"Or what?"

"Or you'll have him heading up the traffic detail on the night shift."

"He knows damn well I can't do that. McCarrie would fight any meddling in the YPD. Look at all the trouble he caused about the Bellino squad."

"Carly, somehow you have to break this up. By the way, isn't he a lot older than she is? How'd she get hooked up with him?"

Carly snorted. "I wish I knew."

When Judge East left, Carly sat somberly in his office. Shortly after, Jodi entered and walked up to his desk. "Are you alright, Carly?" she said.

"Yeah, I'm okay," he said softly.

"Is there anything you want me to do?"

"No." Such a request, not too long ago, would have been met with knowing looks and an afternoon of stealthy passion. Now the mayor sat somberly staring at her, not wanting to think of the pleasures he could have with Jodi, pleasures that he once enjoyed at his call. "I'm going home, Jodi. If anything important turns up, call me."

"Okay, Carly. Are you sure I can't do anything?"

"Yeah," he said.

Virginia Giustino had been waiting for Carly to call her as he usually did. They were to go to a Cavour Club banquet later, and she always needed time to reassure herself that she looked presentable. Carly always looked so youthful for his age. She was always tormented by her own looks that seemed to evaporate before her eyes as she looked into the mirror. She felt dowdy and gray, a pale shadow of the look she once had, the kind that attracted Carly to her, the body that seemed so lush and desirable a long time ago.

She heard the garage door open and looked outside to see Carly's Cadillac going in. In a moment, he was in the kitchen. For a few seconds they stared at each other wordlessly. She had become so tentative lately. All the things that bothered her had eroded what she once was, that attractive, personable, and intelligent self. She had also learned, over the years, to be careful around Carly because of his volatile temper, careful to phrase her words in such a way that they would not elicit an angry outburst from her husband, careful not to imperil his political ambitions. She knew she was always being watched by both Carly's political friends and by his enemies. And worse yet, she was being evaluated as though she were a competitive figure skater: a flaw was magnified, remembered, counted, and always held against her, no matter how much other good she did.

And all along, she made choices, for her lifestyle, for her daughter, choices for Carly. Choices that began as accommodation that gradually reshaped her as a sculptor reshapes a mass of clay. So, she changed, and grew more quiet, and more resigned to her life. And then, all the accommodation became silent capitulation. And as Carly's political ambitions grew, she was less important in his life. He listened to others, like his father, or Judge East. So, she quietly bore the burden of raising their daughter alone and suffering wistfully for missing with

Carly all the little things that Lisa did, all the lovely bits of memories they would never have together.

And she was alone even though they slept together in the same bed. And when the younger women that he admired so much were readily available, she was more alone. And their bed became just one more way they showed their estrangement. It was a forbidding place where sex occurred rarely and usually as a joyless afterthought, an act of surrender, not love. And in every moment with him she sensed the aura of the other women.

And the terrible, final pain came from the mirror. Her hair was graying, her skin more sallow, her eyes devoid of sparkle, and her body without the contours that once made her so attractive. She looked square; she looked tired.

Even though, now, Carly seemed to be trying harder, and it was better, it still was not good. Time was taking its toll. And the intimate joy, so long forgotten, was gone, too — if it was ever more than her imagining. And the gnawing fear that he could betray her again, just on impulse, haunted her and made her afraid.

"Hi," he said, looking away from her and walking to the closet to hang up his coat.

She knew right away that there was something wrong. But this time he was avoiding her gaze, so she knew, from years of knowing, that this was personal, not political. "What's wrong, Carly?" she said without trying to be careful with her words.

He sat heavily in a chair facing her. "Lisa's been shacking up with Chris Laney."

The words made the hair on Ginny's arms tingle. "How do you know?" she said.

"Kel East told me. He overheard some lawyers down at the courthouse…people who weren't friends of mine."

"Oh, God! I never liked him. He's creepy…makes my skin crawl when I'm near him."

"You're one of the few women who feel that way. All the rest want to hop into his bed."

"But where did she meet him? How can she be mixed up with a man like that?"

"I don't know," said Carly weakly.

"We have to stop her, Carly."

"I know. I just don't know how to do it. She won't even talk to me. I know you've talked to her. Will she listen to you now?"

"Not anymore. She feels that I've chosen sides with you against her."

He hesitated for a moment. "Have you?"

"How can you ask me that? I've always been on your side, but that doesn't mean I'm against our daughter."

<hr>

Tommy was feeling better. The days had been bright and cool. The promise of a beautiful Ohio autumn came at the same time as Cleveland Browns, Spring Common, Ohio State, and Notre Dame football. And now, each morning, as he awakened, he realized that he wasn't lonely anymore. And it was not just the delightful, chattering children, and Elly with here marvelous smile and questions. Now, it was the thought that Lucy, who he could only dream about in his darkest moments, was now his. That she had pledged her love to him, that there would be days ahead filled with her presence, days with her special magic.

Maybe my life's too good for me to be a good investigator, he thought. *Maybe I have to be edgy to see things right.* And lately, the words of the dear departed Smokey played over and over in his mind. *What told Smokey that there was something right before everyone's eyes? But what? Could Chris Laney be the undiscovered key? Could he have killed Danny and Neva? It just didn't make sense. Why would a police captain turn into a killer of children? And why wouldn't someone know it?*

Tommy stared out the bay window. It was going to be a nice day in Youngstown — windy, but fair. But some people did know about Laney. Lazarus said he was a killer. And Smokey knew there was something, maybe someone, that everyone had overlooked.

He could hear Lucy arrive to work. But he could also hear her talking to someone. Bumpy was gone for the week? Who? In a moment, his door opened. Lucy peeped in. "Hi," she whispered from the doorway. "Chief Mencken."

Pete followed her introduction into the room. "Hi, Chief," he said to Tommy. It was a funny ritual that had developed between Tommy and a few close friends: Upon greeting him for the first time, they called him "Chief," acknowledging his position. Then, for the rest of their conversations, he was "Tommy." And Tommy, in turn, often did the same with them.

"How's everything, Chief?" Tommy responded.

"Can't wait till Bumpy gets back."

"You're doing fine, Pete. You just don't like wearing two hats."

"Yeah, that narco squad is really getting interesting now."

"So, what's the story on the bombing? Anything?"

"Not much, Tom. It was a pro hit. We can't even pinpoint where the stuff came from, and the FBI's all over it."

Tommy looked outside again. "Pete," he said without looking back to his friend, "that hit on Danny and Neva was done with a .32 automatic, right?"

"Yeah?"

"And we've checked out every gun shop in the Valley, right?"

"That's what Laney said. Why?"

"Did you read all the reports about the murder weapon?"

"Yeah...What's up, Tommy?"

"They gave short shrift to the weapon, Pete. Laney had that squad check out the gun shops, but never followed up on anything."

"But he said that only a few places sold .32 ACP rounds in the last three years, and they were expensive as hell compared to more common rounds. Besides, all the buyers checked out...a couple of World War II vets..."

"There's someplace else they didn't check out," Tommy said.

"But where? I thought they covered their tracks okay on this one, Tom."

"How about the YPD range?"

Pete stared at the chief for several seconds, as though not believing what he had just heard. Tommy nodded to his questioning look. "You think the killer was on the job, Tommy?"

"Hunch, Boyo. All this time I've been recovering from that bomb blast, I've been studying those reports. That squad did everything but check out our range. In fact, you could see Chris Laney's hand in this whole thing: leads not followed, logical questions not asked, investigative procedures not followed, all of them signed at the end of the day. Laney had those guys running in circles. Now why do you suppose he did that?"

"Jesus Christ," Pete muttered. He knew Tommy too well to doubt his instincts.

"What do you want to bet there's a .32 automatic carrier on the YPD?"

"He'd by stupid to flash it now. When the whole world knows

those kids were killed by a .32."

"That's just the point, Pete. No one knows. If you read that pile of bullshit, you realize that a critical piece of evidence is buried in a mass of worthless data. You wouldn't know it unless you were looking for it...unless you suspected that someone deliberately buried it."

Pete eyed his boss. "Jesus, you think Chris Laney's the killer, don't you?"

"Bet the house on it, kid. I just don't know why."

"So what're we gonna do?"

"I'd like you to do me a favor. I can't do it because it would look too suspicious...but I'd like you to go check out the YPD range. Too bad old Vito's gone, because he'd remember back a lot of years. But ask Lorenzo if he can remember anyone shooting a brick of .32s lately."

"God, Laney wouldn't be that dumb, would he?"

"I'm not sure, kid. All I know is that if we find someone who concealed carries a .32 automatic, and has shot it recently, then this game is gonna change a whole lot."

———◆◈◆———

Lisa Giustino couldn't keep her promise to forget Chris Laney. She couldn't forget the coke and she couldn't forget the passion she felt when they made love. Yet, she wasn't sure if she wanted him back, if she wanted his strange aloofness, the lingering doubt that he ever cared for her at all.

So, she dialed his number and waited for him to answer. "Chris," she said, "I'd like to come over to get a few of my things."

"Sure, come on over," he said.

On her way over to see him, she wondered what he would be like. Would he be forgiving? Would he be warm? Would he be cold?

When she arrived at his condominium, he opened the door after she knocked, even though she still had a key.

She entered and faced him in his living room, both of them in awkward silence. "How have you been?" he said, finally.

"Okay," she answered. "How about you?"

"Fair," he said.

"Fair? Why?"

He hesitated for a moment. "Things have been rough at work. Your dad disbanded the special squad I was heading up…and I lost my girl-friend."

"My dad's a real asshole sometimes," she said. "You lost your girl?"

"Yeah. That's the part that hurts."

"Oh, Chris," she said, shrugging. "You can be an asshole, too. I would never leave if you hadn't driven me out."

"Yeah. Sometimes I make dumb mistakes. You want to take off your coat?"

She knew, if she took off her coat, that she would be staying. But without hesitation, she took it off. Laney looked at her and drew a deep breath of satisfaction. She was his again.

He walked over to her and kissed her hungrily. She responded in kind with her lips and her body. In a few minutes, they were in bed.

Later that night, when they lay awake, spent from the sweaty, almost desperate sex, Laney said, "Want to do a few lines?"

"No…I'm going to give that all up," she said quietly.

"Why? Don't you like the way it feels?"

"I like it too much, but I'm getting scared. Sometimes my heart beats too fast, and I can't see things right after we're done."

He shrugged, and then lay back down on the bed. "What did my dad do to you?" she said.

He didn't like to talk about career defeats, especially with her. Especially when it was her father that did the damage to him. "Not just to me, but to our whole squad," he said. "He fucked it all. We were doing our job, and he just pulled the squad. Word is that McCarrie made him do it."

"McCarrie can't make him do anything. He hates him."

"McCarrie must have something on him. Else he would have fired him day one," Laney said. "We have to get rid of that old wino. He's constantly fucking our program up."

"Maybe you should talk to my dad about firing him," she said naively.

Laney snorted. "Your dad has other people he has to listen to."

"Judge East?" she said.

"No. Mose Pagliaro."

"My dad doesn't listen to anybody, not my mother, not my grandfather. When he was..." She stopped, recoiling from her allusion to her grandfather as though he were dead. "Pagliaro? He hardly ever mentions him. Are they friends?"

"No, but Pagliaro helped him get elected."

She shrugged slightly, seeming disinterested in anything relating to her father's politics. None of it ever brought happiness to the family. For Lisa, politics represented only bad things in her life: her father hardly ever home, his temper, his volatility, the fights between him and her mother, the tears her mother shed. "I hate politics. I wish he never was in all this. We were happier before."

"He wants to be governor," Laney said.

"I think he wants to be president," she said thoughtfully.

Laney as quiet. If Carly were governor or something more, maybe he'd be of better use to Carly than he is now. Maybe Carly would appoint him chief of the YPD for starters.

"What are you thinking?" Lisa asked.

"I'm thinking that someday you'll have to choose between me and your father," Laney said, turning toward her.

She didn't answer him. She knew what Carly was; she knew his moods, his temper, his affairs, his ambitions. But somehow, she also knew that he cared about her, enough so that she could fill him with anger when she wanted to. And strangely, she knew he cared about her mother.

Laney was different, uncertain. Lisa could never figure out if Laney cared for anybody. He said he cared for her, but maybe it was just her body that he cared for. Maybe he had to learn caring from her. Or maybe he would never learn, and that was her gamble.

Pete felt a rush as he headed out to the YPD range. It was connected to the station by a concourse that led to the back end of the building. *Jesus, I'm back in homicide again,* he thought contentedly.

Of all the group of friends that ran the YPD, only Pete and Tommy missed the hunt. Smokey was a ramrod-straight, perfect administrator. Bumpy was an organizer and facilitator, able to speak to the hearts of the men he commanded, and able always count on their adoration and respect. Med was a tinkerer, good with his men, too, but never the energy to go outside the station. His legs and knees hurt, and getting in and out of cars during investigations was agony, something to be avoided as years passed. Med had learned to run a clean shop with a carefully chosen crew. He knew more about cars that anyone on the force.

Only Tommy and Pete loved the agonies of investigation. Tommy, when he was an investigator, had the gift of insight. Pete always admired his friend for his instincts, especially since Tommy did not act as though he was special. Tommy was one of those people who always seemed to learn from others, curious and questioning without ego and pretense. He was a master who did not act like one, still more of a student than a teacher. Tommy had the one thing that never threatened his friends and instead earned him their undying respect: humility. He always acted as though he couldn't do his job without them. He always hoped they would be his friends.

Pete entered the storeroom where the ammunition and guns were kept. "Chief?" said Lorenzo. "Ain't seen you here in a long damn time." He was smiling at a man he had known for many years.

"How ya doing, Lorenz?" Pete said. "Thought I'd come down here to see if you earn any of that big money we pay you."

Lorenzo smirked. "You know when I hit the lottery, I'm gone, right?"

"How's the back, kid?" Pete said, more seriously.

"No good to complain," said Lorenzo.

Pete nodded, understanding well that Lorenzo had many painful days since he took a slug in his back and fell down a flight of stairs. "You ever gonna retire, Zoe?"

"Someday, Pete. When I can't handle this range anymore."

"You seem to be doing okay."

"Yeah," Lorenzo said, knowing now that this was more than a chance meeting. Pete was there on a mission. "So, what's up, Chief?"

Pete hesitated a second, then spoke. "You have any .32s back there?"

"For you?"

"Yeah. You got any?"

"Yeah. I keep a few bricks back there. I only order them about once a year...Nobody uses them anymore."

"So why order them?"

"Well, actually, one of our guys comes in here once in a while and blows some rounds."

"Yeah? Who?"

Lorenzo hesitated. "Chris Laney."

Pete's heart began to beat faster, making his words sound breathless as he spoke. "You sure it's Laney, Zoe? No one else?"

"Nah. He carries it as a backup. It's a beautiful little thing...a Seacamp, I think, near like those old Baby Brownings."

"Uh, Zoe, I want you to do me a hell of a favor."

"Yeah? What?"

"I want you to go back into the barrels and get me some of those spent .32s."

"Jesus, Pete, you want me to find a needle in a haystack! That'll take a hundred hours."

"I need them, Lorenz."

"Christ, Pete, he could have been here a month ago, and he doesn't always shoot his backup. You realize how many shells are shot here in a month?"

Pete raised his hands, sweeping away Lorenzo's argument as though clearing his way through a forest, the same Italianate gesture he unconsciously copied from Bumpy over the years. "Zoe, I need those shells. Now are you gonna get 'em for me or not?"

"How many do you need?" said Lorenzo dolefully.

"About a dozen. That should do it."

"It'll take a few days."

"No problem. But get them quick as you can."

"What the hell's this crazy deal about, Pete?"

"I'm just trying to find out some things."

"You want me to invest a week's work into finding some shells that Chris Laney shoots?"

"Zoe, will you get me the fucking shells?"

"Yeah, I will," Lorenzo growled.

"Thanks for the help, kid," Pete said as he turned to leave the range. Then, he stopped and turned back to Lorenzo. "Uh, Zoe, we didn't have this conversation, right?" Lorenzo nodded.

Later, Pete was in his office. Tommy would be glad to hear what he had found out. Sure enough, Laney carried a .32 and was probably the only cop in the YPD that did. Most of the others carried .380 backups or one of the new small nine-millimeter automatics. Tommy's hunch was right.

Down at the range, Lorenzo scowled at his assistant who came in for the afternoon shift. "What's wrong, Sarge?" the young man said. "What the hell are you doing?"

"Looking for .32 shells. Mencken wants 'em."

"What for?"

"I don't know," said Lorenzo disgustedly. "But you may have to man the desk for a couple days while I do this. If I'm lucky, I'll find some in a few hours."

The young officer nodded, and went out to make sure the weapons supplies were stocked.

———⟡———

Chris Laney had been having a bad day. Lisa Giustino was still behaving like a wife, by wanting to be a wife. There would never be a time when she would be satisfied with anything less than marriage. And truth be told, he might someday want that, too. But not now.

He just wasn't ready for it; that was the rub. And when he was ready, Lisa might be too familiar, no longer fresh, no longer discoverable. He will have explored every fold and recess of her body many times over. He will have brought her to heights of ecstasy too many times. She will have thrilled him with her youthful lust…too many times again.

When that day came, after a road long traveled, through days of glorious sameness, she would not be the one. When he was ready, he would need a new body, a fresh passion, an expectation of new wonders, an expectation long lost with Lisa.

He shook his head. It just wasn't worth it. He decided to go down to the range and shoot. He hadn't yet qualified this month, and he would relax as he did something he long enjoyed. The .32 automatic he carried in his pocket was his favorite gun, precisely because no one else on the job had one. And even if it were small, he had learned to be deadly accurate with it at seven yards, something hard to be with such a small gun.

But this time he decided not to shoot the .32. He would shoot his street gun, a Glock .40. He walked casually down the corridor to the elevators, greeting the people he knew, consulting with one of his sergeants who stopped him as he got off the elevator.

As he approached the range, he could hear the booming reports of a large caliber gun going off. The range wouldn't be crowded today. Inside, he greeted the clerk at the desk who said, "Hi, Captain. Gonna do some damage?"

"Yeah. A brick of .40s."

"Gonna do some serious shooting, huh? Not that little backup stuff?"

"Yeah…strictly business."

"That's a new gun, right? Didn't we order it just this year?"

"Yeah. Zoe told me it had good balance." At the mention of his name, Laney was reminded of his old friend Lorenzo who had gotten him so many guns before. "Where is Zoe? You running the range alone?"

"Aw, he's pissed off. He's in the back going through the barrels looking for some shells that Mencken wants."

"What kind of shells?"

"I think he said .32s...like the ones you shoot."

"Mencken wants them? Why didn't Zoe just give him some of the ones we have?"

"Nah, that ain't it. Mencken wants spent shells. That's why Zoe's so pissed. He's back there going through the barrels looking for about a dozen .32s. I don't know what the hell Mencken wants 'em for. Zoe might be there till Christmas."

Suddenly, Laney felt a chill as the hair on his arms began to tingle. It felt as though he had been kicked in the chest by a horse. He was silent for several long seconds. Finally, the officer said, "Captain?" drawing Laney back to the moment. "You need some rounds? Some .40s, did you say? Or was it .32s?"

"Uh, no." Laney looked quickly at his watch. "Oh. I don't think I'm gonna have time to do this. I didn't realize it was so late. I'll have to come down later this week."

The officer shrugged. "Tell Zoe I'll see him later," Laney said as he walked out.

———✦———

Fridays were often quiet in the McCarrie house. Carrie and Mike always seemed to have something to do at school, or church with the youth group. And whenever Tommy was home, he was often alone since Elly would also be doing something for the school or the church. But tonight, they were both home. Tommy read the newspaper in the living room and Elly seemed to by busy out in the kitchen or upstairs in her room.

The quiet calm was pleasing and relaxing. Tommy was drinking a glass of bourbon, feeling secure enough not to start downing a whole bottle. He felt some stiffness ease as he rested and relaxed.

Elly came downstairs, seemingly more heavy-footed than usual, as though in a hurry. Suddenly, she was at the front door and the doorbell rang. Tommy looked up, momentarily perplexed at the intrusion on his solitude. Although he still liked to hear the door-bell ring. There were just too many lonely days in the last few years where no one called except for business. He'd take this any time.

He heard Elly say a soft "hi" to whoever it was. In a moment, he could see Danny standing in the living room, handing his coat to Elly. He was dressed in casual clothes, so he wasn't coming from the YPD station. "Hi, Danny," Tommy said, getting up out of his chair with a questioning look on his face.

He looked at Elly who was now standing beside and slightly be-hind Danny, about three feet from him. This was a strange meeting. Suddenly, Tommy was afraid. "Danny? Is your mother okay?" he said gravely.

"Yeah, Chief, she's fine," he answered, looking over uneasily at Elly.

"Your uncles?"

"No, they're fine. The kids are fine...Everybody's okay."

Tommy looked over at Elly, who stood silent, looking strange, seeming to know what Tommy didn't. Then he looked back at Danny.

"What is this? Is there something wrong?"

"No, there's nothing wrong, Dad," Elly said finally. "We'd like to talk to you about something." She glanced at Danny and smiled weakly, encouraging him with her eyes to speak. She stepped closer to Danny to be right beside him.

With that small gesture, Tommy was able to discern what this meeting was all about. Suddenly his gaze changed from one of abject fear to one of bemused confidence. "We?" he said.

"Elly and I," said Danny. "Uh, Chief... I love Elly and..." Danny glanced over to her. "And she loves me, too."

Tommy stared at the two of them a few seconds. If ever there were two people who should be in love it was these two. He had come to like and respect Danny as he began to know him personally through his years of anguish. He liked the way Danny's being a cop had not hardened him; he liked the way he could be surprised, or hurt, or flustered and be so natural about it. He admired the way he lived — loving and caring for his surviving children, honoring his mother, and upholding his dignity in the face of three tragic losses. He liked the way the losses he suffered and the public disclosure of his pain did not make him cowering or distant or bitter.

That he could have fallen in love with this girl who redeemed Tommy's latter years when he least expected it, this girl so intelligent and sensitive, the girl of endless curiosity and countless questions, the gentle, innocent, and feminine creature who had been hurt and humiliated by an errant husband, and was yet not resentful... All this was a kind of miracle in his life that he never dreamed he'd see. When all hope of living a peaceful life, surrounded by friends and loved ones, seemed like a fond dream born of his loneliness that would never be fulfilled, this girl walked back into his life, and showed her true self to him, the self he never dreamed existed. And now these two gentle people had found in each other a love that they alone could cherish.

But he was not going to let it happen without having some fun. He was too old not to play just a little bit. "What makes you so sure she wants to get involved with a cop?"

Danny was flustered. "Uh, she never said..." Then he stopped, sensing for a second the twinkle, the play in Tommy's demeanor. "Well, hell, you're a cop," he said, gesturing toward Tommy.

"She had no choice about me. She does have a choice about you."

"If I had a choice about either of you, I'd want you both to be accountants or veterinarians," Elly said, catching on earlier than Danny to her father's taunting. She knew him better.

"So where do you go from here?" Tommy said.

"We want to join a nudist commune in Australia," Elly said, taunting her father back.

"Quiet, Ellen. So do you want to do the right thing by my daughter, boyo?"

"Yeah, Chief," Danny said seriously. "You know, I'd just about given up on luck. I was never going to have any... I thought it was my destiny. And then I met her," he said, gesturing to Elly, who was now beaming and smiling broadly.

"You gonna be up to handling her? Once she sets her mind on something, she'll drive you crazy with her questions."

"Yeah, I know. She already does that."

Elly let out a soft huff. Tommy was quiet for a few seconds, looking at the two of them standing before him like two small children, now holding hands. He still found it hard to believe that such a wonderful thing could have happened. Two years ago, when he first met Danny and Neva, he never would have dreamed his life would change the way it did. "Does anybody else know?" he said.

"No. We thought it best to tell you first," Elly said.

"You really love her?" he said to Danny. Danny nodded silently. "And you?" he said to Elly. "This is the real thing?"

"Yeah, Dad," she said softly.

Tommy nodded to himself, seeming to be thinking as he did. "I want you to know something: I never expected something like this to happen after all you've both been through. But I can't think of any two people who deserve each other more than you two." He stopped for a second. "And I'm very happy for you both."

"We have your blessing, then?" Danny said earnestly.

"You're my blessing, son — that you're both part of my life."

Elly ran to Tommy and threw her arms around him. She kissed him tearfully. As he held his daughter in his arms, Tommy stretched his hand behind Elly's back toward Danny. When Elly finally stepped back away from her father, he said to Danny, "So I'll be related to your mother now, huh?"

"Yeah. That's the way the Italians look at it."

"How about your uncles? Would I be related to them, too?"

"Yeah. I'm afraid so," said Danny, already learning some of Elly's taunting techniques to use on Tommy.

"Jesus. I don't know if I can handle that. Connie, okay...but Rino and Lou?"

<hr />

Carly watched the apartment from his car for several minutes. He had to go in there, but he knew it was going to bring on a fight. She was stubborn and she hated him. But he had to get her away from that nut.

He got out of his car and walked to the apartment building. He took the elevator up two flights. As he rode, he noticed that the building was clean and looked well-maintained. He wondered how much it cost her; that is, how much money Ginny was giving her to pay this rent.

At her apartment, he stopped, took a deep breath, then rang the doorbell. It took several minutes, then she opened the door with the night lock still on. She stared at him, dumbfounded at his sudden appearance. "What do you want?" she said coldly.

"I want to talk, Lis," he said softly.

"We don't have anything to talk about. Just go."

"Lisa, we have to talk...for you mother's sake if nothing else."

"Don't use Mommy just to get to me. You've said all you're ever going to say to me already."

"Lisa, do you want me to break this goddamned door down?"

After a few moments of silence, she shut the door and unlatched the night lock. She opened the door and Carly walked in, still angry for what she had done to his dreams for her. He stopped suddenly and looked around the room, the living room of the apartment. There was a kitchen with a counter fronting on the living room, a bedroom and bathroom at the far end of the living room.

He saw several drink glasses and some amber bottles on the kitchen shelf. "Are you here alone?" he said.

"Yes," she answered hesitantly, with just enough of a quaver in her voice to raise his doubts. But he would deal with that later.

"Are you still seeing Laney?" Carly asked, now staring intently at his daughter.

"That's none of your business," she snapped.

"Don't tell me..." He started the words in a rasping yell but tapered off the noise as he tried to control himself. "Don't tell me," he began again, more calmly and softly, "what's my business. You're my business, like it or not."

He was still looking around as he spoke. He smelled smoke. "What are you smoking?"

"Nothing. A cigarette."

"Where? Show me."

"It was a cigarette, and I'm not going to show you a fucking thing."

He recoiled at her language, never having heard her use crude words before, even in her anger. Instinctively, he lifted his hand as if to strike, but he stayed his hand as he watched her face. "What are you going to do? Hit me again?"

He looked at her, wondering how she could have been so alienated from him...as though she were a stranger. "What you need is to be hit. To slap your goddamned foul mouth. Is that the way you're supposed to talk to your father? Did you ever see me talk to my father that way?"

She didn't answer. Instead, she walked away from him. He watched her as she walked. She was acting strange. There was something wrong, something going on. "What's wrong, Lisa?" Carly said.

"There's nothing wrong...except that you're here."

Carly started to look around the room as she studied him. Near an end table next to a love seat there was a small coffee table. On it he could see a slight trace of white, as though someone's hand had swept across the table to wipe away the traces of powder. He turned toward his daughter, and they stared at each other for a few seconds. At the end, Carly shook his head, never taking his eyes from her.

She could feel the hurt she had caused him. Never had he done anything to be repaid as she was doing. She wilted under his glare. "Where is it, Lis?" he said softly.

"Where's what?" she said weakly, knowing that he knew more than she wanted him to. To that lie, he only closed his eyes, not moving his body even a little. The lie had cut into him as though she had stabbed him.

He walked quickly to the end table and pulled out a drawer. Inside, there was a bag of white powder, a spoon, a glass pipe, paper towels, a cheap cigarette lighter, all hastily crabbed together and stuffed into a drawer. He couldn't control his anger. The old fury that he had so long tried to suppress since his election, the natural fury that was at the core of his being, took control of his brain and turned him into a monster.

He pulled the drawer out and held it for a split second. "Where's what? This is what!" he yelled, raising the drawer above his head and throwing it across the room, smashing a lamp and a mirror on the wall, scattering cocaine over the floor, crashing the glass pipes into a glass tabletop and shattering both together.

Chris Laney suddenly appeared in the doorway in undershorts and a T-shirt, amazed at the loud crash that made him come out of the bedroom where he was hidden. "What the fuck's going on here, Carly? Have you lost your goddamned mind?" he snarled.

"You?" Carly turned back to his daughter. "This is the guy you're banging and snorting coke with? Jesus Christ, why didn't you just start fucking Castro or some Colombian drug runner?"

"Get the hell out of here, Carly. Don't you see she doesn't want anything to do with you?"

"You got her on to speed and coke, didn't you. I know you, Laney. I know what you're all about even if Mose is too dumb to know...fucking assassin."

"You two know each other like that?" Lisa said weakly, more confused now by the hatred each man had shown for the other than by the presence of an angry Carly in her living room.

"Yeah. Ask him how many people he's killed, Lis. Innocent people."

"That's enough, Carly. Get out of here before I throw you out."

"You and whose army, asshole?" Carly snarled.

"What is this all about... assassin for who?" Lisa said to Laney.

"That's just your old man's colorful language. He's just jealous of me because I fuck your brains out every night. He'd like to do it himself," Laney said, looking right at Carly, who for a half second didn't realize what Laney had actually said.

Suddenly, Carly lunged at Laney, his hands going for his throat. Laney took a half step sideways and hit Carly on the shoulder and back of the head with a small pistol he held in his hand, concealed from the other two as they talked.

Carly coughed, and for a second, knelt on all fours, stunned by the blow to the head. Then, Laney hit him again, pulling him to his feet and putting his knee deep into Carly's groin.

"Chris, what are you doing? Stop it! You'll kill him, Chris!" Lisa shouted, terrified at the change in Laney. He seemed to be just a brutal thug who enjoyed giving punishment.

But Laney's eyes were glazed. He couldn't hear her; he couldn't hear anyone. He held the helpless Carly erect and hit him in the face with his fist, smashing his nose and jaw and causing blood to flow from his mouth and his nose. "That right, mayor? I fuck your daughter, and you can't?"

He pulled Carly's hair back and turned his face toward Lisa. "See, Lisa? Here's the guy that wants to get into your pants. Here's the old man."

She was crying as he spoke. Carly looked at her with swollen eyes and bloody, mangled face. He said nothing, but stared helplessly at her, his eyes showing more pain than he had endured from the beating. "I'm sorry, Daddy," she said, holding her hand up to her mouth as if to keep from throwing up. "Please, Chris, don't hit him again. Please."

"Honey, he likes it...almost as much as he'd like to fuck you, right, Carly?" Just then, he hit Carly on the back of the neck and sent him spread out face down on the floor. Lisa began to scream. "Shut up!" Laney snarled, "Shut up!" When she didn't stop, he slapped her, backhanded, across the face and the neck. She sprawled across the far end of the room.

"Let her alone, Laney. She didn't do anything to you," Carly said.

"Shut up, asshole," Laney said, turning back to Carly and kicking him in the back.

"Chris, please, let's get out of here," Lisa said, now crying with every word she spoke.

Carly was dazed and bleeding, trying to bring himself erect. Laney stared at him as he struggled to stand up. "Please, Chris, let's go out for a drink," Lisa said.

"I'm not going out," Laney said calmly as he watched Carly.

After a few seconds, Carly started to pull himself up again and Laney raised his pistol as though to strike him down again. Lisa suddenly grabbed his arm and put himself between them, staring at Laney for several seconds. "What are you doing?" she asked in amazement, seeing the controlled and systematic brutality and the deliberate satisfaction on his face, the face of a stranger to her.

"If I go and you don't come with me, it's over, Lisa," Laney said.

"I can't come with you," she said softly. "I don't even know you."

He went into the bedroom for a few minutes, then returned. "You look a mess, Carly...and you'd better think up a good excuse why you're so busted up. You wouldn't want people to know that you walked in on your daughter while she was smoking dope and banging a YPD police officer, would you?"

As he spoke, he was smirking. "You're not the first person to try to fuck me over. You should have known that I don't take any shit from someone in a fight."

In the moment that he left, Carly realized something horrible. In studying Laney's face as he spoke, Carly knew that this was the man who was the enforcer for Mose Pagliaro. When he called him an assassin, it was only based upon instinct, the confluence of vague feelings and experiences. Pagliaro had to have someone who could do his dirty work. He had to have an assassin with no conscience who liked to see people suffer, someone who enjoyed killing. There was no one in Pagliaro's stable who could be that angry. Except Laney.

Laney had all the special gifts: no conscience, a quick, athletic body, good looks, intelligence enough to understand technical matters, enough to get him through law school, enough to advance him quickly in the YPD, and the remorseless cruelty that could make him kill without a pang of conscience, and then lie just to make people suffer.

All the horrible crimes that he suspected of Pagliaro, suddenly became clearly defined. Laney had done the worst of them because Pagliaro needed a pitiless murderer to handle his bad business. The bombing of McCarrie's car. He stopped for a moment and raised his left hand to his swollen mouth, as if not to feel the pain that his thoughts evoked. *My God*, he thought, *Laney killed the Bellino kids.*

⸻

Tommy walked into his office feeling bright and contented. Lucy was there already. They had talked two hours the previous night and still he couldn't wait to hear her voice again. He delighted in hearing her talk to him in the new way, with a looseness and whimsy that grew out of the confidence she had in his love, that grew stronger every time that he touched her.

"Hi," she said.

"Come here," he said grabbing one of her hands and leading her into his office, closing the door behind him. He kissed her and she responded warmly and gently. "You know, this isn't working out," he said.

"What isn't?"

"This weird plan of mine to solve the Bellino case..."

"I never thought much of the idea in the first place," she said, smiling.

"Let's talk tonight, okay?"

"Okay...Tom, I put some papers on your desk. The City Council report's ready if you want to look it over one last time."

"Okay. I'll take care of it," he said.

He was in his office about an hour, drinking coffee and reading through his report to Council, when suddenly his office door swung open. It could only have been Bumpy.

The deputy chief looked confused and tormented. "What's wrong, Bump?" Tommy said, already moving around the front of his desk.

"Tommy, I —"

"Come on, Bump! What's wrong?"

"I just talked to Pete's wife. I called because I thought he was sick...

Pete's missing, Tommy. Nobody's seen him for almost two days."

"Pete?" Tommy said, as though not believing his own words. "How in the hell could nobody miss him for so long?"

"May thought he was over here, and I thought he was home or..." He paused for a moment. "Or doing something for you."

The words almost knocked Tommy down. He closed his eyes. *Doing something for him! Doing something for him! God, it was all happening again.*

In a few steps, Tommy was at the coat rack reaching for his shoulder holster and strapping on the .45. "Where are you going, Tommy? You can't go out there on this. I'll send..."

"Find Laney, Bump. I don't want him to leave this station."

"Laney called in sick, Tommy. He's not here."

Tommy stopped what he was doing and let his head fall back upon his shoulders, facing toward the ceiling. "Jesus Christ. I really blew this one, Liborio," he sighed.

"What're you talking about, Tom?"

"I sent Pete down to the range to find out who's been using .32 automatics. He put Lorenzo on to finding spent shells; I'm sure of it. He was going to check ballistics against the weapon in the Bellino killings. And someone must have found out about it, Bump."

Bumpy took a deep breath. "And you think Laney was using .32s on our range?"

"Bet the house on it, kid. Who else on the force called in sick today?"

"Only Laney," Bumpy said softly. "Jesus Christ." Tommy nodded to himself and began to put on his holster. "Where you going, Tommy?"

"Down to the range to talk to Lorenzo," he said putting on a short leather jacket from the closet. Then he went to the drawer of his desk and took out a pocket holster with the small .25 automatic pistol in it and put it in his pocket.

"What do you want me to do, Tom?"

"We gotta get Lucy out of here. I don't want Pagliaro to get to her somehow. It would be too easy."

"I'll take her home. Jesse's there and she'll be safe."

"Put some of blues out there anyway…and load them up. I want that place covered. There are all irreplaceable there. Couple of other things: Get me a shotgun with a TR barrel. I also want you and Danny and Med wired. Get me one, too, so we can talk easily. And call Danny and Elly and bring them up here to the office. I also want two blues up here in the hall. Get Danny a shotgun, too."

"Okay…Tom?"

"Yeah?"

"You watch yourself. You've got too much to live for now. So be careful."

Tommy nodded. Then, they both walked to the outer office. Lucy took one look at Tommy in his leather jacket and blanched. She stood up without speaking. "You have to go with Bumpy, Luce."

"Where?"

"His house. You're going to stay with Jesse. Call your kids and tell them to stay together…and don't go out. Bumpy will put a squad car wherever they stay." He turned toward Bumpy. "Let's wire them, too."

"But where are you going? What's happened?"

"Pete's missing." Lucy gasped at Tommy's grim news. "We're putting all the people they know out of harm's way."

"My God, Tom, shouldn't someone else be in on this to help you?"

"There will be. But since we're not sure who we can trust yet, the fewer people who know, the better."

"Please be careful," she said, hugging him. He kissed her softly and walked out.

———•—••—•——

Lorenzo was on duty when Tommy walked into the gun shop. There were about four officers shooting that Tommy could see. He could feel the report of one as he walked through the door into Lorenzo's office. The thunderous report sent shock waves through the whole range.

"What the hell's he shooting?" Tommy asked Lorenzo.

"That's one of them SOAE revolvers. He thinks he's a cowboy."

"Do other guys carry pieces like that?"

"Nah. The old-timers like you shoot .45s. Most of the guys shoot 9 millimeters or .40s. And some of the young guys like to play Dirty Harry and carry .357 magnums. This kid's in a class by himself...an ex-MP."

"Anybody shoot smaller rounds?"

"A few guys conceal carry .25s...and Chris Laney carries a .32 back-up."

"For sure?"

"Yeah. Didn't you see them?"

"See what?"

"I sent the shells up to Pete two days ago."

".32s? Who'd you send them with?"

"Laney. He came down and said he knew all about it, so he'd take them up."

"How many did you send?" Tommy sighed.

"Thirteen. You mean you never got 'em?"

"No. He must have forgotten...Listen, do you have any more? Just give me what you have."

"I don't have any more. They're gone."

"Gone?"

"All the barrels are empty. They must have come on my day off to get the shells."

"Didn't Pete say he wanted you to go through the barrels and find some .32s? Why'd you salvage them out?"

"I didn't, Tom. They came and picked them up. Somebody called them. I just thought it was Pete."

"What'd they do with them? Any chance they're still intact?"

"Nah. They smelt them down and sell all that brass back to the ammo companies. If not, they're in a dumpster going down to Dayton. That's where they send 'em sometimes."

Tommy was silent for a few moments. Laney must have disposed of those shells. "Who called the salvage place?"

"They said it was some captain of the YPD."

"They give you a name?"

"Yeah…a Captain Benton."

"Who the hell's that?"

"You got me, Chief. There's never been a command officer of the YPD named Benton, and I've been here twenty-six years."

He did it, Tommy thought. *He must have called and had them take all the shells. No more chance to run ballistics tests on the .32's. No more shells to connect Laney to the Bellino killings.*

"Lorenzo," Tommy said deliberately, "I'm gonna tell you this only once." Lorenzo looked startled. "I don't want you to say a fucking word about these shells to anyone, understand? Not your wife, not your mother, especially not any YPD cops. Got that?"

"Yeah, Chief."

"Cause if I find out you told anyone, I'm gonna cut your balls off, understand?"

Lorenzo looked dumbfounded. "Chief, I..."

Tommy raised his hand to silence him. "Hear what I said, Lorenzo?"

"Yeah, Chief."

"Okay. Now I also want you to report to me...only me...if ever Laney sets foot in this range or talks to you, or belches or farts, I want to know about it."

When he was done, Tommy returned to his office upstairs. Already there were two armed guards outside his door. For a moment, one drew his pistol as Tommy approached, not recognizing the chief in a cap and leather jacket. Then the more experienced one recognized Tommy and gestured to the other man to holster his gun.

"Hi, Chief," he said tentatively.

"Hi, men. You carry on. Watch yourselves."

"Uh, Chief, you have to knock. They've locked it up."

Tommy knocked, and from inside, he heard Danny's voice asking who it was. "It's McCarrie, Danny.

In a second, the door opened, and an ashen-faced Danny let him in. "Any word on Pete?" Tommy asked.

Danny shook his head. "Chief Malatesta just called. No one has seen him," he said.

"Did they bring the shotguns?"

"Yeah. Yours is in your office. Mine's over there," he said, pointing to a table across the room.

Tommy went over to Elly. "Maybe you shouldn't stay here...I was just trying to keep you out of danger."

"Aunt Jesse has all the kids...Danny's and mine. Uncle Bumpy sent blues out for all of them."

"Okay. Later we can get you over to them. Meanwhile, don't leave this office, and don't stand near any windows." He turned to Danny. "Dan, call the Cleveland PD and get some dogs. Send one of our guys up if you have to."

"Dogs?" Elly said. Tommy glance at Danny, who understood the chief's subliminal message. "You think he could be dead, Dad?" she said, her face a mask of horror for thinking what she couldn't imagine just a few hours ago.

"We always have to be ready for the possibility, kid."

"Uh, Chief...Someone else called, a guy named Lazarus," said Danny. "Says for you to come to see him...said you'd know his address."

Tommy nodded, seeming distracted and preoccupied. He went into his office and came out with the shotgun. Just then, the phone rang. Elly answered it and had a strange look on her face as she handed the receiver to Tommy. "It's Carly Giustino; he wants to talk to you."

Tommy answered. "McCarrie here."

"Chief, this is Carly. I have to talk to you about something important. Will you come to my house as soon as you can? You know where I live?"

"Now, Carly? I'm in the middle of something, can't it —"

"I wouldn't call if it wasn't important, Tommy. I have to see you now. This isn't politics...it's about my family."

Tommy hesitated for a moment, thinking if any possible good could come from this. "Okay, Carly, I'll be right over," Tommy muttered.

"What's wrong, Chief?" Danny said, noting Tommy's look of concern.

"I don't know, Danny. Something's wrong in his family. He wants me to go over now."

"Are you going?"

"Yeah, for a short while," Tommy said in a low voice. "You keep that shotgun handy, understand? And if Chris Laney gets within fifty feet of you, blow his goddamned head off."

"Please be careful, Dad," Elly said, hugging him as he was leaving.

"Talk to Lucy, okay? She'll appreciate that."

———————

Tommy rang the doorbell of Carly's home. Virginia Giustino answered the door. "Mrs. Giustino," Tommy said.

She seemed pale and very nervous. "Come in please," she said.

As he stepped into the foyer, Tommy quickly looked around the house. It was beautiful...and expensive, the house of a millionaire.

"He's in here," Virginia said, pointing and beckoning for him to follow her.

She opened the door and announced Tommy before admitting him. She stepped aside and let Tommy have his first look at her husband.

For a few seconds, Tommy stared, horrified, at his face. "Jesus! What the hell happened?"

"I took a beating for telling the truth. How about that for a politician?"

"Who did this, Carly?" Tommy asked, knowing he would not be surprised at the answer.

"Don't you know?" asked Carly.

"I have an idea," Tommy said, cocking his head in affirmation.

Carly paused for a moment, looking away from his old tormenter.

"It was Chris Laney, at my daughter's apartment."

"What did you do to get your head beat in?"

"The fact that he was there was enough." He paused for a few seconds, studying Tommy, waiting to see how much condescension or smugness he could detect. But strangely, he didn't see any. Tommy seemed serious, and professional, but did show skepticism and doubt, and needed more to justify his patience with the man who had been his enemy all his life.

"They were sniffing cocaine, Tommy." Tommy glanced at his wife. She nodded in agreement.

"You saw them?" Tommy said.

"I saw the glass pipe, the cigarette lighter, and the powder. I know what they were doing."

"Did you know that Laney was seeing your daughter?"

He shook his head. "No. Did you?"

"I heard rumors," Tommy said. "Why didn't you file charges?"

"You know I can't. The papers would have a field day with me... And Lisa would be smeared as a drug user."

"So, what do you want?"

"I want Laney nailed to the wall. Correct me if I'm wrong, but YPD captains shouldn't be serving coke to girls half their age, right?"

"Right about that, boyo." Tommy stopped for a moment, looked at Carly's wife and then back at Carly. "Carly, can I talk to you alone?"

Virginia said, "She's my daughter, too, Chief. I should hear everything about her."

"Ginny, please. I'll talk with you later."

"It's not about Lisa, Mrs. Giustino. This is different. By the way, where is she? I'd like to talk to her."

Carly and Ginny looked at each other. "Uh... she went to her apartment to get some things...real quick. She's moving back here."

"Ah, Jesus, Carly, you shouldn't have let her go!"

"Is she in danger, Chief?" Ginny said, her voice faltering at Tommy's outburst.

"You don't think she's in danger from him, do you, Tommy? Why would he hurt her?"

"I sure as hell do, Carly. I've found out a lot of things about him... one, that he has a screw loose, the other that I think he..." Tommy hesitated. "I think he did the Bellino murders."

"Jesus Christ," Carly said in wide-eyed horror and amazement. "I knew it! If he could do those killings, then he —"

"Then he can hurt our daughter," Ginny said in a muffled cry, her hand over her mouth as if to stop the words and the thought that conjured them.

"You think he will, Tommy?"

"He sure could, Carly. He knows I'm on to him, and he's desperate. He didn't report to work today. I don't know where he is."

"Jesus, he could be at Lisa's apartment right now," he said.

"Virginia, go call her," Tommy said. "If she's there, tell her to come home right away. Whatever she does, she can't stay there."

She left the room immediately. Tommy turned back to Carly. "Carly, was Laney in on Pagliaro's drug operation?"

Carly hesitated. To answer these questions was to acknowledge that he was a dirty politician, that all Tommy believed about him was true. But Tommy was a man reputed to be honest, talking about the safety of his daughter. He was there to help...to keep Lisa from harm. "I think he was Pagliaro's distributor and hatchet man, Tommy. I never really knew what he did for him. Pagliaro is a guy who keeps secrets. I don't think even his brother, Nick, knew how much he dealt with the Mob."

"Did he have something to do with the bombing of the YPD station?"

Carly shrugged. "I accused him of it...and we had a big argument, and he denied it."

"You weren't in on any of it?"

"No, Tommy. Believe it or not. All I did was look the other way, and he'd put up money for my campaigns. He never asked me for anything. All he wanted was that I should wink when he did something shady...and keep the heat off."

"What about the Bellino killings? Did you know if he was in on those?"

"No," Carly said, looking more ashamed as he talked. "Tommy, I swear to God I didn't have anything to do with that stuff...and Lisa isn't involved with Pagliaro. She's just hooked on Laney, that son of a bitch." He paused, reflecting on past memories. "You know, even my dad didn't like Pagliaro. He told me that drugs were blood money. He said someday I'd have to turn on Pagliaro...before he turned on me. I'm glad he won't be able to understand any of this."

"Is he that bad?"

Carly nodded. "They say he's not going to live too much longer," he said grimly.

"Carly, is there anything else you know about either Laney or Pagliaro...about the killings and the bombing? What did they have against Danny Bellino? Was I so much of a threat that they had to bomb my car and almost kill my daughter...and kill an innocent old man like Liebowitz?"

Carly hesitated to answer. "You know, I wasn't in on any of that stuff, Tommy. I knew Laney was jealous of Danny, but I never dreamed he'd kill his kids."

Tommy was thoughtful for a few minutes. "I never thought you were a killer, Carly."

Carly nodded in appreciation, looking up at Tommy, who now seemed the one solid hope he had of getting his daughter back safely. Suddenly, Virginia came back into the room and said, "She's not there. I left a message. Where can she be? Do you think she's in danger?"

Tommy didn't answer. But he turned to leave, thinking that he had spent too much time with Carly already. And he had to see Laz first, before he could see the others. He stopped for a minute, turning back to them. "When she comes back, don't let her out of your sight for one minute, understand? Not one minute." They both nodded. "I'm going to send out a squad of blues to her place and have another one stationed outside here. I don't want anyone to come or go... not until this is all done."

Tommy started for the door. It was only then that Carly noticed the way he was dressed. He had never seen Tommy look so grimly ready for action.

"Tommy," he said, "there is something that might be important I never thought of before."

"What is it?"

"I think Laney was having an affair with Danny Bellino's wife. She was the one who was so good looking, right?"

"You sure?"

"All I know is I walked in on Mose talking with Laney about it once. And another time I heard Mose complaining to his brother about the mess Laney had made."

Tommy nodded in appreciation of the news. Then he said, "Remember. Keep your daughter here."

Tommy rang at Laz's door and waited for the old man to open it. Inside, Laz noticed Tommy's outfit and his grim visage. "What's going on, kid?" Laz said softly. There was none of the friendly banter between them this time. Each one had business on his mind.

"We can't find Pete. I sent him to do something for me, and no one's seen him since."

"This have anything to do with Laney?"

"A lot. Those Bellino kids were killed with .32s. Guess who carries one as a backup?"

"Son of a bitch!" Laz spat. "Jesus, Tommy, he could have Pete."

"Yeah," said Tommy. "And he's got a screw loose..."

"You know what I called for? I was talking to some of the cops down at the club. We were just having a drink, and the conversation lit on police. Somebody mentioned Laney, so I did some diggin'. You know this Laney guy was banging Danny Bellino's wife...the one that died?"

Tommy closed his eyes and snorted. Laney did the Bellino killings; there wasn't much doubt anymore. "Is that something everybody knew, Laz?"

"I don't think so...just a few of the old-timers."

Soon, Tommy thanked his old friend and headed out the door. The last time he talked to Danny about his wife, he told him that he believed that she was faithful to him. And now he was in love with Elly. He must never know about Kaye Bellino and Laney.

Nick Pagliaro nervously drove to the southeast side of Youngstown, stopping at the garage in front of his brother's office. He entered the rear of the building and rode up the elevator to Mose's office. His older brother came out of his office to meet him. "What's up?" he asked.

"I wish I knew, Mose. Something's happening, though."

"What are you talking about?" Mose said.

"I just got a call from one of our guys at the police station and they said that something's going on. Shotguns given out; they've gotten some dogs in from Cleveland."

"Dogs? What do they want with dogs?"

"What do you think? Dogs smell things, Mose. They track stuff down."

"Where's McCarrie?"

"No one knows. They say that his office is being guarded by two cops. All this is goddamned strange. I don't like that stuff about dogs, Mose. Hell, a dog can smell anything. I don't want to go to fucking jail."

"Shut up, Nick. You're not going to jail," Mose growled, preoccupied with his own thoughts.

"See, you don't know what can happen. You know McCarrie thinks you're shady. What if he has something on us?"

"He can't have anything on us," Mose spat.

"Don't tell me that, Mose. The guys down at the station say they've never seen anything like this. Malatesta's putting a newly selected team on alert; Mencken hasn't been seen for a few days. McCarrie's not around...and guess what? Laney didn't report to work today."

Mose recoiled at the mention of Laney's name. "Laney? Jesus Christ, Nick, that man's going to put me in an early grave."

"You don't suppose the son of a bitch did something crazy, do you? Jesus, Mose, I hate it when my balls are in the pocket of some guy who's got a screw loose."

"We have to get rid of that fucker, Nick. I'm gonna be up in Cleveland next week. I'll talk to someone."

"Mose, what if they're moving on us? How can we wait to see what will happen?"

"Look, the last thing we should do is panic…"

"Mose? What if Laney fucked up? I mean, really fucked up? What if he has his ass in a sling and McCarrie knows every bit of it?"

Mose didn't answer directly. "I don't know," he said as much to himself as to his brother.

"You don't understand, Mose. If he spills his guts, we're screwed. They could get us on accessories to murder, conspiracy. Hell, who knows what he's been doing? Do you want him to drag us down with him?"

Mose was quiet. Suddenly the great edifice he had constructed was in danger. In danger because of its weakest part, Chris Laney. And even if they didn't have Laney in jail, he was still in a position to ruin them. He had to go.

"Nick, we have to get out of town. Get those phony IDs and take everything we got and put it in the van, all the files especially. Everything that will keep our business and money safe."

"What about Laney?"

"Whatever you do, just let him think that we're okay. And call Mickey. I have a job for him."

"We got problems here, Mose. What are you doing trusting a guy with half a brain?"

"We'll let him do this one and then I'll call Pittsburgh, and they can take care of him… along with Laney… but Laney first."

"Jesus, Mose, we better watch ourselves. If we start killing all these guys, they'll still take us down the tubes, dead or alive."

"Look. I'll get out of town first. You stay back and get everything set up. Shred every paper that can screw us. Close all the accounts in the Valley banks. Transfer the money overseas."

"Me? What if they nail my ass? No! I want to get out with you."

"You want to give up forty million dollars just to go with me? Hell, Nick, the way you cover your tracks, they won't touch you. Just clean it all up and meet me in Costa Rica."

"I don't know, Mose. I don't want to get caught holding the bag while you fly out to some villa somewhere."

"Christ, Nick, have I ever done anything in your whole fucking life that could make you believe that?" Mose spoke earnestly. He also looked scared, and his brother seemed convinced. Nick nodded.

"We have to get Mickey out here. Make sure you call him... I'll also talk to Laney. Remember, you never let him know something's wrong."

<hr />

Tommy called his office. "Any word about Pete?" Tommy asked his daughter.

"Nothing, Dad. How are you?"

"Okay... Did you talk to Lucy and the kids?"

"Aunt Jesse's got them eating better than they have in their whole lives... Lucy, too."

"Is Danny there?"

"Yes. Do you want to talk to him?"

"No. Just tell him I'll be back soon."

On his way back to the station, Tommy agonized over Pete. The terrible foreboding he had was too reliable and instinctive, honed over thirty-three years of being a cop. And if Pete were hurt, or God forbid, if he were dead, it was because Tommy sent him on the errand that cost him his life.

Somehow, Laney had turned into a killer. The young man who was so promising, so physically gifted, had become a monster who could not face reality, who had to kill reality. Somehow, he had gotten hooked up with Kaye Bellino, and somehow he had made her lie to her husband, made her false to him and to their children.

That's what he remembered...no skid marks. Kaye Bellino had driven that car without breaking, knowing she was going to die. Poor woman. She did one final desperate favor for her husband, a headlong crash into the Mahoning.

And Danny, always believing her, loved her sincerely as she slipped away from him...and loved her in her falsehood. And yet that one faithless lie of Kaye Bellino can never be known because to know it would be to know her sin. No. Danny must let bad memories evaporate in the glow of Elly's love and be lost.

But what magic did Chris Laney possess that he could steal Kaye Bellino from a devoted husband and Lisa Giustino from a loving family? What made some men have it all so easy? What excitement did they see in him? What glories did his sexual abilities promise? And why was that enough?

And what made him pistol whip Carly? What did people ever see in Laney that could make them trust him? His appearance? Or maybe his calm and sure belief of his own superiority? Maybe he just walked through life expecting women to be in awe of him, and somehow it accomplished what he wanted.

But what kind of man could work beside a decent, loving husband, and yet be sleeping with his wife? Could the act bring that much pleasure? No. For Laney, a cruel man, the pleasure didn't come from the sexual act itself, it came from the conquest of another man's wife or daughter. Somehow, Laney hated Danny and Carly for what they were, for what their futures promised. Both had beautiful women and Laney took them both. And neither of them knew it. And yet when Carly finally found out, Laney gave the mayor a savage, ritualistic beating.

And Danny? What harm could he do to Danny other than defile his wife? He would not let harm pass if he could inflict more of it. So, what then? Now it was easy to see; he stashed the cocaine in the car a second time. Only that time, he didn't count on the kids catching him doing it. It was all meant for Danny alone. But when it didn't destroy him, when Danny recovered, and when he found a new ally in the chief and all the other command officers, at least Laney had deprived them of the kids.

He had to do it for control, just as he did when he beat up Carly. Laney's soul was possessed of demons who made him a killer, a soul without joy or belief. He hated people for what they had, for the enjoyment of their lives that came so naturally, and for the absence of it in his own life.

When Tommy arrived back at the station, he called Danny aside while Elly talked on the telephone to her kids. "Are the dogs here yet?"

"Yeah, they're here. Where do you want them to go?"

"I'm not sure. I'll let you know. Just make sure they're ready."

"You okay, Chief?"

"Yeah, kid. Why don't you take Elly to Bumpy's place now. All of you can stay there...and don't come in tomorrow. I'll stay in touch with you."

"But what about you? Isn't there some way I can help?"

"You're doing the most important thing of all...keeping Elly and Lucy and all your kids safe. They're going to be your family, Danny.

This'll just give you a head start."

"How long do you think we can do this? Are the kids going to be out of school indefinitely?"

"Pete…Laney…Pagliaro…It can't go on forever. One of them will turn up soon."

———◦◦◦◦◦———

Tommy also talked to Lucy. "I have a couple more things I have to do, then I'll try to see you later tonight. Did you call your kids?"

"Yes. Eddie's at Maria's apartment. Bumpy sent a squad out to watch the place. Where will you sleep, Tom?"

"Maybe there. Bumpy has an extra twin bed I used to sleep on when I was all boozed up. I spent many a night in that room."

"Should I stay here? With Danny and Elly and all the kids, I…"

"Yes. Besides, then maybe I'll get a chance to see you."

———◦◦◦◦◦———

Tommy went down to Meadows' office. His old friend was surprised to see him. "Tommy? What's up? You got all the blues staked out?"

"My house, Bumpy's place, Lucy's daughter's place, and Laney's and Pagliaro's. Danny, Ellie, Lucy, and all the kids are going to stay at Bumpy's tonight."

"What can I do?"

"I want you to take charge of the dogs, for one thing. We have to have someone who knows the investigation to be in charge."

"Hell, I haven't been in investigator for years," Med drawled.

"Med, I need you and I trust you. I think Laney killed those Bellino kids, and I think he knows where Pete is…And I think he took out Leibowitz."

"God damn, does it all fit?"

"He's Pagliaro's enforcer and spy at the YPD. I don't know who's fingering people, but I think Pagliaro calls the shots...and maybe Laney freelances on the side."

"You want me to round up another squad?"

"Yeah, everyone you can trust. And get some guys who are really good shots. Just be ready to move with those dogs when I tell you. Forget the motor room. Stay in touch with Bumpy, okay? And carry your wire."

Med nodded. "Tommy, you watch yourself. Those fuckers won't think twice about blasting you good."

"Yeah, I know. We have to disorient them and take them down one by one. I just hope we're in time for Pete."

"You really think they have Pete?"

"Bet on it, kid."

"What're you doing now?"

"I'm going down to check with Bumpy. Meanwhile, you start doing some checking too. Everyone must know something's up by now. Pete's not around, and neither is Laney. Besides, we got all kinds of blues on special duty. Meanwhile, see if you can find out who is still in Laney's pocket. It'll be nice to know upfront, so we don't place our trust in the wrong guys. Work it out."

Down in Bumpy's office, Tommy sat in a chair near his desk. "So, what do we now?" Bumpy asked.

"Laney and Pagliaro are joined at the hip," Tommy said. "And I'm sure Laney killed the Bellino kids."

"But can we ever make the whole story stand up in court?"

"I don't know. But we've never really concentrated on him...I mean, we've never searched his place, never tailed him, never asked him any questions."

"What should we do?"

"We don't have any time to go by the book. I think he has Pete. He pistol-whipped Carly."

"Carly?"

"Yeah. I was just over there. Laney's been banging Carly's daughter. Both Carly and Lazarus told me so."

"What can I do?"

"First, you have to run this place. Second, you and Med have to keep a couple of good squads handy so we can get all this together. Can you do that while you run the YPD?"

"I can do that...but anything else?"

"Keep those three ladies at your house safe. Put the best blues you have on those stakeouts. Besides, Bump, when I get close to those two guys, something's going to pop...and then I'm gonna need you in the worst way...and fast. *Capish?*"

"*Capish*, kid. But you keep yourself safe, okay? You still carry that little Beretta as well as that .45?"

"Yeah, but I hope I'll never need it."

"You never know, kid. Just carry it."

Tommy was silent for a minute, staring away from Bumpy. "What's is it, Tommy?"

"Remember when Danny and Neva were killed, I asked big Dan about his wife?"

"Yeah. They separated for a short time, right?"

"And he said she never cheated on him. Well, there was no professor that would have been interested in her. They were either women or old men."

"So?"

"No professor...because it was Laney."

"Banging Danny's wife?"

"Yeah. What d'you think?"

Bumpy was thoughtful for a moment, then said, "How do you know this?"

"It kept gnawing at me after Elly checked on her grade transcript at Spring Common. Then Lazarus's grapevine...A few of his guys thought so, and he's never been wrong yet on this case."

"Do you think Danny lied to you?" Bumpy said skeptically.

"No." Tommy shook his head. "But she sure as hell lied to him."

Bumpy nodded in agreement. "Bump, I want to talk to Danny before I leave," said Tommy. "Get everything going as soon as you can."

"Sure," Bumpy said, his face betraying the questions he had. Tommy had to tell him.

"Bump, Danny and Elly want to get married. They told me the other night..."

Bumpy shrugged approval. "The whole world knew they should... probably before they did. Uh...I'm happy for you, Tom. Too bad all this shit is going on...But this won't spoil it. We'll get those bastards."

"Thanks, kid. We'll talk later, okay?"

———✦———

In a few minutes, Danny walked into Bumpy's office. "What's up, Chief?"

"Have a seat, Danny," Tommy said. Danny sat down opposite Tommy, looking awkward and nervous. "I think Laney killed your kids, Danny," Tommy said softly.

Danny gasped. "But why? What did they ever do to him, for God's sake?"

"Nothing…He envied you for Kaye, for Danny and Neva, and for your future in the YPD. I think he was planting cocaine in your car again. It would be a hell of a lot harder for you to explain it the second time. He was trying to get to you, and if the kids got caught, you'd be implicated. Did you ever wonder why the Spring Common police were clued in about the coke in your car? Before anybody else on the YPD was even notified? Danny and Neva must have somehow stumbled upon Laney when he was trying to shaft you again. Anyway, however it went, Laney was scared enough to kill them…and now we're getting close, so he's scared again…and even more dangerous."

"But could he hate me that much? Enough to kill my kids? How could anybody do that to someone he hardly knows?"

"But he did know you…and what you had…and what you would become…Tell me, Dan, where would Laney get the money to put so much coke in your car?"

"I don't know."

"He'd have to have someone fix him up, right?"

"Yeah, I guess. But who? Pagliaro?"

"The green Buick that was tailing me was owned by Mose Pagliaro, right?"

Danny looked back at the chief. "So, they're in this together?" Tommy nodded. Danny took a deep breath. "What about the bomb? Did they do that, too?"

"I'd bet my next paycheck on it, kid. They wanted to get rid of me, too. I was learning too much."

Danny's emotions went from pain to shock to anger. "Do you think we can get them?"

"He took Pete, Danny...and I think...I'm not sure...he's done him in."

"But what did Pete know that could threaten them?"

"Pete was checking out the YPD range for some .32 auto shells... like the ones that killed Danny and Neva. Laney's the only one that uses them for a backup pistol. Pete was going to run some ballistic checks...only Laney found out, and he got Pete. Now Pete's gone, the shell barrels at the range were emptied on Lorenzo's day off – without his knowledge, and Laney's gone, too."

"What are we gonna do?"

"I'm going out to get Mose Pagliaro. I want him to give me Pete."

"But are you going alone? Shouldn't you have someone with you?"

"Not you, kid. Bumpy and Med have pulled a small squad together. When I need them, they'll go to work."

"Chief, I..."

"Danny, this thing could never be your fight. You know that." Danny took a deep breath. "Now, go back and take care of Lucy, my daughter, and those kids," Tommy said.

Mose Pagliaro stirred slightly. He kept thinking about all the things he'd need on his journey. He hoped Nick would remember everything...or at least set things up so they could access their money and stocks from wherever they were. He always had a million in cash ready in a minute. It was always good to have some seed money just in case. He had two million in Switzerland that even Nick didn't know about. Then he also had the six million that they shared between them in gold certificates. So, all he had to do was get out of town...just slip quietly away.

But then he heard the door close. In a moment, Chris Laney was in his office. "We have to talk," Laney said.

"About what?" Mose said as cooly as he could, trying not to betray the turmoil inside him as he sensed the clock doing damage to his best plans.

"McCarrie is after me…and you."

"Why me? I never did anything to him?"

"Except maybe to bomb his car and kill an old friend. Now look, Mose, I'm in no mood to play games. You have blood on your hands as well as I do."

"Did you talk to McCarrie? How in the hell did he know about anything?"

"I don't know, but that secretary of his that you've been fucking must have told him a mouthful."

"Bullshit. She didn't know anything about my operation."

"Don't be so stupid, Mose. She told McCarrie about you, your life, your money."

"I tell you she knows nothing."

"Well, he's been sniffing around the YPD range looking for .32 shells."

"Christ, are you stupid. Why didn't you just leave a calling card? Of all things, you use a rare gun, something they can trace right to your front door."

"I told you: I didn't have a choice. They saw me in their car, and I had to get rid of them. Besides, they won't find any shells. I took care of that."

"Chris, that won't change his mind. He knows you killed those kids and all he's looking for is something to prove it."

"What about you, Mose? If you think they're gonna hang all these killings around my neck without my taking someone with me, you're crazy."

"Get this straight, Chris. I didn't tell you to put that coke in Bellino's car. And I sure as hell didn't tell you to kill those kids or start fucking the mayor's daughter. You're on your own on those."

"Yeah, but you told me they had to be done in. And you're the one that wired the bomb to McCarrie's car to get him off your back. So, just remember one thing, Mr. Clean. If they get me, they get you."

Pagliaro was quiet for a few minutes, trying to counter the logic of the other man, but failing. "So, what do you want?" Pagliaro sighed.

"I want out of here and I need your help."

"How?"

"I have the mayor's daughter at one of the apartments. I want him to give three million to let her go."

"Three million? Is that all? Why not ask for fifty? You're out of your fucking mind."

"Listen. He's worried about his career. He wants to be governor, and he can't afford to get caught up in a sensational news story. Besides, he wants his daughter with him. I think he's got the hots for her."

Mose stared at him for a few seconds, as though seeing Laney for the first time. No wonder Nick hated him so much. This guy was really a creep, someone who killed easily, and thought crude things like no one else, a loner who liked getting the best of helpless people.

"What's wrong?" Laney said.

"How in hell are you gonna get Carly to give you money?"

"I told you, I have his daughter."

"You're crazy, Chris. You think I want to get mixed up in something like that? What are you going to do if he doesn't come up with the money? Kill his daughter?"

"No..." Laney took a few steps toward Mose, and Pagliaro suddenly thought clearly about what could happen to him. This lunatic could screw up his plans to get out of town; he could hurt his chances to recover all his money. "Mose, if you don't help me, I'm gonna take you down with me. I swear to God, if I don't get out of town with a stash, you won't either. You know fucking well McCarrie's gonna get us both if we don't do something first. He'll put every cop in the YPD after us."

Mose was thoughtful for a moment. "What do you want?" he said.

"I want you to hold Carly's daughter at a place where we set up the meet. I'm gonna be behind him in case he decides to set us up."

"What makes you so sure Carly's dumb enough to bring a suitcase full of money and then let you walk free?" Pagliaro said.

"Because he's crazy about Lisa...and because he thinks I'll kill her if I have to."

Mose thought it over frantically. Laney was just as dangerous to him as he was to Carly. But he was also a way to get out clean. Laney was purposeful. Once he knew he had to do something, he did it with all his energy. And right now, he needed someone who could do things that had to be done. "So what do you want?"

"I'm going to meet Carly. I want you to keep Lisa away from him..."

"Until when?"

"Until we have the money. "I'm not sure how it's all going to shake down. But once I get my money, we can be gone."

"But if I'm holding the girl, where are you going to be?"

"I'll be behind him, making damned sure he transfers the money and doesn't run out on us."

"What if he does?"

"Then you don't give up his daughter."

"I don't want to do this, Chris."

"You don't have a choice, Mose."

"I have every choice I ever had."

"Listen, you either do this or go down with me. Remember what I told you."

"Hey! Who the fuck do you think you are? I don't listen to you; you listen to me."

"I don't listen to anybody but myself now. I need money and I get it from Carly, or I get it from you. Take your choice."

"From me? What the hell makes you think you can get it from me? I've paid you greatly for everything you've ever done. You were bought and paid for. You were on call."

"Things have changed, Mose. Now are gonna do this for me or not? Do it the easy way or the hard way. But I don't have a lot of time. For all I know, McCarrie's got that squad on its way now. And your chances of getting away are the same as mine."

Mose took a deep breath, trying not to commit himself. Going it alone meant he would then have two enemies, McCarrie and Laney. Carly would also turn on him in a minute. Going with Laney would get him out of town, divert McCarrie with Laney, and give him and Nick a chance to get out of the country. It wasn't hard to choose...and there might be a way to find Laney once they were out of town...and silence him for good. The Pittsburgh guys owe him one. Laney would be easy.

<hr>

Tommy called Bumpy's house to talk to Lucy. "How are you, kid?" he said.

"I'm okay...Tom?"

"Yeah?"

"Why don't you take Chief Malatesta with you?"

"Because I'm not sure where I'm going. I'm in reactive mode, kid. I have to wait to see what happens," said Tommy.

"But what if you're hurt?"

"I won't get hurt, Luce. I'm gonna track down that son of a bitch and put him in jail."

There was silence on the other end of the line. "Oh, God, please don't get hurt, Tom. I'm so afraid of all this."

As he drove, Tommy thought of the ironies of his life that were so frightening now. Could his life end this way? After spending all those years without love? And then, after finding the love that would illuminate his existence, would he now be killed just before the promise of that happiness would be realized? Jesus, this was bad. He was changing. The worst thing for a cop was to be afraid, to be fearful of losing the future. When cops have too much to lose, they're more vulnerable because their minds aren't right. Maybe they're so worried about preserving the future that they'll lose the keen edge of wariness that keeps them alive, and cunning, and lethal to their enemies.

He sorted, as if to banish the thought. He had to find them. Suddenly his cellular phone rang. It was Bumpy. Tommy's heart sank. "Bump? What up?"

"I just talked to Carly, Tommy...his daughter never came home."

"It's got to be Laney or Pagliaro, Bump. She's their insurance."

"Yeah. I told Carly that she's probably alive."

Carly paced nervously as he waited. Tommy McCarrie had not

called in several hours. Bumpy Malatesta was only a little comforting as they talked. "...Probably still alive."

Jesus, what would he and Ginny do if they lost her? She was all they had. How could they hold together?

Carly shook his head. He was haunted by the thought that they could have had another child, but somehow never did. Ginny once told him, when she was angry with him, that she would never forget that other child that she longed for, something that might have been. But it was something so easy to put off. And now that girl they loved so much, and that he had hurt so much, was in the hands of a madman.

Suddenly, the phone rang. Ginny jumped to get it. So did the police interceptors as the recording began. "Let me talk to Carly," the voice said.

"Is my daughter with you? Is she all right?" Ginny said.

"Let me talk to Carly," the voice snapped, "or I'll hang up right now."

Carly ran to the phone, knowing from Ginny's expression who was on the other end. He grabbed the phone from her. "What do you want?"

"Lisa is here with me," Laney said.

"Where are you, Laney?"

"Come on, Carly. Let's not start the bullshit. Are you gonna listen to me or not?"

"Yeah, I'll listen. Is she okay?"

"She's fine...and if you do what I tell you, she'll stay fine."

"What do you want?"

"It's easy, Carly...money."

"How much?"

"Three million cash. One dime less and you'll never see Lisa again…and don't get cute with marked bills, because Lisa's life depends on it, understand?"

"It'll take me a day or so to get it. Don't hurt her, Chris."

"Just don't fuck with me, Carly, and she won't get hurt. I don't want to do anything to her…unless you try to play any games. You'll keep McCarrie and the YPD out of this if you're smart."

"How will I get in touch with you when I have the money?"

"I'll get in touch with you…and don't be stupid about tracing this call. I didn't become a police captain without knowing something about tapping phone lines."

Carly called Mose Pagliaro on his cellular phone, so Mose answered it, reflexively. "Mose, this is Carly."

"What do you want, Carly?"

"I want you to get that lunatic, Laney, to give up my daughter."

"What are you talking about? Give up your daughter for what?"

"Don't fuck with me, Mose. You know he's crazy and I know he works for you."

"Carly, I'd like to help you, but I just don't know what you're talking about."

"Mose, if any harm comes to my daughter, there won't be enough holes in this world for you to hide in. I'll use my last dime to find you."

"I don't have your daughter, Carly."

Carly was getting angry. He always mistrusted Mose. And he always hated Laney. The two of them together were capable of just about anything. "Mose, I'm in no mood to play games. I'll get the money. Just don't hurt her."

"Look, Carly, enough is enough. I told you I don't have your daughter. Hell, I wouldn't know her if I saw her. So if you have a problem with Laney, that's your business with him, not me. I'm busy now, Carly. I'll talk to you some other time."

When Carly hung up the receiver, he ground his teeth in frustration. They had him by the balls. They had the one thing he cared about most…and they knew it. But this was crazy: Mose was part of kidnapping another dago's daughter? It didn't make sense.

Just then the phone rang, and Carly answered. It was Tommy Mc-Carrie. "You hear anything, Carly?" the older man said.

"I just talked to Mose Pagliaro," he said.

Tommy took a deep breath. "Carly, please, I know you're worried about Lisa, but you have to let our guys know what you're doing. The more you stay off the phone, the better."

"For Christ's sake, Tommy, do you want to hear about my conversation or not?"

"Yeah, Carly, I do…I'm sorry, kid. I know this is a hell of a strain. So what did you find out?"

"He and Laney are planning something; I just know it."

"Laney's always been on the take from him," Tommy muttered.

"But I know they have Lisa, Tommy. Pagliaro told me I was crazy, but he's got her…or he knows where she is."

"Laney's got her," Tommy said.

"Tommy," Carly said hesitantly, "there something strange about this. Pagliaro's a dago. Kidnapping another dago's kid can't be his style. Besides, he's worth a ton of money; why does he want Lisa?"

Tommy was quiet for a moment. *Yes. Why? Why would a smoothie like Pagliaro get involved with rough stuff like a high-profile kidnapping? Carly was right. It wasn't his style.*

"You just told me something, kid. I have to figure out what it means, but what you saw was important. Now, look — stay off the god-damned phone unless you get a call, understand? The boys in the truck have a hook-up. They're recording everything that comes in."

In a few minutes, Tommy was on the phone to Bumpy. "How's Lucy?" he asked.

"She's fine, Tommy. Danny and Elly are there. The kids are all here. She's worried sick about you."

"Tell her I'll talk to her soon…Does Danny have his shotgun?"

"Yeah, and he knows how to use it, too. He's not as good with a handgun as you are, but I remember Smokey telling me he could handle long arms…from days in the service."

"Good. You stand ready, okay? I'm gonna call you sometime soon and I'll want you to run like hell to find me. Bump, if he has her, he's gonna want lots of cover, someplace we'd never think of."

Then Tommy was on his way again. What did Carly say? If he's right, if Pagliaro wasn't involved in the kidnapping, then he was involved as a second stringer with somebody else calling the shots. That had to be Laney. But why would a guy like Pagliaro let a jerk like Laney call the shots? Why is a money man covering for a killer? Only one way. Laney has some leverage on Pagliaro.

Poor old Smokey was right. He sensed that this whole case hinged on something under our nose. That was easy in retrospect. Chris Laney was the killer; he was also the enforcer for Pagliaro, who now had his boss by the balls.

What a perfect setup all along. In the YPD, a captain of detectives could easily cover his tracks all along, could send people on wild goose chases, could muddle and confuse, and cast suspicion on everyone but the killer. It was easy.

Suddenly, his cellular phone rang. "Tommy," Carly said, "I just got a call from Laney. He wants me to meet him tomorrow…with the money."

"How much?" Tommy asked.

"Three million cash."

"Can you get that kind of money?"

"Yeah," he sighed, "but it'll take some time."

"We don't have much, Carly," Tommy said.

"I'll get it."

"Okay. Get it. I'll call you first thing in the morning. The sound truck will monitor every call…so you can sleep tonight." He stopped for a second. "Carly, if she's okay now, he won't harm her until he sees the money."

"I hope to hell you're right, Tommy."

After the call, Tommy called Bumpy. "Bump, I want every airport this side of the Mississippi to know about Laney and Pagliaro…and call the FBI, now that we're dealing with kidnappers."

"Med's already called the State Highway Patrol and all the state police in this part of the country."

"Good…I don't think he'll go until he gets the money. Pagliaro's the one who might take off early."

"He won't go if Laney has something on him, Tom."

"Yeah. If they're working together, then Laney's calling the shots. I wouldn't be surprised if we see one of them soon."

"So, all we do is wait."

"All you do is run everything. Keep Danny with those women and have blues all over the place."

"You take care of yourself, kid."

"I'm gonna get a few hours at the Terrace Motel. Call me there if you hear anything. Carly already has my number. You know, Bump, our one ace in the hole is that these two guys are such crooked bastards, they might turn on each other."

"Yeah. Two snakes in a barrel, huh?"

"Let's hope their true colors show. Get some sleep, kid. We're gonna be busy tomorrow."

At the motel, Tommy checked into one of the police rooms that the YPD had on retainer. He thought of calling Lucy but hesitated. God, he missed seeing her. How easy it was when he had no one, when he was young. Then, he faced danger easily, and the thought of losing the future never entered his mind. The glimmer of what was good in life, what was worth fighting for, hoping for, began with Neva and Danny. Then, in the last two years, Elly and Danny had entered his life, and now suddenly Lucy. And yet, the loss of the young couple, the loss of Smokey, the loss of Liebowitz, the mere notion of what might yet be lost, of happiness unrealized, can make a man hesitate. Maybe it was just a pretty gloss over fear, even over cowardice. Maybe he's afraid of dying at the hands of one of these assassins.

He listened to the sound of his breathing, the sound of his heart beating. God! Where was Pete? As much as Tommy thought the best thoughts, and put the worst out of his mind, he had seen evil triumph over hope too many times.

Now he was in this strange bed, with all the people he cared about at risk. And all he could do was wait. Everything was against him. Pete was a hostage...if he was alive. Lucy and Elly and Danny, all the kids, they could be in danger in a thousand ways he had not thought of. If these madmen could kill Danny and Neva and the others, they could kill again. It had been so long since he played this waiting game. The quiet stole upon him and he relaxed in spite of his fear and doubt. Soon, he was breathing heavily, asleep.

Mose heard a knock on the back door of his house. He knew it wasn't Nick. It had to be Laney. "What's going on?" he said as Laney entered wordlessly.

"Did you see that squad car parked outside, down the street?"

"No! Jesus, are they coming in?"

"No. But they're watching. If we make a false move, they'll nail us."

"How'd you get by them?"

"I know this neighborhood. I came through the alley."

"Did you tell Carly about the money?"

"I told him we'd exchange her for it."

"Then what?"

"Then you and I leave town."

Mose was silent for a minute. He took a deep breath. "Chris, once we're out of here, you go your way, and I go mine."

"I can do that."

Mose nodded. "So where are you gonna do the exchange?"

"Guerin Woods...but you're gonna do it."

"Me? Why the hell should I do it?" Mose said, his voice straining.

"Because I have to be behind them to see that they aren't all wired up...Look, I know you're flush, but I'm not. So, if you want to live to enjoy all the money you've stashed, you'd better let me get my hands on some of my own."

Mose shook his head to himself. Of all the people in the world to be hooked up with, it was this guy, a goddamned wack job. But it wouldn't be for long. He'll get somebody to take him out as soon as they get out of this mess, sooner rather than later.

"When will you bring her?" Mose asked.

"I'm gonna call Carly this evening. When I know he's ready, I'll set up the drop. Then, I'll bring Lisa to you, and then, in our own cars, you and I will drive up to Guerin Woods. Up there, Lisa will stay with you on the North Side where there's a small hill. We'll make Carly come in from the west side and meet us with the money on the little flat near the bottom of the hill. Then, we do two things... watch him drop the money, and then back away from it. I'll grab the money, and you can release Lisa to her old man. I'll be behind them to make damned sure they don't pull any funny stuff. You just be sure you don't let her go unless we have the money."

"Jesus Christ," Mose muttered. "Can't you think of another way to do this? I don't like this kidnapping shit."

"Do you want to do it in town? Where every cop in the YPD can be out there waiting with sniper scopes to nail you? At least we're calling the shots here. They don't know what we're gonna do next and that works in our favor, understand? By the way, Mose, don't try any funny stuff or you'll be dead. I can do it easily."

Mose huffed and nodded. "I'll be carrying, too, Chris. And remember, I have — you might call them *relations* — in Pittsburgh and Cleveland that I've made a lot of money for, and I've clued them in about you. So, if you ever want to enjoy that cash, you better not try to fuck me over somehow. I don't need the money, so if you ever want to live to enjoy it, you'd better do this straight and be out of town before daylight."

The phone rang. Tommy stirred from a fitful sleep and grabbed the receiver. "Yeah?"

It was Bumpy. "Tommy, Carly just got the call. But Laney knows we wired the mayor's house so he's sending him on a goose chase before he finally tells him where to go."

"I figured that. He's too smart to blow this one for himself."

"What do you want us to do?"

"Tell me where the next call will be."

"At the train station at one o'clock."

Tommy snorted. "It's like he's done this before, huh?"

"You gonna be there?"

"Yeah. How's Lucy?"

"Worried sick about you."

"She get any sleep?"

"Not much. Elly and Danny and all the kids are doing okay. The kids are having fun."

"Hell, they might as well... Man, I could sure use a drink."

"Not now, Tommy. After this, we'll all get smashed... at your wedding."

Tommy smiled grimly. "Okay, kid. Just stay wired. We'll see what happens."

"What about that squad, Tommy?"

"Make sure a few of them are at the station... but I don't know, Bump. Something's funny about this."

"Okay. I'll send a few out in street clothes. We'll keep the others to dispatch to the next scene."

"Good. I'll see you later, kid. You help get the YPD going, okay? You and Med are all I've got."

Tommy took a deep breath. Neither man mentioned Pete, even though they were both thinking of him. *Laney's going to die,* Tommy thought. *He's going to make some mistake and do something stupid... or maybe too arrogant... and Danny and Neva will be avenged, and their father would be free to marry someone who really loved him.*

But Tommy knew he had to be careful. He had to be perfect. One bad move could get someone killed. And Tommy knew he had to be a killer and not a victim.

———◆◆◆◆◆———

At the train station, Tommy was early, checking out ways in which the squad could hide themselves and see if Laney would show up.

"Chief?" said the young sergeant as he approached at the head of the small squad. They were coming from the back of the station so that they wouldn't be seen.

"Matuszak, right?" Tommy said. He was glad this young cop was one of the good ones. He had noticed him several times in crises, like at the death scene of Danny and Neva, and he looked concerned and confident. He would make a good assistant to Danny as chief and would succeed him some day if he played his cards right. Pete and Bumpy liked him and that was good enough for Tommy.

"I've been here a while," said Tommy. "Put two guys in that lodge up there...at opposite ends," he said, pointing at an area of the main floor that looked like a mezzanine. "I don't think this is the place where we're going to get the action, but we have to be prepared just in case."

Matuszak left Tommy and began to deploy his men around the station. All were good shots and carried rifles as well as side arms. Tommy too had his venerable .45 as well as Bumpy's small belly gun hidden in a pocket holster.

Tommy found a place near the phones. Everyone waited silently, knowing that they might have to kill someone if necessary.

Tommy called Bumpy to find out if Pagliaro had left his house.

There was no sign of him. All that happened was that Mickey had entered the house, then came out and put the green Buick off the street into Pagliaro's garage.

They waited longer. Finally, Med drove up with Carly in the mayor's unmarked car. Tommy waved to them as they entered. When Carly saw Tommy, he became agitated. "Tommy, what the hell are you doing here? What if you scare him away, for Christ's sake?"

"He's not here, Carly. He wants to talk to you on the phone, remember?"

"He could have someone else here, can't he?"

"Carly, there's no one here. They're alone on this one…and they'd be fools to show up now."

"I'm so damned scared, Tommy."

"Remember one thing, kid. He's a killer, and killers don't live up to promises. He'll fuck you over in a minute and not even think about it."

"So what the hell are we doing here?"

"Trying to outguess, him. You're playing poker, boyo."

"With my daughter's life," he said ruefully.

"It's the only game we can play now, Carly. We just have to keep our eyes open and try to outsmart him."

"It's not a game if Lisa can get killed."

Suddenly the phone rang. Carly paled and began to shake. Tommy signaled to Matuszak to keep everyone ready and watch the lobby for any familiar looking people…like one of Laney's YPD spies.

Tommy nodded to the mayor and squeezed his arm to bolster his courage. "Hello?" Carly said.

"Glad you made it, Carly. Blow a kiss to all the sharpshooters for me, will you? Now listen to me…"

"How do I know if Lisa's all right?" Carly interrupted.

Laney paused for a minute, and suddenly Carly could hear Lisa's voice: "Daddy, I'm okay."

"All right, Carly. Satisfied? Now if you don't listen to me, you'll never see her again. Do you understand what I'm telling you? If you try any more games like you just did at the train station, then your daughter's gone."

"What do you want?" Carly said softly. Carly looked at Tommy who had been standing close to him, his ear as close to the receiver as he could to hear. Tommy nodded to the mayor again. "Carly, I know you got police all around you now, so we aren't going to do any business. But I'm gonna call you later and tell you what to do."

Carly blanched in anger. *What a son of a bitch*, he thought. Laney continued: "...And if you ever want to see her again, you better play this one straight...no cops, no lawyers, no McCarrie, nobody but you and the money. Go home. I'll call you later this afternoon with more instructions." Then, there was a dial tone.

"I'm going home," Carly said resolutely.

"Carly, he's not going to tell you where to go from your house. It'll be another one of those public phone deals. He knows your house is wired."

"Yeah," Carly said. "But like you said, he's calling the shots. And I don't want any cops with me the next time...like we have here, understand?"

"Carly, he's a killer. He can decide to kill Lisa at a moment's notice...even if he has your money. You can't give this guy an even break."

"Don't come near me, Tommy. I don't care about the money. All I want is Lisa back."

"You could lose Lisa and the money … and Laney, if you don't trust me."

"I have to trust myself, Tommy."

Matuszak then drove Carly back to his house. Tommy called Bumpy. "What's up, Tom?"

"Laney was just showing us who's boss. He scared Carly, Bump. Carly wants to go it alone. He thinks he can buy his daughter back without us."

"Oh, shit!" Bumpy said, "What now?"

"We have to play it by the book. We can stay away from him, but we can also do our job. By the way, did you go home?"

"I'm going now. I have to get some sleep or I'm gonna fall down."

"Okay. I'll rest a while, too. Let's put some of the shift captains in charge until we can get our work done."

"Yeah. There's nothing else going on."

—◈—

Elly was wide awake. She stirred and heard the girls breathing heavily in sleep. It seemed strange to be so suddenly alert. She put on a night gown and didn't even put on her slippers so as not to make noise. In the hall, she listened for a few moments to the sounds of sleep from all the rooms.

She decided to go downstairs. She was careful not to make any noise because she didn't want to wake Danny, who was sleeping on the couch downstairs. Though, secretly, she wanted him to be awake so they could talk.

She walked into the sunroom illuminated now only by dim moonlight and was startled to find Lucy there. "Lucy? Are you alright?" she said softly, barely above a whisper.

"Yes," she answered simply.

"Have you been up long?"

"A while," Lucy answered, shrugging as she did.

Elly's eyes were accustomed to the dark, and once while Lucy talked to her, she caught moonlight on her face, glistening off the tears that had streaked down her cheeks. Suddenly, Elly walked over to Lucy and sat on the floor at her feet. Both women had light nightgowns on and were silhouetted against the dim light of the night sky.

"He'll be okay," Elly said. Lucy shook her head, and Elly could see fresh tears. "I know he'll come back safe and sound," said the younger woman, pleading softly.

"You know, Elly, sometimes I think I'm not meant to be happy. All those years I spent with Ed...none of them were like this. I think I could be happy if..." She stopped, as if listening to her own thoughts, then shook her head again. "I'm so afraid that I'm going to lose this one chance."

Elly reached for Lucy's hand and held it. "I think I understand," she said hesitantly. Then she stopped for a few moments. "My marriage was like yours...you know...hoping he would, just once, say thanks or tell me that he loved me, or touch my hand, or ask me how I felt about something. And I waited all those years, and it never happened. The most horrible part of all was knowing that if I waited for a lifetime, he still wouldn't do those things."

Lucy reached out and ran her hand over Elly's hair. And that small gesture helped the two of them know that each understood the feelings of the other. They both knew that there was a chance for happiness for them, and that they held the keys to it...if only Tommy would return safe.

"I'm feeling so sorry for myself that I've forgotten that you've had it hard, too. I'm sorry, Elly," Lucy said softly.

Elly kissed her hand and noticed that Lucy had more tears in her eyes. Lucy saw the look. "You know," she said, "all those years I was married to Ed, I never cried, no matter what, and yet your father...I seem to cry over him all the time." She snorted and smiled.

"That guy in the next room had made me cry a few times, too... and he didn't even know it," Elly responded.

"It must be that happiness and sorrow come together...the price we pay for love," Lucy said.

"I'll pay the price. After living so many years without love or caring, or even emotion, it's worth a few tears once in a while."

———◆◆◆◆———

Carly got the call from Laney that afternoon. "Do you have the money?"

"Yeah. Don't hurt her, Chris. I've got it all ready for you. Just don't hurt her."

"You know, Carly, you're not being very swift about this. I thought we could handle this alone..."

"McCarrie was just trying to help, Chris. But he won't be with me anymore. I'll be alone."

"All right. I'll call you back in a few hours. Then I'll tell you where to go, Carly...but don't try goddamned games. Remember, I have Lisa, and what happens to her depends on you."

Carly's wife had been listening to her husband talk. "What does he want now?" she said.

"Only to know if I had the money...Did Judge East call?"

"Yes. The money's on its way. He says he'll be coming later."

"Did he handle it the way I told him?"

"I'm sure he did ... What about McCarrie?"

"I can't afford to have him involved with this. That goddamned Laney hates him. I think he's afraid of him, too. We can't take the chance that he'll mess this up somehow, just by being there."

"What are we going to tell him if he comes here? Or if he calls?"

"Tell him we can't afford to have something go wrong. Even if he means to help, we have to handle it our way."

"Do you really think Laney will do it?"

"I can't believe he'd hurt her. He just needs money to get out of town."

"Tommy McCarrie thinks he'd kill her."

"He and McCarrie have been feuding forever. They hate each other. I never had much contact with Laney. I dealt with him only through Pagliaro, so he doesn't hate me the way he does McCarrie. So maybe he'll have enough sense to take the money and run."

Tommy called Lucy. "You okay, kid?"

She snorted. "I've been better. Where are you?"

"I caught a few winks at the Hillside Motel. I know this thing's going to happen soon."

There was silence on the line for several seconds. "Lucy?"

"What?" More silence.

"Are you okay?"

"No, I'm not okay. How can you ask me that?"

"I'll be all right, Luce. I promise."

"Those men are killers, and they'll try to kill you before you get them."

"They're going to get each other, Luce."

"Tom, they'll spoil our lives…spoil my last chance for happiness. I almost feel cursed, as though I'm never supposed to be happy."

"You're my last chance for happiness, too, Luce."

"Then what are we doing, Tom? You're in danger, I'm in a strange house under police guard…and we're not together. Even if it all ended now, I'd want to be with you, not have you alone, wandering the streets looking for men who want to kill you."

Tommy didn't answer for a few seconds. Then, he said, "Luce, you know it has to be this way. I couldn't control this…"

"But let someone help you!" she interrupted. He knew she was crying now.

"They are helping me, kid. We just have to find Laney first. And we don't want Carly's daughter ending up like —"

"Like Pete? Is that what you were going to say?"

"I don't know Pete's dead yet," Tommy said softly.

"But you're afraid of it, aren't you?"

"Yeah. Luce, I promise you I won't take any chances. We'll be together as soon as this is over…soon. I have to go now."

"I love you, Tom," she said in a voice muffled by a strange nasal sound of tears clogging her breathing.

Tommy took a deep breath. "Thank you, kid. I love you, too."

<hr />

Laney had called Mose to let him know they when they would meet. "You wait for me at the Berlin Motel on Route 62," Laney said. "You know where it is?"

"Yeah, I know."

"I'll see you at seven o'clock. I want this meet with Carly to be at night."

"How do I know where you are?"

"Cabin 15," Laney said. "Just drive up to it and park. It's open."

"I don't know if I want any part of this," Mose mumbled ruefully.

"Use your head for Christ's sake, Mose!" Laney snarled. "I'm offering you a chance to help me and help yourself. After tonight, you'll never see me again. What more do you want?"

"I don't want to swing for the Bellino kids, that's what."

"Jesus, would you rather swing for Liebowitz? Remember, that one was your idea. Christ, you even made the bomb, Mose." Mose didn't answer. "Face it. You're in up to your neck with me, so don't fuck it up."

"All right, all right. I'll see you at seven."

After he hung up, Mose sat quietly in the dark, thinking about his plight. When you have to deal with guys with screws loose, you always leave yourself open to danger, the weakest links, over which you have so little control, are the minds and personality quirks of the people who do things for you.

He called his brother. "Nick, we have to move fast. This Laney has us by the balls and I'm afraid he's gonna do something stupid…He wants three yards from the mayor, and I have to help him get it."

"When?"

"Tonight."

"I took care of all the transfers. We're covered. We can go tomorrow."

"Okay. I'm going to do this with Laney. But then, that's it. I'll call Pittsburgh tonight if he plays us for suckers."

"Mose, we can get fucked royal here…and we're dealing with a guy who doesn't give a shit about us. So even if you do it yourself, just take care of it. As long as we're out of here tomorrow."

"I'll take care of it," Mose said.

When he was done with his brother, Mose called Mickey Gorman. "Come on over here right away, Mick. I have to talk to you."

When Mickey arrived, he was startled to find Mose in a pair of jeans and a sweater. "What's up?" he asked Mose.

"Not much. How are you?"

"Fine... You call me over here just to chat, Mose?"

"Oh, no," said Mose, acting preoccupied and distracted. "I want you to help me push my car out of the garage. I can't get it started."

"Why don't you just call a garage?"

"Because I need to do something in the garage tonight. I'll call about the car tomorrow."

"What's going on, Mose?"

Mose had to decide how much he could let this dim man know. Finally, he decided that if Mickey could make some money, he could be managed. "Mickey, I'm gonna level with you." Mose stopped to watch Mickey's reaction. Mickey seemed surprised at the intimate tone Mose used on him, a tone he only heard him use on equals, and few at that: the mayor, his brother, Nick, and a few important people.

"About what?" Mickey asked warily. He wasn't used to being addressed as someone sensible enough to deal with Mose's quiet thoughts.

"About you... me, Carly... this whole town."

"What's going on?" Mickey said, more enthusiastic about his new status.

"I'm getting out of town," said Mose. "Carly's changing. I don't trust him anymore. The cops are in for a shake-up. McCarrie's going to roll some heads and Carly's gonna buy it. Everything we had going is gonna change, and I don't want to be going to jail for someone else. Understand?"

"Who's going to jail?"

"You don't think it'll be Carly or McCarrie, do you?"

"Then who?"

"Me, you…anybody they can hang something on. But bet your ass it won't be them."

Mickey shook his head, his wide eyes showing the force of the new ideas on his mind. "But if you go…"

"If I go, who do you think they'll come after next? The mayor? A police captain?" Mickey was silent, tormented about things that he had never thought of and never could process now that they were at his attention. "I have a proposition for you, Mick," said Mose, still using his earnest, intimate tone.

"Oh, no. I don't want no proposition. I just want out of this."

"Listen, Mick. You think Carly's gonna save your ass if the heat's on him? How long do you think it'd take for him to give you up?"

"Carly's been good to me," Mick stammered, shaking his head.

"Sure, as long as you were a slave to him — a gopher. But what if his own ass is in a sling? You think he's gonna say, 'I want to make sure Mickey comes out of this clean, no matter what happens to me?' You know him. Is that Carly's style?"

"I don't know, Mose; I don't know. I'm getting out of here…I don't want no part of this." Mickey started for the door.

"It'll be worth cash money if you help me out," Mose said to Mickey's back.

Mickey turned around slowly. "How much?"

"A lot more than you make now."

"How much?"

"If you do it, it'll get you twenty grand."

Mickey snorted skeptically. "What do you want me to do, kill somebody?"

"No. I'm not real sure what I need out of you. But I guarantee you it won't take you more than a couple of days...maybe just one."

"Don't bullshit me, Mose. I don't need that."

"Look, I have to get out of town...like you. You help me, and I kiss you goodbye with twenty grand in your pocket."

"So, what do you want?"

"I want you to watch this place tonight...all night. But before I go, I want you to push that Buick into the lot at the far end."

"Push it? Why?" Mickey stopped and looked at Mose. He was almost fevered by the decisions that he had made during the last few minutes. He trembled as his mind tried to grapple with the complex maze of ideas that he had to understand for his own safety.

"Don't start it, Mick. Understand?"

Mickey took a deep breath, seemingly amazed that Mose had wired the car. "Here's the key. Just don't start it 'cause it's hot."

"I don't know about this, Mose. You're talking about something that can get me in jail."

"Twenty grand, Mick. Now are you gonna do it or not? I don't have time to negotiate. If you don't want to do it, I'll find someone else."

Mickey was quiet, as though wishing that his mind could comprehend all the complexity about Mose's offer. "Twenty grand, Mick," said Mose sharply. "How about it?"

Mickey took a deep breath, but as he did, he nodded his head. "Good, Mick. Now keep those keys. If Laney comes back here without me...and he's looking for wheels out of town, you give him the keys."

"But that would mean —"

"That would mean you gave him the keys to a car that you don't know anything about. It's not yours and it doesn't have your prints on it...nor mine, either."

"Mose, I…"

"Mick, goddammit, I don't have time for this. Now do you want the money or not? Just say it. I'm not going to ask you again."

"What do you want done?" Mickey said, surrendering to the siren song of Mose's money.

"I'm going out to meet Laney soon. You get that car out of here and keep those keys. When we're done, we'll be back here. I'll give you five grand now, the rest when I get back. Remember, if he comes back alone, you make sure he starts that car." Mickey nodded. "It'll be the fastest twenty grand you've made in your life. Then it'll be a lot easier for you to get out of town."

———◆◆◆———

"Chris, what are you doing?" Lisa said. "How could you do this to me?"

"I haven't done anything to you," Laney snapped. "I'm just getting out of town, and I need some funds."

"I thought you loved me. You said you did."

"Yeah, well, sometimes we say things without thinking."

"Do you hate me? Is that why you've tied me up like a dog? Do you think I'll run away?"

He chuckled. "No, I don't think you'll run away. You'll just hang around until Daddy gives me some money, then you can go back to college for your senior year."

"I loved you, Chris," she said softly. "I would have done anything for you."

"Anything but go against your father for me," he countered.

"Just because I didn't want you to kill him…like you almost did at my apartment?"

"He started it."

"God! You sound like a little boy. He was only thinking of me. You should have known that."

"I don't have time to analyze your father, Lisa. I have to get out of town, and you have to help me."

"I'll help you...Take me with you." He shook his head. "But why? Why can't we be like we were before?"

"Too much water over the dam, Lisa. We can't get those feelings, back."

"You don't know that."

"That's the difference between you and me. The years between us make me know that it's all gone, but let you keep thinking we can keep it going."

"Chris, were you lying all the time? Every word of it?"

"I was saying what made you feel good. Isn't that enough?"

"So I was just one of a long line of girls that you lied to?"

"Do you know any other man my age who hasn't had other women? Grow up, Lisa. It was good while it lasted...and you were the best of them. Let it be enough."

"It would always have been enough, Chris. All you had to do was be honest with me," she said.

He was packing his clothes and rubbing fingerprints off his gun. When he looked over at her and saw tears streaming down her face, she saw him look at her. For a few seconds their eyes met. In that short time, she expected something from him, some spark of concern, some little evidence of caring, but she got nothing. He was preoccupied with his own problems, and her being trussed up and gagged like a doll meant nothing to him.

She had the horrible emptiness of heart that a lover feels when she realizes that the man who had lain in her arms, and had steered her through such turbulent passion, could never say those few, simple, magical words that would make her know the dream of love. And they would never be heard for the worst of all reasons: the dream lover was hollow inside. No amount of educating and sensitizing would make it happen in his heart. No muse would enkindle that desire to make her feel joy and comfort…and love. No amount of wishing would turn her Pinocchio into a human being and give him the heart that she'd dreamed he'd have.

That's why he was dangerous. When he beat Carly, and would have killed him except for her pleading, he was doing something easy, something he enjoyed.

And she realized now that all of those emotions that would set the blood of others to flow faster, and would bring a flush to their faces, and would evoke shame after the deed was done…all of those were one and the same for Chris Laney. Killing someone, making love to someone, hating someone, envying someone, beating someone, lying to someone, were all deeds of the moment, done because it got Chris Laney through a crisis or a need.

That was his secret. He was not betrayed by the emotions that tormented others, that made them hesitate to lie or shrink from violence or regret enjoying evil. He was true only to his moments. What had to be done was done decisively and remorselessly, with never a backward glance. It was then that Lisa Giustino knew that she and her father were in mortal danger.

Med came down to see Tommy, who was using Bumpy's office. "Chief, that squad is ready. All we have to do is hear the order."

"What about the dogs?"

"They're ready, too."

"Anything more about Pete?" Med shook his head. "Okay. Keep me posted. And wait for something big to call Bumpy. He's been up for two days."

"Uh, Tommy, I talked to Danny just a little while ago. He's nervous as a cat, but everything's okay. Elly and Lucy are fine."

"Thanks, Med."

———◆◆◆———

"How's it going?" Mose said to Mickey, who was just coming into the garage.

"The car's out in the lot."

"Good. You lock it?"

"Yeah."

"You keep the keys. Remember, if Laney comes back alone and needs wheels, you give him those keys. And stay the hell away from that car." Mickey nodded.

"Where you going, Mose?"

"I have a chore to do with Laney. You have to keep an eye on this place."

"Okay...Is Carly gonna know about this?"

"The twenty grand is between you and me. Carly's not going to know a fucking thing...unless you're dumb enough to tell him."

"So I could go back and work for him? The job's easy and the pay's good."

"If you want to chance it, do what you want, Mick. I'm gonna be gone."

"Uh, Mose...How about you give me half now and half later?"

Mose looked contemptuously at Mickey. He hated himself for having to deal with a stupid man — and to have that fool negotiate with him just when he knows Mose needs him. "Okay. Five thousand now... and the rest after? If not, then go fuck yourself. I can get lots of guys go for what I'm offering. Did I ever stiff you when you did things for me?"

"This is different."

"You're making it different. Now are you gonna do this or not?"

"Yeah, five thousand. But I want it now."

Chris Laney waited with Lisa Giustino until dark. Then, he called Mose Pagliaro on one of his cell phones to tell him where to meet them. He had given Lisa a sedative and she was quiet. They parked in the rear lot of an old bar on the East Side, and Laney joined Mose in his car. "You know what we have to do?"

"I know I don't like this."

"Look. You have to stop this. We can pull this off in one quick shot. Then we get out of town. Did you pack?"

"Yeah."

"Okay. I'm packed, too. All we do now is call Carly and let him know where to meet us. But we don't tell him the first time, understand? We make sure he comes alone."

"Suppose he brings the cops?"

"We have his daughter, Mose. He'll come alone."

"When are you going to call?"

"Now. You ready?" Mose nodded.

Tommy dozed in Bumpy's office, trying to store up enough rest so that he could be at his best when the last act of the drama unfolds. Suddenly, Sergeant Matuszak knocked on his door and entered. "Chief? The electrovan just intercepted a call to the mayor's house. Laney gave Carly directions to the first stop."

"Where is it?"

"A pay phone booth about a mile from his house."

Tommy was silent for a moment. Finally, he said, "Thanks, Ted. You look after this place while I'm gone. Remember what I told you. Keep things as normal as you can. I don't want anyone to know what's going on."

"Will Chief Malatesta be coming in?" the young man said, blanching at Tommy's charge.

"He'll be coming in soon. When he does, you do what he tells you. You two and Med are running things and keeping a lid on until we find out what Laney's gonna do."

"You gonna be okay, Chief? You need some help?"

"No. I'm not sure what I can do to help Carly, but I have to find some way. Meanwhile, I'm counting on you. Okay?"

Matuszak snorted and nodded, as though convincing himself that he could live up to Tommy's expectations. "Yeah. We'll take care of things."

In a moment, he was gone, and Tommy was again alone in the quiet office. Carly wasn't going to tell them what Laney was telling him to do; he knew that. *So what's going to happen here?* Tommy thought. He has to get Carly in a safe place, somewhere where he can make the exchange and be gone. But will he make the exchange? Jesus. Tommy could think of a dozen reasons why he would. But then a dozen reasons why he wouldn't.

Med knocked and walked in. "Hi, Chief."

"Med," said Tommy in acknowledgment. "What's up?"

"Carly got another call from Laney. It's gonna be one of those maze chases so he can lose us."

"We have anybody who can tail him?"

"We have some guys from that squad. But Laney's sharp, too. He can make Carly lose us…and of course if Laney figures Carly's playing him dumb, then the girl's in trouble."

"Yeah," said Tommy thoughtfully. "And Carly'll go off on us and maybe put her in danger still."

"Bumpy called…he's coming in. And I talked to Danny again. He's going crazy. I told him to hold on a few hours more."

"Good. You know, he must be going nuts. I wonder what I'd be like if it were my kids and my wife?"

"Did Laney kill his wife, Tommy?"

"Nah, Med, she was so screwed up, he didn't have to."

"But that means you think she…"

Tommy held up his hand to silence his friend and keep him from completing his thought. "Laney and Pagliaro have been shedding all the blood around here, kid. That's why I want to nail their asses to the wall."

"Our guys are ready, Tommy. When you tell us, we can move."

"Okay. I'll be giving you a call when this thing shapes up. When's the first call?"

"Six-thirty at some phone near the house."

"Okay. See if our trackers can stay with them. Make sure those dogs are ready."

"Okay. So, this is what you do," Laney told Pagliaro. "You take her and just hold her there until Carly walks out into the clearing with the briefcase. We'll make him show us the money and if everything's kosher, we take off with the money…and I'm telling you, Mose, if this is a set-up or some kind of scam, you blow her fucking head off."

"Where are you gonna be?" said Mose.

"I'm going to be opposite you on the little flat. If anything goes wrong, we can blow them both away. You have your piece?"

"Yeah," said Mose.

"What d'you carry? A .40?"

"Yeah. The .40'll take it right to them."

"Okay, we're ready," said Laney. "Remember, Mose, if we do this fast, we can be in Canada tonight. And I can be in Aruba tomorrow. You can go where you want."

"All right. Let's go."

Laney made the first call to Carly at the pay phones. He knew the sound men were waiting at Carly's house, so all he did was tell him which phone to use…and await further instructions. But Laney was also cunning and experienced and had done some homework. So, when Carly got to the first pay phone, there was a note taped to it with other instructions.

Laney led Carly to several other phones in the city, only to anger the mayor at each stop. Laney would smile at each of Carly's outbursts, knowing that his prey would only have to calm down and be humble again. *He really did love that daughter of his*, Laney thought.

"All right," Laney said to Mose. "We've softened him up. Now let's go out to Guerin Woods and make the swap. I'll call Carly and tell him what I want him to do."

—•••••—

Tommy had been recalling all the things that had been done in the past two years...leading up to this night. This was the ribbon on the package. Danny and Neva, Kaye, Liebowitz, Pete. Laney and Pagliaro had been in one way or another the merchants of death, and to find them was to close the mysteries and put them up on the shelf. Then his life could begin.

But what would he do if they got away? Carly wasn't helping, so they'd have to follow him to the drop...or figure out where it was going to be. Now where would Chris Laney want this drop to be? If it had to be away from other people, if it had to be a place easy to see your quarry, if it had to be light enough, and yet have some dark places. Tommy stood up and went to the window. A clear night, easy to see someone carrying a suitcase. How could you find a place where you can see your mark and not be easily seen yourself? Where are such places in Youngstown? And which of those places would Laney choose?

Suddenly, Med opened the door. "Jesus, Tommy, they lost him!"

"Fuck!" Tommy said, slamming his hand on the windowsill.

"He kept going on all these stops. Then he went into the Park Cliff Mall, and we lost him."

"Did Carly go back to his car?"

"No, it's still there."

"So, Laney planted a car near one of the mall doors," Tommy muttered to himself. He was quiet for a few seconds. Then he said, "Pull the squads from my house and Pagliaro's, Med. Send them out to help the others."

In a moment, he was gone. Laney was sharper than he thought. How else could he have planned this thing? But Pagliaro is sharp, too. He made millions in the Valley, and nobody knew his name. He hit all his enemies and never got his hands dirty. He was smooth enough to fool Lucy, to somehow seem different from all the other men who had come on to her. Smooth enough to get her into his bed.

How smart could they be? How long could they have been planning this? Two cunning, ruthless men who could kill easily, who were smooth and efficient, who were unhindered by conscience or remorse? What could stop them? Can two "snakes in a barrel" pull off a quick strike that will make them rich and set them free? But what's Pagliaro's take in this? He doesn't need the money, so why isn't he out of town? And why does a smart guy who wears silk suits, hang around Youngstown to nail the mayor...for only three million bucks? Pagliaro? He has to be the most reluctant one of the pair; he has everything to lose. And Laney? Three million cash looks good on a cop's salary. This is Laney's show...and Pagliaro's along for the ride.

So where will they go? When Laney killed Danny and Neva, he did it in the dark, in a place he knew. He did it where he could move easily about, on terrain he was comfortable with. It was his ballgame, and the one place he knows is the place where he had done all this before... against Danny and Neva. He was going to Guerin Woods!

Suddenly, Tommy burst out of the office in his dark jacket, the handle of his .45 visible in the holster on his belt. He was walking fast, heading for the garage. "Chief?" both Joe Matuszak and Med Williams said simultaneously.

Tommy turned back to them. "You guys get all those squads ready in a blink. Wait for word. When you hear it, you get out of here as fast as you ever did."

"But take somebody with you, Tommy," Med said.

"No! Because I could be wrong. And this has to be quick and quiet. Just stay on the horn, hear?"

Tommy's car roared out of the YPD garage, still under construction against the effects of the bomb. He had to get to Guerin Woods before Laney and Carly did. He had to be waiting for them. As he drove through the streets in the East Side, he remarked at the decay of the neighborhoods that once bloomed with summer flowers and vegetable gardens, that flew flags on holidays, of churches that had eternal floodlights on the Madonna. Now it was the graveyard of drug addicts and gang losers. And yet, despite the man-made blight, there was a ring of trees and hills and creeks and valleys, the life ring around Youngstown. And in that ring was Guerin Woods.

Tommy trembled slightly as he drove. It had to be Guerin Woods. Laney would go nowhere else. Tommy remembered playing baseball as a boy on a field once mowed out of the weeds, with a shabby backstop and an old well spring off the side of a nearby road...a pipe stuck into the hillside, with a trickle of fine, cold water pouring out day and night.

He had to decide where in the woods they would be. The old overgrown ballfield was out — too open, too accessible. Laney needed privacy, he needed a place where he had control, where he had the advantage. Carly had to be able to get to it too.

Tommy turned out the car lights, then drove down the streets that ringed the woods. He stopped the car. In this moonlight he could see without car lights. He listened with the windows open. Nothing. He waited, then listened again. If this was the place, they weren't here yet.

He had to look around but could only do it after he found the place where he thought they would meet. Tommy began driving again. *Remember, remember,* he called to himself as he drove. From distant memories, he remembered a small ravine, high up on the hill between a trail along the woods and the street bordering it above. In the ravine was a small clearing, a flat terrace off the hillside between the trail and the street. It was not too far from the small wood where Danny and Neva's bodies were found. Tommy had to decide. If Guerin Woods were the place, then this flat terrace, right here between the two access roads, would be it. If Laney knew this area, he would pick this part of the woods because he could come in high and look down on Carly. His car would also be on good road, not a gravel one as Carly's would be. This had to be it.

Tommy parked his car in front of the lone house around a corner from the woods, and slung a small duffle bag over his shoulder, and started walking toward the ravine. Suddenly he stopped and called Bumpy's cellular phone. "Hi, Bump," Tommy said softly.

"Tommy, where are you?"

"Listen, I have to talk softly, so I'm gonna make this quick."

"But where are you?"

"Along Doyle Road in Guerin Woods."

"Why there? You know something about a drop?"

"It's a long story. I'm not sure this is, but it's my best bet."

"We're checking the airport," said Bumpy.

"Good. But he's not going to use the airport. He's gonna drive... probably into Canada."

"So what do we do?"

"I don't know, Bump," Tommy sighed. "We can't tail him... but make sure there's a squad back at Laney's place, although it may not do any good... and make sure the two squads at your place are on alert. Bring the rest all toward Guerin Woods... no sirens, no radios... and whatever you do, don't let Laney see two squad cars together. If he catches on, we're finished."

"Okay, Tom."

"Just stay by the horn, boyo. When I call, we have to be able to move in a second."

"Tommy…I hope you're right about this place."

Tommy snorted. "Me, too, kid."

Tommy drew nearer to the woods, stopping from time to time, to listen. Then he walked into the thicket, cursing himself for stepping into a hole on almost his first step. He knew his right shoe was covered with mud, but he couldn't see to clean it. After a few minutes of walking, he found a spot. He could see if someone came down the hill, away from the street. He cleared some of the underbrush, so that if he wanted to run into the clearing, he could go easily.

He knelt down and listened…and waited. *God help us all if he was wrong*, he thought. In his torment and breathlessness, he thought of Lucy, of what it would be like to hold her in his arms in bed. He shook his head. It seemed as though he was incapable of imagining such happiness. Imagining is the talent of young men who can actually bring their dreams of love to fulfillment. It was never going to happen, he thought. It's not the way my life works. If something can go wrong, it will.

Tommy felt for his watch and pressed the button for the face light… almost nine o'clock. *If they were coming here, why so late?* he thought. *Maybe the drop would be somewhere else, maybe Mill Creek Park? What made him think it wouldn't be Mill Creek Park? It had huge dark places. But it also had park police and lights in most of the accessible areas. It also had traffic from people going through the park to the West Side. But Laney could have known a spot, could have scouted it for weeks, could have set this up long ago.*

But Laney was a creature of impulse if Tommy knew anything about him. Laney wasn't a long-term planner. Those murders were passionate hits, done in fury, heedless of the consequences. From Danny and Neva to Pete, all were done without thought, and only later covered up. Laney didn't scout this. Laney would be here.

Suddenly, he heard a noise on the road over his shoulder. A car was coming slowly, the drone of the motor constant as it approached. Then he heard it stop, and there were no lights anymore. One door slammed, and then another. Now he heard another motor, this time coming from the trail, down the ravine. Two cars? Could it be Carly? He soon saw more lights, and listened as the sound came from the west on the opposite side of the clearing. Then, it stopped as the lights went out.

Tommy reflexively loosened the strap around the .45 automatic in his belt holster. He fingered the safety and released it, then held his breath. He could hear movement, brush crackling, coming from above him on the right. Then for several minutes, there was total silence. Tommy's heart pounded in his ears; he took a breath against the rhythm of his pounding heart. Silence.

He saw movement in the moonlight, at the far end of the ravine. "Chris?" It was Carly's voice calling.

"Daddy? Is that you?" It was Lisa, calling to her father, her voice on the same hillside opposite Tommy but obscured by the brush between them.

"It's me, honey. Everything's going to be okay. Are you alright?"

"I'm okay, Daddy. Please do as they say so you won't get hurt."

"Is Chris there, Lis?"

There was silence. Tommy thought he could hear some words spoken. Why was Lisa the only one talking?

"Lisa?"

"I'm here, Daddy. Oh, Daddy," she wailed, her voice crying the anguish she felt.

"Don't cry, honey. Daddy's here. We're going to be alright." Again, movement in the brush. For several seconds, there was silence. Tommy was standing up now, his gun in his hand.

"Daddy, you have to bring the suitcase into the clearing." Again, more silence.

Carly couldn't move from behind the small mound where he had stopped. He seemed paralyzed, caught by the fear of losing his daughter. She was the blessing he never deserved; she was the joy of his past and the dream of his future. He had to save her. He had to have her back in his arms. He had to bring her back to Ginny.

Carly couldn't wait. All the things he had ever done in his life were scripted. He was always going through motions, and it always came easily. But now there was no script, no Judge East, no father to give him sage advice. This crazy man held his daughter's life in his hands, and suddenly there was nothing to achieve except to get her back.

The thought of losing her was searing his imagination. Nothing could be as bad as this. And to lose her in a terrible way, with her blood splattered in her last moments of agony, was more than he could stand. She was his future. She was the little girl that made him know what it was to be a father. She was the little girl who would touch his face and giggle at the tickle of his beard stubble on her fingers and her palms. This was the little girl he lost as she became a woman, the girl who grew up longing for her preoccupied father until it was too late.

Suddenly, her father was not the man she turned to. Suddenly, she began to long for other men who hardly knew her, who never felt the joy of seeing her angelic beauty in its lost innocence.

But now Carly's time had come and gone. He had been too busy with his career and his big house and his car and his office and his clothes…and his women, who never knew Lisa. And in the aftermath of those lost years, he had argued with her, had cursed at her, and had struck her in that lovely face, driving her out of her only home.

And now her voice had called him Daddy. Suddenly his chance had come again. These lost years seemed to be calling him back into another existence, a time when Lisa would be his little girl again. This would be a new, fresh time, a time to laugh again, a time, for just a moment, when she was his alone and the warmth of her, the beauty of her, the spirit of her would enkindle the total joy of being a father again.

It was Carly's time; it was his chance. And Carly stood up and started to run toward the echo of Lisa's voice, calling to her, running toward the new memories he would make, running toward new dreams, running toward redemption.

Then, he heard her voice again. "Daddy, no. Daddy, he'll kill you. Daddy, no..."

And another voice reverberated in his ears, the voice of Tommy McCarrie, "No, Carly! Get down!" But Carly only heeded the voice of Lisa that giggled when she was a baby, that brought such sunshine and hope into his life.

Shots rang out, careening off trees and rocks, one thudding into Carly's groin, tearing at his organs and making a large and bloody exit wound. But at the same time, there were several more shots. Tommy had fired toward the smoke that enveloped Laney, toward the faint figure that had just let Lisa go a split second before. Tommy's aim was also deadly, smashing the front of Laney's face and scrambling blood and teeth and bone and gray matter into a cavern at the back of his head. He was dead as he fell to earth, backward, one sightless eye open to the forest it could no longer see. Blood oozed from the cavity of the other eye, now gone, and also his shoulder and his neck.

Carly was down on the dirt terrace; he had fallen on his face and with his remaining strength had rolled himself over on his back. Both Tommy and Lisa were running toward him from opposite directions. When Lisa arrived, she cradled her father in her arms, crying loudly and hugging him. Carly winced and spoke in a feeble voice. He too began to cry more softly than Lisa because of the pain in his groin and the weakness of his stomach muscles. Tears welled in his eyes as he spoke. "Are you hurt, Lis?"

"No, Daddy," she said softly.

As he spoke, Tommy arrived and knelt down beside them, lifting away the coat in front of Carly to examine the wound. He looked, and then slowly covered it again with the coat. Carly looked at him, at the grave attention that Tommy paid, and the sad intelligence that had confirmed Carly's worst fears.

"Carly, I've called the life squad. Everything's on the way," Tommy said softly. "Hang on, boyo."

Carly shook his head slightly. "I've had it this time, Tommy."

Lisa moaned and held her father to her, crying uncontrollably. When Carly winced again, Tommy gently laid his hand on Lisa's arm. Carly coughed, and blood trickled from one of his nostrils. He struggled more to speak. "Tommy, she didn't deal those drugs, you know." Tommy nodded. "Help her, please."

"I won't charge her, Carly."

He struggled to make his gaze more direct into Tommy's eyes. "If you take care of her..."

Tommy touched his shoulder to silence and reassure him. "Everything I can to get her off, Carly. You count on it."

Carly nodded slightly. "Tommy, I'm sorry about you and me...I wish we started better."

"Me too, kid," Tommy said softly. At last, Carly seemed relieved.

He took a troubled, deep breath and turned back toward Lisa.

Tommy stood up and backed away from them. This moment was theirs, and he wasn't going to intrude. He turned and ran up the grade toward where he had shot. He had his flashlight on, searching the hillside. As he scanned, he saw the light cast off a figure lying in the bushes. He held his gun ready. As he approached in slow careful steps, he knew the look of a dead body. And when he stopped before the figure, legs twisted and body contorted, he shined the light on Laney's face. But then he gasped. It wasn't Laney's monstrous and pale face that stared into the sky; it was Mose Pagliaro's. Pagliaro? But where was Laney? God, Laney wasn't there! *The other car*, he thought. *It wasn't just a random driver passing by. It had to be Laney...and now he's gone.*

Tommy called Bumpy. "Doyle Road, up the hill from the old playground, Bump. Put those sirens on. Laney isn't here. Alert that squad at Laney's house. I'll shoot up a flare."

"Oh...I'm gonna miss you, baby," Carly said as tears welled up in his eyes.

"Daddy, please. You won't..."

"Let me finish, Lis. I have to talk." Lisa ran her hand down her father's cheeks, brushing the hair back off his forehead. "You used to do that when you were a baby," he said, smiling weakly. "It tickled, huh?"

She smiled and grimaced through her tears. "You know, I loved you every minute, baby. I never stopped."

She kissed him. "I know you did, Daddy. I know."

He coughed again, this time fighting off the pain and the struggle to breathe as the blood collected in his mouth. "Find a nice guy, Lis... only one...and take care of him. Make him into someone."

"I will, Daddy."

He struggled to take one more deep breath. "Tell your mom I always loved her. I just didn't know how much until too late." He stopped, the rattle in his voice more insistent and ominous. "She and you were the best things..."

This time there was no more breath to take. The blood had filled his mouth, and all the muscles were gone. He couldn't take that final breath. His eyes rolled in his head, and he went limp in her arms.

She began to cry aloud into the forest as Tommy drew near again. It was a wail that only loving women could call in their anguish, the wail he had known from his childhood when he went to home wakes and could hear the all-night mourners. In the distance, beyond the wail, he could hear the police and rescue sirens coming doggedly but too late. He looked back at Pagliaro's body and sneered. It wasn't right that these evil men could cause such suffering. And yet it had become his life's work.

Tommy crouched down and put his hand on Lisa's shoulder as she held her father's head in her arms. The girl moved herself toward his hand in acknowledgment of his kind presence. He stayed with her as the sirens came closer to the moment.

———◦❭❬◦———

The flares Tommy had shot lent an eerie, shimmering paleness to the scene. In a few minutes the rescue squad came down the hill, frantically crashing through the undergrowth to the clearing where Carly lay in Lisa's arms. As they drew near, Tommy stood erect to meet the emergency unit.

"Lisa," he said, laying his hand under her elbow, urging her up, "these people have to tend to your dad. Here," he said, helping her release Carly's head to the men who put the mayor on a stretcher.

As Bumpy and Med approached him, Tommy was holding the girl in his arms as she cried softly. "Lisa, this is Chief Malatesta and Sergeant Williams. We're going to take you home to your mom."

Bumpy hugged her and said, "Let's go, honey."

"You handle this for now, Bump. I'll talk to the family later. Med, take care of all this. If Laney did come, he bailed out during the excitement. And now he's on his way. He has to get out of town without the stash. Stay wired, kid."

"I'll be in touch, Tommy."

Tommy ran up the hill, getting one of the blues to ride him to his car. He had to get to Laney's house as soon as possible.

Meanwhile, in the clearing, Med stood watching as the men secured Carly's body into the ambulance. Just then, one of the squad members came up to Med. "Sarge, there was a suitcase full of money down over that little mound there."

"How much? A lot?"

"More than you and I have. It's packed with hundreds... Look," he said as one of the blues brought the suitcase up to Med.

"Thanks, son, keep looking around," Med said, turning his back to the life squad. As they were laying Carly onto a gurney, one of the men lifted him from the shoulder. When they set the body down, he realized his hand was coated with blood.

"Sergeant, this man also has a back wound," he said.

"What?" said Med.

"He was shot in the back. Look," he said, holding up his bloody hand.

"Wait," said Med, coming to the ambulance. When they turned Carly's body over, they saw the wound. The paramedic was right.

The paramedic crew chief, a man named O'Hara, walked up to them. "What's wrong, Med?"

"The mayor took a back shot, too," said Med.

"How'd that happen? Wasn't he running up the hill?"

"Yeah...Have a look at this, Teddy," said Med, gesturing to Carly's body.

Teddy loosened the shirt and trousers on the body, noting the large wound cavity in the mayor's groin. "This looks like two different guns, Med. These wounds are different." Med closely followed Teddy's finger as he pointed out the differences between the wounds. "This one's a .45 or a .40...but that back one's from something smaller, like a .380."

"Or maybe even a .32, huh?" said Med.

"Yeah, could be, but they're rare. Anyway, I'll lay money there were two different guns here."

"What the hell is this?" said Med to himself. "Thanks, Teddy." There had to be two assassins that got Carly. Someone got him with a back shot.

"Tommy?" Med said, calling his boss who was speeding toward Laney's house.

"Yeah, Med?"

"Something's wrong here. Carly took a back shot from a gun that the medics don't think was a .40. But maybe a smaller caliber, more like a .380 or..."

Tommy interrupted. "Or like maybe a hot .32?"

"Laney must have been there, Tom. He had to be the other killer."

"So, he shot Carly and then took the money and ran."

"Not so, Tommy. My guys found the suitcase and it was flush."

Tommy was quiet again. "Okay, Med. Stay in touch."

Tommy slammed his hands against the steering wheel. What was he going to do now? He pulled the car over to a curb and sat quietly, staring out at the lights mounting the hills and streets of the city. "Damn it. What am I going to do?" he muttered aloud. "Laney won't go home. He has to know we've covered his condo...and he missed his chance at the money. He must have panicked when he saw my shots."

Tommy grew quiet again. What would Laney do now? He needs money to get out of town. He doesn't want to leave and then have to work for a living. It'll be too easy to get caught. So, what's his play? He needs something, and the two people he could have gotten it from are dead in Guerin Woods. And he knows he can't go home. His only move must have been to kill Carly and then Pagliaro and make off with the money.

Suddenly, Tommy started. He put the car in drive and made a turn at the next intersection. He was heading for Pagliaro's house. Pagliaro had money and he was a dope dealer. One of those two things had to be in his house...and Laney was desperate.

⸙

On the way to Mose's house, Chris Laney cursed himself for panicking. Who the hell was that on the hillside? Was it McCarrie, for Christ's sake? It sounded like him. But who else could it be? And what was he doing there? How in hell, of all the places in the world, did he end up in Guerin Woods? That bastard Mose must have told him. But why? What sense could that make?

He looked at his watch...quarter after ten. He had to do this fast and be on the way out of Youngstown as soon as he could. He'd take one of Mose's cars, one of the other ones he seldom used. That would throw them off the trail for a little while. He could be in Canada not long after midnight. Then, he could be on a plane by morning. It wouldn't be hard once he got going and had some money. His own would get him through several weeks. It wouldn't be bad. But he needed a meal ticket, and none of his savings would accomplish that. He sure as hell never intended to work for a living anymore.

As he neared Pagliaro's house, he slowed down, surveying the area. It looked okay, but still he took a turn around the block, just to be sure. In this old, shabby neighborhood there were plenty of dark places. And in this neighborhood, people keep their doors locked and minded their own business. They had come to know that noises in the night bespoke danger. That dark movements, as long as they were in someone else's yard, were to be ignored, in hopes that the danger was meant for a neighbor rather than for them.

An alley stretched between several streets of Mose's block and passed through the block adjacent to Mose's house and garage. The garage was a triple, fronting on the alley, and overlooking a small blacktop lot on the other side.

He noticed a lone parked car at the far end of the lot. It was becoming cloudy, but still there was light enough to see the outline. It was Mose's green Buick.

He parked his car in a space just off the street at the far end of the alley, away from Mose's place. Then he quietly walked through the alley and entered the gate next to Mose's garage. He took out a handkerchief and drew his gun. If the door wasn't open, he knew how to get through it. The door was locked.

With a quick hit and a grab with the handkerchief, the glass was broken enough for him to reach inside and to undo the lock. He was satisfied at how easily and quietly he did the job.

He walked down the few steps of the enclosed porch and opened it into Mose's office. He took one step inside and suddenly he heard the sound of a hammer being pulled near his ear and a soft voice saying, "Don't move." Then he was shoved from the back against the wall of the entry to the porch. He struck the wall and turned instinctively back toward the voice.

"Chris? What the hell are you doing here?" It was Mickey.

"Jesus, Mick, you scared the hell out of me. Why're you here?"

"I'm watching the place for Mose..." Mickey was excited. His thought patterns were slow and chaotic. That was always his problem: he could never put pieces of impressions together into a clear idea. Luckily, he didn't have to do it often because Carly or Mose did all his thinking for him. Mickey still pointed the revolver at Laney. "I asked you what you were doing here, Chris," he said more coldly.

"I'm here to pick up something Mose left me."

"Mose didn't leave you no package," Mickey growled, still dimly trying to sort out the noise from the strange events that he beheld.

"Mick, you gotta believe this: Mose is dead. So is Carly. They shot each other up in Guerin Woods where Mose had Carly's daughter and Carly was supposed to drop a satchel of money for him."

"Bullshit! Mose and the mayor? No way!"

"Turn on the fucking radio, Mick. I tell you they're both gone... I'll tell you something else. You better get your ass out of town tonight or else you're gonna have your balls in McCarrie's vice."

"Me? What did I do? I never..."

"Fuck, man, you prints are all over Carly's house and all over this place. Everybody knows you're Carly's bodyguard... and a lot of people know what you do for Mose. You want the Mob guys to know that you gave Mose up to Carly? Mose made them a lot of money."

Mickey lowered the gun, holding it in his hand facing the floor.

"Shit!" he muttered in dazed confusion, like an animal caught in a trap that couldn't realize what had happened to it. "He was gonna pay me twenty grand," he muttered.

"Hell, Mick, I'll pay you that. But you have to help me get the fuck out of here."

"Where you going?"

"Somewhere where McCarrie can't get me. Somewhere where nobody knows who the hell I am."

"And you'll give me twenty grand?" Mickey said, feeling smug after he pocketed the early five grand from Mose, and now conned Laney out of another twenty grand.

"Yeah...I told you. But I have to find my package first. Remember, Mick, I'm all you got. Mose is done for."

"So what do you want me to do?"

"Go get that green Buick in the lot by the alley. Bring it up to the garage." Mickey blanched. "What's wrong? You have a key?"

"Uh, yeah."

"Then what's wrong? Is something wrong?"

"Nothin' is wrong. What are you gonna do?"

"I'll be putting some stuff in suitcases. You come back when you're done, and I'll give you some things to load into the car."

"Yeah...okay." Again, Mickey hesitated in the same dim, tormented way that he had done before.

"Now what?"

"Nothing."

"Mick, do you know where Mose's safe and stash is?"

"No," Mickey said fearfully.

"Goddammit, Mick, we have to get the fuck out of here. In a few minutes this place is going to be loaded with cops. Now, do you know or not?"

"Uh, I think he kept everything upstairs. He had some special closet. I heard him slip it out once. He never knew I heard it."

"Okay, I'll find it. Now get going."

Laney ran up the stairs to Mose's apartment. When he reached the top of the stairs he stopped and exhaled slowly. What a beautiful place. Man, Mose was shrewd. He never let on he lived like this.

First, Laney ran into all the rooms. There were two bedrooms and a library, a kitchen, a living room, and a small dining room, all of them beautiful. It had to be one of the bedrooms. He knew Mose's room was a small suite, and the other bedroom had the look of a guest room. In Mose's bedroom, he looked at all the things on his dresser, all the pictures, the bookcase full of books. He started slowly touching and examining each one, but before long he was throwing them out on to the floor. He turned over the mattress... nothing. He started through the drawers. Still nothing. More drawers. Nothing again.

In a few minutes, everything in Mose's bedroom was turned over. In one drawer he found eleven hundred dollars and some credit cards assigned to Mose's real estate company. He pocketed those. On the dresser in a small vase, he found seven hundred dollars in fifties. He snorted. *Imagine not caring about a few thousand bucks. Thousands are not what he needed, not for a lifetime.*

Then he saw the closets. One smaller one that he ransacked in a few minutes. He found another small box filled with hundreds. He didn't bother to count it, but he knew it was more than Mose had promised Mickey. Good. Mickey was covered. Now he had to find some real money for himself.

But there was one more closet, a huge walk-in with shelves along the walls and rods going sideways holding suits and trousers and shoes and more ties and sweaters. Laney whistled. This was a movie star's closet. Suddenly he looked at his watch. It was eleven o'clock and he began to draw faster breaths. This was taking longer than he thought. He wanted to be near Lake Erie by now, well on his way to Ontario.

He started frantically going through the shoes and then the suits. But as he littered the floor and stumbled through the debris, he realized that he wasn't going to find what he was looking for. He found bonds and stock certificates and papers, all worth money, but nothing easy, nothing liquid. In a few moments more he had cleared the room and left a pile in the center. Where did he keep the serious money?

He stood in the bedroom, looking all around him at the mess he had created. Then he saw a spot in the dresser that he had not seen. When he felt with his hand he found money again. This time a wad of hundreds... several thousand. He stuffed all the money into his pockets.

Again, he stood still, surveying all that he had done. But where was the big money? Could it be in a safe? No. A safe would be too obvious. Besides Mose was like a squirrel, burying money all over the place. So, where? He went back into the small closet and looked carefully at what he saw in it. There was nothing unusual here... nothing.

He tried the large, walk-in closet. *Where would you hide something in here?* he asked himself. He started pressing down with his feet on the floor. Slowly, he covered every part of the floor. But always the feeling was the same: the floor was intact as he swung his weight up and down on the balls of his feet.

What else? If it were in this closet, it could be in the walls or the ceiling. But he carefully looked at the ceiling. It was seamless and intact. He began pressing and knocking on the walls. Where the hell was Mickey? What was taking him so long?

All that he could see was solid, even at the corners. All resisted the push he would make on their surfaces. Where could it be? He knew Mose had to have easy access. He surveyed the scene again. Then, suddenly he saw it: a sturdy wooden box by the door with sweater boxes on it. A stepstool in a closet? Quickly he threw off the boxes and pulled the box away from the wall. He stepped up and began to press the area above the door. This time it yielded slightly to his touch. He began to pound with the heel of his hand all along the wall, and each time the wall would give at his blow. He grew excited, his heart pounding in his chest and his fists pounding furiously against the soft wall.

Finally, he saw a crack that became a seam as he pounded. He pressed in and then grabbed a piece of the wall board and pulled. The whole panel above the door gave, and finally came free. Laney gasped. About two dozen bags altogether, Mose's insurance policy. About eight thick bundles of hundreds and some dope in two different shades of clear plastic. He stuffed as many wads of hundreds as he could into his pockets. Then, he opened a clear zip-lock bag that was taped shut and rolled into a compact bundle. He stuck a wet finger into the bag and then flicked the excess off and brought it to his lips. Cocaine. Then he grabbed one of the pink shaded clear bags. Again, he tested. He stood still a few seconds. Jesus, it was heroin. There were about five pink bags of heroin and seventeen clear ones of cocaine...all weighing about a kilo.

Laney felt a flush. He smiled to himself. This was his ticket out of town, the pass to the good life. He hurriedly grabbed a large suitcase from the other closet and stuffed the dope and the rest of the money into it. He smiled at his good fortune.

As he headed downstairs, he gave grudging recognition to Mose Pagliaro. He knew how to keep aces in the hole. Mose was always ready for a fall back, like a fox with two ways out of his den. And he liked the quiet way Mose managed his wealth, never showy, but enjoyable and satisfying, nonetheless. He decided that he would act that way in Ecuador...keep it low, keep it safe, keep it sure.

Where the hell was Mickey? he thought. Even in his euphoria, he was bothered by Mickey, who he never liked or trusted. *I wonder if that asshole took off. After all I said to him, after I promised him twenty grand for a few hours work.*

Mickey, himself, was confused and harried by the turn of events. Mose was dead...and Carly. Now what should he do? How does he know he can trust Laney not to give him up? He never liked him anyway. He was always a smart ass. And what about the wired car? Should he tell him? Or let him blow his ass to kingdom come? Mickey waited outside, shifting back and forth from one foot to the next. He wanted this thing to be okay. He had to have that extra twenty grand. It would really make his life better if he had it.

"Mick?" Chris whispered as he came outside. No answer. "Mick? Where the fuck are you?" Still no answer. Laney cursed and carried the suitcase and the briefcase into the garage. Mickey waited quietly, hoping Laney would decide to take his own car. He walked quietly back into the house.

Laney closed the garage door behind him. Only one light was lit... over a small workbench in the garage. He opened the suitcase again and counted the bags. He wiped the powder and dust off each one. Where the fuck was Mickey with that car? He went to the garage window and looked out. Mickey had not moved the car. Damn, he thought again silently, he must have run out on me.

Suddenly, his whole world began to unravel with a few softspoken words. "How's it going, Captain?"

He turned toward the voice and confronted his worst demon. Tommy McCarrie was sitting on the hood of Mose's Jeep, pointing a .45 automatic at him. Laney reflexively closed the suitcase. "Don't even think about moving, Chris. I'll kill you before you take a half step."

Laney looked around the garage. McCarrie was alone. He sighed, even relaxing slightly from the horror of being discovered. "How'd you know I was here?"

"Just a hunch. Mose was gone...Whatever he had in this house was there for the taking. You got greedy, boyo."

Laney closed his eyes. This wasn't happening, he thought. It can't be that this old drunk had outsmarted him. "Was that you out in Guerin Woods?"

"Yeah," Tommy said.

"But how'd you know? Who told you? Were you wired somehow?"

"Again, a hunch," Tommy said, motioning with the gun for Laney to move away from the workbench. "You'd been out there before, right?"

"What do you mean?"

"I mean with Danny and Neva."

"And that was enough to make you go out there and wait?"

"I could have been wrong," Tommy said, smiling. "I gambled."

Laney didn't answer. After a few minutes of staring at his tormentor, he said, "So shoot me if you're gonna do it. Get it over with!"

"Why'd you kill those two kids, Chris? Why did you ruin something so innocent and clean?" Laney stared at him, but didn't answer. Finally, he shook his head. He didn't want to say that he had no good reason. "Couldn't you find some other way to do their father in besides killing those kids?" Tommy asked, his voice now showing emotion.

"They got in the way," Laney said cooly. "She came upon me as I was loading their car the second time."

"You just could have shot her. You didn't have to mutilate her."

"She called me a devil…and I knew you had the hots for her, too," he said with a smirk.

Tommy's face contorted. "You sick fuck," he growled. He was losing control. His hand was shaking.

"Why don't you shoot, Chief? You know in court I'm gonna tell the world that I not only killed his kids, but I was fucking Danny's wife. What are you waiting for?"

The rage in Tommy was transforming him. Laney's smirk, the easy admission of brutality, had changed Tommy from cop to avenging angel. "You miserable bastard," Tommy snarled, "I don't know whether to kill you myself or to give you over to the Mafia and let them torture you."

Just at that moment, Mickey opened the door and walked in. "Chris, I think you…" In that split second, Laney grabbed Mickey and swung one of his arms around so that Mickey faced front, and Laney held a .32 to his neck.

"Now," said Laney softly to Tommy, "now you can take your best shot." Tommy was frozen. "What are you waiting for, Chief? Why don't you shoot?"

Mickey was frightened. "Tommy, no. He wants you to kill me. Don't do it, Tommy. I ain't no part of this. I didn't kill nobody!"

"Go ahead, Tommy," Laney taunted. "Shoot!"

Tommy raised his .45. "Fuck it, Captain. This bullet'll go through him and get you anyway," he said coldly.

For a split-second Laney hesitated, knowing that Tommy was right about the .45. "Tommy, for Christ's sake!" Mickey screamed. "Don't kill me just to get him. I didn't do nothin' to deserve this!"

Tommy seemed to aim, but hesitated, then slowly lowered his gun. Mickey breathed a slight sigh as Tommy moved. "Lay it down, Chief," said Laney. Tommy hesitated, cursing himself silently for not killing Mickey and getting Laney in the bargain. "Drop it."

Tommy set the gun on the floor. "Just tell me one thing, Chris. Did you do all of them? Danny, Neva, Leibowitz...Pete?"

It was the one thing Laney didn't expect; a chance to make McCarrie's last minutes of life even more wretched than they were now. He loosened his hold on Mickey's neck slightly. "I did them all but Leibowitz. Mose did that. He's an old demolitions man. And he wanted to show everyone that he could take you out. With you gone, he'd own the Valley. Besides, you were stumbling into his operation...getting too close."

"But why Neva? Why did you have to do her like that...to mangle her so?"

"Because she spit on me...and she called me some name."

"But you killed Danny before her eyes, didn't you? What'd you expect?"

"It was more than that. She called me some spik name...She said you'd get me for what I did. How about that? So here we are, huh?"

While they were talking, Mickey was watching Tommy, puzzled and terrified. He seemed dazed to be still alive, but also afraid that instead of being killed by Tommy, he'd be dispatched by Laney in a second of heartless, cold efficiency.

But Tommy twice did something that even Mickey in his dim perceptions could understand. It was the old East Side sign, used on the playground so many times, used in barfights since before he was born. Twice, Tommy closed his eyes and pushed his right shoulder forward. It looked like a tic, but it wasn't. It was the old East Side sign you gave to a buddy in a tense confrontation...a shoulder and two blinks and you hit the dirt. He studied Tommy. No blinks. Tommy kept talking, flashing one glance at Mickey, their eyes meeting in a second of communication. They knew each understood the other. "And Kaye Bellino? Did you have to defile everything about Danny? What'd he ever do to you?"

"I wanted to queer your plans. You could see it in Malatesta's eyes. Even Smolenski and Mencken liked him. They promoted him faster than me. And I know that even though I outranked him, and even though I had a law degree, you were going to make him chief."

"And Pete?" Tommy said, blinking twice, quickly and obviously, easily understood a second late by Mickey, but not to Laney, who was younger and not from the East Side.

Suddenly, Mickey reared back, putting Laney off balance, and then he grabbed Laney's arm and pulled him on top of him as he lunged at the floor. Laney tried to keep his balance, and pulled back away from Mickey, stumbling on one knee and having to brace himself to keep from falling on a collapsed left leg that had slipped beneath him. Laney tried to get the pistol around to shoot at Mickey, but he stumbled backward. Tommy in those passing seconds, because he knew what was coming, had drawn the tiny .25 automatic that Bumpy had given him as a pocket gun. He fired twice at Laney, missing once and hitting him in the left buttock as he twisted to pull at the door behind him. Then Tommy shot again, deliberately hitting Laney in the same buttock, the bullet tearing through the muscle and lodging near the other. Laney screamed.

"The gun, Mickey!" Tommy said, getting Mickey to sweep Laney's gun toward Tommy with his leg. Tommy retrieved his .45.

Mickey jumped up, hearing Laney screaming and seeing Tommy

standing again with the formidable .45 once more trained upon his chest. "Don't move, Mickey," Tommy said softly. "We still ain't buddies, you and me." Mickey was relieved only a little, but at least he was not dead. He also knew that Tommy wouldn't kill him with the same nonchalance as Laney would. "Pick him up and lean him against the car there," Tommy said.

Mickey reached down to Laney and tried to pull him erect, but he stopped as Laney screamed again. "Pull that bastard up, I said," Tommy growled.

"But he's dying, for Christ's sake, Tommy," Mickey pleaded.

"He'll live a while. It was only some shots in the ass. Pull him up!"

Mickey pulled the screaming Laney up and draped him face down across the front of the big Cadillac that was Pagliaro's society car. "You son of a bitch!" Laney screamed at Tommy. "Just shoot me. What are you waiting for?"

"I already shot you, Laney," Tommy said. "Mickey, you have the keys to that green Buick out there in the lot?"

"Yeah, but I..."

"Go get it and bring it up here by the garage door."

"I can't, Tommy," Mickey said.

Tommy raised the .45 toward Mickey's face. "Why the fuck not?" Tommy said.

"It's, uh... It's wired."

Tommy stared at Mickey for a few seconds. "Did you set it?" he said softly.

"No. It was Mose. That was his thing. He's the one who set the —"

"The one in the YPD garage, right?" Tommy said, finishing for him.

"Yeah," Mickey said sheepishly. "Laney watched, and Mose wired it in."

"Did you help him load this one?" Tommy said.

"No. He had it done before he called me. He told me that if Laney came back alone, I was supposed to give him the key to that car."

Tommy smiled tightly. "A barrel full of snakes," he said to himself. He was quiet for a few seconds, trying to decide what he had to do. Finally, he said, "Okay, Mickey, I'm gonna give you the biggest break of your miserable life...something you sure as hell don't deserve."

"Yeah...okay, Tommy. Anything you say."

"You have to do one thing for me." Tommy raised a single index finger in front of Mickey's face as though to hypnotize him.

"Yeah...okay," said Mickey doubtfully. "What?"

Tommy pointed toward the overhead door. "You take this piece of dogshit down to that Buick..."

"No, Tommy, I told you..."

"Shut up, Mick! Now listen to me. You take him down to that Buick, open the driver's door, stuff the key in his mouth, prop this fucker against the door, and then run as fast as your legs can carry you...unless you want to go to hell tonight."

"He won't do it, Tommy. Why would he blow himself up?"

"It's a long story, Mick. He'll do it. Won't you, Laney?"

"Fuck you, McCarrie. Fuck you! You're gonna have to kill me yourself. I'm not doing it."

"Slap him on the ass, Mickey," Tommy said softly. Mickey hesitated, questioning Tommy's order. "I said slap him on the ass!"

Mickey halfheartedly slapped Laney and the younger man shrieked and moaned, cursing Tommy.

"Did you feel anything, Captain? How about in the front?" Laney just stared back at him with glazed eyes. "You know what, Laney? You'll never feel anything down there again." Tommy was pointing to him.

"You're lucky you can piss with that dick. It's gone. The nerves are blown to pieces. It's worthless now."

Laney moaned and cried at the same time. Mickey looked at Tommy in amazement, as though seeing the chief clearly for the first time. "So, I'm gonna give you a break, Captain. See, you can go to trial and then, if you're lucky, might get life in prison. But even if you get life, you're gonna go to Meershan State and live like an animal until you die. And we're gonna get the word out to all the swell kids at Meershan that you don't have a real dick anymore. And then your nights are gonna get interesting.

"See, you're gonna be a punching bag for every horny cutthroat in that place. Hell, you're gonna be the next best thing to a piece of female ass...the guy with the useless dick."

Tommy stopped, and studied Laney's face, contorted in agony, more from the horror of what Tommy conjured up than from the pain of his injuries. "So choose," Tommy said, pointing the finger again. "You want the whole world to know that the killer cop, the animal that mutilated that girl, the guy with the worthless dick, is going to be in the pen? Hell, they'll be taking reservations!"

Laney buried his face in his hands and began quietly sobbing. Tommy knew what he was going to do. And Tommy was satisfied. Danny would never know about Kaye. He'd just know that part of his life was over now, and a new and happy part would begin with Elly. And all Tommy's secrets would go to the grave with Laney...if there would be anything left of him to bury.

"Mickey," Tommy said, "after you get him down there, you have till daylight to get out of town. If I ever see you again, I'll cut you to pieces, understand? Not Youngstown, not Ohio, nowhere near here. If you ever come back, you might as well wear a bullseye on your chest, because you're gonna be target practice for the whole YPD…a gopher for a cop killer."

"No problem, Tommy, no problem. I'm gone." He winced when he spoke, looking confused and agitated.

"What's wrong?"

"I don't have any money. All I got's just five grand. I…"

"See what he has in his pockets," said Tommy gesturing toward Laney. Mickey roughly searched Laney's pockets and suddenly his expression changed. He pulled wads of hundred dollar bills out and knocked the bound stacks of hundreds on the floor, heedless of Laney's agonized screams.

"Leave that money on the floor. Those wads'll do you," Tommy growled. "Now get going."

"What if he doesn't start it up?"

"He'll do it. He doesn't have any choice. Just remember to give him those keys and lean him toward the driver's seat."

"Then, that's it? That's all you want me to do?"

"That's all, besides get out of town," Tommy said. "You're flush now. Make the best of it, Mick."

Tommy turned to Chris Laney. "Did you ever think you'd go like this, Chris?" he said with a smirk. "You have the stink of death all about you…or did you crap your pants?"

Tommy glanced at Mickey to give him the command to take Laney. Mickey pressed the opener button and then roughly grabbed Laney and started walking, dragging Laney who was crying and screaming and cursing as they went. After going about ten yards, Mickey turned to Tommy. "This is rough," he said, resisting Laney's thrashing and lunging. His legs were getting numb; he was losing blood and probably going into shock.

"Hurry, Mickey," Tommy said, leaving the garage and closing both doors. There was a wall near the back of Pagliaro's house, about forty yards from the green Buick. The walls were dirt reservoirs against the hillside, terracing the house yards up and down the hill. Tommy climbed the embankment and stood watching against a thick old tree growing on the corner of the wall.

Laney fell down once, and Mickey picked him up roughly and kept him walking, half dragging him as he screamed. Finally, as they neared the Buick, Mickey propped Laney against the back of the car and went to the driver's side to open the door. He did it quickly and returned for Laney. Tommy watched intently. He had a perfect vantage to see it all. Mickey, taking Tommy's words literally, tried to stuff the keys into Laney's mouth, but when Laney protested, he stuffed them into a shirt pocket. Then he tilted Laney toward the open door.

In a second, Mickey was gone, heading toward the alley and running as fast as he could toward his car. Tommy knew he would never see Mickey again.

Laney had braced himself at the door, unwilling to enter and sit down. He cursed and screamed, pounding the roof of the car. The scream was like music to Tommy ears. The hatred he held for Laney for what he did to Neva was being sated by the picture of this broken creature, suffering through a decision that so few people have to make in life...and making the decision out of despair. *I wonder what he's thinking*, Tommy thought.

With his eyes still intent on Laney, Tommy called Bumpy on the phone. "Tommy, where the hell are you?"

"I'm at Pagliaro's, Bump."

"What the hell's going on? Are you okay?"

"I'm fine, kid. The story's over. Better send some fire trucks and a couple of squads out here to case this place. There's about fifty pounds of dope in the garage. What you find in the house might be even more interesting."

"But where's Laney? What happened?"

"He and I had a serious disagreement."

"Is he alive?"

"Yeah, but his chances don't look too good…Bump, send somebody out to Guerin Woods with those dogs. See if Pete's out there. And pick up Nick Pagliaro; he'll have a lot to tell us."

"Tommy, are you okay?" Bumpy asked, troubled by the strange, callous calm of his old friend.

"I'm fine…" Laney, who had gotten into the car and dragged himself out twice, had been sitting in the car for several minutes. Tommy watched intently, stepping behind the tree and using it as a shield.

"Tom?"

Suddenly there was a fireball and a shock wave that thumped against Tommy. He grunted as he struggled to see the car disintegrate. Everything about it was in flames. There was total destruction; Pagliaro wanted his revenge to be permanent.

"Tommy, Tommy, Tommy!" Bumpy shrieked. "Tommy!"

"I'm okay, Bump. It's all right."

"But what was that explosion?"

"Two snakes in a barrel, Bump. It's a long story. And Chris Laney isn't with us anymore."

"Jesus Christ, what did you do, Tommy?"

"Not much. I'll tell you about it. Get some people out here, okay? These neighbors are gonna be scared by all the broken windows."

Tommy sat in the darkness of his office, barely able to see except for the ambient light cast by the signs and streetlights outside below. He was as tired as he had ever been. His chest was sore as he breathed. His shoulders and neck were stiff and ached at every movement.

He didn't know what to do. He wanted to go, but he couldn't make himself get up and leave. He wanted to give in to the weariness he felt, imagining that his terrible fatigue was what people felt just before dying, just before giving in for the last time.

But he couldn't give in. Bumpy had said it: he had too much to live for. But it was as though he was afraid of happiness, somehow afraid that he might be too old and heartsick to enjoy what life now promised. He was afraid...

Suddenly, the door opened and the light from the outer office illuminated Lucy in the few seconds it took to open and shut the door. She came over to him and stood in front of him a few feet away. "Tom...Bumpy just told me...The dogs found Pete's body in the field where you said. He was shot with a .32."

Tommy let his eyes drop closed, surrendering to the awful news. He put his head in his hands, and in a few seconds let out a low and weak wail. Lucy rushed to him and held his head in her arms. He began to sob against her, his face buried in her groin, his arms clutching her around her hips.

For a long time, they remained in the embrace. Lucy, when she could, kissing him on the crown of his head as he clung to her. Finally, she knelt down in front of him, her face level with his, their eyes meeting, her breath close enough for him to feel against his face. She looked at him as though she were going to speak. But she said nothing for several seconds, her eyes studying the face she had loved for so long, seeming not to believe what the future promised them.

"Will you marry me, Tom?"

He studied the lovely face before him. His eyes roaming from her forehead to her eyes to her lips to her chin. "Do you know what you're asking? I'm almost ten years older than you are," he said softly.

"I know what I'm asking," she said, nodding to show him as if he couldn't believe her words. "I want you to sleep with me in my bed tonight... and wake up beside me every morning of your life. I love you, Tommy."

Tommy took a deep breath, then stood up, marveling at the good fortune that was his. How strange that life mixes such joy in one hand and sorrow in the other. He nodded to her.

"Let's go home, kid," he said.

About the Author

Donald Greco grew up in Youngstown, Ohio, and has lived in Ohio all his life, fulfilling a career as a fifth-grade schoolteacher, a high school geometry teacher, and later as a professor of mathematics. He always dreamed of writing stories, so quietly, in his spare time, he wrote novels throughout his adult life. The only one who knew of his secret passion was his beloved wife, Angie, who sadly passed away several years ago. He is still a resident of Ohio and is the father of three sons and five grandchildren. He published his first children's book, *What Ever Happened to the Smooth-Tongued Cats?* in 2022. The first novel in his *Youngstown Quintet Series, Abramo's Gift,* was originally published in 2008. The series' long-awaited final installment, *The Ghost Hawk,* was published in 2024. Greco plans to re-release the entire *Youngstown Quintet,* with *Abramo's Gift* and *Tommy the Quarterback* now available.

greconovels.com
dongreconovels@gmail.com

www.ingramcontent.com/pod-product-compliance
Lightning Source LLC
Chambersburg PA
CBHW050120030726
47505CB00007B/1957